A CORNUCOPIA OF
DUNDERHEADS

A CORNUCOPIA OF DUNDERHEADS

A Parody of the Novel A CONFEDERACY OF DUNCES by John Kennedy Toole, with a Foreword by Franz-Heinrich Katecki

John Kennedy Toole Jr.

Printed in the United States of America

This Baidarka Boy edition is published by arrangement with Brooklyn Bridge University Press.

Excerpts from *A Cornucopia of Dunderheads* appeared in *Pseudocopula* (June 2015).

Library of Sexual Congress Cataloging-in-Publication Data

Toole, John Kennedy Jr., 1969
    A cornucopia of dunderheads
      1.   Title.
[PUBES3570.054C69   2015]   813'.54 15-408

ISBN: 0692572376
ISBN 13: 9780692572375

Baidarka Boy
an imprint of Brooklyn Bridge University Press
1 Base of the Bridge Road
Brooklyn, NY 11201

Distributed by Lost Horizon Productions, LLC

12 13 14 15 16   56 55 54 53 52 51

For
Mom, Julie, and James Keith

Foreword

Perhaps the best way to introduce this novel—which upon my eighty-second reading of it astounds me even more than the first—is to tell of my first encounter with it. It was a dreary November morning, and I had just arrived at the world's smallest university, Brooklyn Bridge University, a sedevacantist institution that sits at the base of the Brooklyn Bridge on the Brooklyn side of New York City. Here at the university, I work as dean of three colleges, provost, ombudsman, and men's head basketball coach, and I teach scores of classes, most notably Armenian, Russian, French, philology, archaeology, Koine Greek, Latin, Yiddish, Aramaic, Hebrew, Chinese (Mandarin and Cantonese), English literature (with an emphasis on the plays of William Shakespeare, the sermons of John Donne, and the poetry of Gerard Manley Hopkins), Austrian School economics (with a particular emphasis on the work of the late Murray Rothbard and on the work of the way too late Ludwig von Mises), theology (with an emphasis on sacerdotal Christian sects, especially those that existed in Iraq) and philosophy (with an emphasis on the works of Aristotle, especially as they pertain to syllogistic reasoning, and on the works of Thomas Aquinas, especially as they pertain to the number of angelic beings that can inhabit a given physical space, micro or macro). These are my duties, among others. (By the way, I am the university's janitor every other Tuesday.)

As for other faculty, there is only one: a blind Portuguese named Dr. Paco de DaSilva, who teaches higher-level mathematics, midlevel astronomy, lower-level physics, and scores of other science courses and who coaches the chess team and who has never been late for a day of work, save for the day when a Nepalese veterinarian inadvertently gave Dr. de DaSilva's neutered seeing-eye dog too strong a dose of canine testosterone, thereby causing the seeing-eye dog to go on a sexual rampage that involved anything within reach of the seeing-eye dog's leash, including Dr. de DaSilva's legs. Suffice to say, several dogs, numerous cats, a Vietnamese potbellied pig, a recently disabled police officer, and an elderly woman were never the same. Dr. de DaSilva had another incident with the neutered seeing-eye dog, which subsequently died of a coronary. But I digress. That is another story altogether, a story that will have to be told at a later time under the proper and due circumstances.

And on that dreary November morning, there was no traffic on the East River, save for what appeared to be an Eskimo paddling a canoe, a man whom I espied from the window of my cramped office. Not believing my eyes, I used my binoculars to get a better look, and it was, indeed, a man—not an Eskimo, from the looks of him, but a dark-skinned man nonetheless— who had a steely, determined look. He was in a baidarka, not a canoe, and when he neared the United Nations building, he stopped, looked up at the building, and then raised a middle finger at it. This caused me to chuckle, given my intense hatred of the United Nations and given my intense hatred of its generally genocidal and specifically antihuman campaigns and policies. The man then paddled the baidarka diagonally across the river, heading towards the university. I reasoned that he would reach the Brooklyn shore, disembark his baidarka, and, being the tourist that he probably was, would maunder around this section of Brooklyn or even walk across the bridge, as many tourists are wont to do, even on dreary mornings like that one.

I put my binoculars back into the top right-hand drawer of my desk. I wasn't scheduled to teach for the next two hours, and after reviewing my notes pertaining to a graduate seminar that I would be teaching that morning (*The Cat in the Hat* as *The Protocols of the Learned Elders of Zion*: the Semantics and Semiotics of Questionable and Potential Anti-Semitism in Postmodern Children's Literature), I checked my e-mail, drank three cups of Whorebucks coffee, pared my fingernails, and wondered if I should get a pet cat, preferably a Russian blue.

I was interrupted from my thoughts by Mrs. Means, Brooklyn Bridge University's receptionist, transcriptionist, administrator, registrar, bookkeeper, bouncer, and women's lacrosse team coach. She was scowling, and I asked her if the electric company was threatening to cut off our power once again or if she was constipated, and she replied that no, neither of those things was the issue; what was bothering her was a man who was now sitting in the sole chair in Mrs. Means's small office, demanding that he be allowed to see me. I told Mrs. Means that I was not interested in speaking with another Jehovah's Witness who, I assumed, had somehow stumbled his way from the printing presses of his faith up the road and who was hoping to convert me to his Arian heresy.

Mrs. Means assured me that the man waiting in her office was not a Jehovah's Witness.

"He says that you're his last hope," Mrs. Means said.

"Perhaps he needs to see a priest, preferably a sedevacantist," I said.

"I think that you should see him," Mrs. Means said. "He said that he's paddled all the way down here from Maine."

"Paddled all the way from Maine!" I stood. "You must be joking, Mrs. Means!"

"I'm as serious as the heart attack that killed Dr. de DaSilva's neutered seeing-eye dog, Dr. Katecki."

And now I frowned. "Oh, all right. Send that gentleman in here, Mrs. Means, with the caveat that I can speak with him for only ten minutes, if that. And if he is a surreptitious Jehovah's Witness, I will not hesitate to boot him immediately from my office!"

Mrs. Means replied that she would tell the man these very things, and she turned and headed down the stairwell to her small office.

I sat down at my desk and did a Craigslist search for Russian blues that might be up for adoption. I stopped. I sensed that someone was staring at me. And when I looked up, I discovered that my senses were correct. There he was, the dark-skinned man who had paddled his baidarka on the East River and who had raised a middle finger at the United Nations building. He was stocky—not chubby, but stocky in a muscular way—and I made a face, sensing that I had seen or met this man somewhere before. In his hands he had a Kinko's photocopy box, and from the way that he held the box, I knew that it contained a somewhat hefty manuscript, somewhere, I assumed, in the range of 120,000 to 130,000 words. (I would later discover that my assumption was correct.)

I stood, and he gently placed the photocopy box atop my cluttered desk and extended his hand, which I shook. Like his face, his handshake was cold, steely, determined. I motioned for him to have a seat, which he did, and I sat down. I then asked why he wanted to see me.

And he began to tell me his story, beginning with the suicide of his alleged father in March 1969, and then the most recent events of his, this paddler's, life, the first being his Micmac mother's death two months earlier and the second being a book that he told me that the world had to read. Before he could tell me what he had written and why he had written it, Mrs. Means appeared at my door, telling me that I was late for my graduate seminar.

I told Mrs. Means to reschedule the seminar for the following morning; I was not to be disturbed for the remainder of that day. With that, I closed the door, sat down at my desk, and bade the man, who called himself John Kennedy Toole Jr., to continue with his story.

The story was long, and though he told the story well, and though he told the story in order, the story was still somewhat convoluted, given the number of adventures and misadventures that he had had. For one thing, this man was claiming to be the illegitimate son of John Kennedy Toole,[1] author of the very well-known novel *A Confederacy of Dunces* (the Pulitzer Prize winner for fiction in 1981) and author of the lesser-known work *The Neon Bible.* According to Toole the Younger, Toole the Elder met a female American Indian student from Maine while he was driving around the United States on his last ride, Toole the Elder having given up hope of ever seeing *A Confederacy of Dunces* published and having entered a despair that he would never be able to escape.[2] For a biology project, Nona, a Micmac student, was exploring river basins in lower Mississippi with two female

1 The author John Kennedy Toole was born on December 17, 1937, in New Orleans, Louisiana, and committed suicide on or around March 26, 1969, near Biloxi, Mississippi.

2 Cf. *Butterfly in the Typewriter: The Tragic Life of John Kennedy Toole and the Remarkable Story of A Confederacy of Dunces* by Cory MacLauchlin (Da Capo Press, 2013) for the most current, and most definitive, biography about Toole the Elder. An excellent memoir is *Ken & Thelma: The Story of A Confederacy of Dunces* by Joel L. Fletcher (Pelican, 2005).

Choctaws she had met at what would become Haskell Indian Junior College.[3]

According to Toole the Younger, Toole the Elder and Nona got along so well that they had a one-night stand that produced Toole the Younger, who said that he was born on December 17, 1969, almost nine months after the suicide of Toole the Elder and the exact day that would have been Toole the Elder's thirty-second birthday.

And then I realized why I had sensed that I had met or seen Toole the Younger. The previous year I attended a Modern Language Association convention in New Orleans, and a guest speaker gave a presentation about the use of first-intention words in *A Confederacy of Dunces*. After the speaker's presentation, I purchased a monograph of her work, which had a photograph of John Kennedy Toole (a high school picture, I believe). Toole the Younger is the spitting image of Toole the Elder, save that Toole the Younger has a very dark complexion (thanks to his Micmac mother), a slightly wider brow (thanks to his Micmac mother), and a nose that hints of the Romanesque (thanks to his Micmac mother).

I asked Toole the Younger about the book that he had written. Was it a biography of his late alleged father? Was it a hagiography of that man? Was it Toole the Younger's autobiography? What, exactly, was this thing about? And was Toole the Younger hoping to garner publicity for himself and somehow obtain money from the estate of Toole the Elder?

---

3 This institution is in Lawrence, Kansas, and is now known as Haskell Indian Nations University. Note that I use the terminology *American Indian* and not *Native American*. American Indian activist and author Russell Means preferred to be called an American Indian. Cf. *Where White Men Fear to Tread: The Autobiography of Russell Means* by Russell Means and Marvin Wolf (St. Martin's Griffin, 1995) and other media (writings, interviews, and speeches) by Means.

"Don't be ridiculous," Toole the Younger replied, and though his facial expression showed a stoicism that Marcus Aurelius himself would have admired, I could tell that the last question bothered Toole the Younger immensely. "I don't need anything from his estate or from his family. They don't owe me anything, and I don't owe them anything."

"You haven't answered the question," I said. "What, exactly, have you written? What is it that you want so desperately for the world to read?"

And then Toole the Younger told me that he had written a parody of *A Confederacy of Dunces*. Toole the Younger said that no one had ever written a parody like this one, one that was a very transformative work of art, something unique and quite distinct from *A Confederacy of Dunces*, yet at the same time, because this new work used characters from Toole the Elder's novel, complemented *A Confederacy of Dunces* because of the new work's parodic nature and intent.

I then asked Toole the Younger why, of all people on this earth, he had come to me.

Toole the Younger's explanation was rather lengthy, but to make a long story short, here is the essence: years earlier he had contacted and met with several agents and publishers within greater New York City, and an editor at a major publishing firm in midtown Manhattan showed interest, as did a literary agent in uptown Manhattan. The literary agent and the publishing firm drafted a contract, knowing that the parody had the potential to become a bestseller, but unfortunately for them, Toole the Younger did not accept the terms of the contract.

For one thing, Toole the Younger believed that the publisher wanted to eviscerate the parody by making it "politically correct," thus making it more palatable, and thus more marketable, to the general, feeble-minded public. Being an antiauthoritarian, and believing in the freedom of the press and in the freedom of the artist, Toole the Younger continued to refuse the terms, even though the major publishing firm repeatedly redrafted the contract and offered to pay Toole the Younger an initial payment of a cool $1 million. The literary agent, of course, did her best to get Toole the Younger to sign the contract, even dropping to her knees and offering to perform a sexual act on him, but he played the cigar-store wooden Indian and would not budge, and he subsequently fired his literary agent and told the major publishing firm that he was no longer interested in its services, its lucrative offers, or anything else that it might have to offer.

And for another thing, Toole the Younger wasn't so sure that he wanted to support "the big guys." The corporate media, by way of the totalitarian powers that be, are attempting to stifle artistic expression, especially artistic expression divergent from what the corporate media (by way of the totalitarian powers that be) want to foist upon a gullible public. Toole the Younger wanted nothing to do with foisting anything upon anybody.

Thus, Toole the Younger decided to go the academic route.

That, however, was a more arduous route and, subsequently, a more futile route than the commercial route that he had previously undertaken.

Toole the Younger came to discover that he did not care for the presses of modern American universities, which he came to consider indoctrination centers, not institutions of education, with all of these so-called places of learning publishing what Toole the Younger called "politically correct tripe." The academic publishers wanted to eviscerate the parody even further than the major publishing firm in New York City had wanted; if one hasn't noticed, the politically correct left does not have a sense of humor. (Here's a joke that Dr. de DaSilva told me his first day at Brooklyn Bridge University: he had picked up the recently published *The Leftist Joke Book* [the Braille edition, of course], only to discover that the pages were blank. I had a hearty laugh. Did you, dear reader?) Besides wanting to eviscerate the parody, the academic publishers wanted to turn the parody's protagonist, Ignatius J. Reilly, into something that he was not and clearly could never be: a politically correct eco-warrior who renounces proper theology and geometry and who comes out of the closet as a homosexual with transgender proclivities.

The worst offenders were a public university in Kansas, several public and private West Coast universities, and all East Coast universities. In effect, Toole told them what they could do with their so-called revisions, put away the parody, and returned to rural Maine, where he hunted, fished, and perfected his baidarka navigational skills by making forays to Newfoundland and to Nova Scotia.

Fast-forward two years. Tragedy struck: Toole the Younger's mother (who had told him his true identity when Toole the Younger turned twenty-one) died of pancreatic cancer. It was a vicious blow to the literary upstart, who decided that he could no longer wait to see his parodic novel published but had to act and to act quickly.

Hence, he spent a week going through his marketing notes, wondering what literary agents or publishers he should contact, when he found my name at the bottom of the list, Toole the Younger never having contacted me because of his frustration with all academic media. Nonetheless, Toole the Younger sensed that I and my singular university might be able to help him. So, Toole the Younger went online, researched my background more extensively, compiled a list of my four hundred or so articles published in academic journals and in Yiddish weekly newspapers, read critical reviews of my work, and then read my essay "The Ideological and Theological Demesnes of John Calvin: Determinism as Manichean Comedy in Protestant-Era Geneva" in the philosophical-philological journal *Pseudocopula* (June 2008). Convinced that I was a scholar with a sense of humor (or perhaps a sense of humor that was a scholar), Toole the Younger decided that he had to see me.

"Why not just contact me first by way of e-mail?" I asked. "What if I don't like your parody? Wouldn't your paddling from Maine thus be in vain?"

"Do you always rhyme?" he asked.

"Only when the Seussian mood strikes me," I replied.

"You must read this novel today," he said. "There is no other work like it. And you must see to it that this parody is published. And I am *not* taking no for an answer, Dr. Katecki."

By his steely, determined look, I knew that he was not going to take no for an answer. So I promised him that I would read the parody. We shook hands, and Toole the Younger said that he was going to paddle his baidarka to New Jersey and camp somewhere near Fort Lee; he would return the next day, by way of his baidarka and the East River, to see what I thought of the parody.

After Toole the Younger left my office, I stood at my office window and watched him paddle down the East River until he became a speck on the horizon and vanished. Given that I had rescheduled the graduate seminar, and given that I had no other classes to teach that day, I opened the Kinko's photocopy box that Toole the Younger had placed atop my desk.

Within the photocopy box was a smudged manuscript, a work that had been typed, I assumed by studying the font, on an Olivetti typewriter. (I later discovered that my assumption was correct.) I briefly glanced at the cover page and then read the opening paragraphs. Soon I was lost in the parodic world that John Kennedy Toole Jr. had created.

To say that I could not put the parody down would be an understatement. I chuckled. I laughed. I cried. And I began rereading the parody after I completed my first reading of its 120,000 words, and, in the middle of my second reading, I discovered that the time was nearing midnight. I knew that I should probably return to my studio apartment in Coney Island to get the rest that I needed, but Toole the Younger's words would not let me go. I read and read and read until dawn arrived, when I could read no further.

I showered in the men's locker room and then excitedly told Mrs. Means and Dr. de DaSilva, upon their arrivals at Brooklyn Bridge University, that we had a book to publish.

Toole the Younger appeared at my office later that morning. I told him that we had a deal.

Hence, you now have *A Cornucopia of Dunderheads*[4] by John Kennedy Toole Jr., courtesy of Brooklyn Bridge University Press, in your hands (or feet, or however you are holding this parodic novel), dear reader.

Some might wonder if this parody, unauthorized in the sense that Toole the Younger did not seek anyone's permission to craft this parodic work and authorized in the sense that he had the legal right and the artistic right to do so, should have been published. If you are one of those people, continue to read. You'll discover not only why this parody should be published but why this parody needs to be made available to the world now, in this turbulent period of world history.

But first, before we get into that discussion, we need to discuss what differentiates a satire from a parody.

---

4 Toole the Younger uses an extensive amount of wordplay in this novel; and there are several homages, too. Those that come to mind are to the novelist Anthony Burgess, the filmmaker Paul Morrissey, and several others. Also, for the dream sequence involving Ignatius, Myrna, Dr. Ingloss, and the group therapy group, Toole the Younger borrows from *Psychopathia Sexualis* by Richard Von Krafft-Ebing (Bell Publishing Company, 1965). In addition, Toole the Younger takes artistic license wherever he deems it necessary.

A satire is a comedic work that mocks a person or people or institution or period of time with biting, often exaggerated humor. A satire exploits the human and social and political foibles of its times, as the Soviet-era writer Mikhail Bulgakov does in *The Master and Margarita* (Grove Press, 1994) and as Swinging London-era Joe Orton does in his plays, most notably *What the Butler Saw* (Methuen Drama, 1969).

A parody, on the other hand, mocks a specific work of art (playfully or meanly), typically by exaggeration of the parodied work's theme, characterization, plot, or style, or some combination thereof. Parodies can parody serious works of art, satires, and even other parodies. The parodic songs of Weird Al Yankovic come to mind (my personal favorite is "Smells Like Nirvana"), as do those of Allan Sherman, about whom I am writing a critical biography when I am not doing my Tuesday janitorial duties. In terms of the literary, Ernest Hemingway's *The Torrents of Spring* (Scribner, 1998) enters the fray. Hemingway's parody mocks the work and writing style of Sherwood Anderson, whose work I read whenever I am constipated; Anderson's prose, for whatever reason, unblocks my blocked bowels. (Theodore Dreiser's work has much the same effect on me.)[5]

Thus, *A Confederacy of Dunces* by John Kennedy Toole is a satire. And thus, *A Cornucopia of Dunderheads* by John Kennedy Toole Jr. is a parody.

Now that we have discussed this differentiation, we need to discuss copyright law as it pertains to *Dunderheads*. In a truly free and freely true society, such laws need not exist. Such, however, is not the case in our times. Thus, accordingly, we must discuss legal reasoning and legal cases that set the precedent for the defense of parody as a commercial art form.

The doctrine of fair use pertains to one's usage of the copyrighted works of another. According to Wikipedia, fair use is the

---

5 If you, dear reader, suffer constipation, I recommend Anderson's *Winesburg, Ohio* (Dover Thrift Editions, 1995), and Dreiser's *An American Tragedy* (Signet Classics, 2010) as suitable remedies.

limitations of and exception to the exclusive rights granted by copyright law to the author of a creative work. The United States Supreme Court ruled unequivocally in Campbell v. Acuff-Rose Music, Inc., 510 US 569 (1994) that parody can qualify as fair use under 17 USC § 107 (Limitations on exclusive rights: fair use) of the Copyright Act of 1976. According to the Supreme Court, parody provides social benefit "by shedding light on an earlier work, and in the process, creating a new one" (which is what John Kennedy Toole Jr. has done in his parodic novel *Dunderheads*). Thus, *Dunderheads* is a transformative work. (In other words, dear reader, *Dunderheads* is NOT a sequel to *Dunces*. The novel *Dunderheads* parodies the thematic elements, characters, plot, plot devices, language, and style of *Dunces*, with the setting in *Dunderheads*, however, being New York City, not New Orleans.)

In addition, the Supreme Court's decision pertaining to Campbell v. Acuff-Rose Music, Inc., allows for parodies to be made for commercial purposes. (Campbell v. Acuff-Rose Music, Inc., by the way, is a case in which 2 Live Crew, a rap group, did a parody of Roy Orbison's "Oh, Pretty Woman." According to Wikipedia, the group's manager asked Acuff-Rose Music, Inc., for a license to use Orbison's song for a parodic work by the members of 2 Live Crew; Acuff-Rose Music, Inc., refused to grant the rappers a license, but 2 Live Crew nonetheless produced and released the parody. Long story short: there was a lawsuit or two, and the Supreme Court ruled in favor of 2 Live Crew.)

According to Wikipedia's entry about the aforementioned case, the Supreme Court ruled that parodies rarely substitute for the original work, since the two works serve different market functions. In other words, *Dunces* serves the market for satire. *Dunderheads*, on the other hand, serves the market for parody. (Even though *Dunces* is a comedic work, and even though *Dunderheads* is a comedic work, the two works are entirely different. As shown, satires are not parodies, and parodies are not satires.)

Another case provides legal precedent for what Toole the Younger has done in *Dunderheads*. SunTrust Bank v. Houghton Mifflin Co., 252 F. 3d 1165 (11th Cir. 2001), opinion at 268 F. 3d 1257, was a case decided by the United States Court of Appeals for the Eleventh Circuit against the owner of Margaret Mitchell's *Gone with the Wind*, vacating an injunction prohibiting the publisher of Alice Randall's *The Wind Done Gone* from distributing the book, according to Wikipedia. And, according to Wikipedia, the case arguably stands for the principle that the creation and publication of a carefully written parodic novel in the United States counts as fair use. Despite stating that substantial portions of Mitchell's work were used, the Court of Appeals found that the likely outcome of a full adjudication of the rights involved was a finding of fair use, according to Wikipedia.

In permitting parody without permission, according to Wikipedia, the decision in SunTrust follows the previous Supreme Court decision in Campbell v. Acuff-Rose Music, Inc., in which the Supreme Court ruled that 2 Live Crew's unlicensed use of the bass line from Roy Orbison's "Oh, Pretty Woman" constituted fair use, even though 2 Live Crew's work was a commercial use; this ruling thereby extends the legal principle and precedent from songs to novels. According to Wikipedia, SunTrust is a binding precedent.

We could review other cases and precedents, dear reader, but the two aforementioned cases suffice for the legal protection that Toole the Younger needs in regards to the publication of *A Cornucopia of Dunderheads*. As for real-world examples of parody, here are a few: *Fifty Shames of Earl Grey: A Parody* by Fanny Merkin and Andrew Shaffer (Da Capo Press, 2012), *Fifty Sheds of Grey* by C. T. Grey (St. Martin's Griffin, 2012), *The Hunger Pains: A Parody* by Harvard Lampoon (Touchstone, 2012), *Bored of the Rings: A Parody* by Harvard Lampoon (Touchstone, 2012), *Nightlight: A Parody* by Harvard Lampoon (Vintage, 2009), among numerous others.

Now, on to the artistic reasons for why Toole the Younger wrote *A Cornucopia of Dunderheads.*

We live in a fascistic, Orwellian, decadent world, one in which the definitions of words are being mutated constantly by the totalitarian powers that be (university committees, political groups, activists, politicians, globalists, demagogues, you name it) so that the totalitarian powers that be can control us, either in actual prisons or in prisons of thought. As I write this, the totalitarian powers that be are doing their best to remove the First Amendment rights of the US citizenry. Examples of this are so-called free speech zones, so-called hate speech laws, and the potential taxing of citizens for using trademarked names like Disney. (Insane? Wait until you get a bill from Disney, the government, or both after you mention Disney in an e-mail monitored courtesy of the National Security Agency.)

Eventually, if the totalitarian powers that be have their way, satire and parody will go the way of the dinosaur, not from a lack of interest in these works but because the creation of them will be illegal. Do you remember reading earlier that the politically correct left does not have a sense of humor? The truth is that no statist (left wing or right wing) has a sense of humor. And each statist wants to be taken seriously; no, no, no, you must never mock them or laugh at them. Hence, their hatred of satire and parody, especially the latter.

And hence, why John Kennedy Toole Jr. wrote *A Cornucopia of Dunderheads*: this parody is a slap to the face of the totalitarians.

Some might argue that it were better that this novel had never been written, that, somehow, *Dunderheads* is a mockery of the work and memory of Toole the Elder. Toole the Younger begs to differ. If you, dear reader, read carefully, you'll see that playfulness, not meanness, motivates Toole the Younger.

I must leave you with an exquisite, important note, dear reader: *Dunderheads*, like *Dunces*, is not a politically correct novel. If anything, *Dunderheads*, because it is a parody, exaggerates its political incorrectness.[6, 7, 8]

Much has been said about *A Confederacy of Dunces*, and much more can be said. At its heart, *Dunces* is an anarchic novel; Ignatius does not act, *per se*, but reacts; but the point is, he does do something. Unfortunately, the editor Robert Gottlieb failed to understand this.

I hope that you enjoy *A Cornucopia of Dunderheads*, a literary masterpiece and a testament that comedic genius still exists, even in the darkest of times like ours.

> Franz-Heinrich Katecki, BA, BASc, BCJ, BCL, BEd, BFA, BS, BSc, DCL, DD, DLit, DPhil, DPT, DSc, DUniv, FdA, FdSC, JD, LLB, LLBean, LLD, LLM, MA, MBA, MCD, MD, MEd, MFA, MJur, MLib, MPA, MRes, MS, MSc, MSt, MTh, MTL, PhD, ThD

---

6 Real comedy, to paraphrase George Carlin, cannot be politically correct. Cf. the work of Carlin, the work of Richard Pryor, and the work of Lenny Bruce.

7 In *Dunces*, blacks are the predominant racial minority group. In *Dunderheads*, however, Puerto Ricans and Chinese are the predominant racial minority groups, and Jews are the predominant ethnic-religious minority group. Note that I do not use the terminology *African American* or *European American*. The former terminology is a misnomer because not all Africans were or are of Negroid descent. Likewise, the latter terminology is a misnomer, in that not all Europeans were or are of Caucasoid descent.

8 In the spirit of *Dunces*, *Dunderheads* employs the politically incorrect language of the 1960s and parodies the homophobia in *Dunces* by exaggerating that homophobia. Rest assured, dear reader, neither Toole the Younger nor I are racists or anti-Semites or homophobes, though an idiot or two, not having read this foreword and its footnotes completely and understandingly, and not understanding this parody, might make such false accusations.

The use of traveling is to regulate imagination by reality, and instead of thinking how things may be, to see them as they are.

—SAMUEL JOHNSON, *ANECDOTES OF SAMUEL JOHNSON*

Southern political personalities, like sweet corn, travel badly. They lose flavor with every hundred yards away from the patch. By the time they reach New York, they are like Golden Bantam that has been trucked up from Texas—stale and unprofitable. The consumer forgets that the corn tastes different where it grows.

—A. J. LIEBLING, *THE EARL OF LOUISIANA*

One

A green hunting cap squeezed the top of the fleshy blimp of a head. Green earflaps stuck out, one flap up, the other down, not like two turn signals indicating two directions at once, but like middle fingers thrust out angrily at a chaotic world. Full, pursed lips smacked, and the mouth attached to them craved potato chips, one of Mr. Clyde's foot-longs, and a Dr. Nut. Underneath the green visor of the hunting cap, Ignatius J. Reilly's supercilious blue and yellow eyes stared at the back of Myrna Minkoff's head. Myrna and Ignatius had just arrived in her battered Renault at her mother and father's house.

A Colonial Revival house among several, the Minkoff estate stood on Valentine Avenue in the Bedford Park area of the Bronx. Before arriving in the Bronx, Ignatius had imagined that the area would be teeming with unwashed Eastern Europeans (Jews, Russians, Magyars, Transylvanians, Slovaks, Czechs, Serbs, Croats, Bulgarians, Moldovans, Montenegrins, Szgany), immigrants living in gray and graying tenements under gray and graying skies, with the Jewish immigrants arguing incomprehensibly, to the untrained ear, in Yiddish one to another. Ignatius had attempted to imagine the odors of the immigrants, but his own peculiar odor—one like well-used orange pekoe tea bags—got in the way of his olfactory imagination. From the initial looks of things, it seemed that his initial ruminations were false.

Grunting, Ignatius struggled to sit up in the backseat of the dilapidated Renault. His nemesis-friend Myrna, who had helped him to escape New Orleans, looked over her shoulder at him. Though she had been driving for days, she had an indefatigable corona of energy that only rescuers have. Ignatius had fought her off at several rest stops. Fortunately, he had kept his virginity inviolate.

"You okay, Ignatius?"

"How else would I be doing under such circumstances?" Ignatius said, doing his best not to bellow. He pushed aside the shattered remains of Myrna's guitar, which he had inadvertently destroyed during a rest stop in Pittsburgh. "Of course I'm doing well. We have escaped incestuous New Orleans and entered the holy land of Gotham, where I am to be purified. A few days in bed and a few hearty meals, and I shall be more than ready to face this oh-so-cruel world."

"Remember what we talked about?" Myrna winked at him, yet her expression was quite serious. "You're hostile because of your sexual repression. We're going to work on that by working on that virginity problem of yours, right?"

"Good heavens, please, not now," Ignatius said, clutching his chest, pretending that he might suffer a coronary. His belly gurgled, and he shuddered at the thought of his seeing Myrna nude. "I'm not sure that my worldview is ready. Your body is like that of an odalisque in a seraglio, you minx, and the thought of my piercing you almost drives me into a wanton lust."

"Huh?"

"So this is the grand, famed Minkoff estate?" Ignatius asked, wanting to change the subject. Cupping his paws on the cold passenger-side window, he formed binoculars through which he peered. The Minkoff estate indeed. It was evening; the sun had set almost half an hour earlier, and the white house had a bluish hue to it now. "It appears that your father has done exceptionally well as a pawnbroker."

"That sounds like another anti-Semitic remark, Ignatius," Myrna said, glowering, "and one, quite frankly, that I do not appreciate. My father is not a pawnbroker. He owns a restaurant supply business. He's bourgeois through and through, but I can't help that. My group therapy group is helping me to overcome the stigma of having been raised in an overly white, overly Jewish, and overly privileged household."

"Yuss, of course," Ignatius said, slipping into the Mayfair accent that he had used to fool Gus Levy. Then Ignatius spoke in his normal voice, sans the supercilious tone. "It is dinnertime, I assume, is it not? This ride has been so enervating that I'm most willing to eat anything, including matzah ball soup and other fine Jewish delicacies."

"What is it with all of these anti-Semitic remarks, Ignatius?" Myrna said peevishly. She put on her black horn-rimmed glasses, which weren't real glasses but which she wore to emphasize her commitment to the cause at hand. "Because if you are going to keep making remarks like these, I might have a good mind to turn this car around and take you back to New Orleans." She paused, staring thoughtfully at him. "I thought we were getting along for once. I thought I was getting through to you for once. I thought you were beginning to see the light for once, especially in the sexual sense, considering that horrid, cloistered existence that you were living down there in New Orleans." She blinked. "Anyway, no more anti-Semitic remarks, okay?"

"I have absolutely nothing but positive things to say about the Jews, especially when they addecimate and especially in regards to their forays into things sexual, as witnessed by our dear friend and colleague, the late Sigmund Freud," Ignatius said imperiously as he straightened the earflaps on his green hunting cap, lonely for New Orleans but certainly not wanting to go back there, especially under those current dire circumstances. "It's terribly cold. I would like to go inside and get warm and partake of a repast that will adimpleate an ill lad who's been traveling up the Eastern Seaboard."

In the living room of the Minkoff house, Mr. Minkoff and Mrs. Minkoff peered through the front window at the idling

Renault. Mr. Minkoff shook his head in disgust and sat down in his recliner and kicked up his slipper-encased feet onto an ottoman while simultaneously slipping his hands into that day's edition of the *New York Times*. Mrs. Minkoff handed him his lit Peterson briar pipe, the stem of which he inserted into a corner of his mouth without thanking her. Mrs. Minkoff noted how stern and authoritarian he appeared, especially because of his receding hairline and because of the reading glasses that he was wearing. She loved Mr. Minkoff even more when he looked stern and authoritarian. Myrna, fortunately, had inherited her father's looks.

Mrs. Minkoff sat down on a sofa and looked at Mr. Minkoff, who was reading an article about Puerto Ricans and homosexuals warring against one another in lower Manhattan.

"Did Myrna say that he was Jewish?" Mrs. Minkoff asked.

"Who?" he asked.

"That man that Myrna brought home." Mrs. Minkoff blinked, forgetting the question that she had just asked her husband. "What was I talking about, Bernard?"

"You were asking if what the cat dragged in was Jewish," he answered, exhaling cumulus clouds of cherry-vanilla smoke through his nostrils and putting aside the front section of the paper and flipping to the business section. "How the hell should I know if he's Jewish? You want me to ask him to drop his pants so that I can see if he's circumcised?"

"Even if he is circumcised, that doesn't mean that he's Jewish," Mrs. Minkoff said. "Most gentile men are circumcised these days, from what I've heard, and these men certainly aren't Jewish."

"No, gentile men certainly aren't Jewish," Mr. Minkoff said in a voice that mimicked hers, almost sounding as if he were imitating Stan Laurel. Then he returned to his normal voice. "I can't believe that we're having this conversation, Miriam. I used to wonder why Myrna was such a dingbat. Now I think I understand why."

"What were we talking about?"

"Oh, to hell with it."

Outside, Ignatius did his best to navigate his ursine frame up a sidewalk buckled by the roots of now-dormant oaks. A thin coating of ice covered the sidewalk, like light frosting on an expensive birthday cake, and his tree-trunk-like legs, which had always been weak as far as he could remember, could barely transverse this new, strange terrain in which he found himself. Myrna held on to one of his heavy arms and dragged him forward, one inch at a time. Ignatius wobbled in his boots. His ursine body threatened to thump butt-first or to pitch face-first.

"Do be careful!" Ignatius wailed, looking as if he were standing on a surfboard and riding a wave to a sunny Californian shore. "You're going to kill me, you minx!"

"Quit fighting," Myrna said, as if speaking to a paramour who didn't want to be ravished. "Jesus, you would think we were climbing Mount Everest or something."

"Oh, my God!" Ignatius bellowed, feeling his pyloric valve about to seal. "Oh, no!"

"What, Ignatius?"

"Oh, oh, oh!" Ignatius bellowed, and then it happened: Ignatius farted, his flatulence filling the air with a noxious, sulfurous gas generated from too many bowls of greasy chili and too many cheap hot dogs eaten at the last truck stop.

Mrs. Minkoff watched from the front window. In the front yard, Myrna gagged and hopped about, as if in terpsichorean rapture. Mrs. Minkoff wondered if the wobbly man had just proposed to Myrna. Mrs. Minkoff certainly hoped so, and she certainly hoped that he was Jewish.

Myrna leaned over and vomited, steam rising from the remnants of her last meal—corned beef and hash browns and a pot of black, bitter coffee—which she had had at the truck stop. Ignatius slipped, yelped like Oliver Hardy, and plunged face-first into the snow. He squalled, flailing his arms and legs as if he were making a snow angel.

Myrna stood and wiped her forehead, which was dotted with perspiration. Her breath formed clouds that vanished just as quickly as they formed. It was getting darker, and she thought that she heard Negro carolers singing somewhere in the distance.

"I'm beginning to wonder if this was such a good idea," she said. "You know, Ignatius, that I believe in saving the world, and that means saving everyone, including you. But I'm not so sure that you can be saved. Sometimes you seem to be your old nasty self, and at other times you behave like a saint. When I take you to meet my group therapy group, we'll have to work on that dichotomy, which—as Freud might say—has something to do with repressed homosexuality or the onset of paranoid schizophrenia."

Ignatius pretended that he didn't hear her. Instead, he crawled through the snow like a battle-weary soldier making his way across a field laced with land mines. Fortuna had played gambits with him his entire life, spinning him into numerous cycles. But the Wreck of the Plymouth had been the start of a vicious cycle unlike any other that he had had in his relatively short life. When he had the time, he would write an essay about the evils of modern devices and contrivances, particularly the Plymouth. If only his mother had had an elegantly carved cabriolet from Paris instead of a mass-manufactured vehicle from Detroit, then none of this would have occurred.

Myrna reached down and placed her hand under his armpit.

"What do you think you're doing!" Ignatius squealed.

"Ignatius, come on, stand up," she said, tired like Ignatius and wanting to get inside where it was warm. "It's been a long week for both of us. Let's get inside, get warm, and get something to eat."

Ignatius frowned and bit the end of his bushy black mustache, which needed trimming. He sat up gingerly on his knees as he held Myrna's outstretched hand.

Mrs. Minkoff watched the goings-on. She smiled. Mr. Minkoff now stood at her side, the stem of the Peterson briar pipe affixed to a corner of his mouth, as if the pipe were a permanent feature.

"What's happening?" he asked.

"He's proposed to Myrna!" Mrs. Minkoff yelled excitedly. "Our baby's getting married! Mother, oh, Mother, where are you! Mother! Mother—"

"Your mother's in bed where she belongs," Mr. Minkoff said, shuddering at the thought of the toothless and gray and weird-smelling Grandmother Horowitz, as they called Mrs. Minkoff's wizened mother. Before Myrna had taken off for New Orleans to rescue Ignatius, she and Grandmother Horowitz began to discuss their favorite sexual positions. Subsequently Mr. Minkoff had had several nightmares in which he engaged in bestial acts with his mother-in-law, acts that would have put Sodom and Gomorrah to shame, acts that not even the owners of the smoky and oily porno shops and theaters throughout New York City could imagine. "Let her rest. If that big lug is stupid enough to propose to Myrna, we can announce it to Grandmother Horowitz and the rest of the world later."

The front door opened, and Myrna stepped into the foyer, stamping her booted feet and ridding them of snow. Ignatius entered, gasping, his green hunting cap askew, and Myrna closed and locked the front door behind them.

"*Chez* Minkoff," Ignatius said, studying the foyer and its hallway with his supercilious blue and yellow eyes. He thought that he smelled potato pancakes and borscht and cayenne peppers. He wrinkled his nose, cataloging the intermixing scents, unsure, however, in which categories the scents belonged. "Of course, it is time to eat our magnificent dinner. I shall require a repast fit for a king, perhaps even fit for a gypsy king, something along the lines of a steamed grouse or a corned gamecock or two. Being that this is a Jewish household, however, I assume the offerings might be a bit paltry and not as elegant, but I'll have to make do. And afterward, you can take me to my room, preferably one with a large bed in which I can begin my extensive and intensive ruminations once again. Speaking of which, my Big Chief tablets—"

"Come meet my parents," Myrna said, ignoring what she would have called anti-Semitic remarks because she was too tired. She took Ignatius by the hand and led him from the foyer into the adjoining living room.

Mrs. Minkoff was sitting on the sofa, hands in her lap, smiling amiably at the two. Mr. Minkoff stood at a bar, pouring himself a shot of Maker's Mark. He had a feeling that he was going to have a lot of drinking in store for him the next few days. He downed the shot and then poured himself another without offering any to his wife, to Myrna, or to the huge strange-looking man standing in the middle of the living room.

"Dad, Mom, please meet Ignatius," Myrna said. "He's my new pet project. Ignatius, these are my parents."

Ignatius stared at Mr. Minkoff and Mrs. Minkoff, who, in turn, stared back at him.

"That's funny, you don't look Jewish," Mrs. Minkoff said to Ignatius.

"That's because he's not Jewish," Mr. Minkoff said, scowling, removing the stem of the pipe from the corner of his mouth and offering his hand to Ignatius and then retracting the hand, thinking the better of it. "Another of Myrna's projects, huh?" He turned to Myrna. "Like that epileptic Negro banjo player you brought here? After what he did at the dinner table, it's a wonder your mother and I can ever eat again."

"I would never touch such a horrid instrument," Ignatius said, insulted by Mr. Minkoff's insolence and lack of proper theology and geometry. What did he, Ignatius, look like? A picaro from a Mark Twain novel, of all things? "The banjo is a tinny abomination. Besides, the music that one plays on a banjo is contrary to my worldview, which is that of the medievalist. I play the *lute*, not the banjo."

"The flute?" Mrs. Minkoff said, beaming. "That's such a lovely instrument."

"He didn't say flute. He said lute, whatever the hell that is," Mr. Minkoff said. "Sounds like something one of those commie, radical beatniks down there in Greenwich Village plays. The news is on. Go get the table set for dinner, Miriam. And while you're at it, forget to wake up that dingbat mother of yours."

"Are you strict in your dietary observations?" Mrs. Minkoff asked Ignatius.

"Jesus Christ," Mr. Minkoff said, shaking his head. "I told you, he isn't Jewish. Are you Jewish, Ignacio?"

"Ignatius," Myrna said angrily, emphasizing her point with her hands. "His name's Ignatius. And no, he isn't Jewish. Why do you always insist on insulting my friends whenever I bring them home, Dad?"

"It must be because I've been reading too many stories about Puerto Rican gang leaders in the *New York Times*," Mr. Minkoff said solemnly, reaching down and turning on a large-screen television set. A dot appeared on the screen, and then the color set hummed, and Walter Cronkite stared at his viewers, the anchorman intoning solemnly about that day's events. "Excuse me for living, especially in this household of dingbat women."

"That's another thing I want to talk to you about," Myrna said forcefully, forgetting Ignatius and walking up to her father and wagging a finger in his reddened face. "It's your sexist attitudes towards women. Has it ever occurred to you that women are going to be running the world one day, Dad?"

"With the way things are screwed up, I thought that they were already running it," Mr. Minkoff said irascibly, sitting down in his recliner. He frowned and motioned for silence with both hands.

"It's a wonder that I haven't already gone insane. Now, quiet. Walter is on, and you know what that means."

"Yeah, yeah," Myrna said, throwing up her hands in mock surrender. "It means that we have to be quiet while the high holy reactionary gives us his prefabricated, regurgitated mass-media views of the world."

"Would you happen to have any hot cocoa ready?" Ignatius said to Mrs. Minkoff before she stepped into the kitchen.

"No, but I can make some for you if you want, Ignacio."

"That would be truly lovely," Ignatius said, finding himself truly liking the Spanish version of his name and truly desiring hot cocoa and truly desiring a means of escape from the palpable tension in the living room. It seemed as if things were about to explode into a conflict like one brewing in some godforsaken country in Southeast Asia. "Would you happen to have marshmallows, too?"

"I think we do, but I'm not sure if they're kosher," Mrs. Minkoff said, leading the way to the kitchen. "Why don't you follow me, and we'll find out."

"I would be most delighted to do that," Ignatius said, and he felt tempted to comment negatively about the tasteless prints of modern art adorning the living room walls and the dining room walls but decided against it. There would be a time and a place for dealing with the Minkoffs.

Myrna sat down next to her father's recliner, like an acolyte sitting at the feet of an adept. A Mutual of New York commercial played, and Mr. Minkoff unzipped a leather pouch, from which he retrieved a bolus of cherry-vanilla tobacco that he placed into the bowl of his pipe. He lit his pipe and then looked at Myrna, who was looking up at him with sad puppy-dog eyes.

"What?" he said irritably. "What did I do now?"

"I need money, Dad."

"You always need money. When don't you need money?" He puffed as another commercial—one advertising a sporty-looking Corvair—played. The car looked nifty. More important, it looked safe. Mr. Minkoff thought that he might like to own one someday.

"I'm being serious, Dad. Ignatius is in big trouble."

Mr. Minkoff raised an eyebrow. "Jesus, don't tell me that you brought home an escapee from some Louisiana penitentiary. Is that what you've done, Myrna?"

"Keep it down, Dad," Myrna said cautiously, motioning with her hands. "I don't want him to hear us—"

"What kind of trouble is that lug in?"

"Personal trouble," Myrna replied, making the kind of face that she made before entering a protest, especially one whose points she did not understand. "The kind of trouble that's going to require a lot of money. His mother's insane and plans to marry a Ku Klux Klan member, and she was going to send Ignatius to an asylum, of all things."

"He looks like he belongs in one," Mr. Minkoff said, and he motioned for Myrna to become quiet because Walter Cronkite was on. "That or a zoo. Just let me watch the news, all right? We can discuss this later."

"It's always later with you."

"Quiet! Walter's on!"

II

A man with a racing form in one hand leaned against a rail in Battery Park. Across the winter waves of the Atlantic stood the Statue of Liberty, fulgent in nocturnal illumination as sea breezes battered it and lower Manhattan. A fireplug of a beat cop, Irish by birth and irate by winter, trudged by, truncheon in hand. The beat cop gave the man with a racing form a hard, questioning look. The man with the racing form stared back at the beat cop until the beat cop looked away.

The man with the racing form sniffled, feeling the onset of a bad head cold. He hadn't been feeling well the past month or so. He wondered if he might have caught a bug in one of the many dives that he had been frequenting during his two-month sojourn in New Orleans. Great architecture, especially Jackson Square, and great food, especially those dressed po' boys, but that city had the strangest people, that was for sure. It seemed to be a perpetual Mardi Gras or a never-ending confederacy of dunces. For no particular reason, he thought about that one night in November, when he had been in the Night of Joy in the French Quarter, and he thought about that strange fat man wearing a green hunting cap and his saddened little mother, who had shared her macaroons and wine cakes with the joint's denizens. The man with the racing form wondered what had become of the pair, and when one of the many cabs honked, the remembrance left his mind like a snowflake batted away by a harsh wind.

He blinked. A tropaean wind blew into Battery Park, and he shuddered, hunching his shoulders against the subzero wind chill. Nick the Nose should have been there by now. Nick the Nose should have known better than to be late. Nick the Nose should have been doing this job, that's what Nick the Nose should have been doing. And he, the man with the racing form, should have been at the Algonquin Hotel, sitting in bed and drinking hot toddies.

The man placed the racing form into an oversized pocket in his pea coat, adjusted a heavy muffler encircling his neck, and turned, scanning through winter-watery eyes the numerous executives and office workers hurrying by. A Salvation Army band played "God Rest Ye Merry, Gentlemen" on a corner, and a man wearing a creosote-colored Cossack cap and a long winter coat tossed two quarters into a red Salvation Army bucket, each coin plinking.

The man with the racing form sniffled. The New York City air tasted like copper. He could tell that this head cold was going to be an especially bad one.

"Hey," Nick the Nose said, appearing from the dark, his murine teeth gleaming yellow under street light. He reeked of stale cigarette smoke and was wearing a seedy topcoat that looked as if he'd just stolen it off a corpse. He picked his nose, wiped his finger on his pants, and rubbed his hands together. "Cold as hell out heh. You must be him. What da hell you doin' out heh, man?"

"Wad do you dink?" the man with the racing form said. "Drop's subosed to be here."

"You Russian or sumpin, man?"

"Screw you," the man with the racing form said. "I'm gedding a code."

"Shut it," Nick the Nose said, his murine eyes bugging out. "You ain't supposed to be talkin' about no codes, got me?"

"Screw you," the man with the racing form said. "Code, a code. I have a code. Unastan?"

"Oh, oh, a cold, a cold," the murine, balding, hunched-over man said, finally understanding. "Gotcha. Look, let's go across da street to Joseph's Lounge. They got great ouzo dere. Ouzo's good for da cold. Ya like ouzo, do ya?"

"You subosed to be here. Vy—"

"Come on, man." And the murine man grabbed the other operative's arm and dragged the other operative across the street.

The oak-paneled interior of Joseph's Lounge was dark and musky-odored. Dour-faced businessmen wearing finely tailored suits stood at the bar, intermingling with cherubic-faced clerks fresh from their Wall Street jobs. The man with the racing form noticed that there were not any women in the bar. That made him nervous. When a bar didn't have women, it meant one of two things: either the place was becoming a queer joint or was already a queer joint. The man with the racing form did not like queers or queer joints. Queers and queer joints always spelled trouble with a capital T.

He looked suspiciously at Nick the Nose, who was leading the way to one of the many unoccupied booths in the back. Nick the Nose kept his hands too long on the shoulders of the men whom the rat-faced man was gently pushing aside. The man with the racing form did not like the way that Nick the Nose touched—make that lovingly fondled—the men.

Nick the Nose sat down in a corner booth, and the man with the racing form slid into the opposite seat. Nick the Nose snapped his fingers at a cross-eyed Negro waiter. The lanky waiter sauntered to the table, a hand on his waist, the other hand supporting an elliptical serving tray. Nick the Nose ordered two ouzos, served steaming hot. The cross-eyed Negro nodded and went to place the order. The man with the racing form sniffled and unwrapped a cloth napkin, from which he removed a knife, a spoon, and a fork, and wiped his philtrum with the cloth.

"We play like we's normal, havin' us a good time," Nick the Nose said. "By da way, sailor, what's yer name?"

"It idn't sailor, dad's for sure," the man with the racing form said, his refined Yale sensibilities offended by this impertinent Brooklyn rat. "Id's Henley."

"Ids Henley? Interestin' name. Ids Henley, go figure."

"No, no," Henley said. He sneezed into the cloth napkin, and the cross-eyed Negro waiter, who was lankily walking by, blessed Henley in a voice as high as Little Richard's. "Henley. Dad's all you need to know."

"Oh, oh, Henley, Henley, gotcha, right," Nick the Nose said, winking. Then he peered at Henley, Nick the Nose's murine eyes intense in his murine face. "Okay, after we finish da drinks, you slip it to me. You heads out, then I heads out, got it?"

Henley nodded and wheezed. He was tired of being a government operative. And he was tired of traveling. A Cuban had almost gunned down Henley in Omaha, and a cast and crew of mafioso characters in Kansas City had almost killed him. He hadn't particularly liked the characters there. They had been real creeps, all right. Just as Nick the Nose was a real creep.

The cross-eyed Negro waiter arrived with two large shot glasses filled with steaming ouzo. After thanking the waiter, Nick the Nose raised his shot, saluted Henley, and downed the ouzo in one gulp.

"G'head, g'head," the rat-faced man said, smiling, revealing crooked, yellow teeth. "Drink it. It'll kill the crap what's ailin' you."

Henley picked up the shot, took a sip of the steaming ouzo, and gagged, spitting the licorice-flavored alcohol onto Nick the Nose, who glowered.

"Jeezus," Nick the Nose said, wiping the grimy sleeves of his seedy topcoat. "You'd think I was tryin' to pi-son you or sumpin. Why the hell didn't ya say ya didn't like ouzo?"

"Shud up," Henley said, struggling to catch his breath, eyes watery. He wondered if he were going to catch pneumonia. "Just be quied, otay? I need dime do dink."

Henley leaned back in the booth, near an oaken panel that felt warm, and closed his eyes, imagining the warm bed at the Algonquin Hotel and the hot toddies that he would imbibe before he went to sleep. If all went according to plan, he'd be on a jet the next day, heading back home to Santa Barbara and to his loving wife, who believed that he was a traveling pharmaceuticals salesman.

When Henley awoke, he found Nick the Nose staring at him.

"You been out twenty minutes," Nick the Nose said, pointing a stained index finger at his cheap wristwatch. He had downed Henley's shot of ouzo and had ordered another one, and after finishing that drink, had lined up the three empty shot glasses on the edge of the oak table. "I gotta get outta here. You wastin' my time, man—"

"Shud up," Henley said, feeling a little stronger, thanks to the rest. He reached into an interior pocket of his pea coat, removed a palimpsest from the pocket, and handed the coriaceous paper underneath the table to Nick the Nose.

"Don't lose id," Henley said, sniffling. "Unastan? You lose id, we in big drouble."

"No worries," Nick the Nose said, placing the slip of paper into his wallet, which he placed somewhere in his seedy topcoat. "Now, head on outta heh. I leave in a few minutes, after I have a couple more of dem ouzos."

"You just get dat delivered," Henley said angrily, irritated that he was speaking like that impertinent, rat-faced man.

"Bye!" Nick the Nose called after Henley, who didn't acknowledge the farewell and who waded his way through a throng of executives and clerks chatting loudly one with another.

Outside Joseph's Lounge, Henley hailed a cab. He felt thankful that its interior was warm and inviting, and he felt thankful that the mumbling Montenegrin driver didn't care to converse. Henley decided to sleep on the way to the Algonquin Hotel.

Meanwhile, Nick the Nose drank two more ouzos and flirted with the cross-eyed Negro waiter, who was either too straight or too stupid to know that he, Nick the Nose, was flirting. Disgusted, but yet feeling turned on and wanting action, Nick the Nose paid his tab and hurried out into the night, hunching the collar of his seedy topcoat against the bitter night air.

He was nearing an alley when a man lurking near its entrance wolf-whistled. Nick the Nose turned, and the man, a macho, mustachioed Puerto Rican wearing a black work tog and a black stocking cap, stepped out of the shadows.

"What?" Nick the Nose said expectantly.

"You very cute," the man said. "You like sucky-suck?"

"You kiddin' me?" Nick the Nose answered melodically. "I dig that, man. Yer place or mine, sailor?"

"No, here," the macho man said, motioning at the alley.

Nick the Nose leered. An alley was nice. A beat cop had almost caught Nick the Nose one time in an alley, and Nick the Nose had pleasured himself frequently with the remembrance of that encounter. How he adored macho men.

Nick the Nose stepped into the alley, its sole illumination a blue light at a back door. Snow began to dust the alley, and Nick the Nose felt snowflakes collecting atop his balding head.

"Who's first?" he said, turning, his eyes widening in horror because the Puerto Rican held the tip of a glimmering switchblade less than one thousandth of a millimeter away from the operative's prominent nose.

"Okay, *puto*, give me wallet," the Puerto Rican said, eyes glowing demoniacally as he waved the gleaming blade menacingly in the operative's face. "*No problemas, sî?*"

Nick the Nose's heart pounded, and Nick the Nose knew that he couldn't give the Puerto Rican the wallet. It contained the palimpsest that would allow the hidden elite to take complete, irrevocable control of the world.

"Sure, sure, no problem," Nick the Nose said, stepping back, his trembling hand reaching inside his seedy topcoat. "I got it right heh for ya, pal."

Instead of removing the wallet from his seedy topcoat, however, Nick the Nose removed a black police-issue Smith & Wesson .38, which he pointed at his would-be mugger.

"Come and get it, spic," Nick the Nose said.

The Puerto Rican dropped the switchblade and ran. Nick the Nose gave chase and fired. The round missed the Puerto Rican's head and grazed an ice-caked alley wall. The wind carried the ricochet into the December night.

"You come back heh!" Nick the Nose shouted above a howling December wind. "You bastud! You come back!"

The Puerto Rican ran into a slick street, dodging a cab that blared its horn. Nick the Nose fired another shot. On the sidewalk across the street, an elderly woman wearing a purple dress, a purple coat, and a purple pillbox hat screamed. Still angry and unaware of what he was doing because of his adrenaline rush, Nick the Nose fired shots until he emptied the pistol the way a nineteen-year-old college stud's testicles emptied themselves in a Tijuana bordello.

"Goddammit!" Nick the Nose said, not aware that a major plot twist was about to occur.

Suddenly he realized that he was in the middle of the street and that speeding traffic was hurrying at and around him. Drivers honked horns at him, and a cab driver rolled down his window and shouted obscenities at Nick the Nose and told the operative to get the hell out of the street.

Then Nick the Nose saw it, it being a Greyhound Scenicruiser that bore straight down at him.

"Holy shit," Nick the Nose said as the bus's brakes screeched.

The bus came to a screeching, swerving halt, just missing the operative's murine nose by one thousandth of a millimeter.

The operative's eyes crossed, he groaned, and he fainted, not falling face-first, which is typically how someone faints, but falling backwards, as if providing a bit of comedic relief telegraphed several times throughout a novel set in New Orleans. The pudgy, irate Irish beat cop shoved people out of the way as he ran to the downed operative.

The door to the Scenicruiser popped open, and people ran out of vehicles and from the sidewalk to aid the man who had fainted. The driver of the bus knelt beside Nick the Nose, felt for a pulse on the operative's neck, and then yelled for an ambulance. A *New York Times* photographer, who happened to be on his way to his nephew's bar mitzvah, snapped photographs of the operative and the gathering people.

Meanwhile, while no one was paying attention, the operative's wallet slipped out of a ripped pocket in his seedy topcoat and slid down to the snow-slickened street. A cold, harsh wind blew the wallet open and tugged at the jagged edge of the palimpsest. The wind blew again, tugged the palimpsest out of the wallet, and carried the coriaceous paper up into the December night, possibly to nowhere in particular or possibly as a plot device in this parody.

III

Officer Patrick Aloysius "Paddy" Magoohan entered a warehouse-sized room, heading to his sergeant's battered desk. The sergeant's battered desk sat in the Battery Park Precinct, and around the battered desk sat other battered desks, behind which sat battered police officers. On nearby battered benches sat handcuffed Negress prostitutes and next to them their handcuffed handler, a gum-snapping white man who reminded Magoohan of Father O'Malley, a pug-nosed priest who had given Magoohan his first communion.

Magoohan then noticed three Puerto Rican men sitting on a battered bench opposite that on which the Negress prostitutes and their white pimp sat. What Magoohan didn't know was that one of the Puerto Ricans was El Lobo Macho, the man who had attempted to mug the operative. And what Magoohan didn't know was that the other men, Guapo and Chico, were El Lobo Macho's lieutenants in El Lobo Macho's antihomosexual campaign and its reign of terror in lower Manhattan. And what Magoohan didn't know was that the three Puerto Ricans were surreptitiously using picks to free their wrists from the handcuffs that held the men prisoner.

The macho, mustachioed El Lobo Macho scowled, and Magoohan scowled back. You don't scare me, Magoohan thought. Not in the least, you PR prick.

Magoohan then remembered that Sergeant Scarletti was waiting. This was no time for stopping and thinking, that was for sure.

Magoohan wound his way through a maze of battered desks until he reached a battered desk in a corner of the warehouse-sized room. Behind the battered desk sat Sergeant Scarletti, a simian man in his late forties who would be dead two years later from a massive coronary while he was in bed with one of the aforementioned Negress prostitutes.

"Officer Magoohan reportin' as ordered," Magoohan said obediently, standing at rigid attention in front of the sergeant's desk.

Sergeant Scarletti didn't acknowledge Magoohan. Instead, the sergeant signed one form, then another form, and then opened a manila folder, into which he slid the forms.

As the sergeant worked, Magoohan couldn't help but day-dream. His thoughts took him back to his childhood, when he had decided to become a cop like his mother's brother, Uncle Mick, who had been a tough, no-nonsense man who hadn't tak-en guff off anyone and who knew when to wield a skull-cracking baton when the time came. Even though Uncle Mick had wal-loped Magoohan hundreds of times, Magoohan, like an abused wife, felt a deep sympathy, and an even deeper empathy, for the man, whose wife shot and killed him during a domestic dispute.

"Sergeant Scarletti?"

"Just stand dere and keep your goddamn trap shut if you know what's good for you," Sergeant Scarletti said. "You do know what's good for you, don't yas, Magoohan?"

"Sure, Sergeant, I know what's good for me."

"Didn't I just tell you to keep your goddamn trap shut?"

"Yes, sir, you did tell me to keep my goddamn trap shut."

"So why you still talking?" Sergeant Scarletti asked, peering with his mean little simian eyes at Magoohan.

"On account you asked me a question, Sergeant Scarletti," Magoohan replied. "I figured if I didn't answer, you'd yell at me."

"Just shuddup, okay?"

"Shuddin' up, Sergeant Scarletti."

Sergeant Scarletti jotted a note on a pad and then flipped open a manila folder while Magoohan continued to stand at attention. Sergeant Scarletti often made Magoohan stand at attention, sometimes up to forty minutes, whenever Magoohan got into trouble. Magoohan's father had often punished Magoohan the same way.

But Magoohan's father, Joe Magoohan, had not been a cop. Joe Magoohan had worked at the Bowery Brew Brewery, and, after having downed thirteen Bowery Brew beers in less than half an hour at a bar one evening, had placed an empty beer glass to his ear, as if the glass were a seashell, and exclaimed, "I can hear the brewery calling to me!" Whereupon Joe Magoohan had marched to the Bowery Brew Brewery, ascended two flights of metal stairs leading to a huge vat, and fell into its frothy contents, his body discovered the next day by a jaded Jamaican janitor whose hair changed from black to gray that very morning. Paddy Magoohan had been a mere thirteen when his father drowned.

"Do you know why you're here?" Sergeant Scarletti said, looking up from his paperwork.

"On account of something I done?" Magoohan asked, unsure of what he should be saying that moment. "I don't know, Sergeant. Would ya please tell me?"

Sergeant Scarletti lowered his pencil. "Are you Jewish, Magoohan?"

"You know I'm Irish," the Irish beat cop said. "Why you asking me a question like that for, Sergeant?"

"I'm asking da questions here, Magoohan, not you. So answer da goddamn question."

"No, sir, I ain't Jewish."

"You know why I asked you if you was Jewish, Magoohan?"

"No, sir, why?"

"Because you're a putz, Magoohan," Sergeant Scarletti said. "A real friggin' royal putz. Some Puerto Rican was acting up again, and you didn't catch 'im. Why didn't you catch 'im, Magoohan?"

"He was gone before I got dere," Magoohan said. "Guy was firing at him, and then this bus almost nails dis guy's ass, and he faints. What was I supposed to do, Sergeant?"

"You was supposed to catch me a Puerto Rican sonofabitch, that was what you was supposed to do," Sergeant Scarletti said. "These PRs are having a major war with da queers. Me, I'd prefer that they kill each other off. But we gotta deal with first things first, and the first thing we gotta deal with is the PRs. After we deal with them, we'll deal with da queers."

"I'm right wid you, Sergeant."

Sergeant Scarletti scowled. "If you was with me, you woulda done what I said and brought me in one of them PRs. But you dropped the ball, Magoohan. And didn't I warn you?"

"You warned me, Sergeant, sure, you warned me."

"You Polish, Magoohan?"

"Why you asking me that for, Sergeant?"

"You never learn, do you, Magoohan?"

Magoohan sighed softly. "No, Sergeant, I ain't Polish."

Sergeant Scarletti made a face, mimicking Magoohan's expression. "'No, Sergeant, I ain't Polish. No, Sergeant, I ain't Polish.' Well, you are now, Magoohan. You're a Polack."

"Okay, I'm a Polack," Magoohan said, hoping that, with his agreeing, Sergeant Scarletti's anger would be assuaged.

"No, you ain't a Polack," Sergeant Scarletti said. "You're a dumb Polack, got me?"

"All right, I'm a dumb Polack. I agree with you one hundred percent, Sergeant Scarletti. If you say I'm a dumb Polack, I'm a dumb Polack."

"Shuddup, you dumb Polack," Sergeant Scarletti said, looking down at his paperwork and jotting a note. "You know why you're a dumb Polack?"

"No, sir, I don't know why," Magoohan said, hoping that he had scored points by responding correctly.

"Because you're going to be working with a dumb Polack," the sergeant said. "And since I ain't no dumb Polack, and since we don't have no dumb Polacks in this precinct, thank God, you're gonna be working in a different precinct."

"Different precinct, Sergeant? I worked hard to get into dis precinct."

Sergeant Scarletti's mean little simian eyes peered at Magoohan, and Magoohan felt his heart beat faster.

"We don't want you here no more," Sergeant Scarletti said. "Your new sergeant is another dumb Polack, and his name is Sergeant Dumbrowski. And Sergeant Dumbrowski works in Greenwich Village, where there's all sorts of interestin' characters. What do you think about that, Magoohan? Do them apples suit you?"

Magoohan's head swam. He didn't want to work in Greenwich Village. It was a place where beatniks, poets, folksingers, Jewish radicals, and queers hung out. And Magoohan detested the latter.

Much as he hated Puerto Ricans—and Magoohan hated them with a passion—he truly detested queers. He used to tell his high school friends that Hitler's mistake was using Jews instead of queers.

"Seems like you don't like it, but tough titty toenails," Sergeant Scarletti said. "Get yer stuff outta your locker, and head on down to the Greenwich Village Precinct first thing tomorrow morning. The dumb Polack's waiting for you, and believe me, Magoohan, if you mess up one more time, you're gonna be off the force, you fat little redheaded mick. Now, get the hell outta here."

Magoohan snapped his heels together, stiffened his back, and saluted Sergeant Scarletti. Sergeant Scarletti, however, sneered and returned to his paperwork. Grimacing, Magoohan turned. He had a feeling that something, some divinity, something up there, or something down there, had it in for him. And that something was going to make his life miserable, at least in the near and foreseeable future.

Magoohan wound his way through the labyrinthine maze of battered desks in the Battery Park Precinct, he and the other police officers failing to notice that the three Puerto Ricans were no longer handcuffed, and furthermore, were no longer sitting on the battered bench.

Greenwich Village? Magoohan shuddered at the thought of working with a Polack named Sergeant Dumbrowski. But Magoohan shuddered even more at the thought of doing a beat among all those queers.

IV

Arctic winds assaulted lower Manhattan, slicing and sluicing their way around and over buildings like white-water rapids over smoothened stones. The winds blew harder, thus causing the falling snow to become more blinding, and if someone could have miniaturized the setting, it would have made for an enchanting, and enchanted, snow globe.

A lone man wearing a long emerald-green coat and carrying a ledger hurried past the Washington Arch, pausing briefly before hurrying onto Fifth Avenue. A few minutes later, he rounded a corner on W. Eighth Street, and two minutes later he stopped in front of a tavern. He lowered an emerald-green hood and stared at the establishment, always amazed whenever he saw it.

The man, whose hair was dyed a brilliant orange and whose eyebrows had been plucked and whose face was covered with a hint of pancake, studied the face of the Stone Carver Inn. The place belonged to him, but that had not always been the case. In fact, he had started out in the place as a bar back, eventually worked himself up to bartender, and then purchased the place at a steal after Al Lenae, the bar's previous owner, was arrested and sent to jail for pandering.

Grenadine Roe stared at the tavern's sign, whose wording was spelled in gilded, Old English lettering. He smiled. Then he opened the tavern door, leaving the brutish winter behind him, and entered a pleasant warmth that was comparable to that of a mother's womb.

Inside the tavern, he settled down into a chartreuse leatherette booth and removed his emerald-green coat, which he had purchased in New Orleans. Giacomo, the tavern's janitor, mumbled to himself as he pushed a dry mop across the floor. Frank, the bartender, wiped dry a freshly washed wineglass and hung it up on a rack. The glass touched another of its kind and tinkled. Grenadine slapped the chartreuse booth's table.

"Do be careful with that!" Grenadine said to Frank bitchily. "Don't you understand, you silly man! You could absolutely ruin my establishment if you aren't more careful!"

"Jeezus," Frank said, wiping his brow with the back of his forearm, which was as hairy as an ape's. As far as he knew, he was the only straight working in the place. He worked there only because he made twice as much as he could at any other bar. "Yer actin' like I'm tryin' to destroy yer place or sumpin, Grenadine, sir."

"That's *Miss* Roe to you," Grenadine said. "If I want to be called sir, I'll wear pants."

"But you is wearing pants," Frank said, emphasizing his point with a pointing finger. "Purple pants. Just take a look yerself."

Grenadine looked down. Indeed, he was wearing purple pants. Tight purple pants. In fact, very tight purple pants. He chuckled.

"You're right, Frank, for once," Grenadine said in a voice that hinted of a Midwestern twang. "You Italian sweethearts are so observant, aren't you? That's what makes you so endearing. You can go back to calling me Grenadine."

"Thanks, I guess," Frank, who was married and who had three kids, said, picking up another wineglass, which he began to towel dry.

Grenadine placed the ledger onto the table and by the ledger a red ballpoint pen. Giacomo stumbled by, muttering, his tan eyes glassy and bloodshot.

"Another long night, Giacomo?" Grenadine asked.

Giacomo stopped, turned, and peered down at Grenadine. Grenadine wasn't sure what race Giacomo was. Sometimes he looked Negroid, sometimes he looked Italian, sometimes he looked American Indian, sometimes he looked like a mixture of these three things, sometimes none of those three things.

"Whad?" Giacomo said.

"You know, the only reason I hired you was because you looked so adorable, and if I didn't take you in, the police were going to arrest you on trumped-up charges of loitering near a public urinal."

Giacomo's sad eyes and sad expression showed that he did not understand.

"You've been smoking marijuana again, haven't you, my dear?"

"I have to smoke weed cuz otherwise I get depressed, boss, cuz I miss Miss Maggie."

"Miss Maggie?" Grenadine said, raising an eyebrow. "Since when you did become enamored with a woman, Giacomo? Or is this what the queen calls herself?"

"My snake," Giacomo said, hurt that Grenadine could never remember the snake or the snake's name. "Miss Maggie's my boa constrictor."

"You ask me, you have more of a garter snake," Grenadine said, chuckling meanly. He reached into his purse, from which he retrieved a pair of Wayfarer sunglasses that he had found the previous summer in Central Park. He stood and put the sunglasses on Giacomo.

"That's better," Grenadine said, putting a finger to his chin, thrusting out his hip. "Now no one can tell that you're stoned."

"But I can't see, boss."

"Just make do," Grenadine said, sitting down and looking at the figures in the ledger. The fine handwriting was very ornate, similar to italic. His mother, bless her soul, had told him that he wrote as beautifully as Leonardo da Vinci. "I'm sure that if you work it, it'll work you, Giacomo."

Giacomo pushed the dry mop and bumped into a table, causing the black plastic ashtray upon the table to fall to the floor, where the ashtray clattered.

"Do be careful!" a horrified Grenadine shrieked, throwing his hands to the sides of his face. "Do you know how much those things cost, you idiot!"

Giacomo removed the sunglasses.

"Put those back on!" Grenadine screamed, standing, jabbing an index finger at Giacomo, the finger's newly manicured nail gleaming green. "I do not want to see you without those sunglasses! If the undercover cops come in here and see you with those eyes, they're going to think that we're dealing Mary Jane out of this place! And I will not have my establishment ruined!"

Giacomo obediently put the sunglasses back into place and stooped down and reached around on the floor like a blind man. Grenadine sighed, went over, and bent down. He scooped up the fallen ashtray, which he thrust into Giacomo's outstretched, grasping hand.

"Now you have the ashtray," Grenadine said. "Now put it back onto the table."

Giacomo felt with his other hand.

"Why aren't you standing up?" Grenadine asked, becoming more frustrated.

Giacomo's hand brushed a chair and then clasped Grenadine's crotch. Unsure of what it was, but believing, nonetheless, that it would give him aid in standing, Giacomo squeezed tightly.

Grenadine screamed in anger and then squealed in pain. "Let go of me, you moron!" he screeched two octaves above his normal range. "What the hell do you think you're doing!"

Giacomo released his hold on Grenadine's crotch. Grenadine exhaled loudly and fell backwards into a chair and took deep breaths and cupped his freshly squeezed testicles. Giacomo reached out with his hands, attempting to find something to help him to stand.

"Oh, take those things off, you brute," Grenadine said, voice one octave lower than before, the effects of the painful squeeze dissipating. "We'll find another way to disguise your eyes. Who would believe that someone would wear sunglasses all day long, year in, year out? That's utterly preposterous."

Frank placed a glass of soda water with a twist of lime in front of Grenadine. Grenadine grumbled his thanks.

Giacomo placed the Wayfarer sunglasses onto the table. "You going to fire me, boss?"

"Do you want to be fired, Giacomo?" Grenadine said, making a face. "Why do you always ask me the silliest, stupidest questions, Giacomo?"

"Who can say?" Giacomo shrugged. "Sometimes I think that you don't like me too much. And I don't blame you. I'm shiftless, for the most part. Anyway, I'd still probably end up here no matter what."

"You make it sound as if the universe is playing tricks," Grenadine said.

"It plays tricks with all of us," Giacomo said. "But what can we do? We think we direct our lives, but then we end up in places like the Stone Carver Inn."

"You wax poetical," Grenadine said, "yet philosophical."

"Can I help it?" Giacomo shrugged. "It's my nature."

"I wish he would wax," Frank said from behind the bar. "The goddamn bar needs polishing. All he does is push that broom around."

"Dry mop," Giacomo said, correcting Frank the bartender. "A broom is different—"

"Oh, shut yer goddamn trap," the bartender said, shaking his head in disgust. "You irritate the hell out of me, Giacomo, you know that? Philosophize on that, you goddamn jerk-off."

Without saying a word, Giacomo retrieved his dry mop and began pushing it dutifully across the floor and whistled softly the melody of a Japanese miners' song. Grenadine lurched over to the booth, knees together, hand covering his crotch, and slowly eased himself into the booth, wincing as he did so.

The figures in his ledger looked great, save for the payouts that he was making to the cops. Those bastards, they wanted more and more and more. They were never satisfied. Before you knew it, they or the Mob would attempt to take over the tavern. And that was one thing that he, Grenadine Roe, would never allow. The Stone Carver Inn was his place. The Stone Carver Inn was his home. The Stone Carver Inn was his establishment.

"Frank, over here, please," Grenadine said, closing the ledger.

Frank hustled over, damp dish towel in hand. "Whad is it, Grenadine?"

"Have a seat, Frank."

Afraid that his boss might be making a pass, Frank nonetheless slid into a seat across from Grenadine's.

Grenadine stared at a far green wall. "We need to make more money, Frank."

"We do?"

Grenadine nodded. "We're doing a booming business, but we've got problems. *Blue* problems, if you get my drift. Any ideas on how we can handle those problems, Frank?"

Frank squinted. He had heard of female problems—hell, his wife had those every twenty-eight days or so, and Christ, was she murder at those times—but never blue problems. Perhaps what Grenadine meant was *blues* problems. After all, at the Stone Carver Inn they played bebop and other styles of jazz, even a Frances Faye album or two. Perhaps Grenadine wanted something that was more befitting a juke joint.

"I think I got it," Frank said, snapping his fingers, leaning forward, eyes wide.

"What do you have, my dear?"

"Shaky Lemon McCoy," the bartender said.

"What?"

"Not a what, a who," the bartender said. "Shaky Lemon McCoy. He's a spade banjo player who sings the blues. Whenever I pass by the hospital and other places, I see him playing. Got himself a hat in front of him and his banjo in hand. Guy can play a mean blues banjo. Only problem is that he throws a fit every once in a while."

"What are you talking about?" Grenadine said. "I tell you the kind of problems we're having, and your solution is an epileptic banjo player who sings the blues? I'm not following this logic, my dear."

"You said you had blues problems," Frank said. "And I understand why you would. Me, I get tired of listenin' to John Coltrane, Thelonius Monk, and Frances Faye all the goddamn time. Guy's gotta have variety, right? Right. So, you want blues."

"I wasn't talking about blues problems, I was talking about *blue* problems," Grenadine said, closing his eyes, wanting to smash his forehead several times against one of the walls in his establishment. If it wasn't the cops trying to drive him crazy, it was either Giacomo or Frank. "*Blue* problems are *cop* problems. We're having problems with the *cops*, Frank. Now do you understand?"

"We got queer cops hanging out here?" Frank said, stunned. "You coulda fooled me."

"Oh, Jesus!" Grenadine closed his eyes and slapped his forehead.

"Got a headache, Grenadine?"

"I didn't until now," Grenadine said, opening his eyes, which he blinked rapidly because of his frustration. "You take the cake, my dear, and then some. Tell me, did you ever consider brain surgery?"

"Doing it or having it done, Grenadine?"

"Never mind." Grenadine waved his hand. "Run along. I'll figure this out on my own."

Frank shrugged, dutifully stood, and headed back to his station. Giacomo pushed the dry mop past Grenadine's booth.

"Giacomo, dear."

Giacomo stopped. "Yes, boss?"

"Tell me, my dear, if you owned this tavern and wanted to bring in extra income, how would you do it?"

"That's easy, boss. I'd deal weed out of the back office. If you want, I can do it. You can make lots of money."

"Do you have any other ways, Giacomo? If so, please enlighten me."

"Well, the acts around here are pretty lame, truth be told," Giacomo said. "You been placing ads, and you always seeking new acts. You ask me, you need to have a exotic drag act—like, say, three Puerto Rican drag queens."

Grenadine slapped the table, causing Frank to jump. "Delicious, delicious! That's it, Giacomo! It's absolutely delicious!"

"I would say so," said Giacomo, who went back to dry-mopping the tavern floor.

"We'll call it Las Tres Amigas," Grenadine said. "Exotic, dark-skinned sisters whom these fair-skinned queens will come to lust after. It will be the greatest show on earth. *The* greatest show, I guarantee that. Now to find the three Puerto Ricans—"

El Lobo Macho, Guapo, and Chico ran into the tavern as a convenient plot device, having, by mistake, taken the subway to Greenwich Village. Unbeknown to Grenadine, a dutiful cop had been chasing the three from Battery Park to Greenwich Village after a wizened jail janitor had alerted the cop.

"Speak of the devil!" Grenadine said, clapping his hands. "Look at the gift that the angels hath bequeathed us!"

"*Qué?*" El Lobo Macho said, looking around the dimly lit tavern, unsure into what he and his two compatriots had stepped. "What is this place?"

"You've entered the Stone Carver Inn," Grenadine said, approaching the three and extending his fine elegant hand. His green fingernails reflected what little light there was, making the fingernails look like emeralds against fine black velvet. "I'm sure you're here about the job."

"Job?" Guapo asked. "Job? *Trabajo?* What kind of place is this, man?"

"Actually, woman," Grenadine said, "or soon to be, if Christine Jorgensen and her sisters get their way with me. Please, come have a seat. We have much to discuss."

The Puerto Rican gang leader and his two friends looked at Grenadine suspiciously and then looked at Frank, who was drying another wineglass, and then at Giacomo, who was pushing his dry mop across the floor for the umpteenth time as he muttered to himself.

"Ay, ay, ay, what the hell is this?" Chico said in Spanish. "I think we are in the lair of the faggots."

"Ay, I agree," Guapo replied, also in Spanish. He reached into a coat pocket and fingered an Italian stiletto that the police had failed to find. "You want us to cut these bastards, Macho?"

"No, no, no," El Lobo Macho said, also in Spanish. "Let us see what this faggot wants."

Grenadine watched in amusement.

"I see that you dears are discussing what you want in regards to wages," the tavern owner said, motioning for the three to have a seat in the booth. "Come, let us discuss our thirty pieces of silver and all that you must do to earn them."

El Lobo Macho nodded, and he and his two friends slunk into the booth. Grenadine sat down in the opposite seat and extended his hands, indicating something of great importance.

"You three lovelies are the exact thing that I am seeking," he said, winking at El Lobo Macho, whom Grenadine found adorable: a darling machismo who yet had a feminine side.

Then Grenadine cleared his throat. "Now, you'll be working Thursday, Friday, and Saturday evenings and doing a matinee on Sunday. That might seem like a lot, but believe you me, your two hours of performance are going to be over in no time at all."

"What you want us to do?" a sneering Chico asked in broken English.

"Why, what else?" Grenadine said. "Perform. You three are responding to the ad that I put in the *Village Voice*, aren't you?"

"Oh, *sí*," El Lobo Macho said. "Yeah, we looking for jobs. We need work. *Sí*, that is right, we are not here because a cop is after us but because we need *trabajo*, I mean, work. Yes, *señor*. We looking for work. The cop is not after us."

Grenadine frowned. "That won't do."

"*Qué?*" El Lobo Macho asked suspiciously. He stroked his mustache, his proudest accomplishment. "You look at me funny. What the matter? I have something on my face you do not like?"

"That mustache," Grenadine said, shaking his head, "is absolutely out of this world, but I'm afraid that it's going to have to go."

"*Por qué?*" El Lobo Macho said. "I mean, why? Why I need shave? I be working in the kitchen, washing you dishes. Why must I shave? This does not make sense. Many Latinos with mustaches wash dishes in kitchens. Is a law that says that I cannot have a mustache if I am to work in you kitchen?"

"Kitchen!" Grenadine exclaimed. "My heavens, why on earth would I have you three darlings working in a hot, steam-softened kitchen?" He motioned at the empty stage, where Giacomo was now sitting on a stool, staring at a wall and drooling. "You're going to be my star performers. You're going to make this place come alive. What's more, you're going to help me to get the cops off my back."

El Lobo Macho looked at Guapo, who looked at Chico, who looked at El Lobo Macho. They spoke quietly in Spanish. Grenadine wished that he had spent more time paying attention in his high school Spanish class.

"This is a good place to infiltrate," El Lobo Macho said to the two. "We wage our campaign here. We are guerilla fighters, like Fidel Castro and Che Guevara."

"Do not compare me to those Cuban faggots," Guapo said, frowning. "I do not like to be compared to Cubans or Dominicans or Mexicans or Bolivians or Venezuelans. I am a proud Puerto Rican. No, make that, I am a fiercely proud Puerto Rican."

"Ay, I agree, you idiot," El Lobo Macho said, tempted to tap Guapo in the forehead but deciding to play it cool in front of the tavern owner. "Yes, you are a fiercely proud Puerto Rican, and I am a fiercely proud Puerto Rican."

"Do not forget me," Chico said. "I am a fiercely proud Puerto Rican, too."

"Okay, you are a fiercely proud Puerto Rican, too," El Lobo Macho conceded. "But work on it. You have a long ways to go, you runt."

"I might be small, but inside I am a giant," Chico replied, pouting.

"You are a—never mind," El Lobo Macho said. He would deal with Chico and his insolence later. "This faggot wants to hire us. I say we take whatever jobs he offers us."

"Ay, I agree," Guapo said.

"Ay, I agree, too," Chico said.

El Lobo Macho looked into Grenadine's eyes. "We not performers, but we learn quickly," El Lobo Macho said, reverting to English. "You like Puerto Rican songs, *puto?*"

"You can dance to whatever you want," Grenadine said, beaming, utterly delighted that these three young Puerto Rican men had just agreed to perform in drag. "Are you comfortable wearing stage clothes?"

"We wear whatever," Guapo said, waving his hand nonchalantly.

"Do you like standard or push-up?" Grenadine asked. He himself was a push-up man; he desired that these three applicants be push-up men—rather, women—too. "I'm open to either, provided, of course, that you look cute. That, of course, is the main thing."

"We wear whatever," El Lobo Macho said.

"I just said that," Guapo said.

Face reddening, El Lobo Macho glowered at Guapo. Guapo gulped. He knew that he had pushed El Lobo Macho too far.

The gang leader returned his attention to Grenadine.

"Do you like high heels?" Grenadine asked.

"*Qué?*" El Lobo Macho asked.

"You want us to dress like *putos*, no?" Guapo asked.

"Are you out of your *puto* mind?" Chico said.

Grenadine chuckled, not knowing that the three Puerto Ricans would have just as easily cut him to ribbons with switchblades as look at him.

"You're so angry when you're cute," Grenadine said, making a limp-wristed motion. "Look, my dears, we have costumes in the back. Giacomo will show you to the dressing room. Find dresses that fit you. We'll worry about the high heels later, after you've adjusted to wearing dresses. It can take some time, though, in my case, it came rather naturally." Grenadine snapped his fingers. "Giacomo, please take these darling ladies to the dressing room. We must see how they look in drag."

Dry mop in hand, Giacomo motioned, with a nod of his head, for the three Puerto Ricans to follow. They did, El Lobo Macho leading the way, followed by Guapo, followed by Chico.

After they were gone, Frank shook his head and looked down at the bar.

"I don't like it when you do that," Grenadine said. "When you shake your head, Frank, it means that something bad is coming. You're prescient that way. I'm not sure if all Italian men are prescient that way—I would that they weren't, but if they were, I suppose I could live with it—and your prescience is upsetting to me. Pray tell, my dear, what irks you?"

"Puerto Ricans," Frank said, drying his last wineglass. "You can't trust 'em. Ever. All they're good for is groping women on subways and living on the dole and robbing purple-lipped hebes who have their arms full of groceries."

"These are very fine gentlemen, Frank, who will make very fine women."

"You honestly believe that, Grenadine?" Frank said, finishing with the wineglass and hanging it up. He stepped back and put his hands on his waist, admiring his work. His wineglasses were always shiny, always spotless. His father, God rest his soul, had been a bartender, too, and had taught Frank a Sicilian trick for keeping wineglasses shiny and spot-free. Frank believed that he must have felt the way Michelangelo felt after completing the Sistine Chapel.

"Frank, dear. We were speaking."

Frank blinked and then looked at Grenadine.

"Why do you say such horrible things about these dear, dear men, Frank?"

"Because they're trouble, that's why," Frank said, emphasizing his point with his large Italian hands. "You mark my words. They're going to ruin your establishment, Grenadine, if ya ain't careful. And you ain't bein' careful, leastways not that I can see. You want my advice?"

"Not really, but since we're on the subject, do please tell me what's on your mind," Grenadine said, curling the fingers of a hand and looking at the fine, polish-tipped nails.

Frank stepped out from behind the bar and walked over and sat down in the booth with Grenadine.

"You gotta listen to me for once, Grenadine," Frank said imploringly. "If you don't, I'm outta a good job. And I don't want to be outta a good job. Good jobs is hard to come by. Real hard to come by."

"Perhaps you should speak to my own self-interest," Grenadine said. "You're a wonderful bartender, Frank, but you must remember, it's my interests, not yours, that ultimately count."

"Then get rid of those bums and save your establishment," Frank said. "Before you know it, we'll be overrun with PRs. They'll be playing calypso or whatever the hell it is they play down there on that island. We'll be able to sell only rum because that's all they drink. No more wine! Can you imagine!" Frank felt himself on the verge of tears. "Do you want that to happen to the Stone Carver Inn? Do you want this to become a PR hangout, Grenadine?"

"It is an idea," Grenadine said, giving the notion serious thought. "After all, the white sisters do get tiring after a while. One can only listen to so much to talk about the newest fashions in Paris and London. Mind you, the closet queens from Wall Street and elsewhere are a hoot to watch, but in the end—oh, my, I think there's a potential pun there, Frank—it all becomes boring. Everything gay is effeminate, and everything effeminate is ephemeral, and everything ephemeral comes to an end."

Grenadine sighed, feeling rueful as he studied the empty tavern and imagined it as it would appear that evening, full of merry and happy-go-lucky queers calling each other names like tacky bitch and fudge packer while these queens drank endless rounds of daiquiris. He leaned towards Frank. "We need new blood, Frank. I'm tired of the same old, same old. Trust me on this one, please."

"You're making a big mistake, Grenadine. I'm tellin' ya."

Giacomo stumbled in, clasping his left triceps.

"What's wrong, Giacomo?" Grenadine said, rushing over to the wounded janitor.

Giacomo slumped in a chair. "One of them hit me. Seems he don't like the idea of wearing a brassiere. It was white. Maybe he prefers black."

"See what I mean?" Frank said, returning to his station.

"Oh, shut up, Frank," Grenadine said, and he attended to the wound that Giacomo had received. "I'm sure it was just an accident."

"I don't think so, boss," Giacomo said. "I think you're going to have serious problems."

"See what I mean?" Frank said.

Grenadine stamped his foot. "Oh, do shut up, Frank!"

V

Done with his self-pleasuring, Ignatius removed his rubber glove and belched. He sat up in the bed in the sole guest room in the Minkoff house, pleased that his pyloric valve wasn't acting up, especially after a dinner of takeout Chinese. Mr. Minkoff had been forced to get the takeout when Mrs. Minkoff, having forgotten that a roast was in the oven, burned that night's dinner. Ignatius didn't know who General Tso was, but whoever he was, he certainly made good chicken. Ignatius imagined that General Tso was a world-weary, mustachioed man who had been forced to flee communist China. Ignatius was certain that he and General Tso would get along very well, should blind Fortuna ever bring the two men onto the same path.

Ignatius was wearing stained, yellowed pajamas that he had brought with him from New Orleans. The twin-sized bed, which groaned occasionally because of his heft, felt warm and pleasant, and the just-turned-on lamp on the small nightstand reminded Ignatius of his old room. Ignatius missed his house on Constantinople Street. Ignatius missed his desk. Ignatius missed his mother (pre-Claude *roué*, of course). Ignatius missed New Orleans. Ignatius missed the mighty Mississippi. Ignatius missed seeing shows at the Prytania, and Ignatius missed calling Doris Day a cheap, floozy callet, which she was most certainly was. After all, no woman of proper theology and geometry would ever act in the horrid films for which Doris Day had sold her paltry, wretched soul.

Ignatius studied a Big Chief tablet resting on his huge gut, wet the tip of a freshly sharpened pencil that he had filched from Mr. Minkoff's desk, and opened the Big Chief tablet. Ignatius scrawled furiously, the words coming with little effort, as if they had been raging water held back by a New Orleans dam that might give way at any time on a late August day.

Hell is paved with good intentions.
—SAMUEL JOHNSON

From the trenches of Alsace-Lorraine:

Your warrior finds himself tossed about once again by that wanton Fortuna, spun into another cycle on her horrid wheel. O Boethius! Where is your consolation, especially in these, these wretched days of the Philistines, whose bastions I am about to storm!

Your warrior had much time to do soul-searching during the journey from New Orleans to Gotham. Myrna minx, bless her sex-starved soul, made several sexual advances during the trip, but I was able to rebuff her by pretending that I was having epileptic episodes brought on by the thought of my dear mother's reactionary psychosis. Fortunately, Myrna was able to deal with her sexual frustrations and peccadilloes in several places, most notably in a small coastal town in North Carolina, behind a barn affixed to a crab shack where men spin yarns and imbibe the infamous John Barleycorn. I dare not attempt to imagine what she was doing with those three lumberjacks behind that barn, but, suffice to say, after the fact, the minx seemed content not to talk about sex or sexual matters for quite some time as we pursued our way up the Eastern Seaboard.

Gotham is much to my liking, though quite honestly I was expecting—perhaps hoping—to find a hearty, healthy, unwashed immigrant population into which I could easily blend. I do not speak Yiddish or Ladino, of course, so my finding a hiding place in the Jewish ghetto is obviously out of the question, as is that of finding a home in the Negro ghetto, my foray at Levy Pants showing that I do not fit in well into that specious subculture. Perhaps there are other Southern medievalists like me in this vast, glorious Gotham, men and women who, spurned by this horrid modern world, have come to Gotham as a means of either undermining this metropolis or perhaps as a way of escaping the horrible circumstances into which Fortuna has driven them. If these people are here, I intend to find them. And if they are not here, I will be the start of a new enclave for them, a bastion of medievalism in a world of modernity gone amok. Fortuna has had her way with me, but, eventually, the cycle must turn, and it must turn upward. Nothing can stay down forever. This doughboy takes reassurance in that.

My current living conditions are beyond what I expected; Madam Minkoff, who reminds me of my own mother in terms of mental capacity, is, nonetheless, a very hospitable host, though I cannot, for whatever reason, convince her that I am not Jewish. At dinner I had to repeat to her at least six times that I was at one time a devout, church-attending Roman Catholic dedicated to the Church and especially to Hroswitha. But never Jewish. (Though I have not attended mass in years, I am, nonetheless, one of the elect, in that I hold to the ancient rites of the Church.) Perhaps Madam Minkoff believes that I am Jewish because of all the horrendous suffering that I have had to endure. After all, are not the Jews the most vilely persecuted people on the face of this planet? And have they not been unfortunate wanderers for centuries, working as pawnbrokers and tap dancers and haberdashers? These were occupations in which the Jews could save their pennies, hiding them in their bill-stained palms from the lesser, stupider gentiles, who attempted to keep down these noble, hook-nosed, itinerant people. I do not have a hook nose, and I do not have gold coins stashed away in the back of a synagogue, but I do know suffering. In that way I am a Jew, I suppose. (After all, were not the early Christians Jews? Though St. Paul, as he says in Galatians, no longer practices the religion of the Jews, I am assured that he would take bagels and lox and gefilte fish over a foot-long any day of the week, if given the chance. On the other hand, he might come to enjoy a foot-long as much as I have.)

Mr. Minkoff reminds me considerably of Gus Levy, in that both are very highly frustrated men. Mr. Minkoff refused to speak to anyone throughout dinner, though his chirpy wife did her best to enliven the dinner conversation with a story of how Mr. Minkoff almost won a yoyo contest in Central Park but ended up hitting himself in the groin with the yoyo and getting the yoyo's string wrapped around his neck, and he surely would have strangled himself to death had not a meandering *mohel*—a Jewish man who performs circumcisions—cut the string with the surgical weapon that he, the circumciser, wielded so delicately and so aptly and so artistically. Mr. Minkoff's face turned a bright red during the telling of this tale, and he excused himself and said that he was going to his study. I assume that he went there to count his money.

Grandmother Horowitz, who smells pleasantly of orange rinds and of garlic, reminds me considerably of Madam Minkoff, though I do not understand what this dear grandmother meant when she whispered into my ear (I was sitting between her and Myrna minx) and asked if I wanted to "snap her garters." I am certain that this "snapping of garters" is a Jewish custom, given the proclivity of these people to earn their livings as the makers of garments and undergarments. (Mr. Minkoff runs a restaurant supply business, by the way, dear reader. Given that I will need at least a month, if not more, of bed rest, and given that I will need several months to complete a review of my journey from New Orleans to Gotham, I cannot, at this time, help him with his business and financial endeavors. Nonetheless, given the chance, I can, and shall, help this man as a means of thanks for his hospitality, though, while I was in his presence, he gave me glaring looks and shook his head one or two times. A quick nota bene: Mr. Minkoff's lineaments, especially when he frowns or scowls, remind me of the English comedian Stan Laurel.)

Back to the main issue at hand: I shall have to learn more about this Jewish custom, this "snapping of garters." In addition, Grandmother Horowitz asked, in that whispery voice of hers, if I wanted to talk about my "favorite positions." I am assuming that this refers to the stances of worshippers in synagogues. Perhaps, like Madam Minkoff, Grandmother Horowitz believes that I am Jewish. And, perhaps, she and I can talk about our "favorite positions," should that time come, but first and foremost I will have to instruct her about the positions of the Roman Catholic faith, the positions of which I am well versed. If need be, I will direct her to a priest who can instruct her about positions. I am certain that she will thus be satisfied. (Nonetheless, I must ensure that the priest is a worthy man, unlike the priest in my former parish, who refused to perform the sacramental rites for my beloved Rex.)

The exertion of this evening's writing has taken its toll on me. Bear in mind, dear reader, that your doughboy has been on the run for nearly a week, fleeing a mother who has fallen prey to a lecherous Joe McCarthy epigone, an imbecile redneck lout who wandered around train tracks at night, switching boxcars and wondering, during his fervid lustful periods, when he would find a way to steal away someone's dear mother and consequently ruin that household. Suffice to say, Fortuna's Wheel applies not only to this doughboy but to that horrid homewrecker and to all others who have unduly afflicted your humble narrator. May they soon get their comeuppance.

Your doughboy must get ready to enter tomorrow's trenches; hence, he is signing off for this evening.

Yours truly,
Doughboy Dave

Two

Ignatius refused to get out of bed, despite Myrna's best efforts. Mrs. Minkoff checked his temperature—first wanting to insert a thermometer into the crack dividing Ignatius's huge pink ass cheeks, much to Ignatius's protestations, and then settling for placing the thermometer underneath Ignatius's huge pink tongue—and told Ignatius that he wasn't running a fever. Nonetheless, Ignatius said, it was probably best that he spend time recuperating, at least for the remainder of that week, if not longer. Myrna said that she was going to speak to her group therapy group that morning about Ignatius, and Mrs. Minkoff said that Ignatius had probably eaten something the previous evening that wasn't kosher and heartily apologized to Ignatius for his feeling unwell. Ignatius, wanting Myrna and Mrs. Minkoff to leave the small bedroom, complained that his pyloric valve was about to seal, and Myrna hurried herself and her mother out of the guest room.

Mr. Minkoff was sitting at a small breakfast table in a small breakfast nook, attempting to enjoy his small breakfast of eggs, bacon, and coffee. Myrna told him good-bye, and Mr. Minkoff grunted and turned a page in the *New York Times* and glanced at an article about a man who had almost been killed the previous evening by a Greyhound Scenicruiser in Battery Park. A photograph showed the man sprawled out on the street, arms splayed, as if he had been crucified. Mr. Minkoff grunted again. He knew what it felt like to be crucified, having lived all those years in a house full of dingbat women. Mr. Minkoff then flipped the page to an article about a rumored new invention, a pill that prevented conception.

"Just what I needed to read," he said in disgust, folding the paper and tossing it aside and pushing the plate containing the remnants of his breakfast out of the way. Mrs. Minkoff, who was sitting across the circular table from him, smiled. "You think it's funny, Miriam?"

"Is what funny, Bernard?" Mrs. Minkoff asked, blinking.

"They've supposedly invented a pill to keep women from getting pregnant," Mr. Minkoff said. "Myrna spends ninety percent of her time thinking about sex. Now, with this new pill, it's going to become a full-time obsession for her. Before you know it, the whole world will be full of Myrna Minkoffs evangelizing this new pill."

"Was it kosher?"

"What?" He frowned. "Was what kosher? The pill?"

"No, that Chinese food we had last night."

Mr. Minkoff made a face. "What does that have to do with anything?"

"Irving is sick," Mrs. Minkoff replied seriously, shaking her head ruefully. "He isn't running a fever, but his system is delicate, you know. Orthodox Jews aren't meant to eat nonkosher foods."

Mr. Minkoff glowered and stood. He donned his heavy overcoat and his mouton Cossack cap. It was time to go to the office.

"How many times do I have to tell you?" he said. "Ignacio isn't Jewish. I'll be back tonight. While I'm gone, be sure to give that dingbat mother of yours a bath. She's beginning to stink up the place. Better yet, let her stay in the tub and fall asleep. Maybe she'll do us all a favor and drown. And while you're at it, you might want to put a little more pressure on our darling, unwashed daughter so that she goes out and finds a job—a real job." Mr. Minkoff ground his teeth together. "And that goes for that big fat slob, too!"

Mr. Minkoff slammed the front door. Ignatius, who had been listening in the hallway, stepped into the nook; he was wearing a tattered bathrobe, pajamas, and a pair of slippers with perforated soles. He yawned and stretched his arms, and Mrs. Minkoff smiled at him as he sat down at the circular table.

"Feeling better?" Mrs. Minkoff said.

"Much, thank you," Ignatius said. "I'm assuming that you'll serve me my breakfast, yes?"

"Of course, Irving." Mrs. Minkoff made a face. "I thought you said you weren't feeling well."

"Alas, I am not," Ignatius said, making a face, pretending that he was ill, causing Mrs. Minkoff to make a face of pity. "But I do need a repast, perhaps not one fit for a king but something most certainly better than one of Mr. Clyde's foot-longs."

"Mr. Clyde's what?"

"Never mind," Ignatius said, feigning a smile, his empty belly growling and desiring to be satiated. "I see that Papa Minkoff had eggs, bacon, and coffee. I would like eggs, bacon, toast, and tea, three bags if you would. I am famished, what with the exertions of my getting to Gotham. If, after this meal, I have enough strength, I endeavor to write a treatise on the Jewish household and its kind treatment of gentile visitors."

Mrs. Minkoff stood. "I understood the breakfast part, but the other part I didn't understand, Irving."

"Ignatius."

"Who?"

"My breakfast, please," Ignatius said, doing his best to control his exasperation.

Mrs. Minkoff entered the kitchen, and, wearing an oversized bathrobe, Grandmother Horowitz entered the breakfast nook, mumbled to herself, and squinted. She sat down at the table, her bones cracking audibly. She adjusted herself in her chair, farted loudly but with no foul odor, and reached underneath her robe with a claw of an arthritic hand and scratched her private parts. Ignatius watched, fascinated by the elderly woman's audacity. There might not be hope for the rest of the Minkoff clan, but Ignatius sensed that there might be for Grandmother Horowitz. Perhaps, given the right circumstances, he would be able to turn Grandmother Horowitz against Myrna minx.

It took a few seconds for the synaptic pulses in Grandmother Horowitz's brain to fire up, but when they did, Grandmother Horowitz recognized the obese man with the greasy thick black hair and blue and yellow eyes to whom she had been sexually attracted the previous evening. Grandmother Horowitz smacked her lips and winked at Ignatius, who raised an eyebrow. "You think about what I said last night, honey?"

"Very much so," Ignatius replied, "though I must say I am not familiar with the Jewish custom of the 'snapping of garters.'"

"Snapping garters is snapping garters, regardless of who does the snapping," Grandmother Horowitz said, snapping her toothless gums together, emphasizing her point. "You either snap them or you don't."

"I, for one, have never snapped garters, though perhaps I might have had a chance to do so, had they manufactured them at Levy Pants."

"Levy? Pants? Tight pants that show off the package?" She winked at him, but to Ignatius it looked as if she had something caught in her eye and was doing her best to get it out.

"No, it's an abysmal factory run by an inept office manager who couldn't tie his shoelaces and a harridan of a senile old woman who attempted to ruin Gus Levy, the owner of the factory," Ignatius said, shuddering at the thought of Mr. Gonzalez and that horrid office environment and his, Ignatius's, botched attempt at starting a revolution. Perhaps, however, he, Ignatius, should have given it another chance; after all, Rome wasn't built in a day, and it took Castro one or two times before he took Cuba. "It's part of a past that I'm doing my best to forget, Grandmother Horowitz."

Mrs. Minkoff appeared, holding in her dishwater-reddened hands a white plate, upon which squatted a bowl of steaming oatmeal.

"Good heavens, oatmeal!" Ignatius said, flabbergasted. "I thought that I ordered eggs, bacon, toast, and a mug of steaming tea, madam!"

Mrs. Minkoff placed the plate supporting the bowl of oatmeal in front of Ignatius and then placed a large silvery spoon into the center of the bowl. The spoon stood straight in the stiff, thick oatmeal like the never-ending erection of a nineteen-year-old man. Grandmother Horowitz leered at the spoon, which gleamed.

"Yes, Irving, oatmeal," Mrs. Minkoff said, sitting down. She blinked at her mother. "Oh, good morning, Mother. I hope that you slept well."

"As well as could be," Grandmother Horowitz said, waving fingers that reeked of smegma.

Ignatius's face pale-greened. "Pray tell, what is that horrid odor?"

"I just smell oatmeal," said Mrs. Minkoff, and that's all Mrs. Minkoff did smell because she was getting over a head cold that Mr. Minkoff had given to her two weeks earlier. "Please, eat your oatmeal. The fiber's good for your bowels, according to *Reader's Digest*. Do you read *Reader's Digest*, Irving?"

"It's Ignatius, and no, I do not read that horrid, reactionary, fascistic magazine, which, as far as I can tell, is the publishing arm of the CIA," Ignatius said, making a face, his hungry belly deciding for him that he would partake of the steaming oatmeal, which he spooned into his mouth, the gustatory capabilities of his large pink tongue noting a hint of cinnamon and a delicate touch of brown sugar. "*Reader's Digest* is a root cause of the problems in our country, you see, what with this magazine's false views of societal hierarchy and its egalitarian leanings. I put it on par with Billy Graham and 'Turkey in the Straw,' if even that."

"Doesn't he just sound like a rabbi?" Mrs. Minkoff said to Grandmother Horowitz. "Myrna needs a nice Jewish boy like you."

"I dated a rabbinical student," Grandmother Horowitz said, staring into space, remembering the many men she had had throughout her long, lust-filled life. "He had a schlong the size of one of those bananas Farinelli used to sell at his market."

"Mother, please, you and Myrna—"

"Maybe I was thinking about Farinelli's schlong—"

"Mother, please, not in front of Irving, the man who's going to marry Myrna—"

"Marry Myrna minx!" Ignatius sputtered and wiped his mouth with the sleeve of his maculate robe. "Oh, my God! Oh, my God! Marry Myrna! Marry Myrna minx! Marry Myrna minx Minkoff! Pray tell, madam, whatever gave you the idea that I would ever marry your daughter!"

"Because I saw you two last night, right after you arrived," Mrs. Minkoff said, blinking, perplexed. "You were holding her hand, and you proposed to her. She was dancing about in joy. I was hoping that she was going to say something about the marriage proposal last night, but she didn't, and she didn't say anything this morning." Mrs. Minkoff smiled. "You're going to make a wonderful son-in-law, Irving."

Ignatius groaned. His pyloric valve sealed. The bed, he had to get back to the bed.

He stood and stumbled into the living room, which spun. He lumbered one way, then another, as Mrs. Minkoff ran over to help him, yelling at him to calm down. Ignatius bellowed like a newly castrated steer, and his hefty body slammed into a china cabinet. The china cabinet teetered one way, then tottered the other. Ignatius's eyes crossed, and he fainted, landing on his back with a large thud that reverberated throughout the house. Mrs. Minkoff screamed because his collapse caused the china cabinet, which was about to teeter back into place, to totter. The china cabinet pitched face-first onto the floor, the cabinet's contents of rare cups, saucers, and plates exploding into thousands of shards.

Mrs. Minkoff chewed her knuckles. The china had been Mr. Minkoff's long-dead mother's china. Mr. Minkoff treasured that china as a reminder of his late beloved mother, who had fled Bolshevik Russia and to whom Mr. Minkoff had been utterly devoted, to the point where she had almost overwhelmed his life.

"Oh, no!" Mrs. Minkoff said, shaking her head, tears flooding her eyes and spilling down her paled cheeks. "Bernard's going to be furious!"

Ignatius awakened. He moaned. He felt a cold sweat envelop his body. He wanted to sleep for the next two days, dreaming only of Rex, if he dreamed of anything at all.

Grandmother Horowitz—who reeked of orange rinds, garlic, and smegma—curled up next to Ignatius. He was too weak to protest, too weak to even care. He closed his eyes, but that didn't stop the room from spinning. Marry Myrna minx? Descending to, and entering, the final circle of Dante's Inferno would be much more preferable.

"Oh, no!" Mrs. Minkoff said, more tears coming to her eyes. "How am I going to explain this to Bernard!"

II

Magoohan stood in a charity hospital in Greenwich Village and wrinkled his porcine nose in distaste. Sergeant Dumbrowski had sent Magoohan to the hospital to interview Nick the Nose, given that he had been taken to that hospital. Sergeant Dumbrowski suspected that Nick the Nose was a suspicious queer and wanted him arrested.

In the hospital, doctors, nurses, and interns hurried about, oblivious to Magoohan's presence, and spoke animatedly one with another or attended to urgent hospital business. The beat cop had just spoken with a receptionist, a sour-faced woman, and Magoohan now had the room number of the injured man.

Magoohan sighed. Hospitals were so depressing, especially since his beloved mother, Agnes Sowards Magoohan, God rest her soul, had died in one. (He had inherited her porcine features, particularly her eyes, jowls, and nose.) This hospital, in particular, depressed Magoohan because of its patients, many of whom were blacks and Puerto Ricans. Even the Christmas ornaments adorning the hallways couldn't make Magoohan feel better.

Magoohan grunted and went to find an elevator. As the elevator ascended, he thought about how he would question the queer. If the queer refused to answer the questions, Magoohan decided that he would beat the queer over the head with his, Magoohan's, well-used truncheon. Magoohan had cracked many heads with the truncheon, his treasured possession. With each head that Magoohan cracked, the truncheon seemed to become shinier. Magoohan relished the day when the truncheon would radiate at its most fulgent.

The elevator continued to ascend jerkily, and Magoohan removed his truncheon from its holster and stroked his truncheon, unaware that two nurses and a doctor were eying him suspiciously, wondering if, indeed, Magoohan was a cop. After all, he was barely five feet tall, and he was so pudgy that he looked as if he probably couldn't run more than twenty feet before collapsing. Perhaps, they surmised, he was a deviant who had escaped from the psychiatric ward and absconded with a beat policeman's uniform. Magoohan, noticing their stares, glowered at them, and the three looked away, the doctor nervously clearing his throat. Magoohan holstered his truncheon authoritatively.

Magoohan got off on the twelfth floor and followed directional signs in a hallway and made his way through a labyrinthine passageway that frustrated him. It figured that the queer asshole would end up in a ward like this one. Didn't he, Magoohan, have enough trouble with his new beat and his new sergeant, that dumb Polack, Sergeant Dumbrowski? Magoohan made a mental note to put Polacks on his list of enemies, right below queers.

The door to room 1234 was open, and Magoohan barreled his way into the room without announcing himself. Nick the Nose, the sole occupant of the hospital room, was sitting up in bed, reading the funnies. The beat cop removed a pad and a ballpoint pen from the front pocket of his blue coat. He flipped open the pad to a blank page and clicked the ballpoint pen with the meat of his winter-reddened thumb.

Nick the Nose folded the funnies and stared quizzically at the fiery-haired, fiery-faced, fiery-tempered policeman. He, the operative, had hoped that he could leave the hospital that morning. The doctor had said, however, that a cop was scheduled to come by to get an interview.

"I'm Officer Magoohan," Magoohan said, clearing his throat, noting that the room smelled unpleasantly of petroleum jelly. "They sent me heh to find out what happened last night, on account things don't look too kosher, you get my meanin'?"

"Some spic, he tried ta mug me," Nick the Nose said defensively. "Ain't my fault I hadda run out in da street and almost got killed by a bus."

"Right," Magoohan said, scrawling notes in an illegible hand. His mother, God rest her soul, had rued not sending him to a Catholic school, where he could have learned better penmanship. "What was you doing down deh?"

"Workin', what else? A guy's gotta work, right?"

"What kinda work?"

"My own business," the operative said. "I make deliveries."

"What kinda deliveries?"

"Whatever kind my customers want."

"You like to dress up like a cowboy at midnight sometimes?" Magoohan asked, eyeing Nick the Nose suspiciously, who, the beat officer surmised, had something fairy about him.

"What?" Nick the Nose said incredulously.

"You heard me. You hang out at da theaters at midnight, dressed up like some fairy cowboy?"

Nick the Nose shrugged, doing his best to look confused. "Whatcha gettin' at?"

"You a queer or sumpin?" Magoohan asked menacingly, taking a step forward. "I bet you is. You look like a little queer. You was doing something dirty out there in them streets, wasn't you?"

"No way, sir, no way," Nick the Nose said, getting aroused at the sight of the fiery, impertinent little cop. Several scenarios involving the cop—most of them bondage scenes—played through the operative's mind. "I like girls."

"You do, huh? What kinda girls you like?"

"All sorts."

"Yeah? That a fact? You like female spics?"

"You bet."

"What about female wops?" Magoohan said, seeing if he could trap the man into admitting that he was queer. "You ever do it with a female wop?"

Nick the Nose felt irritated; he didn't like it when someone used pejoratives against Italians, especially when it was a mick who was doing it.

"Did you ever—"

"I'm into micks," the operative said defensively. "I got sumpin about red hair."

Magoohan glowered. "You getting smart with me, pal?"

"Just answerin' yer questions, Officer."

"So you like Irish women," the cop said, flipping the paper in the pad and scrawling on a fresh sheet. "I bet you like Irish women."

"What's dis all about?" Nick the Nose said. "You heh to discuss girls or what?"

"I'm supposed to ask you what you was doing out on dat street," Magoohan said, scrawling notes to himself, one of which was to get jock-itch powder at the drugstore on his way home. "But before I does, I need to know what ya's all about. So what da hell was goin' on?"

"Some spic tried to mug me," Nick the Nose said angrily. "I was goin' home—"

"Where's home?" said Magoohan, scrawling illegibly.

Nick the Nose felt tempted to say, "Home is where da the heart is, sailor," but decided against it after eyeing the phallic-shaped truncheon holstered at the Irish beat cop's side. Nick the Nose shuddered, and Magoohan made another note, one about getting condoms before he went to see Rita the Heater.

"Well?" Magoohan said after a few seconds had passed.

"Oh, yeah, yeah, yeah," the operative said. "Da Village. I live in da Village, but I'm originally from Brooklyn."

Magoohan frowned.

"I say sumpin wrong?" Nick the Nose asked suspiciously.

"Maybe," the beat cop said. "Now, about this spic. Gimme a description."

"Height about six feet, weight about one ninety-five, great facial features for a spic, he could've been the spic version of Rock Hudson, you ask me," Nick the Nose said, remembering vividly the details of his sexy would-be assailant and feeling the start of tumescence. What a bruiser! "You like Rock Hudson?"

"Sure do," Magoohan said. "Hey, what kinda question is dat? Whaddaya mean by that? What does Rock Hudson have ta do wid it?"

"Nuttin," Nick the Nose said. "I don't mean diddly by it."

"Diddly? Ain't that a queer code word of some sort?" The beat cop eyed the operative suspiciously. "You into Judy Garland? You collect her records?"

Nick the Nose shook his head, looking solemn, doing his best to lie to the beat cop.

"You have a thing about red shoes?"

"No, sir, I hate 'em."

"You sure about dat?" The Irish beat cop moved closer to the bed, pen and pad in hand, scribbling. "Are you sure you sure about dat?"

"Positive," Nick the Nose said, and he wished that he had his snub-nosed .38 on him in case the beat cop decided to attack. "I don't know nuttin about Judy Garland or quiche or drag queens or nuttin like that."

"What else can you tell me about da spic?"

"He hadda mustache, a curly black mustache," Nick the Nose said fondly.

Magoohan raised an eyebrow. This might be leading to something big, and Magoohan unconsciously stroked his truncheon.

"You pulled a piece on him," Magoohan said, remembering where he was.

"Glad I had it, too. He was gonna kill me."

"Wid what? His bare hands?"

"No, switchblade. About twelve inches long, you ask me."

"I ain't askin' you," Magoohan said irascibly, subconsciously miffed by the phallic, Freudian reference. "Let's see some ID."

"Why? You know who I am."

Magoohan scowled. "Just get me the goddamn ID."

"Sure, sure."

Nick the Nose picked up his wallet from a dresser next to the bed. He flipped open his wallet and handed the beat cop a grimy driver's license, which the beat cop held up to the light.

The beat cop offered the driver's license back to Nick the Nose, who noticed that something was missing in his wallet.

"Whatsa matta?" Magoohan asked as Nick the Nose shook his wallet violently, vainly attempting to find the palimpsest that Henley had given to him.

"I lost it!" Nick the Nose babbled hysterically. "Where da hell is it!"

"I gave you back yer license—"

"That ain't what I'm talkin about," Nick the Nose said, dropping the wallet and ransacking the items on top of the dresser. The operative tossed aside small containers of petroleum jelly, a torn surgical glove, and half-filled vials of red nail polish, items that had been in the pockets of his seedy topcoat. "I need it—"

"What the hell you talkin' about?" Magoohan asked, getting flustered because he got flustered whenever others got flustered.

"Where the hell could it be!" said Nick the Nose, who hopped out of the bed and on his hands and knees explored the tessellated floor. Dust balls wafted in several directions as he searched diligently for the parchment.

Magoohan squatted next to the frantic operative. "Find what yer lookin' for?" the beat cop asked. "What's cookin'?"

"I think my friggin goose is cookin', dat's what's cookin'!"

III

Henley was sitting up in his warm bed in his warm room at the warm Algonquin Hotel. He sniffled, thankful that the job was finally over. Soon he planned to catch a jet to Los Angeles, where, at the airport, he would get into his Alfa Romeo and head up the coastal highway to Santa Barbara, where his beautiful and loving wife was waiting for him. Henley took another sip of his tea—Lipton's, into which room service had stirred several teaspoons of honey and squirted several squirts of lemon—and felt thankful that the little rat-faced queer, Nick the Nose, now had the ball in his court.

Just as he was thinking about Nick the Nose, there was a knock on the door of room 322. After donning a robe, Henley picked up his black .38 and sniffled, his silk pajamas feeling pleasantly smooth and providing the only comfort that he felt. There was another knock on the door. Henley walked along the side of the wall, cautiously approaching the door. There was another knock on the door, and this time the knock wasn't patient but demanding.

"Go avay," Henley said, coughing. "I'b sleebin."

"Open up," Walpole, another operative, said. "We need to talk."

"Oh, holy Ghrist," Henley said, pocketing the .38, wiping his nose with a tissue, and opening the door. Redolent of a winter morning and mentholated cigarettes, Walpole, Henley's field supervisor, entered the room. Henley closed the door and locked it. Walpole's overcoat was way too tight for his odobenine body, and his bowler looked extremely belittling on his odobenine head. "Whad is id?"

"Big trouble," Walpole said, taking a seat in a faux King Louis XIV chair. He tugged both ends of his mustache, which looked like tusks. "That little queer lost the recipe."

"Whad!"

"You heard me, Henley," Walpole said. "The little queer lost the recipe."

"Oh, my Dod!" Henley sniffled and climbed into bed, hoping that Walpole would get the hell out of there and go find the palimpsest himself.

"Come on, get out of bed," Walpole said, standing, popping a wintergreen-flavored lozenge into his mouth. "You need to find that recipe." He paused for emphasis. "Or else."

"Cand you see that I got a code?" Henley said, wiping his red nose, his philtrum and nostrils irritated a brilliant red from the many tissues into which he had been sneezing and wheezing. "Ged somebody else, for Ghrist's sake."

"It's up to you and Nick the Nose," Henley's field superior said. "You either find that recipe or you and that little queer are dead men. Do you understand me, Henley?"

Henley groaned. He wanted to be back in beautiful California. He wanted to be back with his beautiful wife. He wanted to be back underneath the beautiful orange trees in his beautiful back-yard, near a beautiful, crescent-shaped swimming pool that cast beautiful, sapphire-like patterns onto his beautiful living room wall. The last place that he wanted to be was New York City, look-ing for a small, recently discovered slip of paper that was the key to a new global world order, a new aeon, a new beginning for his kind, the hidden elite.

Henley shuddered. He closed his eyes; it would be so easy now to walk over to the window, open it, and jump out. Much easier than going out into the bitter cold of New York City in a nearly hopeless, very vain search for the palimpsest. He imagined his knocking that little queer's yellow murine teeth into the back of that little queer's throat.

Henley opened his eyes. He sniffled, groaned, and shuffled towards the bathroom. He paused before entering. Before he left the hotel room, he would take a long hot shower. And then he would have two shots of whiskey.

"You going to take all day?" Walpole asked impatiently.

"Jud a momid," Henley said, entering the bathroom.

After closing the bathroom door, he looked into the bath-room mirror and saw rheumy eyes, a rcd nose, and red, swollen cheeks. He groaned. Henley closed the lid on the toilet and sat down. His joints ached, his bones ached, his muscles ached, his throat ached, and his thoughts ached. Slowly, he peeled off his robe and, slowly, he removed his pajama tops, then his pajama bottoms, and then his plaid boxers, which his beautiful wife in beautiful Santa Barbara had purchased for him.

Taking a scalding shower, Henley did his best not to weep from the deep frustration that he was feeling. If and when he got the chance, he was going to take care of Nick the Nose. He, Henley, was going to ensure that that little queer never screwed up again.

IV

Dr. Ingloss stroked his white french-fork beard and nodded. He nodded a lot, especially when he was leading his group therapy group, as he was doing now.

Dr. Ingloss, who had studied Freud and Adler and Reich and a host of other unproven psychological theorists, headed the Ingloss Institute for Psycho-Sexual Research, headquartered in Greenwich Village. He, Myrna, and the rest of the group had just finished listening to Mrs. Murray.

Mrs. Murray, a retiree and a widow, was considering having sexual intercourse with an ex-convict who lived down the hallway from her and who had just been released from Sing Sing. Myrna, one of Dr. Ingloss's favorite patients, had told Mrs. Murray to go ahead and sleep with the man, who had done time for aggravated robbery, felony battery, rape, arson, and one or two other charges that Mrs. Murray didn't remember. After all, as Myrna had often said, ex-cons often made the best sexual partners. To Dr. Ingloss, Myrna's advice sounded wonderful and brilliant, if not wonderfully brilliant.

"Your turn, Myrna," he said, pointing at her with his pen. "What would you like to share with the group this week? You must have a lot to say, given your recent absence."

"He's here," Myrna said, smiling, beaming like a savior.

"Who?" asked Mrs. Murray. "Fred, my ex-con?"

"No, no," Myrna said, gesticulating, eyes wide in amazement and joy. "I rescued Ignatius! He's here, staying with me in the Bronx!"

Dr. Ingloss and the group therapy group—Leonard, Ralph, and the aforementioned Mrs. Murray—applauded Myrna, who felt as if she had finally and truly rescued someone. Mrs. Murray patted Myrna's back, and Ralph, who was attempting to overcome chronic masturbation, stuck two fingers into his mouth and whistled. Dr. Ingloss motioned for his patients to calm down and then motioned for Myrna to continue.

"I would have brought him today, but he's not feeling well," Myrna said. "We barely escaped his deranged mother and her racist, fascist fiancé who, because of their own pathologies, were going to send Ignatius to a barbaric, so-called mental institution. It's a wonder we got out of there without being lynched by the Ku Klux Klan."

"What do you think that Ignatius is experiencing now, considering all that you've told us about him?" Dr. Ingloss inquired.

"For a while, I thought that he might be suffering from a Ganser syndrome," Myrna said, after giving Dr. Ingloss's question deep consideration. "See, he's been cooped up in that small home on Constantinople Street for many years, living like a sexually repressed monk."

Dr. Ingloss nodded sympathetically. "Do go on, Myrna."

"Of course, the drive in my Renault wasn't a pleasant ride, to say the least. I thought that Ignatius was reverting to his old nasty self. Sometimes I sensed that he was doing his best to hold his tongue because, in many ways, I had the power. After all, it was my car, and after all, I was helping him to escape that horrible situation down there in New Orleans."

"Interesting," Dr. Ingloss said, and he flipped open his moleskin notebook and jotted a few notes.

"Yes," Myrna said, and she crossed her arms, shaking her head. "Sometimes, though, I wonder about him and his mother. Freud had a lot to say about the subject, but I'm not sure that he encountered anyone or anything like Ignatius J. Reilly."

"A very interesting angle," Dr. Ingloss said, jotting.

"I hate to think about Ignatius in that way," Myrna said, concerned about the welfare of her friend and her newfound pet project, "but the truth is the truth, right?"

"It is indeed," Dr. Ingloss said, scribbling, feeling excited about the prospects of working on Ignatius. Perhaps, the good doctor reasoned, there might be an award of some sort, even, perhaps, the Nobel. But the real reward he wanted was to get into Myrna's pants. "What else can you tell us about Ignatius?"

"He seems to be making progress," Myrna said, wondering if she were subconsciously lying to herself. "Today, for instance, he insisted on staying home because he wants, as he says, to recharge his psychic energy. I take this to mean that he might have been reading Reich, whose work on sexuality I am coming more and more to admire greatly."

"Reich is great, indeed," Dr. Ingloss said paternalistically, drawing doodles of how he envisioned Myrna's bare breasts. "I believe that you need to bring Ignatius here, once he has fully recovered from your sojourn."

"Have you laid him?" Mrs. Murray said, giving Myrna a suspicious look.

"I tried to several times. Why?"

"Because you just said that I should screw Fred," the older, sexually frustrated, dour-faced Irishwoman said. "Why the hell should I follow your advice if you're not banging someone yourself?"

"I said that I tried," Myrna said defensively, if not somewhat sadly. "It's not like I can rape Ignatius or something like that, even though I've given that very serious consideration, especially when he enters one of his anti-Semitic moods. He's huge like a bear, and he's clumsy like a bull elephant, and I'm afraid that if I tried something on him, he might pass out and suffocate me."

"Must you be so graphic?" Leonard, a WASP CPA, asked. "That is just so, so horrible, Myrna Minkoff, the way you sometimes describe such things."

"Says the closeted homosexual who thinks about pluking Francesca, his mom's black poodle."

"That was only a dream," Leonard said, sniffing, miffed at Myrna. "A dream is a dream. A fantasy is a fantasy. As for me, you can call me whatever you want. Sticks and stones may break my bones, but names can never hurt me, Myrna Minkoff. You, on the other hand, are talking about something that's grotesque, that's horrid—"

"Sex is never horrid," Myrna said, and now she felt extremely angry, as she did whenever she received a rejection letter from one of the many sirs, the editors to whom she sent her articles and letters of proletarian protest. "It's a biological necessity, and it's now becoming a means of power for women, especially us deeply oppressed minority women who are doing our best to save the world and everyone in it. We are discovering that instead of pleasing men, we should be focused first and foremost on pleasing ourselves." She blinked, then looked at Mrs. Murray. "That's why I say that Mrs. Murray should go ahead and bang that ex-convict. He has as a lot of pent-up emotion, among other things. Mrs. Murray can transmute that sexual energy into something positive, something feminine, something dynamic for herself and for the world."

"I don't have any idea what you're talking about," Leonard said, crossing his arms and legs and looking up at a corner of the room, from which hung several cobwebs whose creators had died months before. "And quite frankly, I don't believe that you do either, Myrna Minkoff. Is it me, or does anyone else not understand what Myrna Minkoff's getting at?"

"I like what Myrna's saying, I think," Mrs. Murray said, not understanding a single word that Myrna had said, but believing, nonetheless, that she, Mrs. Murray, understood. In fact, no one in the room, including Dr. Ingloss, understood what Myrna had said, especially Myrna herself.

"There might be a few small holes here and there," Mrs. Murray continued, "but if we all work at it, like Dr. Ingloss says, we can make those holes tighter and tighter, and we can shake the long thing that's been holding us back by passive-aggressively refusing to extend itself. In the long view, everyone becomes happier, I think."

Ralph, the chronic masturbator, held up his left hand, which was closed into a fist. Two painted, globular eyes that had long eyelashes ornamented the index finger, as did a rouged upper lip, and on the thumb appeared a rouged lower lip.

The hand was Miss Kitty, which was about to speak, the thumb moving with each high-pitched pronunciation. "I couldn't agree with you more, Mrs. Murray. You deserve a hand!"

"I agree with her, too, Miss Kitty," Dr. Ingloss said. "And like you, I think that we should all give Mrs. Murray a hand."

"I second that most handily!" said Miss Kitty.

Dr. Ingloss and the group therapy group, excluding Leonard, applauded.

"Very well then," Dr. Ingloss said. "I believe that we should call it a day." Everyone began to stand, including Myrna. "Myrna, I'd like a word with you."

"Sure thing, Dr. Ingloss."

After everyone left, Dr. Ingloss spoke with Myrna in a hallway. "Myrna, I believe that Ignatius can help us to grow, not only as individuals, but, more important, as a collective."

"I think that we can save him," Myrna said.

"I'm sure that we can," Dr. Ingloss said, loving her smile but loving even more the cleavage that he promised would soon be his.

V

It took two hours for Ignatius to rise from the floor. Mrs. Minkoff, who worked feverishly to put the china back together, made noises of fuss and extreme worry. Perhaps, she thought, her husband was correct about Irwin. The epileptic Negro banjo player, after all, hadn't done the damage that Irwin had done.

Mrs. Minkoff implored Ignatius to help her to right the cabinet, but Ignatius excused himself, saying that he needed to get back to bed because that morning's shock had caused his pyloric valve to seal. Lying in bed, and having donned a rubber glove, Ignatius heard Mrs. Minkoff move about downstairs and then pleasured himself. But the phantasms of his long-dead dog, Rex, did not come to Ignatius's mind; now he envisioned the smashing of teacups. Ignatius closed his eyes, grimaced, and shuddered. Afterwards, he washed his hands, went downstairs to the kitchen, and prepared orange pekoe tea.

Feeling the onset of a migraine because of a very difficult day at the office, Mr. Minkoff arrived home around five that evening. That day, Mr. Minkoff had done his best not to think about Ignatius and his strange body odor, but the imagery, almost biblical in its intensity, had refused to leave Mr. Minkoff's mind. Mr. Minkoff wondered if he should attend psychotherapy, and, thinking of his daughter and her group therapy group, shuddered at the thought and decided against it.

Mr. Minkoff wanted to go to bed early. Instead of being able to go to bed early, however, Mr. Minkoff, to his utmost horror, found his frantic wife hurrying about, discovered a snoozing-on-the-floor Grandmother Horowitz with her robe open, and saw the destroyed china cabinet and its shattered remains.

"What the hell happened here!" Mr. Minkoff yelled, shaking his head in horror. "Did you clowns get into a fight that ended up breaking out into a hockey match! What's gotten into you people!"

Mrs. Minkoff cleared her throat and began, "It was the strangest thing—"

"The blame, my dear Mr. Minkoff, indubitably falls upon Grandmother Horowitz," said Ignatius, who appeared in the entry, chewing at potato chip crumbs that hung in his mustache. "It seems that she had a fit and, in what seemed to be an overly excited state of ecstasy, knocked over the china cabinet. I recommend a stay in the local hospital for her. She seems helpless and beyond repair, like Miss Trixie."

"Who the hell is Miss Trixie?" Mr. Minkoff demanded to know. "Is she responsible for this?"

"Miss Trixie," Ignatius intoned solemnly, "is a former colleague of mine who did her best, through nefarious, passive-aggressive means, to undermine Levy Pants, a company headquartered in New Orleans. If you were to ask me, I would say that Grandmother Horowitz is like Miss Trixie in many ways."

"I'm not asking you," Mr. Minkoff said, walking around the ruined china cabinet, shaking his head. What would happen next? Would Ignacio appear on a nationally famous, if not internationally famous, television show and wreak further havoc in the lives of the Minkoffs?

"But Irwin, it wasn't Mother who did it," Mrs. Minkoff protested. "It was you. You went into a tizzy after I told you that you would make a good son-in-law—"

"What!" Mr. Minkoff yelled, and now the headache that had threatened to become a migraine was now no longer threatening to become a migraine but had now become a full-blown migraine. His temples throbbed, he was short of breath, and he felt as if he might vomit at any moment. "This jerk's actually going to marry Myrna!"

"Of course not," Ignatius said imperiously, sipping his seventeenth cup of orange pekoe tea that day. "The minx and I would never entertain such an idea. First and foremost, she is a Hunter-educated Bolshevik whose worldview never was, and never can be, compatible with mine. Second, the minx is concerned solely and strictly with mere fornication—"

"Would you shut the hell up?" Mr. Minkoff said, face purpling, clenched hands trembling. Mr. Minkoff did his best not to strike the fat slob in the face. "When I want to you to speak to me, I'll let you know."

"Of course," Ignatius replied, finishing his tea, unaware of how angry and on the verge of having a nervous breakdown Mr. Minkoff was.

The front door opened, and Myrna hurried in, bringing with her a gust of December. After she closed the door, she stamped her booted feet in the front entrance, and then she tromped into the living room.

"Look at what your friend did," Mr. Minkoff said, pointing at the destroyed china cabinet. "Do you know how much this china meant to me? It was my mother's, for God's sake, my dear departed mother's!"

Myrna looked away from her father and at Ignatius. "Did you do this, Ignatius?"

"Of course not," Ignatius said, eructating. "Grandmother Horowitz was having a seizure of some sort."

"That must be true," Mrs. Minkoff said, blinking, having forgotten Ignatius's involvement. "Irwin's a rabbi, and rabbis don't lie."

"I can't believe I'm hearing these things in my own house!" Mr. Minkoff said, slapping his forehead. "When did this place become a frigging madhouse, can anyone please tell me that!"

"I would assume that it occurred when Myrna reached puberty," Ignatius said, "and, like a monkey, she has not been able to contain her wanton lust ever since."

Mr. Minkoff groaned and sank to the floor. He buried his face in his hands and did his best not to sob. Grandmother Horowitz stirred in her sleep and farted loudly, filling the room with a foul, sulfurous odor. Ignatius bellowed and hurried out, followed by Myrna and Mrs. Minkoff.

Mr. Minkoff shook his head. Why, why, why had things gone so wrong? "Can't we for once have something resembling normality or normalcy or whatever the hell the word is?" Mr. Minkoff said. "For Christ's sake, why can't things be normal for once?"

Grandmother Horowitz snorted in her sleep and rolled over.

"Things could be normal," Myrna said, reappearing with Mrs. Minkoff, now that the foul odor had left the room, "if you weren't such a reactionary against change. The world, as you probably are discovering, Dad, goes beyond anything Walter Cronkite could ever imagine. On top of that, the world is changing more quickly and is going to keep changing quickly, whether you like it or not."

Mr. Minkoff stood. "I'm going to take a couple of my migraine pills, and then I'm going to bed."

Ignatius peered into the room. "If I do say so myself, I am ready for another cup of orange pekoe tea."

"Of course, Irwin," Mrs. Minkoff said absentmindedly, taking the cup from his paws and going into the kitchen. A fatigued Mr. Minkoff exited.

"We need to talk," Myrna said to Ignatius.

"Pray tell, about what?" Ignatius asked suspiciously.

"My group therapy group," Myrna answered. "Dr. Ingloss wants to talk to you about your Ganser syndrome."

"Dr. Ganser wants to do what with my Ingloss?" Ignatius said, his blue and yellow eyes crossing. "What's an Ingloss? And who is Dr. Ganser?"

"It's Dr. Ingloss, and he wants to discuss your sexual problems with my group therapy group," Myrna said. "On top of that, and this is my own diagnosis, you are suffering from delayed ejaculation."

"Oh, my God!" Ignatius said, gagging. He felt woozy and decided not to stand, fearful that he might faint again and wreak further havoc, which he knew that he couldn't blame on the minx. He lay back on the sofa, aspirating. "How have I entered the next circle so soon? What cruel trick has Fortuna played on me?"

"Is she a masturbatory fantasy?" Myrna asked, sitting next to Ignatius. "What does she look like? Is she a prostitute, maybe one that you met in the French Quarter?"

Grandmother Horowitz snorted in her sleep. Ignatius gasped for air, almost hyperventilating, not wanting to hear any more.

"I need to go to bed," he said, struggling to stand, but his bad knees gave out, and he sank to the floor. He crawled towards stairs ascending to the second floor of the quaint Colonial Revival house. "I must rest my very battered and very wearied nerves."

Meanwhile, Mr. Minkoff was lying in bed.

There was a knock on the bedroom door. "Are you all right, Bernard?"

"I'm fine," Mr. Minkoff said to his wife as he wiped his brow with a tissue. His forehead felt hot, and his hands felt cold, and a cold sweat covered his body.

"Are you sure you don't want your dinner?"

"Please do not use that word!" Mr. Minkoff yelled. "The thought of food makes me want to puke!"

"I didn't know that dinner was such a bad word, Bernard."

"Oh, to hell with it!" Mr. Minkoff replied. "Leave me alone!"

Then suddenly an idea came to him, an idea that was like a plot twist in a parody of a satire.

"Get Myrna and that lug in the living room right now!" Mr. Minkoff yelled to Mrs. Minkoff, who was still standing at the bedroom door. "I've got something to say to the both of them!"

• *Three*

Magoohan hated Sergeant Scarletti. Magoohan hated Sergeant Dumbrowski. And Magoohan hated Greenwich Village. He hated the fairies who lived there. He hated the beatniks who lived there. He hated the intellectuals who lived there. In fact, he hated everyone and anything and everything to do with Greenwich Village. And, in fact, Magoohan's hatred has been mentioned enough, so this parody will move along accordingly.

Sergeant Dumbrowski had chewed out Magoohan earlier that morning for Magoohan's failing to bring in Nick the Nose as a suspicious character. Magoohan protested that he had nothing on the fairy. Sergeant Dumbrowski said that Magoohan was sassing too much. And so, as punishment, Sergeant Dumbrowski said that Magoohan would from here on out be working in disguise.

And so later that morning, Magoohan found himself hiding behind the Washington Arch, the beat cop dressed as Robin Hood: green tights, a green leather cap, and green leather chausses that had pointed toes, in accordance with Sergeant Dumbrowski's orders.

Magoohan, who was also wearing sunglasses, had been following Nick the Nose. The diminutive man had left his apartment half an hour earlier. The little rat-like man then met a walrus-like man in a park. Like the little fairy, the walrus-like man was a suspicious character. He was wearing clothes that fit too tightly and wore a bowler that looked too small on his walrus-like head. The two men parted, and Magoohan thought about following the walrus-like man, but the man looked as if he could put up a good fight. Magoohan decided on an easier target, and so he followed Nick the Nose, Magoohan huffing and puffing from tree to tree until he arrived at the arch, which was decorated with Christmas lights and ornaments.

Nick the Nose didn't know that Magoohan was following. What Nick the Nose did know was that he had to find that palimpsest. They, by way of Walpole, had told Nick the Nose to go out and find it—or else.

Besides the loss of the palimpsest, the gray cityscape, too, depressed Nick the Nose. Grayish-black snow adorned the roofs of cars and buildings, and from a chimney arose acrid smoke. He heard three women arguing in a ground-floor apartment, and then he heard the smashing of dishes. The air tasted of bitter metal, and a corner of Nick the Nose's mouth twitched in displeasure at the taste. Hunching his shoulders in his seedy topcoat, he tacked against a cold wind and entered the Paradise Diner. Following, Magoohan crossed the street.

Nick the Nose rubbed his hands together, cupped them, and blew hot air into them. A waitress, a woman with a shallow chest and a small waist and extremely large buttocks and thighs, asked him if he wanted a seat at the counter or wanted a booth.

"Corner booth," Nick the Nose said, and she led him to a corner booth, where he sat down, ordered a coffee and food, and then reached into a pocket of his seedy topcoat, from which he removed a bottle of codeine-infused cough syrup. He uncapped the bottle and took two large gulps of the liquid. The cherry-flavored liquid soothed his aching throat and gave it a pleasant-tasting coating that attenuated the nasty metallic taste of December.

Magoohan took a seat at the counter. Magoohan rubbed his hands together. Magoohan nudged the bridge of his sunglasses with a pudgy finger.

The suspect occupied a corner booth, Magoohan duly scrawled on a page in his pad. That fairy sure did look like someone who could be a communist. Or worse.

Magoohan lowered his sunglasses when a Negro counterman asked Magoohan what he was going to have. Magoohan said that he would have a coffee, no cream, no sugar.

"Where yer band of Merry Men?" the counterman asked, smiling.

"Funny," Magoohan said, gritting his teeth, looking at the corner booth where Nick the Nose, who was absentmindedly picking his nose, was sitting. "Hurry it up, will ya?"

"You sound like some kind of po-lice," the Negro counterman said, shaking his head, backing away from Magoohan. "I don't want nothing to do with no po-lice—"

"Keep it down, will ya?" Magoohan said, doing his best to keep his voice low. "I ain't no po-lice. I'm an actor, like."

"Like that garde-avant shit?" the Negro counterman said, looking even more perplexed. "I has a hard enough time understandin' Shakerod and that cat Kentucky Williams, let alone all that other weird white people shit."

"Just get me my goddamn order." Magoohan grimaced. "And be snappy about it, okay?"

The Negro counterman shook his head, poured Magoohan his coffee, and went to take orders from other diners sitting at the counter.

Nick the Nose noticed the man in the Robin Hood outfit. Nick the Nose frowned; the man seemed vaguely familiar.

Magoohan, noticing Nick the Nose's stare, looked away and scratched a cheek, which stung from a touch of frostbite. A diner next to Magoohan asked for the salt, and Magoohan grunted and grudgingly passed it.

The big-bottomed waitress brought Nick the Nose his order of eggs and hash browns and coffee. The agent sipped his coffee, his hands no longer trembling because the comforting codeine had kicked in. The diner door opened, and Henley entered with a gust of December trailing after him.

Nick the Nose waved at Henley. Henley grimaced, wheezed loudly, and hacked into his silk handkerchief.

"Hey, Ids," Nick the Nose said, running a finger underneath his nose. "How's it hangin'?"

"How the hell ya think?" Henley said, sliding into the opposite seat. "Vere's da paber?"

"I'm gonna find it," Nick the Nose said, "rest assured of dat."

"You bedder," Henley said, glowering at the little homosexual.

The big-bottomed waitress appeared and asked Henley if he would have anything. Henley said that he would have an orange juice. The waitress told Henley that he'd better be careful; it sounded as if he might be coming down with pneumonia. Henley waved her away. Then Henley rubbed his rheumy eyes with a paper napkin and sniffled.

"Otay, you ead, I drink my jude, and den we go to Baddery Pahk," Henley said, sniffling and thinking about his college days at Yale, where he had studied drama, sculled, and been a member of Skull and Bones. "Ids godda be dere."

"You know, you soundin' more and more Brooklyn," Nick the Nose said, taking an overly loud sip of his heavily creamed coffee. "And you ain't dere, Ids, youse here."

"Whad?"

"You said, 'Ids godda be dere.' Well, yer Ids, and you ain't dere, yer heh."

"Screw you," Henley was able to enunciate. "Godda make a phode call."

Magoohan, who had been watching the two suspicious characters, left his seat at the counter after Henley exited the booth in search of a public telephone. Magoohan pretended that he was heading to the restroom in the back of the diner. When he neared Nick the Nose's booth, Magoohan slid right next to Nick the Nose, who jumped.

"What hell da hell is dis?" Nick the Nose said.

"Keep your goddamn trap shut," Magoohan hissed.

Nick the Nose frowned. "Do I know you?"

"Yeah, yeah, we met. At the hospital. I interrogatived you."

"What da hell is dat?"

"I asked ya questions about ya acc'dent," Magoohan said. The Robin Hood costume felt itchy, especially in the crotch, but Magoohan held back from scratching his package, though he desperately wanted to.

"You da cop?"

"Keep it down," the beat cop said. "Whad are you doin' here? Who's that fancy creep yer with?"

Shaking her head, the big-bottomed waitress peered down at Magoohan.

"Whad?" Magoohan said.

"You ain't supposed to do dat in heh," she said, tsk-tsking. "You want to cruise, you go to one of them queer bars. This ain't the place for it."

"You calling me queer?" Magoohan said defensively, wanting to slap the server silly.

"Who's wearin' da Robin Hood getup?" she replied, and she placed a small glass of orange juice onto the table. "Now, you gonna leave, or am I gonna have to call Mike?"

Magoohan scowled. "This is official business, you bitch."

"Mike!" the big-bottomed waitress hollered. "Mike, I need youse, on account of dis queer's cruisin' our client and causin' me problems!"

And before Magoohan knew it, Mike, a bald, enraged Serbian who owned the Paradise Diner and who was a former strongman in his native country, grabbed Magoohan by the nape of his neck and by the seat of his green tights, dragged him through the diner, and threw a squealing and protesting Magoohan out the door and onto a stack of snow-encrusted garbage cans, which scattered and clattered into the icy street.

"Whad was dad all about?" Henley said, taking his seat and sniffling.

"You got me," the seedy operative said, and in his seedy pants pocket his finger played with the trigger of a switchblade.

Meanwhile, Myrna and Ignatius trudged down a bitterly cold, ice-covered street in Greenwich Village. Myrna had a rolled-up *New York Times* underneath an arm. A billboard proclaimed BOWERY BREW BEATS ALL!

"This is so unfair of my father," she said. "And so reactionary of him, too. How am I supposed to help you if we both have to work?"

"Why aren't we using your car?"

"As I told you, Ignatius, no one drives in New York City. You take a cab, ride the bus, or use the subway."

"Oh, my God, then why aren't we in a cab!"

"Ignatius, we don't have the money."

"Perhaps just one of us should work," Ignatius said, his teeth chattering like the chattering teeth one might purchase at a dime store.

"You heard Dad," Myrna said. "If we're to stay there, we both have to work. And he doesn't want us to work at his place because of the revolution that I attempted to start with a union organizer in one of the back rooms of my dad's offices."

"Why don't we stay with one of your radical friends?" Ignatius said, groaning. "This is becoming most unbearable."

"My friends won't let me live with them." Myrna's exhaled breath formed a cloud that hung evanescently in the winter cityscape, and the cloud vanished just as another formed. "And I'd get us our own place, Ignatius, but I don't have the money."

"Don't have the money?" Ignatius said, his pyloric valve feeling as if it might seal. "What do you mean you don't have any money? I thought that all Jews, especially Jewesses, had money."

"You'd better watch it with the anti-Semitic remarks," Myrna said. "That Levy Pants letterhead thing is still irking the hell out of me."

A dwarf trundling a bundle of newspapers almost ran into Ignatius.

"Watch it, pal," the dwarf said in a basso profundo, continuing his journey.

"Such rudeness," Ignatius intoned. "But such is Gotham, I suppose."

"What is it with this 'Gotham' business, Ignatius?"

"Surely you've heard of Batman," Ignatius said. "Gotham is his home. He's the only modern-day hero of our times. His morality is black and white, with no grays in between."

"You sound like my dad," Myrna said, and across the street she saw a mover unload a settee from the back of a van. His back was V-shaped and tapered at the waist, and he had a blue collar hardiness that she always found alluring. She wondered if he would be good in bed. "This is depressing, applying for jobs."

Ignatius agreed with her, but it was too cold for him to speak. His teeth chattered, and he hunched his shoulders. An Atlantic wind came in from the north, blowing through Greenwich Village and flowing around its buildings like water around boulders in a frigid stream.

"Please," Ignatius said, "can't we find a warm place to sit? My pyloric valve is about to seal, and I feel as if I might faint from my exertions."

Myrna nodded at the Paradise Diner. "We'll go in there, Ignatius, and hang out for a while. Who knows, we might find something in there that rescues us."

As they entered the diner, Magoohan stepped out from a neighboring alley. Ignatius raised an eyebrow.

"I didn't know that they celebrated Mardi Gras here," Ignatius said, shaking his head in wonder. Gotham was, indeed, such an exotic land. "Pray tell, are you a hot dog vendor? And if so, how do you withstand the frigidness of Gotham while wearing those clothes, pray tell?"

Magoohan frowned, not understanding what Ignatius had said.

"Pardon my friend," Myrna said, taking Ignatius by his mitten-encased paw. "He's suffering from an Oedipal complex, and this means that he's probably suffering from latent homosexuality."

"Oh, my God!" Ignatius bellowed, and he felt like vomiting onto the dirty snow. "I'm not sure how much more of this modernity nonsense I can take—"

"You callin' me a queer?" Magoohan asked Myrna. "You think I'm a queer because I'm wearin' this funny getup?"

"For someone dressed in green tights and a green cap and funny little green shoes, you sure are reactionary," Myrna said, leading Ignatius into the diner. "Come on, Ignatius, we need to get warm."

Magoohan attempted to show them that he was a police officer, but his badge fell out of his hands. The beat cop sputtered and reached down to pick up his badge, but the pointed chausses gave out on the icy sidewalk, and he pitched face-forward onto a mound of sooty snow. Magoohan gagged, groaned, and sat up. He didn't like that Jewish girl. And he didn't like that fat guy, who had intense blue and yellow eyes and that uppity accent and that uppity way of speaking.

Myrna sat down in a booth after she and Ignatius were escorted there by the big-bottomed waitress. Ignatius attempted to squeeze himself into the opposite seat. He wheezed and huffed until Myrna grabbed the table and pulled it towards her so that Ignatius had more room.

He exhaled loudly. "It does smell delicious, like a bakery," he said, looking around and admiring his new environs, particularly the diner's steamed windows. "But the theology and geometry are off-kilter. This painting, for instance"—and he pointed at an abstract painting done in red acrylics and black acrylics—"shows the worldview of Gotham, a worldview that is fractured and impure and that needs correction."

Myrna ran fingers through her greasy hair. "What are you talking about, Ignatius?"

"Worldviews," Ignatius said, and he thought of Boethius and all that the great Christian philosopher had had to endure at the hands of his enemies before being put to death. "Art, or what pretends to be art, is never neutral. It can never be neutral, unlike the utilitarian, which, of course, is not art because it's utilitarian."

"I wonder if this would be a good place to hold a meeting," Myrna said, looking at the stage at the other end of the diner. "I bet lots of people have lots of meetings here."

"I was talking about worldviews," Ignatius said, peeved at her inattention. "False worldviews almost caused me to be imprisoned unjustly in what is euphemistically called a sanitarium, but which of course should properly be called an insane asylum." He cleared his throat; his mouth watered as his olfactory and gustatory capabilities came alive, especially when he smelled ham, bacon, eggs, coffee, and cinnamon rolls. "Shall we be served soon?"

Myrna snapped her fingers, and the big-bottomed waitress turned and glowered at Myrna. Myrna pointed down at the table, indicating that she and Ignatius wanted service. The waitress told Myrna to hold her horses and hurried off to serve other patrons.

"As I was saying—"

"I have a great idea, Ignatius."

"What great idea?"

"Getting even with Dad and his bourgeois ways," Myrna said, staring at the stage. "It could all begin here."

"What could begin here? What are you talking about?"

"What else?" Myrna said, turning to Ignatius, no longer looking dejected. "The revolution. We could start the revolution here."

Nick the Nose and Henley walked by the booth in which Ignatius and Myrna were sitting, and Henley coughed into his silk handkerchief. Ignatius noticed the murine features of the smaller of the two men, features that Ignatius did not particularly like, while noting that the murine man's topcoat showed a leaning towards proper theology and geometry. Ignatius wondered if he had just seen a kindred soul among the autochthonous inhabitants of lower Manhattan. And Henley frowned, wondering where he had seen this strange fat man with the green hunting cap.

The big-bottomed waitress appeared and took Myrna's order and Ignatius's order: black coffee and a hot bagel with cream cheese for Myrna, a stack of blueberry pancakes and a pot of orange pekoe tea for Ignatius. Ignatius attempted to speak with the big-bottomed waitress about how brutally cold the weather was in Gotham, but the big-bottomed waitress scowled and hurried away.

"I want to stay away from stages," Ignatius said, remembering Darlene's cockatoo at the Night of Joy. "For that matter, I want to stay away from clothing manufacturers, too."

"All this time that I've been rescuing you, we never really talked about what happened in New Orleans," Myrna said. "Was all of this brought on by the homosexual dreams that you were having?"

"What?" Ignatius sputtered. "How dare you—"

"Keep it down, Ignatius," Myrna said, leaning across the table. "Sometimes I wonder if I should have rescued you. Sometimes it seems like you're returning to your old nasty self."

Ignatius held his breath to quell his anger. Fortuna had brought him to this point. He had to be careful. The minx, after all, was his only link to safety. He could not afford to anger her. He knew that. He would play her game, and he would play it well. And he would play it better than her. Before she knew it, she and her family would be in his cold-bitten hands.

"Your work has not been in vain," Ignatius said in an attempt to assuage her doubt. "In fact, my sexual repression, as you call it, is about to lift." He peered at motley attired people. "I have a wonderful idea. I believe that you should go out and seek work while I stay here, or, barring this place, perhaps there is a nearby movie theater where I could wait. I'm sure that some wretched new Doris Day film has been released, and if so, then I must see it. I must keep up my critical review faculties, meaning, ultimately, that I must maintain my cultural imperative."

"No, we'll have our coffee and whatever, and then we'll go answer another ad," Myrna said, looking down at want ads, which she had spread on the table. She frowned; why weren't there ever any ads for revolutionaries or activists? She circled an ad for an insurance claims adjuster and then moved on to other ads seeking professional help.

The big-bottomed waitress brought them their orders, and Ignatius dug into his meal like a ravenous bear. All the hustle and bustle of Gotham—buses, subways, cars, cabs, pedestrians—had enervated him, and he wolfed down his meal, his stomach howling with delight as it received the warming victuals. After he finished his gorging, Ignatius drank his tea, and, for a moment, he thought about his old room, and he wondered how his mother was doing.

"I think I found it!" Myrna exclaimed, drawing a red circle around an ad, as if the tip of the red pen were a motorcyclist looping a circuit. "I think that I've found the work that we're seeking, Ignatius!"

"Please don't tell me it's at a pants factory!" Ignatius said, shuddering. "Oh, my God! To be around people like Mr. Gonzalez and Miss Trixie!"

"It's in Chinatown," Myrna said. "At a fortune cookie company. They're seeking a writer and an editorial assistant. If we work it right, we can get jobs on the line and get the peasants to join us in the revolution." Myrna stared ahead, as if at a faraway land. "I've always been intrigued by Chinese peasantry. They are, after all, the most exploited people in the world, after the Jews, of course. At least the WASP reactionaries allowed us to start clothing factories. All the Chinese ever got were restaurants and laundry services."

"That's actually not a very bad deal, if one really considers it," Ignatius intoned solemnly, thinking of a passage in *The Consolation of Philosophy*. "One time, when my mother was sane, long before she met Claude *roué*, she took the laundry to a Chinese man whose establishment was next to a fresh fish market. Unfortunately, our clothes ended up smelling like red snapper." Ignatius eructated. "Perhaps Mr. Duk Dong should have considered opening his laundry next to a perfumery."

"Can't you just see it, Ignatius? We can help all of those oppressed Chinese workers. They've lived under a repressive form of communism brought about in part, I bet, by the male patriarchy that seems to rule the Far East."

Ignatius sighed. The hot meal and hot tea were making him tired. He wanted to curl up in the bed in the guest room and sleep for many hours and afterwards, perhaps, write five hundred words or so of the treatise that he planned to write about Gotham: its inhabitants, its mores, its splendor, its hope, its ultimate downfall because of the decadence pervading Western culture. Of course, such a treatise, if written correctly, might turn into an autobiography of sorts. Perhaps, Ignatius thought, he should start with his birth in New Orleans and progress through his childhood in a private Catholic school and then move on to his being forced to attend public schools after the loss of his father. Of course he, Ignatius, would provide excruciatingly delightful details about his course of study at Tulane and all that he had had to endure there, especially under Dr. Talc. Most of all, however, he, Ignatius, would devote two chapters—no, make that three—to his foray on the Greyhound Scenicruiser, that monocoque monstrosity. In fact, come to think of it, that subject warranted its own book—

"Have you heard one word of what I've been saying, Ignatius?" Myrna said, peering directly into Ignatius's face.

"Of course, of course," Ignatius said. "I agree. We must take over the factory."

"That's not what I was talking about," Myrna said, making a face. "I was talking about Grandmother Horowitz and her need for sexual release."

"Oh." What he really meant to say was, "Oh, my God!"

"Do you think that you'd be up to it, Ignatius? I believe that it would do the both of you a world of good. Orgasms, you know, can heal anything."

Ignatius felt nauseated. He rolled up a paw into a fist and put the fist to his mouth and coughed, pretending that he couldn't answer Myrna. At just the right moment, a Negro—who was wearing a black balaclava and camouflage fatigues and spit-polished jump boots and who was sitting at the counter and staring at the ceiling and muttering to himself—caught Myrna's attention, and she got up to go speak to him.

Myrna had not touched her breakfast, and Ignatius ate her bagel, reveling at how marvelous the cream cheese tasted.

"It's time to go," Myrna said a few minutes later, gathering up the want ads with her ink-smeared palms and fingers. She haphazardly rolled up the newspaper and put the newspaper underneath her arm. "We need to get to Chinatown. And I have a date tonight."

"Date? With whom?"

"Rastajaq," she said. "He's a revolutionary from an African country that I've never heard of but that sounds fascinating."

"I take it that this Othello is like that African with whom you had a dalliance, Ungba-Bunga, the semiotician—"

"That was Ongah," Myrna said, and she pressed her lips together tightly, not happy to be reminded of her former lover. "Needless to say, some myths are not true."

"I believe I should stay here, where it's warm—"

"We'll get warm on the subway, Ignatius. Now let's get going to Chinatown."

Myrna opened the diner door, and a frigid blast of winter wind whipped her face. Ignatius shivered uncontrollably. O Fortuna, Fortuna, why hast thou done this to me, blind Fortuna!

Magoohan appeared from the alley, having failed earlier to see Nick the Nose and Henley exit the diner. Magoohan sniffed and wiped his philtrum with a stubby index finger. "You two dere."

Myrna turned. "Oh, you again."

"Good heavens!" Ignatius said, teeth chattering, face having crimsoned because of the hypenemious city. "Robin Hood sans his Merry Men once again. Come to take from the poor, you simpleton, and give to the rich?"

"You two characters are comin' in wid me," Magoohan said, and he reached for Myrna, who leaped aside and screeched loudly.

"Keep it down!" Magoohan said, handcuffs in hand, moving towards her. "You take it easy, or I'm takin' it out on you—"

"Rape!" Myrna screamed. "Please, someone help me, help me! I'm being raped! Rape!"

Magoohan held up his hands. "Shuddup, I'm a cop—"

"Please, someone, help!" Ignatius bellowed, following Myrna's lead. "Oh, my God, this wanton homosexual is attempting to rape this young minx! Someone help, please!"

Onlookers gathered around the three, and two cops rushed forward, truncheons drawn. Magoohan smiled when he saw the two cops, whom he didn't know. Magoohan reasoned that help had now arrived.

"What the hell's goin' on heh?" asked the older of the two cops, whose gray eyes matched the pallor of his face. "What's all this about rape?"

Myrna thrust her finger angrily at Magoohan. "He tried to rape me—"

"The hell I did," Magoohan said, and he dropped the handcuffs and came after Myrna with his pudgy hands. "Why, I oughtta choke the living—"

"Hold it right there, buddy," the second cop said, extending his truncheon. "Let's see some ID."

"I'm a cop, you assholes—"

"Then show us your badge."

"Yeah, yeah, sure thing." Magoohan reached into his tights for the badge. He frowned. He moved his hand around in his tights, from the back to the front, all over and all around, slow at first, then fast as he realized that he had lost his badge.

"It seems to me that not only is he a wanton homosexual, but he's performing an onanistic obscenity right before our very eyes," a pointing Ignatius said to the gray-faced, older cop. "Arrest this pantywaist, and give him the bastinado in some hovel of a barren jail! That is what this deviant deserves!"

"I don't understand a word of what you just said," the gray-faced, older cop said to Ignatius, and then the cop looked at Magoohan. "But to me, you look like some previated prevert playing with himself in front of these honest, hardworking people. Now, let's see some ID, Tinker Bell!"

"I'm a cop, you friggin' idiot, you can call—"

"I think he's getting ready to pull a gun, Sarge," the younger cop said.

"The hell he is!" the gray-faced, older cop snarled.

The two cops set upon a protesting Magoohan, fustigating him with their truncheons. Magoohan grunted, holding up his hands to ward off the blows. The crowd applauded the two cops, and Myrna grabbed Ignatius by a paw, leading him away.

"It's time to get to Chinatown," she said.

Ignatius, remembering his interaction with Mancuso in front of the D. H. Holmes, nodded in agreement.

II

Ignatius adjusted his behemoth behind in the guest bed, which groaned because of his immense weight. He opened a Big Chief tablet, wet the tip of a freshly sharpened pencil with the tip of his giant pink tongue, and began writing, the words flowing smoothly like the Hudson River in summer.

> Vision is the art of seeing things invisible.
> —Jonathan Swift

Fortuna has seen to it that more and more glitches enter my world, with my hardly knowing what to do with them. Madam Minkoff has become an ally, albeit an unwitting one, while Myrna minx does her best to convert her so-called bourgeois family into a Marxist cell while, at the same time, doing her best to liberate Grandmother Horowitz from what the minx calls "sexual frustration." I shudder at all that the minx's parents, especially Mr. Minkoff, have had to endure because of her.

Nonetheless, I must always keep in mind that Myrna minx Minkoff, while professing loyalty and fidelity to your beloved Carl, can turn on this boy in but an instant. Her Marxist neuroses, coupled with what I see as a libido that can never be satiated, might drive her over the edge, much as the evil and vile Claude Robichaux and the equally evil and vile Santa Battaglia drove my once loving and adoring mother over the edge.

All was going well until this evening, when Mr. Minkoff and Myrna got into a heated argument, which escalated into a shouting match in the living room. Because of an unfortunate incident, he believes that Myrna and I must pay for the damages. (Of course, dear reader, this is not Myrna minx's fault. On the contrary, the fault lies solely and exclusively with Madam Minkoff, who had the audacity to suggest that I, your dear canvasser, would somehow end up in the nuptial embraces of that infernal minx.)

Myrna, because of her Marxist principles, does not want to pay for the damages incurred to the late Grandmother Minkoff's china. Consequently, Mr. Minkoff threatened to cut off Myrna's funding. Consequently, Mr. Minkoff threatened to cut off Myrna's hair. Consequently, Mr. Minkoff threatened to cut off Myrna, period. And because of that, I, your humble narrator and friend, am very anxious. Should the minx lose her home, then I, too, shall lose my home. I lost my home on Constantinople Street in New Orleans. Must I, for whatever reason, lose the humble abode that I now inhabit?

Alas, unless the minx and I can find work—and find work soon—it seems as if we are going to lose our home. (The good news, if this can be called good news, is that the minx and I have interviews tomorrow morning at the Charlie Chan Chinese Fortune Cookie Company in the heart of what is colloquially known as Chinatown. The minx intends to start a Maoist revolution. I intend to sleep.)

Ah, back to the main point: Myrna screamed that she was going to move to Vermont, where a group of her radical Negro friends were establishing a commune, if Mr. Minkoff continued to make his threats. Mr. Minkoff's face paled but then turned a brilliant red, to the point where he himself could have been a Christmas lawn ornament in one of his gentile neighbors' yards. He told her to go to hell, and she left the house after slamming the front door and was gone for two hours. From her appearance after she came back, it seemed that she found a longshoreman to provide the relief that she so desperately needed. She is, of course, one given to uninhibited sexual acts for which she has a strong proclivity. (She certainly did not get this proclivity from Mr. or Madam Minkoff. The question is: from whom?)

Grandmother Horowitz has taken a stronger fancy to me and has suggested that we spend time alone in her bedroom, not only in the discussion of the snapping of her garters but in the discussion of the number sixty-nine, which seems to hold a strange fascination for her. From my own scant readings about Judaic culture, I am given to the understanding that these people are fascinated with numerology and with anything related to the Cabala, a form of ancient Jewish mysticism. What puzzles me is Grandmother Horowitz's interest in such a subject; after all, most Cabalists, from what I understand, are married Jewish men forty or older. Nonetheless, given the current level of stress in the Minkoff household, I am not sure yet whether I shall, or should, meet with Grandmother Horowitz in private.

I have much work to do here in the Minkoff household, of course, before I even begin thinking about the taking of Gotham. That minx must learn her lesson; that is a given. And I must set Mr. and Madam Minkoff on the correct path. I do not believe that it is too late for them to correct their ways. Then it won't be too long before I have Myrna minx in her rightful place.

A quick aside about Mr. Minkoff: I happened to pass by his study, where, I assume, he goes over his books. I was shocked, however, to see that he was watching a Laurel and Hardy movie on television. Mind you, dear reader, I have nothing against these men, who, in their own way, in their own time, were doing their best to bring a proper theology and geometry to the world. The shock, of course, is not in that but in the fact that our apoplectic Mr. Minkoff has taken such an interest in them. In fact, as I watched his watching the set, his lips were moving each time Stan Laurel spoke. I cannot assay why Mr. Minkoff would do that; suffice to say, his worldview seems to be changing and seems to be changing quite rapidly, all for the better. (Time will tell, they say. Perhaps they should say, time and the devil will tell. We shall, indeed, see if Mr. Minkoff is serious.)

Another aside: I miss New Orleans terribly. Is it Odysseus who says that it is not good for a man to wander? Perhaps it is something that someone says to Odysseus. Whether Odysseus says it, or whether someone says it to him, is beside the point. The saying is quite true. It is not good for a man to wander, save if he is strolling a mere block or two from his domicile, preferably in my beloved New Orleans.

Your hardworking canvasser is weary after another long day. With that, I must sign off, bidding you a fond adieu and a hearty auf Wiedersehen.

With warmest regards,
Carl, Your Neighborhood
Canvasser

A quick PS. A sexual deviant accosted Myrna and me in Greenwich Village. At least blind Fortuna intervened, saving the day. For a moment I was afraid that a new

Mancuso had entered my life. It seems now, however, that my momentary worries were unjustified.

I am yawning, and my eyelids are heavy. And for now, and for certain, Carl the Canvasser must get his much needed sleep!

III

Nick the Nose and Henley foraged in the alley in which the Puerto Rican had attempted to mug Nick the Nose. The two operatives had spent two hours searching the ice-cave-like alley for the palimpsest.

Henley sniffled, feeling as if he were going to die; perspiration dotted his forehead, his joints ached, and even though he was wearing heavy winter clothing, he felt the New York City winter pierce him to the marrow. What he wanted more than anything was to be back in beautiful Santa Barbara, where he and his beautiful wife could sip beautiful vodka martinis and eat handfuls of beautiful cashews while he and his beautiful wife watched the beautiful sunsets on the beautiful Pacific Ocean.

"Why didn't dey just make a copy?" Nick the Nose asked, shaking his head. "Like a dedaction or whatever the hell they call it, Ids."

"Id idn't Ids," Henley said, and he coughed violently, so violently, in fact, that he had to lean against an ice-coated alley wall. He spat phlegm, which tasted sweet, into a lidless garbage can. "And ids a redagshun, not a dedagshun. And dey cand becobs id mud rebain hidden."

"Ah, I gotcha, Ids," Nick the Nose said. "It's like dere's only one copy in the world on account they want to keep whadever it is secret, and they don't want no one else to know what it is."

"Eggs-actly," Henley replied, sniffing.

"Now what, Ids?"

Henley was about to say that his name wasn't Ids, but he chose, instead, to focus on the job at hand.

"We comtinue da serge da area," Henley said, coughing, waving his hand. "Loog eberywhere."

"And what if we doesn't find it?" Nick the Nose asked. "Then what, Ids?"

"Beer ded," Henley said. "Dads what be are."

And then the palimpsest floated in front of Henley's face. He reached for it, and, as part of this parody, a winter wind whipped the palimpsest north.

"Abber id!" Henley yelled, hacking phlegm, wheezing as he ran, wondering if Sisyphus felt the same way after rolling the boulder up the hill. "Abber id!"

And the two operatives went after the palimpsest, which was sometimes within reach. But before either of the operatives could grab the palimpsest, the winter wind snatched it away.

And Henley waved his hands, and the two operatives chased after their lost treasure.

IV

From his perch on a tenement rooftop that morning, El Lobo Macho peered down at a street in lower-west Manhattan, vigilant, as always, for any signs that *la putería* might be attempting to infest his neighborhood. A neighbor, Mr. Gomez, who was dressed as Santa Claus, stumbled drunkenly into a parked car.

Guapo appeared and saluted. El Lobo Macho returned the salute.

"Any faggots about?" El Lobo Macho asked in Spanish, twisting the ends of his mustache, feeling macho because his mustache, which was as thick and as curly as the hairs on a Latina's nether regions, inherently meant that he was macho. He was a man. A real man. He did not eat quiche or any other sissy foods. He had sex at least two times a day with his woman, Lucia, for a minimum of fourteen times a week. If that did not prove that he was macho, then nothing else would.

"None that I can see," Guapo replied in Spanish. "You know, it is very cold up here. I think I will go home."

"It is too cold up here? You let a little cold put fear into your heart?"

"If I am afraid of anything, it is getting pneumonia," Guapo said. "I had pneumonia last year. I do not want to catch pneumonia this year."

"Are you sure that you are not a faggot, Guapo?"

Guapo sighed. It was as if homosexuality were all that El Lobo Macho could ever think about.

"I told you I am cold," Guapo answered coldly. "What does this have to do with being a homosexual?"

"I have my reasons for asking," said El Lobo Macho, who was looking at rows of skyscrapers that composed the island of Manhattan. "I believe that they are infiltrating everything and that we must be aware. You have read *The Protocols of the Learned Elders of Zion*, have you not?"

"Is that not about the Jews?"

El Lobo Macho nodded. "It is, but I believe that the author made a mistake. He should have called it *The Protocols of the Learned Elders of Queerdom*." El Lobo Macho motioned with his hand at the wide expanse of Manhattan. "They are out there, and they are waiting. They want to take over the world. When they do, everything will be inverted. It is a conspiracy of some sort. That I know."

"And you have proof of this conspiracy?"

"Is not the existence of Greenwich Village proof enough?" El Lobo Macho asked rhetorically. "Look, my friend, I am worried for you. I do not believe that you understand the seriousness of this mission. I have done my best to convey the seriousness of this mission to you and to others. I want to ensure that our people are protected. If we are, and the other races embrace the faggots, then we will become dominant, as we were meant to become dominant. We Puerto Ricans shall rule the world, and everyone will bow down to us."

"That is the part that I do not understand," Guapo said, baffled. "You say that we will rule the world. But if the faggots outnumber us and control all the military resources and all the natural resources, among other things, then how are we going to take over? You sound like a madman in Death Valley, envisioning an Armageddon between the blacks and the whites and playing bad folk music and murdering innocent people in the Hollywood Hills."

"Are you saying that I am insane?" El Lobo Macho asked angrily.

"Not at all," Guapo replied cautiously. "I am saying that, while I follow you, I do not understand all your ways, El Lobo Macho. You are enigmatic at times. It is as if you are speaking in aphorisms or parables. There seems to be a wisdom there, but if there is, I cannot fathom it."

"It is because I am a genius," El Lobo Macho replied, puffing up his pectoral muscles to emphasize his point. "And it is because I am doing the will of God."

"God has told you all these things?" Guapo asked.

"I believe that He has," El Lobo Macho said, playing with his mustache the way that he played with the pubic hairs of Lucia. "Before I go to sleep at night, I hear a voice, and it tells me many things."

"Like what?"

"The things that I have told you, among others," El Lobo Macho replied. "Things like buying the next Corvair and how wonderful Wonder Bread is for us all."

Guapo made a face. He did not like Wonder Bread. Though its taste was slightly appealing, Guapo wondered if Wonder

Bread really had all the nutrients that it claimed to have. He missed Puerto Rico and its Caribbean waters and its natural foods.

"Perhaps someone's television is on while you are sleeping," Guapo said. "Perhaps you are hearing television commercials advertising the cheap and finally unsatisfying vanities of the Western world."

"Are you saying that God does not speak to me?" El Lobo Macho asked, a deep, red, fiery anger emanating from the depths of his taut belly. "Are you saying that I am a liar?"

"Not at all, El Lobo Macho," Guapo said, taking an involuntary step back and holding up his hands. "I am not saying these things at all. I believe you. I believe that you are hearing the words of God Himself."

Guapo's words assuaged El Lobo Macho's anger. El Lobo Macho lit a cigarette, enjoying the lit tobacco and the cold air that he inhaled.

"Of course I am hearing the voice of God," El Lobo Macho said. "Whose voice could it be?"

"And what else does He say to you?"

"That I am to preserve our people and get rid of the faggots, no matter how I do it. And I will, God help me, the Blessed Virgin help me, the saints help me."

El Lobo Macho crossed himself, and Guapo followed suit.

"What are we going to do today?" Guapo asked.

"We shall continue our sojourn into the enemy's territory," El Lobo Macho said. "We shall continue to work for that faggot."

"Did God tell you we were to do that?" Guapo asked, hoping that the answer would be no.

"Not yet," El Lobo Macho said, "but I have the feeling that He will."

"Ah," said Guapo. "Sometimes I think that life is like a comedic novel with no real plot, set in a Mediterranean-like city somewhere within the United States, with a loose series of incidents that are somehow tied up at the end, when everything is said and done."

El Lobo Macho scowled. "You wax poetic, Guapo. And poetry is the domain of the faggots."

"God forbid," Guapo replied. "A true man never speaks about poetry, let alone thinks about it."

"Well said," El Lobo Macho said. "Let us get Chico. It is time for us to depart for our practice."

And with that, the two exited the tenement roof.

· *Four*

Myrna and Ignatius entered the fray that was called Chinatown. The air was redolent of fried rice, fried pork, and fried beef. Ignatius's mouth watered. Myrna looked about, attempting to get her bearings. Around them, people, the majority of them Chinese, scurried, their shoulders hunched against the frigid December winds that assaulted everything and everyone.

"I think it was this way," Myrna said, pointing up a street. "When we get there for our interviews, let me do the talking, all right, Ignatius?"

"I, I, I—"

"What is it, Ignatius?"

"I just want to get warm," Ignatius said, hugging himself, pretending that his arms were the arms of his dear mother (pre-Claude *roué*, of course). "It feels as if we've leaped into the Ninth Circle. I expect to see Satan himself at any moment, shedding never-ending tears for the sins that he committed against a most holy God."

Myrna shook her head and began walking, Ignatius struggling to keep up. "You know, Ignatius, I think you're going to back to your old reactionary ways. I had hopes for you. I thought that you would come through and get over the neuroses that you were suffering in New Orleans." She held out her arms. "Look about you, Ignatius. Life is going on around you. Don't you want to partake in this? Don't you want to start a revolution?"

Ignatius's head pounded with the onset of a migraine. This cold was colder than cold. In other words, Gotham was hell. If only, however, there had been the heat of hell. Contrary to what the plebeians imagined, hell was not a roaring lake of fire; on the contrary, hell was a long walk through a Chinese neighborhood in Gotham on a bitterly, bitterly cold winter's day with an overly privileged fellow traveler who, upon turning thirty or so, would more than likely give up her revolutionary ideas and settle down into a life of selling real estate after marrying a Jewish stockbroker.

"Are you going to partake of life or not?" Myrna asked snappily. "I have to have that commitment from you, Ignatius."

"Of course," Ignatius said, and his teeth chattered while he suppressed a loud groan. "I've given up my medievalism and the idea that there is any sort of orderly universe. All is relative. There are no absolutes. If we are to have justice, then we must make it for ourselves." His breaths were coming out quicker, forming cumulus clouds that quickly died after the birth of another cumulus cloud. "Revolution is at hand! We must liberate the Chinese! We must overthrow Western culture!"

"That's the spirit, Ignatius! Now you're getting out of your cloistered shell!"

An elderly, stooped-over Chinese gentleman, with tan eyes that looked very sad, shook his head as he passed the two would-be revolutionaries. Overhead, the sky grayed darker, and a light snow fell. Fortunately, the winds started to attenuate.

"We're almost there," Myrna said as she led the way, "just like one of my potential multiple orgasms. I can feel that we're going to do a lot of good, Ignatius." She stopped and blinked. "I thought I recognized this street. By the way, they say that the Chinese are very good at sex. I intend to find out."

Ignatius shivered, too cold to reply, and the two turned a corner and headed up another street, which was lined with pleasantly aromatic Chinese restaurants and steam-emitting dry cleaners.

Myrna stopped in front of a building, red ideograms ornamenting its brick walls.

"I think this is it," Myrna said. "Do you understand what these things mean?"

"How can I!" Ignatius bellowed, hugging himself. "I'm going to die if we don't get warm soon! Can't you understand that!"

"You're not used to a real winter, that's your problem," Myrna said, taking him by the paw. "Come on, Ignatius, let's go in. We'll get you warm."

They entered the small, well-heated front office that they had entered the previous day, Myrna closing the door behind them. Christmas streamers festooned the walls, on which also hung several framed photographs of Chinese gentlemen in business suits. A Chinese woman sitting at a desk and writing ideograms in a ledger looked up. She peered at the two as if they were aliens who had just arrived from Alpha Centauri. She had not been at the desk the previous day.

"May I help you?" the woman asked.

"Do you speak English?" Myrna said loudly, as if the woman were deaf. "We are here for jobs. Two jobs." Myrna held up two fingers, a gesture that in Hong Kong would have been taken as an up-yours.

"I asked if I could help you," the frowning woman said in a prim, proper, precise Transatlantic accent, "and I spoke in English. Why then did you ask me if I could speak English when I had already spoken it? Are you so racist to believe that each Chinese person you meet speaks Pidgin English?"

"Please pardon her seeming rudeness," Ignatius said, rubbing his hands together, his mouth watering because of the smell of freshly baked fortune cookies that filled the warm lobby. "She doesn't mean to be insulting. She believes that she is saving the world. Yesterday we applied for jobs, and we are here for our interviews."

"Ah, of course," the woman said, opening a desk drawer and taking out the two applications that Myrna and Ignatius had completed the previous day. "You are the professional writers, correct?"

"I've tried several times to get published, but the editors and publishers in this city are too reactionary," Myrna said, scratching her crotch. "This bourgeois culture is not ready for sexual liberation. Do you know, for instance, that most of the housewives in this city have never had an orgasm? I wrote several tracts about this very subject but was driven out of Brooklyn by a bunch of angry Negroes and surly Hasidic Jews who thought that I was a government spy."

The Chinese woman blinked, unsure how to answer this strange woman and her stranger companion. "Are you sure that you're professional writers?" the woman asked, doubtful.

"I am an observer of our times," Ignatius said royally, expanding his chest, wanting to appear as regal as possible. "My worldview comes close to that of Confucianism, if that's any help."

"What happened to the woman who was working the desk yesterday?" Myrna asked. "Let me guess, she was rising in this company and reached the glass ceiling, and now you've sent her to slave away with the other workers, right?"

Ignatius rolled his eyes. The Chinese woman scowled.

"She was a temporary replacement while I was in Hong Kong," the woman said. "Not that that is any of your business. I am Mrs. Wang, the head receptionist, by the way. You do not sound as if you want to work but rather have come here to cause trouble."

"I, for one, earnestly seek earnest employment," Ignatius said. "Shall I have my interview?"

Myrna gave Ignatius a look that showed that she felt betrayed in some amorphous way or another.

"And I want an interview, too," Myrna said to Mrs. Wang. "If Ignatius gets one, then I get one, glass ceiling or not."

"Very well then," Mrs. Wang said in her well-clipped accent. She pushed a button on an intercom, which buzzed.

"Miss Ping?" Mrs. Wang said in Cantonese. "This is Mrs. Wang. Our two interviewees are here to speak with Mr. Pong. And be forewarned: they are crazy white devils, especially the female."

Miss Ping giggled. "Aren't they all?" she answered in Cantonese.

"This is serious business, Miss Ping," Mrs. Wang said sternly. "Mr. Pong desires to make Charlie Chan fortune cookies the number one fortune cookie on the market. This is not a duty to be taken lightly. I, for one, am tired of your obnoxious, so-called attempts at levity, Miss Ping."

Miss Ping giggled and said, in Cantonese, that she would be down.

"This-uh way," Miss Ping said to Ignatius and Myrna, who were sitting on a sofa in the small reception area while Mrs. Wang used an abacus. "Mr. Pong is-er waiting-uh you." She laughed a phocine laugh.

Ignatius, Myrna helping him to rise off the sofa, frowned.

"I fail to see the humor in this situation," he said. "Pray tell, what is so humorous, my fine little mongoloid friend?"

"She believes that she's funny," Mrs. Wang said, not looking up for her ledger. "You will eventually get used to her, as we all have, if you are chosen to work here."

Miss Ping led the way into Mr. Pong's office and closed the door behind her, giggling and apologizing for her undue sense of humor.

Mr. Pong, a slick-haired, cross-eyed man who was wearing thick-lensed glasses (lenses so thick that the glasses appeared as if they came from a novelty shop), rose from a chair behind his desk and motioned with a sweep of his hand for Ignatius and Myrna to have seats in the two chairs in front of the desk. Ignatius's ursine ass got stuck in the chair. He struggled and grunted in displeasure and disapproval.

"I believe that you need to get chairs more befitting a native of the United States," Ignatius said imperiously. "After all, if I am to partake of this interview in comfort, I must be able to move around slightly in this chair, which, I'm afraid, will rise with me when I rise."

"Let us cut to the chase," Mr. Pong said in a crisp English accent that he had acquired at St. Stephen's College Preparatory School in Hong Kong. He sat down in his chair, feigned a smile, and did his best to appear friendly to the two white devil kooks sitting in front of him. "I am seeking a writer and an editorial assistant. The writer must be someone who can create the most imaginative, most tantalizing fortune cookie messages ever written. As you two are probably aware, fortune cookie messages tend to be trite or rather boring. 'You are a hardworking, energetic person,' 'You will meet a tall, dark, and handsome stranger,' and so forth.

"Now that I am the head of the Charlie Chan Chinese Fortune Cookie Company, I desire to take this company in a new direction. For instance, I created new flavors. We now have chocolate-flavored fortune cookies, strawberry-flavored fortune cookies, vanilla-flavored fortune cookies, raspberry-flavored fortune cookies, banana-flavored fortune cookies, and tutti-frutti-flavored fortune cookies, among other flavors that are, as you Americans are fond of saying, in the works." He smiled, proud of his accomplishments. "But the flavoring is not enough. I want to expand the horizons of the Charlie Chan Chinese Fortune Cookie Company so that the messages that the fortune cookies contain truly affect humanity in a positive manner—"

"Are you familiar with Boethius?" Ignatius said. "He's a philosopher—"

"I do not know who that is," Mr. Pong said, glancing at his watch; he had a meeting to attend in twenty minutes, and he felt edgy because he hated to be rushed. "The point is, I want the messages of the fortune cookies created by the Charlie Chan Chinese Fortune Cookie Company to resonate with the world. With these messages, I intend to conquer the fortune cookie market in North America, Central America, and South America. With these messages, I intend to conquer the fortune cookie market in Europe. With these messages, I intend to conquer the fortune cookie market in Asia." He stared at a picture of his father on the far wall, a picture of a tranquil-looking man attired in traditional Chinese clothing. "Now, if I were to hire you, would you two be able to create the kind of messages that I am seeking? That is the relevant question at hand."

"Speaking for myself, I can say that I am the writer whom you are seeking," Ignatius said, and from the background came the whirring and grinding of bakery equipment and along with those sounds the very pleasant fragrances of baking fortune cookies. Ignatius's mouth watered. He had never wanted a job, yet he had never wanted a job so badly. "I could be your in-house philosopher, Mr. Pong. Miss Minkoff could be my editorial factotum. I can assure you, we will create fortune cookie messages that will take over the entire world. As Miss Minkoff can tell you, we are both revolutionaries in our respective fields."

"I need evidence," Mr. Pong said after taking a quick glance at his watch, and he pushed a slip of paper and a pen towards Ignatius. "Show me what you can do."

Ignatius picked up the pen, thought for a moment, and then carefully copied, from memory, a quote from Boethius's *The Consolation of Philosophy*. Ignatius wrote in italic, a font that nuns had taught him when he was in elementary school. After he finished, Ignatius politely slid the slip of paper to Mr. Pong, who took it and held it out, his lips moving as he read silently.

After he finished reading the quote, Mr. Pong leaned back in his black high-backed chair. The fingers of both his hands met, forming a thoughtful steeple. He exhaled a sigh. A tear formed at the corner of one of his eyes, and he wiped away the tear. He shook his head, bewildered, wondering how a white devil barbarian could compose verse as pure and as direct as that written by Confucius.

"This is unbelievably beautiful," Mr. Pong said, quoting what Ignatius had written:

Thou dost bind
The elements in balanced harmony,
So that the hot and cold, the moist and dry,
Contend not; nor the pure fire leaping up
Escape, or weight of waters whelm the earth.

"What can I say?" Mr. Pong said, amazed at what he had just quoted. "I must have you on staff immediately. In fact, I am going to make you vice president. You can start tomorrow, can't you, Mr., Mr.—" and Mr. Pong looked at Ignatius's application. "Ah, yes, Mr. Reilly."

"My salary," Ignatius said. Myrna nudged him, and Ignatius continued: "Corrected; *our* salaries. What yen do you offer us, our fine little Oriental friend?"

"For you, Mr., Mr.—," and Mr. Pong looked down again at the application and then up at Ignatius, "for you, Mr. Reilly, we offer two hundred dollars a week. And for your editorial assistant"— he looked down at Myrna's application and then up at her—"ah, yes, for Miss Minkoffed we offer sixty dollars a week."

"He gets two hundred dollars a week, and I'm getting only sixty dollars a week!" Myrna said. "How unjust! How sexist! How dare you!"

"But he is the writer, Miss Minkoffed," Mr. Pong said solemnly, holding out his hands, as if in supplication. "What am I supposed to do?"

"I should be paid as much as Ignatius," Myrna said contemptuously. "And I can prove it."

"Oh? How?"

"Ignatius, leave the office."

"Good heavens! Help me out of this chair!"

Ignatius waited in the warm outer office, hearing a groan or two and wondering what exactly it was that Myrna was telling Mr. Pong. When the two stepped into the outer office, Ignatius saw Myrna wipe her mouth with her sleeve. Mr. Pong, who was smiling, told Miss Ping that he was going outside to smoke a cigarette. Whatever Myrna had said, it seemed to have done the trick.

"We start tomorrow at nine, Ignatius," she said. "Let's go to the Village and see if we can find Rastajaq. I think that he's working on a plan to overthrow his oppressive government."

II

Irene Reilly poured herself another glass of muscatel. She had been drinking all morning and crying all morning at her kitchen table. Claude Robichaux, her fiancé, had done his best to console her since Ignatius's recent disappearance. But Mr. Robichaux's talk of "communiss" did not relieve Mrs. Reilly of the guilt and sorrow that she was feeling. Unable to console her, Mr. Robichaux had spoken with Santa Battaglia, who went to see Mrs. Reilly. If anything, Santa's visit seemed to make the maroon-haired Mrs. Reilly even more depressed. In fact, that very morning, she hadn't answered her telephone, which had rung thirteen times already. And there had been a knock on the front door—from the sounds of it, her fiancé—but she refused to answer the door, preferring instead to sit in the kitchen in the dark, sipping muscatel, crying, sniffling, and wondering why her feet were aching, given that she had not done any walking that week. Perhaps it was because she had been wearing her bowling shoes more than she should have, she reasoned.

Mrs. Reilly downed the last drops of muscatel and wiped her mouth with the back of her hand. She flipped open a photograph album that she had placed on the kitchen table oilcloth two days earlier.

The photographs in the front of the album showed Ignatius at a few weeks old, a dour, fat baby whose facial expressions seemed to suggest that he was questioning the probity and the propriety of the world. From seated poses, the pictures progressed to photographs showing Ignatius's first attempts at walking; many of these photographs showed an enraged child who did not want to walk and who had tired of falling down. After these came photographs of Ignatius's participation in a wedding as a ring bearer, because the ring girl—Mrs. Reilly had done her best to remember the girl's name, but the name would not come—had had an anxiety attack, and subsequently Ignatius volunteered to carry the ring to the couple, a young butcher who lived down the street and who was marrying a woman who had immigrated from Poland. The wedding had proceeded well until Ignatius scolded the priest for saying the prayers incorrectly in Latin and for reeking of alcohol. The horrified Mrs. Reilly and the laughing Mr. Reilly had taken Ignatius home, where Mr. Reilly and Ignatius sat in the kitchen and ate vanilla ice cream, while Mrs. Reilly sat in the living room and wondered when Ignatius was going to cause a scandal.

From the wedding pictures, Mrs. Reilly navigated to pictures of Ignatius at All Souls, his elementary school. In many of the pictures, he was shown holding prizes from the contests that the sisters had held; one photograph, in particular, caused Mrs. Reilly to smile. It was a photograph of Ignatius dressed as a medieval scholar and holding in his hands what looked like a scholar's tome. Mrs. Reilly adjusted her reading glasses and squinted at the photograph in the dimness of the kitchen, struggling to see what the spine of the book said. *The Condolences of Phyllis*, or something like that. She wondered if it was still in Ignatius's room.

There was a knock on the back door. Mrs. Reilly sighed. And then another knock, this one more frantic, more urgent.

"Irene, we need to talk," she heard Mr. Robichaux say. "And don't worry none, I'm not gonna speak about any more communiss."

Mrs. Reilly stood on wobbly feet and stumbled to the back door, which she unlatched and opened. Mr. Robichaux was standing there. The sky was a light gray, it was lightly drizzling, and though it was winter, the air felt lightly warm, more like spring in Kansas, a state that Mr. Reilly and Mrs. Reilly had driven through during their honeymoon. Mrs. Reilly blinked.

"I been trying to reach you all day," Mr. Robichaux said, sounding as if he were on the verge of tears. "You have me worried, Irene. I was afraid you done gone after your boy."

"I don't know where Ignatius is," Mrs. Reilly answered blandly, blinking, the warm, tropical air having a soporific effect on her. "And so I can't go after Ignatius if I don't know where he is."

"Mind if I come in?"

"Suit yourself, Claude."

Mrs. Reilly turned on the light in the kitchen and sat down in her chair at the kitchen table. On the oilcloth rested the photograph album, which was open to the picture of Ignatius dressed as a medieval scholar. Mr. Robichaux sat down in the other chair and studied the picture.

"That ain't a communiss costume, is it?" Mr. Robichaux asked. "I know your boy is crazy, Irene, but it's one thing to be crazy and to be a communiss all at once."

"He ain't a communiss," Mrs. Reilly said, closing the photograph album. "And yes, I know, Ignatius is crazy. But I also know that I love my boy. I want him back home here with me."

"You got me, Irene," Mr. Robichaux said, taking her hands in his hands, which, because of the many years that he had spent working as an Illinois Central brakeman, doing carpentry for his neighbors, and doing endless plumbing chores on his rental properties, had the tan color and toughness of a Mexican leather saddle. He stroked the backs of her liver-spotted hands with his heavily callused fingertips. "And you always gonna have me, if you want me."

"Oh, Claude," Mrs. Reilly said, and she sighed and then started to cry. She squeezed Mr. Robichaux's hands, and Mr. Robichaux squeezed her hands, not knowing what else to do. He had learned that when dealing with a woman, it was best not to say anything or do anything but to sit there and give the impression that he understood.

A few minutes passed, and Mrs. Reilly removed her small hands from Mr. Robichaux's big hands, and she wiped at her tears with a worn dish towel. She sniffled and then put the towel on top of the oilcloth, which was dotted with blackened-crisp toast crumbs.

"I'm gonna find me my boy," Mrs. Reilly said, staring ahead, eyes set like flint. "I'm going to find me my boy, no matter how long it takes."

"I'll help you," Mr. Robichaux said. "Even if he is a communiss, he is your boy, Irene."

"Ignatius ain't no communiss, Claude. I don't want to hear another word of it."

"Whatever you say, Irene." He put a weathered hand on her bare knee and squeezed. "I'm here for you."

Mrs. Reilly swiped away Mr. Robichaux's hand. "Now to figure out where Ignatius went."

"You said that he was always talking about that bus ride to Baton Rouge." Mr. Robichaux blinked, looking stupid because he was stupid. "Do you think that he went back to Baton Rouge?"

"I don't know," Mrs. Reilly said, sighing. "He could have gone anywhere and everywhere, knowing Ignatius. Angelo told me that he and his police friends are looking for Ignatius far and wide. They done gone back to the factory, they done gone back to the Night of Joy, they done gone back to the D. H. Holmes, they done gone back to the weenie man, they even done gone back to Ignatius's old elementary school, All Souls, where he did so well when he was a young boy and loved his momma." She sniffled, about to cry, but regained her composure, thanks in large part to the muscatel. "No, they ain't seen hide nor hair of him. Miss Annie next door, though, she said that she saw a strange car in front of the house the night that Ignatius disappeared."

"What kind of car?" Mr. Robichaux asked. "Was it the kind of car that a communiss would drive?"

"You and your communiss," Mrs. Reilly said, shaking her head angrily. "Sometimes I'm a wonder why I ever accepted your marriage proposal, Claude. If all you going to do is speak about communiss all day long, why, I'm not sure I want to be around that."

"I don't mean nothing by it," Mr. Robichaux said, attempting to diffuse the situation; his sweetheart's anger reminded Mr. Robichaux of the anger of his former conductor on the railroad, a man who had threatened to tie a ligature around Mr. Robichaux's testicles if Mr. Robichaux kept up with the talk about communists. "It's just a habit, Irene, like a man's getting up early in the morning and soaking his nuts in ice water."

"Soaking his nuts? What kind of nuts? Walnuts?" Mrs. Reilly asked, baffled. "Pistachios? Cashews? Almonds? Peanuts? Now why would a man soak his peanuts in ice water first thing in the morning, Claude?"

"Wrong example," Mr. Robichaux said, blushing slightly. When he and Mrs. Reilly married, he would have to keep that habit, and several others, hidden from her.

"Miss Annie said it was a small, ferrin-looking car," Mrs. Reilly said. "She said she couldn't make out the driver but thought that it was a woman. I bet it could have been a Mardi Gras, the way Ignatius been carrying on that week."

"I got a question, Irene."

"What is it, Claude?"

"With all the trouble that he gave you, and what with his nasty disposition and all his nasty ways, why you want a boy like that around? He done broke your heart over and over again. It don't make sense to want a boy like that back. You ask me, it's too bad you didn't have other chirren, Irene. They would've taken care of you the way that mine take care of me."

"Claude, for as rich as you are, you say some of the dumbest things," Mrs. Reilly said. "Why do you think that I want Ignatius back? He's my boy. Ain't that a good enough reason?"

"I suppose it is, Irene."

"If it wasn't a Mardi Gras who came after Ignatius, it could have been one of them Night of Joy hookers," she said, her face pained with an expression that only the faces of mothers can express. "Ignatius hanging out with women of the evening! And him with all that moralizing and all!"

"Perhaps he was lonely," Mr. Robichaux said, and he remembered the many lonely nights that had tempted him to find a hooker, but he had refrained from doing so, thanks to the training that he had received in the army during World War I. "A lonely boy will do crazy things, Irene. And what's worse is a lonely girl. You can't imagine some of the things that a lonely girl would do."

"Like what, Claude?"

"How about running off with a Negro boy to California?" Mr. Robichaux said. "Happened to Mr. Zuckerman's daughter. Her fiancé, some accounting student at Tulane, broke off the engagement, and a week later, Beulah—that's her name—Beulah took off with a Negro boy she met in the Third Ward."

"Horrible," Mrs. Reilly said, shaking her head. "What's this world coming to?"

"Do you think that Ignatius ran off with a Negro girl?"

Mrs. Reilly frowned. "Are you leading this back to talk about communiss, Claude?"

"No, not at all, Irene. Just asking. Instead of looking in the white neighborhoods and all, maybe Angelo and his police friends should be looking in the Negro parts."

"Ignatius'd stick out like a sore thumb in a Negro neighborhood, Claude. Besides, Ignatius don't look like a Negro."

"He put on black face, he might look like a very large Negro, Irene."

She snapped her fingers.

"What?" Mr. Robichaux said loudly, almost yelling, startled out of the few wits that he had.

"Myrna Minkoff!" Mrs. Reilly said, and she nodded her head. "I bet you a dollar to a donut that that small, ferrin-looking car belongs to Myrna Minkoff!"

"Who's Myrna Minkoff?" Mr. Robichaux asked. The name sounded exotic, like something from Eastern Europe. If so, this Myrna Minkoff, whoever she was, was probably a communist.

Mrs. Reilly stood. "You wait right here, Claude. I'll be right back."

"Where you going, Irene?"

"Ignatius's room. Just wait here a sec, hon."

Mr. Robichaux waited, hearing her entering a more distant part of the house, and wondered what she was going to show him upon her return, which occurred about two minutes later.

Mrs. Reilly's face was red and her breathing stertorous, as if she'd sprinted in a race.

"I found these in Ignatius's room," Mrs. Reilly said, spilling letters written by Myrna Minkoff onto the oilcloth covering the kitchen table. Many of the letters, like the oilcloth, were greasy or slick to the touch, as if the letters had been written in a coal bin or on the pavement of a gasoline station. "She and that boy used to write each other like they was lovers, let me tell you."

Mr. Robichaux picked up one of the envelopes and squinted at it.

"Myrna's people are New York City people," Mrs. Reilly said. "They a lot like us because they sound a lot like us. I guess we have a commoner lineage, probably on the Spanish side of things. You knew I was part Spanish, didn't you?"

"No, I didn't know that, Irene. I would've guessed you was Irish."

"I am mostly Irish, Claude. And Mr. Reilly, well, he had some Spanish blood and Creole blood in him, too," Mrs. Reilly said fiercely and independently. "That's why Ignatius's middle name is Jacques. And Myrna, I bet, she probably has Spanish blood in her, too, from the looks of it."

"So this Myrna character and Ignatius is related?" Mr. Robichaux asked innocently.

"No, no, no," Mrs. Reilly said, irritated. Why did everyone make things so difficult? If only Ignatius had got him a good job instead of that rinky-dink thing at that pants factory, maybe he wouldn't have become a disgraceful and disgraced hot dog vendor in the French Quarter. Maybe this whole thing might never have occurred. "Ignatius and Myrna ain't directly related by a long shot. I was just saying that there was a commoner ground." She paused for a moment, wondering how Mr. Robichaux was going to take the news. "I think I forgot to tell you that she's Jewish."

Mr. Robichaux frowned. He didn't like what he was hearing. For starters, everyone knew that the Jews were behind the international conspiracy to bring communism to the Western world. Weren't seven or eight of the founders of communism Jewish? Mr. Robichaux tried to remember what he had read in his John Birch newsletters but couldn't remember. That was beside the point. More than likely, Ignatius was dating a communist. If he wasn't a communist now, he would be a communist soon. Communists, especially Jewish ones, had a way of infiltrating everything, even things like the New Orleans Cotton Exchange, from what Mr. Robichaux had heard.

Mrs. Reilly was staring at him, her eyes expectant. He was tempted to go on a diatribe against communists but decided against it. It was better to play this thing cool. He would deal with the communism issues later.

"Well, the only thing I can say is that I feel for her," Mr. Robichaux said. "Anyone who can't eat bacon, why, that's horrible. God, you know, don't allow Jews to eat bacon. God must really dislike Jews."

Mrs. Reilly nodded her head in agreement because she was sympathetic to Mr. Robichaux's reasoning. She picked up a smudged envelope, which smelled musty. Mrs. Reilly ignored the scent and looked at the postmark and then at the address.

"I'm going to go through these letters and see if I can find me a phone number," Mrs. Reilly said, removing a stained letter from its smudged envelope. "And if I can't find it, why, I'll speak with the operator and see if I can get in touch with Myrna's people that way."

"You want me to go through the letters with you, Irene?"

"No, Claude, this is something I'm going to have to do," Mrs. Reilly replied earnestly. "I'm Ignatius's momma, after all."

"I'll come by later this afternoon," Mr. Robichaux said, standing.

But Mrs. Reilly didn't answer him. She was busy with the letter, her lips moving as she silently read the letter in search of a telephone number. Her eyes widened in surprise at the things that she was reading.

"Have a good morning, Irene."

Mrs. Reilly continued to read.

Feeling rueful, Mr. Robichaux scooped up his baseball cap. He exited the kitchen and stepped into the backyard.

The sky had grayed darker, and clouds that looked like black ink dispersing in water came rolling in from the east. It looked as if it were going to rain and rain hard.

Mr. Robichaux zipped up his jacket and headed to the pickup truck parked in front of the Reilly house on Constantinople Street.

III

Ignatius and Myrna arrived at the Charlie Chan Chinese Fortune Cookie Company fifteen minutes before the factory opened. Outside the factory, factory workers, all of them Chinese, smoked cigarettes. Myrna attempted to talk to the workers about the need for revolution ("Mao now!" she kept repeating over and over again) and for the need to start the revolution at the factory as soon as possible, but the workers, through facial expressions and hand gestures, indicated that they did not understand what she was saying. Dejected, Myrna turned and went to join Ignatius, who was standing near the front door and shaking uncontrollably, even though he was wearing layer upon layer of clothing, enough to make him look like a clothed volleyball with a head encased in a green hunting cap.

One of the Chinese workers, a man, jabbed his lit cigarette at the two.

"Did you understand a word of what she was saying?" he said in Cantonese to a woman standing next to him, a woman who, like him, was smoking.

"Nothing," the woman replied in Cantonese, tired of the cold. "She is what we call a crazy foreign devil."

"Back in the old country, yes, she would be a crazy foreign devil," the man said, taking a deep drag off his Chesterfield. He didn't know it, but he would be dead of lung cancer in fifteen years; the woman to whom he was speaking would die from a stroke a year after he died. He exhaled a cloud of bitter smoke. "But we are in her country. She cannot be a crazy foreign devil, then. She is just a crazy devil."

The woman raised an eyebrow. "True. And she kept mentioning something about Mao."

"Mao?"

"Something like"—and now she spoke in broken English—"'How now, Mao?'"

"Interesting," the man said. "When I attempted to learn English at night school, they had us learn simple rhymes."

"Oh, really?"

"Yes." He smiled, remembering fondly his night school class taught by a woman who resembled Veronica Lake, a teacher whom he fondly remembered and whom he wanted to fondle. "Ah, yes, I remember one of them quite well. " And now he spoke in broken English: "'How now, brown Mao?'"

"'How now, brown Mao?'" the woman repeated in broken English. Then she reverted to Cantonese. "What on earth does it mean?"

"I am not sure," the puzzled man said in Cantonese. "But I am sure that if we were being taught it, it had to be something of some significance to these round-eyed devils."

Myrna blew hot air into her cupped hands. Ignatius's teeth chattered.

"I suggest we get here later!" Ignatius said. "This cold is utterly killing me! Oh, my God, I can't feel my feet or my hands! They're frostbitten! What have you done to me!"

"Quiet it down, Ignatius," Myrna said, peering at the workers, who continued to smoke and chat amiably one with another. "Isn't it amazing how even oppressed people can find joy in this world?"

"What are you talking about?" Ignatius said, face bluing. "I don't see any antebellum slaves out on the streets, working the cotton fields and singing spirituals that promise them a better life in the next world."

Myrna pointed at the Chinese workers. "I mean them, Ignatius, these downtrodden Asians who are forced to live this way. Mr. Pong should be ashamed of himself, the way he treats his own kind, as if they were coolie laborers. Well, that's going to end today."

"Oh, I wish they would open that door!" Ignatius said. "I don't know how much more of this I can bear!"

Just then the front door opened, and Miss Ping's face appeared. Blinking, she peered at the two of them.

"Do-uh come-er in," she said, opening the door a bit wider, and Ignatius barreled in past her into an overly warm front office, followed by Myrna, who, believing that the secretary, like Mr. Pong, was a traitor to her own kind, gave the secretary a mean look.

Miss Ping closed the front door. "We have-er your office uh-ready, Mr. Lei-ly and Miss-er Minkoffed."

"Office?" Ignatius said, grateful for the news that he had an office but ungrateful for having to share it with Myrna. "I must have my own office. I need privacy so that I can create."

Miss Ping blinked. "Lil-ly, Mr. Lei-ly?" Then she laughed her phocine laugh. "Uh-pardon me. Sometimes-er I like-uh to make-er joke-uh."

"We can deal with your so-called sense of humor later," Ignatius said condescendingly. "Suffice to say, we must deal with my immediate needs. I must have a pot of scalding-hot tea brought to me immediately. Normally I would not drink hot tea at this time of the morning, but given the barbaric weather in Gotham, I must have something that brings the requisite heat that my inner workings require. Of course, the mind is superior to the body, which is a vessel for the mind, and typically I do not take the unneeded or unwanted—"

"One office will do fine," Myrna said, elbowing Ignatius, who grunted from the impact of the blow to his heavily insulated ribs. "We are not going to get special treatment, especially because of the way you exploit your peasant workers, you race traitor. Can you show us where we're going to be working in this slave pit?"

Miss Ping, who didn't understand what Myrna had just said, smiled, turned, and lead the way down a hallway that went by offices filled with Chinese men and Chinese women who were working abacuses and making detailed notes in thick ledgers and chatting quickly and softly one to another in Cantonese. The hallway twisted one way, then another, following a labyrinthine path until Miss Ping, Myrna, and Ignatius arrived at a cramped office in the back of the building.

"The bathroom is-uh here," Miss Ping said, motioning with a hand at a thin door to the left of the cramped office. "We-uh hope-er to own-er the Em-uh-pire Stat-er Building someday. Oh, my-er, a pun!" Miss Ping laughed her phocine laugh. "Pardon-uh me for that-er pun-er. I must-uh learn-er to control-er joking."

"What pun?" Ignatius asked, wondering if he had missed something.

Miss Ping blinked. Myrna frowned at Ignatius and then feigned a smile at Miss Ping.

"Don't pay any attention to Ignatius," Myrna said. "He was almost locked up in an insane asylum by his reactionary mother and her crazy boyfriend, an inveterate Klansman. Ignatius and I will probably go back to New Orleans and overthrow the reactionaries, once we've completed our work here."

"Oh, I-uh see." Miss Ping blinked and smiled. "Please, make-er yourself-uh at home. I-uh be back with-er tea, Mr. Lei-ly and Miss-er Minkoffed."

Ignatius removed his heavy coat in the cramped office, gasping as he did so because his several layers of clothing made mobility of any sort an onerous task. Myrna slipped out of her knee-length coat and let it slide to the floor, which was cluttered with manila folders containing old receipts and yellowed warehousing paperwork. Ignatius bumped into a stack of empty file boxes, which tumbled down upon him and Myrna. Ignatius bellowed, and Myrna waved her arms and screamed. There was the sound of hurried feet in the labyrinthine hallway, and a baffled Miss Ping appeared.

"Oh, I-uh see," she said, smiling. "You are-er eager to get-er to work, so you-uh get-er into-uh box." She laughed her phocine laugh. "You are-er not-uh the typical white-er devil, are-er you? You-er ready to work. I like-er that. We-uh like-er that. Mrs. Wang-er like-er that. Mr. Pong-er like-er that. Charlie-uh Chan-er Chinese-er Fortune-uh Cookie-er Company-er like-er that."

"Those things could have killed me, madam." Ignatius touched the crown of his head, his hand trembling. "Do you realize that I had the misfortune of working at Levy Pants in New Orleans? Do you know that Levy Pants has a very serious issue regarding worker safety? Do you know that I almost died after sitting down on a stool—a stool, of all things? Do you know, Madam Dragon Lady, that the Charlie Chan Chinese Fortune Cookie Company must show the utmost respect if I am to work in these environs?" Ignatius made a sweep with one of his ursine paws. "Suffice to say, this clutter must be dealt with immediately. And I need that pot of scalding-hot tea, too, and preferably a room with a bed in it. Before I begin my endeavors here, I must have rest for the remainder of this morning. Gotham is proving to be more and more like Dante's wretched Inferno, and I've the feeling that we are, indeed, coming closer and closer to the Ninth Circle of Hell, if we have not already entered it."

"You like-er tea?" Miss Ping asked, blinking. She chuckled. "Of-uh course. You must-er have tea. You think like-er a Chinese." She hurried away.

"What about me?" Myrna said, making a face, feeling hurt. "What am I, chopped liver?"

"I beg your pardon?"

"Me," Myrna said. "What about me? What if those boxes had injured me?" She dusted the long sleeves of her peasant's blouse. "Why do you get the royal treatment? This isn't fair. There is a glass ceiling." She looked up at a cracked ceiling, glowered, and then looked at Ignatius. "I've a mind to go and protest this place and you, and I'd do it, too, Ignatius, but I don't have any money, and Dad won't give me any more until we get that china paid for."

Ignatius ignored her and went around the huge desk in the cramped office, barely squeezing past a stack of boxes stuffed with paperwork. He huffed, and he sweated, and he wiped his brow with the back of a meaty paw. The roller chair behind the desk seemed stable, and he gingerly sat down in the chair.

"Have you heard a word that I've been saying?" Myrna asked, arms crossed.

"Each and every word, my dear callet," Ignatius said, turning in the chair slowly, looking out the office's sole window, which was covered with a light gelicide, at a brick alley wall. Stuck to the brick alley wall was the palimpsest that Nick the Nose had lost and for which he and Henley were searching. Ignatius studied the palimpsest, wondering why the December winds hadn't blown it away.

"Ignatius?"

"Yuss?" he said in his Mayfair accent, turning and facing Myrna.

"I've been talking to you for almost five minutes, and all you do is grunt," she said, sitting down on the edge of the cluttered desk. Her peasant's skirt rode up her leg and revealed her ample thigh. "You're like my dad. All he does is grunt and pretend that he's listening."

The palimpsest, for whatever reason, would not leave Ignatius's mind. The paper looked ancient and sacred, and, from its appearance, might have been part of a rimestock. Ignatius wanted to hold the palimpsest. He wanted to read it. And he sensed, for no apparent reason, that the palimpsest might hold the key to his undoing Myrna minx once for all, his returning triumphantly to New Orleans, and a score of other wonders that blind Fortuna probably had in store for him. And then his thoughts drifted back to New Orleans, as if he were lying peacefully on a bed upon the Mississippi River, which was snaking its way slowly and pleasantly into the heart of his beloved city, and then he drifted into a daydream about his long-dead Rex, and then Ignatius felt himself becoming excited, and his breathing became stertorous.

"Ignatius!"

"What!" Ignatius bellowed.

"Miss Ping wants to know if you want sugar or cream or both in your tea."

Miss Ping was standing in the cramped office, holding a tray on which rested an ornate red ceramic teapot and two red ceramic cups. Steam twirled up from the spout of the teapot. She blinked and smiled and then laughed her phocine laugh.

"Now you-uh want-er coffee," Miss Ping said, pushing aside reams of paper from atop the desk and placing the tray on top of the desk while papers slowly ascended and then descended, arcing one way, then another. "You-er try to a-fool me to believe-uh you-uh Chinese. But you-uh want-er coffee." She laughed so hard that tears came to her eyes, and she turned, placing her hands to her mouth, unable to control her laughter. "I be-uh right-uh back. I try-uh not-er to be-uh so funny."

After Miss Ping left the small office, Ignatius removed his copy of *The Consolation of Philosophy* from an interior coat pocket.

He read the first page.

"What are you doing, Ignatius?"

"What else, my dear minx?" Ignatius said, looking briefly at her. "Starting my life's work. But before that"—and now he looked out the window at the palimpsest affixed to the alley wall—"we must get Miss Ping to get a group of wogs to go and obtain that parchment. I've a feeling that its message is one of great importance."

"I'm going to go meet with the workers," Myrna said, turning to leave the office. "The sooner we get the revolution started, the better."

But Ignatius didn't hear her. He was staring at the palimpsest, wondering how in the world it was able to stay affixed to the wall. Blind Fortuna willing, he would have that parchment in his paws very soon.

IV

Grenadine shook his head in disappointment. He stood up from the bar and walked over to the stage and wagged a long index finger at the three Puerto Rican men dressed in drag.

"Your rhythm is way, way off, my dears," Grenadine said, wondering when Frank was going to return from the dentist's. Grenadine hopped up onto the stage. "It's all about rhythm. Now, follow me."

He motioned at Giacomo, who turned on a record player, speakers on each side of the stage hissing as a stylus followed a groove of a vinyl record. Latin music played, and Grenadine rotated his hips in perfect sync with it.

"One-two-three, girls, one-two-three, girls, one-two-three, girls! One-two-three, girls, one-two-three, girls, one-two-three, kick!"

El Lobo Macho wanted to kick Grenadine's *cojones* up into the back of Grenadine's throat but did not do so. After all, he, El Lobo Macho, was on a sacred mission from God. God wanted El Lobo Macho to eliminate *la putería* from the face of the earth. But first to deal with the ones in Greenwich Village and then to take care of the grandest *puto* of them all, Grenadine Roe.

A Latina sang like a songbird, her singing filling the winter-laced air of the Stone Carver Inn with notes of blue, green, yellow, red, and orange. Grenadine felt as if he were back in the Caribbean, when he had spent a summer working a civilian job at an army base. There, he had ended up as a teacher's assistant for army sergeants who had graduate degrees in English from institutions like Tulane and Columbia. About half the teachers had been of Grenadine's orientation, for which Grenadine had been thankful. One of the sergeants, Grenadine's favorite, had nicknamed Grenadine "Pip." The sergeant had been a good person, a good mimic, and a good friend. Grenadine hoped that this sergeant was doing well, wherever he was.

"Now to see you dears in action," Grenadine said, hopping off the stage and hurrying back to the bar, where he turned around quickly, as if he were doing a pirouette for an audition at Julliard. "Now, from the top. One-two-three, one-two-three, one-two-three—"

"*No mas*," Chico said in exasperation, taking off his red wig and throwing it down onto the stage. He wiped off thickly applied purple lipstick with the back of his hand and spat in disgust. "I ain't no *puto*. I ain't gonna dance."

"You gonna dance, or I gonna kill you," El Lobo Macho said, having a difficult time balancing on high heels that pinched his walnut-sized toes. Ay, ay, ay, it was a wonder how his mother, from whom he had filched the high heels, had been able to walk around all day in those things. "We in this together, *amigo*. You don't dance, then I gonna kill you."

"Kill me for what?" Chico whined. "I ain't no *puto*. I ain't no dancer. I come here to—"

El Lobo Macho slapped Chico before Chico could finish the sentence. Grenadine, who was watching, gasped upon seeing the abuse, yet felt aroused by the thought of El Lobo Macho's bare anger and bare brutality. Grenadine clapped his hands together and squealed in delight. Giacomo frowned, and an ecstatic Grenadine rushed to the stage.

"That's it!" Grenadine said. "You lovely beasts have found the answer!"

"Answer to what?" El Lobo Macho asked, raising his fist and looking at it in surprise, as if it were a space alien that had caught El Lobo Macho off guard. He undid his fist and lowered his hand. "You sound like you died and gone to heaven, *Señorita* Roe."

"Oh, this is much, much better than heaven," Grenadine said ecstatically, pacing. "Most drag acts, you see, are filled with pretty men pretending to be pretty women. But this act is the complete, absolute opposite of that. You three are the most macho brutes that I have ever seen. Yet, there's a definite femininity in the way that you treat one another."

"You callin' me a *puto, puto?*" Guapo furiously spat at Grenadine. The Puerto Rican gang member jumped off the stage and rushed towards Grenadine. Giacomo stepped in between the two men, holding out his arms to protect Grenadine.

"I'm not calling you anything, my dear," Grenadine said, guiding Giacomo gently to the side with the push of a long finger. "What I am saying is that this act is going to go beyond your typical drag queen revue. No, we're going to go the rough-trade route. After your dancing, you three are going to beat one another silly onstage, and all the queens who are watching are going to be driven to lust, and this means more sales at our bar and more queens coming to the show!" Grenadine beamed. "Now, what do you girls think of that!"

"You saying we gonna box each other?" El Lobo Macho asked. He kicked off his high heels and stepped off the stage and stood next to Guapo, who was standing in front of Grenadine. "We fight, we gonna kill each other, *cabrón*. There won't be no show."

"You won't really be fighting," Grenadine said to El Lobo Macho. "You'll be pretending, like actors. For instance, you'll throw a punch at him, and he, in turn, will take a cat o' nine tails to you." Grenadine chuckled. "Oh, my, I even have a new name for the show." Grenadine held up his hands, spelling out the words as he spoke. "'Decadence from the South of the Border, with Las Tres Amigas.' Of course, we'll need to get the title translated into Spanish."

"But we Puerto Ricans," Chico said, joining his two fellow gang members. "We ain't no Mexicans, and we ain't from south of no border."

"No one will know the difference," Grenadine answered, and he took a swig of the pink-colored ladyfinger that he had been drinking. "It's going to be *the* drag show of the century, I can tell you that."

Giacomo nudged Grenadine.

"What?" Grenadine asked.

"Mind if I have a word with you, boss?"

"Later, Giacomo. This is urgent business."

"I think we need to talk now, boss."

Grenadine made tossing motions with his feminine hands. "Oh, all right. If it's *that* urgent, Giacomo, then I suppose we had better talk, hadn't we?"

In the back office, Grenadine sat down behind his desk. He motioned for Giacomo to have a seat. Giacomo didn't take the seat.

"Oh, my, this must be serious," Grenadine said sagaciously. "Pray tell, what's on your mind, my dear boy?"

"You know I been touched by God," the janitor replied, "and touched several times."

"I wish He would touch me. I'd prefer it to touching myself."

Grenadine giggled. Not understanding the joke, Giacomo stared at Grenadine. Grenadine cleared his throat and motioned for the janitor to continue.

"God don't like the looks of this, and I don't like the looks of this if God don't like the looks of this," Giacomo said. "Something bad is going to happen if you let those three PRs take the stage. They're gonna ruin the show, they're gonna ruin the Stone Carver Inn, and they're gonna ruin you, boss, if you ain't careful."

"So this is a warning from God?"

"I think it is." Giacomo's eyes crossed as he considered Grenadine's question. "At least I think it is."

"Well, God has been mistaken before," Grenadine said, standing. "We'll have no more talk of these so-called messages, Giacomo. I haven't run this successful venture without having some clue as to what the public wants." Now Grenadine was getting serious, and he was getting angry as he thought of all the naysayers from his past. "Grandfather said that I was too much of a 'sissy boy' to make it in the world of business, and my father—oh, my father, rest his dear, departed soul—believed that I would end up working as a dressmaker. Well, I showed them. Grandmother told me that I had what it took to make it, and Mother believed so too, and let me tell you, those are two of the toughest women I have ever known. They believed in me when Grandfather and Father didn't believe in me and when God didn't believe in me. Now, get back to it. I'm going to ask you to put more elbow grease into your work, Giacomo. As for me, I'm going to go choreograph our girls."

Giacomo wanted to drop to his knees and to plead with Grenadine not to go on with the show. But the janitor knew that it was useless. The show, as they said on Broadway and in Hollywood, must go on.

Giacomo sighed and exited Grenadine's office and stepped into an alley. The janitor removed a kiseru from a pocket in his dungarees and filled the bowl with a combination of cheap tobacco that he'd purchased at a drugstore and marijuana that he'd purchased from a Jamaican in Spanish Harlem. Giacomo lit the kiseru and took a deep, meditative drag.

He looked up at an aluminum-gray sky that canopied the alley.

"I tried to tell him, God," Giacomo said, shaking his head. "You told me what would happen. You told me to warn him. Did I warn him? I warned him, Lord! Warned, warned, warned! "

Giacomo exhaled a nimbus of smoke whose coloring resembled that of the overhead sky. "What else can I do, God? Nothing. Nothing, nothing, nothing." And to anyone who saw him, they might have said that it looked as if Giacomo were going to cry.

After he finished smoking his kiseru, he scraped the oily remnants out of the bowl with a thumb, put the kiseru back into a pocket of his dungarees, and grudgingly went back to work.

V

Mrs. Reilly stood in a hallway and stared at the heavy black telephone resting in the telephone nook. She had purchased the telephone when Mr. Reilly was still alive. That was so long ago. He had been dead for over twenty years, and whenever she saw Mr. Robichaux, she inexorably thought of Mr. Reilly because Mrs. Reilly compared any potential suitor to her long-dead husband. So far, Mr. Robichaux was running a close second to Mr. Reilly. But now was not the time to think about comparisons. Now was the time to deal with the Ignatius situation. Mrs. Reilly picked up the telephone receiver, dialed O, and waited for the operator to answer.

A New Orleans operator asked Mrs. Reilly how she was doing, Mrs. Reilly said that she was doing fine and that she needed to find a telephone number in New York City, the New Orleans operator called Mrs. Reilly sugar and told Mrs. Reilly to be patient, and the New Orleans operator placed a call to a New York City operator, who spoke in a flat, nasally accent, and asked the New Orleans operator what did she want, and the New Orleans operator said that she had a customer on the line who was trying to get a number somewhere in New York City, could the New York City operator please help the customer in New Orleans? The New York City operator replied that yeah, sure, she would be willing to help, and then Mrs. Reilly was speaking with the New York City operator.

"What's the name?" the New York City operator asked in a demanding tone.

"Last name is Minkoff," Mrs. Reilly said, peering down at a stained envelope that she held. She squinted, not only because the light in the hallway was dim, but because she needed new reading glasses. "Myrna lives in the Bronchitis with her parents. She's taken my boy out of New Orleans, I bet you a dollar to a donut."

"What's that name again?"

"Minkoff is her last name. M-i-n-k-o-f-f."

"Minkoff," the operator said, and there was a long silence, and Mrs. Reilly wondered if she had been disconnected.

"Hello?" Mrs. Reilly said. "You there?"

"Still here. We have eighteen Minkoffs in the Bronx. Do you have an exact street address?"

Mrs. Reilly squinted and read the scrawl that was Myrna's handwriting. The New York City operator waited patiently as Mrs. Reilly read the address, and then there was another long pause, and then the operator spoke, saying that she had the telephone number of a J. Bernard Minkoff.

Mrs. Minkoff replied that it was probably Myrna's papa, and so the New York City operator read the number, and Mrs. Reilly jotted down the number on the envelope with a stub of one of Ignatius's pencils. Mrs. Reilly asked for the area code, the New York City operator gave Mrs. Reilly the area code, and Mrs. Reilly then thanked the New York City operator, hung up, and dialed the number of the Minkoff residence.

A phone rang several times, and Mrs. Reilly was on the verge of hanging up when someone answered the line.

"Hello?" Mrs. Minkoff asked.

"This is Irene Reilly," Mrs. Reilly said. "You don't know me."

"No, I don't know you. Who are you again?"

"Irene Reilly. I live in New Orleans."

"That's funny, our houseguest is from New Orleans."

There was the groaning of a woman in the background, and Mrs. Reilly heard the woman on the telephone put her hand over the telephone receiver and, in a muffled voice, say, "Mother, please, not now!"

Then Mrs. Minkoff was back on the line. "Sometimes Mother gets too excited. They do that when they get older, you know, just like kids."

"Speaking of children," Mrs. Reilly said, "I'm looking for my boy."

"Who?"

"Ignatius, my boy."

"Isaiah? He's your son?"

"No, Ignatius is," Mrs. Reilly said, getting impatient. "I think he run off to New York City with your Myrna, if you're Myrna's momma."

"Yes, I'm her mother, and I didn't know that he had run away from anything," Mrs. Minkoff replied. "I thought that Isaiah was here to start his congregation. He's so brilliant, and I'm sure that you're a very proud Jewish mother."

"I ain't Jewish," Mrs. Reilly said. "Is Ignatius going around telling everyone he's Jewish? It wouldn't surprise me. That boy gets into so much trouble, it ain't funny."

"Isaiah is a convert? No wonder he doesn't look Jewish. He's working a job with Myrna somewhere in Manhattan."

The only Manhattan of which Mrs. Reilly knew was Manhattan, Kansas, and nearby Fort Riley, where her one of her cousins had been stationed with the Big Red One.

There was another loud groan, and Mrs. Minkoff yelled at her mother to stop, and Mrs. Reilly winced and removed the telephone receiver from her ear.

Mrs. Reilly looked hesitatingly at the receiver and then put the receiver back to her ear.

"That's the fifth time today," Mrs. Minkoff said. "Sometimes Bernard says that Mother should have been born a rabbit."

"Is Ignatius causing you too much trouble?"

"Isaiah is a joy to have around," Mrs. Minkoff said. "He's doing wonders for Myrna. She has a job, a real job, and she seems happy with it. Mother has taken a very strong liking to Isaiah, who does his best to instruct her in spiritual matters and so forth."

"I'm having me a hard time believing what I'm hearing," Mrs. Reilly said, not believing what she was hearing. "Ignatius ain't capable of taking care of himself, let alone no one else. You sure you have the right Ignatius?"

"Does Isaiah have blue eyes with yellow flecks and a big black mustache?" Mrs. Minkoff said.

"That he does."

"And does Isaiah like to eat hot dogs and drink lots of sodas?"

"That he does," Mrs. Reilly answered. "I bet he's been asking for Dr. Nut since he's been there."

"He has been, but I don't know what that is. None of the kosher stores around here carry it."

"I still ain't sure if it's Ignatius," Mrs. Reilly responded. "What else can you tell me?"

"And does Isaiah like to watch a lot of television and comment about how godawful our culture is?"

"That's my boy, all right," Mrs. Reilly said, knowing without a doubt that it was, indeed, Ignatius. "Can you do me a favor, hon?"

"What's that, Mrs. Rothstein?"

"It's Reilly, hon, not Rothstein."

"That's right, Isaiah is a convert."

"About the favor—"

"What message would you like to leave Isaiah, Mrs. Rothstein?"

Mrs. Reilly's eyes crossed in anger, and her face turned a bright red, and she wanted to stamp the floor in her bowling shoes, but instead she held her breath and slowly exhaled to a count of ten, something that she had learned from *Reader's Digest.*

"Please don't say nothing to Ignatius," Mrs. Reilly said. "I am going to get me up there to New York City to speak to that boy."

"It's going to be a surprise visit, right?"

"That's right, hon," Mrs. Reilly said. "And I want it to remain a surprise. You can't mention one word of this to Ignatius."

"I won't breathe one word to Isaiah," Mrs. Minkoff said, ecstatic. "It's going to be wonderful to meet the mother of the world's foremost Talmud scholar. He's a fine Orthodox rabbi."

Mrs. Reilly didn't know what Mrs. Minkoff meant, but Ignatius had studied a considerable amount at Tulane and had earned himself a master's. As for the Orthodox rabbits or whatever they were, Mrs. Reilly would learn to deal with them later; if Ignatius wanted to raise Orthodox rabbits, he was welcome to do so, provided that he did so down in New Orleans.

"Thank you," Mrs. Reilly said. "Now remember, babe, you made a promise. You can't breathe one word of this to Ignatius."

"Cross my heart," Mrs. Minkoff said.

"All right. I'll be up there in a day or two. Just you keep an eye on Ignatius, and make sure he don't go nowhere, all right?"

"I will, Mrs. Rothstein." There was another loud groan in the background, and Mrs. Minkoff screamed at her mother, telling her to stop pleasuring herself. "Take care, and have a wonderful day. I had better get back to Mother. She is getting way out of control."

"Bye for now," Mrs. Reilly said, and then there was the hollow sound of the line's disconnecting.

That Ignatius. Of course he would pretend to be Jewish. It wasn't bad enough that he had almost ruined a man's factory and then dressed up like a Mardi Gras and destroyed the Night of Joy.

Mrs. Reilly dialed Mr. Robichaux's number. It was time to leave New Orleans.

• *Five*

Mr. Minkoff had gone to bed earlier than normal, his head pounding because of a migraine. He had been having a lot of migraines recently. This worried Mrs. Minkoff, who was watching television that Sunday evening with Ignatius. Grandmother Horowitz had fallen asleep in her rocker on the other side of the room, and Myrna was upstairs, working on her plans for overthrowing the imperialistic Mr. Pong.

Mrs. Minkoff and Ignatius were watching *The Ed Sullivan Show*. Ignatius, who was eating potato chips, grabbed a handful and shoved them into his maw. He chewed, famished because of his exertions the previous week at the fortune cookie company. Potato chip crumbs hung in his mustache, and his large pink tongue picked out the crumbs.

"Can you believe the vacuity of it all?" Ignatius swallowed and pointed at the color television set. "Ed Sullivan is, of course, one of the reasons for the decline and fall of our age."

"I'm worried about Bernard," Mrs. Minkoff said. "He's been watching a lot of Laurel and Hardy on television. And now he's talking like Stan Laurel."

"Who would ever believe that a monkey could add?" Ignatius said, not paying attention to Mrs. Minkoff and shoving another handful of potato chips into his maw. "And who would find such a thing entertaining? It's like the fraternities and sororities at Tulane University, my alma mater. These 'frat boys' got their biggest laugh when someone cupped his hand underneath his armpit and did a rendition of 'The Star-Spangled Banner.'" Ignatius swallowed and shoveled another handful of potato chips into his maw. "What's to become of our world if hideous things like this continue?"

"I don't know, Ichabod," Mrs. Minkoff said. She paused. "I think that someone is going crazy."

Ignatius peered at the woman.

"You believe that I am going crazy?" Ignatius asked, infuriated.

"No, no, not you, Ichabod—Bernard," Mrs. Minkoff said. "He's been staring at the walls a lot, asking them where he went wrong."

"Are they answering?"

"No, they're not, Ichabod."

"Then I wouldn't worry about it," Ignatius said. A tufted capuchin and its trainer left the stage, and two baby elephants dressed in tutus appeared and drew a loud round of applause from the audience. "Back in New Orleans, at my dear home on Constantinople Street, I used to talk to the walls as I pieced together my masterpiece, my *raison d'être*. Suffice to say, my speaking to the walls was my way of composing. A monastic cell is the best thing for composing, after all is said and done. 'Sit in thy cell, and thy cell shall teach thee all' is quite apropos, you know."

"He's been talking about guns a lot, too," Mrs. Minkoff said, watching the two baby elephants but not observing them. "He keeps saying that there is only one way to end it all."

"Look at that idiot in the audience!" Ignatius bellowed, thrusting his finger at the screen, his outburst reverberating throughout the living room. Grandmother Horowitz grunted in her sleep. "He is probably a man who buys tailor-made clothes and despises all things old. He is what one would call a success. He probably has a color television set, much as you do, and probably drinks martinis after a day of selling heating and venting systems. Let me tell you—"

"Ichabod?"

"Yes," Ignatius said, looking at Mrs. Minkoff; she was beginning to remind him more and more of his dear mother, wherever she was at that moment. And then he thought about the palimpsest for which four workers at the Charlie Chan Chinese Fortune Cookie Company had risked their lives; a ladder had slipped and slid on the ice-slickened alley wall as the men made their ascent to obtain the parchment.

"I'm scared, Ichabod. I'm afraid that Bernard is going to do something drastic."

"And should I be alarmed?" Ignatius asked suspiciously. "Do you believe that he is thinking of doing something drastic to me?"

"No, no," Mrs. Minkoff said. "I think he's going to do something to himself."

"Oh, well, that's a different thing altogether," Ignatius said. "Perhaps I should lend him my copy of *The Consolation of Philosophy*. It might help him to understand the futility of living in the modern world. We do, of course, exist in a horrid, horrid time. We have contrivances and gadgets of all sorts, yet we fail to connect in any real manner. And even though we seem to have everything, we ultimately do not have anything when one looks at it from a proper theological and geometrical perspective." Ignatius cleared his throat and licked his lips, which tasted pleasantly of salt. "First thing Monday morning, I shall present the book to him. Perhaps he can read it when he's not busy counting his money or snooping into the affairs of his sweatshop employees."

"Are you really going to do that for him?" Mrs. Minkoff asked hopefully.

"Of course. Why wouldn't I?"

"You're a good rabbi, Ichabod," Mrs. Minkoff said. "I can tell that you're the kind of rabbi who's going to take care of his congregation. And if you weren't a rabbi, Ichabod, I would say that you would make a great psychologist. You are very compassionate and very caring. You're a real *mensch*. It's a wonder some nice Jewish girl hasn't come along and married you, you're such a catch." Mrs. Minkoff sniffled, and she wiped a tear at a corner of an eye with a tissue. "It's too bad you and Myrna aren't going to be married. You two would have such beautiful children."

The thought of procreating with Myrna Minkoff caused Ignatius to gag. The room began to spin wildly, and the potato chips that he had just eaten threatened to disgorge themselves from his massive stomach. He leaned back, closed his eyes, and took deep breaths.

"Are you all right, Ichabod?"

Ed Sullivan said that the next act was a lion tamer who was going to thrill the audience with a new routine.

Slowly, Ignatius opened his eyes and peered at Mrs. Minkoff.

"You must never mention Myrna and marriage in the same breath, ever, ever again," he said. "The thought utterly revolts me."

"I see. You will not marry because of your utmost devotion to God. That's very noble, Ichabod. There are very few men who can say that."

"Indeed there are," Ignatius said, sitting back up. He was thankful that his pyloric valve hadn't sealed, that the room no longer spun, and that the potato chips were settling nicely in his stomach. "Of course I am a man of God, Whom this world opposes. I owe my utmost dedication to Him and His ways, which we are not to question."

"How true," Mrs. Minkoff said, amazed by her houseguest's wisdom.

"It doesn't appear as if that lion tamer is holding his own very well," Ignatius said, motioning with an ursine paw at the television set. The lion tamer nervously snapped his whips at lions that encircled him. The screen cut to Ed Sullivan, who was in the audience and who said that there were minor technical difficulties.

"I don't blame them. Only a moron would step into a cage like that. If you ask me, he gets what he deserves."

"How true," Mrs. Minkoff said automatically.

Ed Sullivan spoke with a member of the audience, a dour man who said that he was from Manhattan, Kansas, and who said that he didn't understand why they had named a part of New York City after his hometown. The people in the audience, including Ed Sullivan, laughed, believing that the man was joking. The man blinked, perplexed by the reaction of the audience. Meanwhile, in the background, lions roared, and the lion tamer snapped a whip, nervously ordering the beasts to obey his commands.

"Nay, nay, nay!" Ignatius said, giving a thumbs-down. "Feed him to the lions!"

"Yes, feed him to the lions!" Mrs. Minkoff yelled exuberantly. If Ichabod said that someone needed to be fed to the lions, then they needed to be fed to the lions. After all, Ichabod was a kind, compassionate rabbi, and rabbis always knew what was best.

Ed Sullivan was speaking with a woman when the screams of a man ended Ed Sullivan's impromptu interview. The television screen went momentarily blank, and then a television commercial for Tareyton cigarettes appeared, and a man with a mock-blackened eye winked at the screen before lighting a cigarette.

"It's too bad that the hillbillies aren't on," Ignatius said. "They tell the truth about the decline and fall of our culture."

"Are they Jewish, Ichabod?"

"Not to my knowledge," Ignatius replied. "I believe that they're devout backwoods Catholics, given their worldviews. Mind you, at least they do not have the mindsets of Protestant hillbillies. Can you imagine there one day being a television show about rednecks in Louisiana, showing how these long-bearded Protestant rubes live off the duck whistles they manufacture?" He shuddered. "The thought is patently absurd."

"At least they're Catholic hillbillies," Mrs. Minkoff said in agreement with Ignatius, not knowing what she was saying but wanting to please this brilliant rabbi with her utmost being. "I like Jed and Granny and Elly May and Jethro. He's such a handsome boy."

"Perhaps Myrna should consider marrying him."

"That's not a bad idea, Ichabod."

"It is a very good idea," Ignatius said.

"I'm still worried about Bernard, Ichabod," Mrs. Minkoff said abjectly.

"The commercial is still on, but after the commercial's over, you must be quiet," Ignatius responded bravely.

"Do you think he needs to go back to the *shul?*" Mrs. Minkoff asked candidly.

"I believe that you're going to need to be quiet very soon," Ignatius said decidedly.

"Do your parents come to you when they have problems?" Mrs. Minkoff asked enigmatically.

"Ah, another commercial," Ignatius said forcefully.

"You don't mind if I snuggle up next to you, do you, Ichabod?" Mrs. Minkoff asked gregariously.

"Please, I do need my personal space," Ignatius answered haughtily.

"Please, Ichabod, I need the comfort of someone at this time," Mrs. Minkoff said imploringly.

"Perhaps you should get Jethro," Ignatius answered jokingly.

"I don't believe that he's available," Mrs. Minkoff said kaleidoscopically.

"I'm sure he's not," Ignatius said laughingly.

"Are you sure Bernard does not need to go back to the *shul?*" Mrs. Minkoff asked meaningfully.

"I do not recommend modern religion or its contrivances," Ignatius said nobly.

"Are you sure?" Mrs. Minkoff asked openly.

"I am positive, now be quiet, the commercial's almost over," Ignatius said patiently.

"We live in such a strange world," Mrs. Minkoff said quixotically.

"I agree," Ignatius said raspingly.

"Anymore, I'm not sure what's going on," Mrs. Minkoff said sagaciously.

"Please, the commercial is almost over," Ignatius said testily.

"Of course, Ichabod," Mrs. Minkoff said understandably.

"Oh, another commercial," Ignatius said vehemently.

"Oh, that's so wrong," Mrs. Minkoff answered willfully.

"Modernity and its so-called contrivances almost drive me to the point of schizophrenic paranoia," Ignatius said xenophobically.

"Am I far away enough from you now?" Mrs. Minkoff asked yieldingly.

"You're fine, and now be quiet because Ed Sullivan is back on the television set," Ignatius replied zealously.

Ignatius and Mrs. Minkoff returned their full attention to the television set. Neither the lion tamer nor his lions were to be seen anywhere, and Ed Sullivan was wiping his brow with a silk handkerchief and telling the television audience that there had been a minor accident and that everything was under control, even though he kept looking nervously to the side of the stage.

"He reminds me of Bernard in many ways," Mrs. Minkoff said, pointing at the screen. "I wonder if Mr. Sullivan, though, wants to buy a gun."

"He probably already has one," Ignatius said, "and it's in his pocket, and no, he is not glad to see you, Madam Minkoff. Now, if you would please be quiet, I would like to enjoy the rest of this modern drivel foisted upon a willingly and willfully stupid and gullible public."

"Of course, Ichabod, I will respect the demands of the rabbi," Mrs. Minkoff said, wondering what had happened to make Ed Sullivan so nervous.

There was the roaring of a lion, and the lion tamer screamed in agony somewhere offstage, and Ed Sullivan made a motion with his hand for the cameras to cut. A commercial appeared, this one for a cruise to the Caribbean, with stops in Haiti, the Dominican Republic, Puerto Rico, Bermuda, and Jamaica. A three-man Calypso band played, extolling the pleasures and virtues of visiting these paradises.

And then Ed Sullivan appeared once again, heartily apologizing, saying that his crew was having technical difficulties and that the show would resume in a few moments. He disappeared from the television screen and was replaced with three Negress singers standing in the center of a stage and moving in rhythm to a tinkling piano intro. And the three Negresses sang:

See the way he walks down the street
Watch the way he shuffles his feet
My, he holds his head up high
When he goes walking by, he's my guy

Ignatius slapped his cheeks. "Oh, my God! I can't believe the utter horror of it all!"

White teenagers and white go-go dancers danced as the Negresses continued:

When he holds my hand, I'm so proud
'Cause he's not just one of the crowd
My baby's always the one to try the things they've never done
And just because of that, they say

"Can you believe the vacuity that they are foisting upon us and the youth of our once-great nation!" Ignatius snarled, thrusting an accusing finger at the television set. "Is it any wonder that our culture is so degraded! That is the problem with our society: that which should be mocked is praised, and that which should be praised is mocked!"

"It is horrible," Mrs. Minkoff said, not sure why it was horrible but knowing that it was horrible because Ichabod said that it was horrible, after all. "Should we change the channel?"

"Of course not," Ignatius said. "I must observe this balderdash to ensure that my critical faculties are still intact."

The Negresses continued:

He's a rebel, and he'll never ever be any good
He's a rebel 'cause he never ever does what he should
But just because he doesn't do what everybody else does
That's no reason why I can't give him all my love

And then the Negresses vanished, replaced by a smiling, flushed, and unnerved Ed Sullivan, who welcomed his next guest, a standup comedian from Hoboken. Unbeknown to Ed Sullivan, two ambulance attendants had stepped onto the stage and were pushing a covered gurney.

And then an idea came to Ignatius. Of course, that was it! Ignatius smiled. He leaned back, believing that he had the answer not only to putting Myrna Minkoff minx into her rightful place, but in bringing about the revolution that he, Ignatius, wanted to foist upon the world.

"Go prepare me a pot of tea!" Ignatius barked at Mrs. Minkoff the way a Puerto Rican army sergeant barked orders at draftees teaching English-as-a-second-language classes. "I believe that I have found my eureka, Madam Minkoff! I believe that I have found the very thing that will justify my *raison d'être*!"

"You want a dish of raisins, too?" Mrs. Minkoff asked, blinking.

"I believe that I now understand why that wanton Fortuna was playing her dastardly games with me," Ignatius said, ignoring Mrs. Minkoff and Mrs. Minkoff's question. "It now makes sense. I was taken from the gullet of my monastic life into the bowels of New Orleans. From the bowels of New Orleans I entered the rectum of New York City. And from the rectum of New York City I shall be expelled into the toilet bowl of the world." Ignatius's blue and yellow eyes sparkled like shimmering pond water on a summer's day. "Why didn't I see it before? Why didn't I hear it before? Why didn't I understand that if I am going to bring about global change, I must use the one and only appropriate means for doing so?"

"Are you constipated, Ichabod?" Mrs. Minkoff asked.

Ignatius blinked. "What an absurd question. Why on earth would you ask that, Madam Minkoff?"

"I didn't understand a thing you said, but you made it sound like you were having trouble with your bowels," Mrs. Minkoff said. "At first I thought you were talking about your vowels, but then you said something about your raisins being in debt, so I figured you wanted roughage in your system, but something sweet, too, and at a cheaper price."

Was she playing games with him? Could she be trusted? Ignatius studied her earnest, stupid face. Of course she could be trusted. How could she not be trusted?

Ignatius leaned towards her conspiratorially. "What I am about to say to you, Madam Minkoff, must be kept in the strictest of confidences. You cannot tell anyone, do you understand me? This must especially remain hidden from Myrna minx, at least for now."

Mrs. Minkoff nodded and crossed her heart and swore that she would rather die than reveal the secret that he, Ichabod, was about to tell her.

"I am going to cure this vile world of its infections once for all," Ignatius whispered. "I was working through the wrong muse—namely, Calliope. She is not my muse here. She cannot be. I need Euterpe. Through her, and with her aid, I shall bring about the world's much needed revolution."

"You're not a communist, are you?" Mrs. Minkoff asked, very frightened. "We have enough trouble as it is with Myrna. I don't think that Bernard could stomach another communist living under this roof."

"I can assure you, dear madam, that I have no desire whatsoever to be a fellow traveler," Ignatius said, feeling renewed and revitalized by his new discovery. "You are going shopping tomorrow, are you not, Madam Minkoff?"

"I always shop on Mondays because that's the day that I take the laundry out," she replied.

"Do you have a pad of paper and a pen?"

"I thought you wanted your pot of tea, Ichabod."

"That can wait. Get me a pen and a pad of paper. I am going to give you a shopping list."

Mrs. Minkoff smiled, stood, and went to get the items. Ignatius returned his attention to the television set. Ed Sullivan was on-screen again, sweating profusely, saying that a man had not just been mauled to death by lions, no, no, that was all part of the act, and to please come back the next week for another very big show.

I will give them a very big show, Ignatius thought. He smiled and listened to Mrs. Minkoff's rummaging in the kitchen. Everything was falling into place.

II

Mr. Minkoff was sitting in his office chair and was staring out his office window. His secretary, Mrs. Andrews, stepped into his office with legal documents in hand. She studied her boss silently and wondered what he was thinking. For the past week or so he had been acting differently. For one thing, he didn't drink coffee any longer. For another, he had not said one angry word to anyone during that entire time. And that worried Mrs. Andrews, who knew that Mr. Minkoff was typically a screamer.

"Mr. Minkoff?"

He turned to look at her. He had a vacant stare. Her husband, a World War II US Army vet, had had that kind of stare, what they called the thousand-yard stare.

"These papers need to be signed," she said. "Mr. Delaney said that they can't wait any longer."

Mr. Minkoff grunted for her to bring him the papers. Mrs. Andrews walked over to the desk and placed the legal documents in front of him and indicated the lines where he was to sign.

Mr. Minkoff uncapped a fountain pen, tested the tip of the pen on blotter paper, and then scrawled his signature on the documents, one document after the other, signing them so quickly that it seemed as if he had gone into a fugue. Horrified, Mrs. Andrews stepped back, not sure how to react. Mr. Minkoff, after all, had once taken great pride in his signature. In fact, at the company, when someone spoke of a fancy signature, it was not called a John Hancock, it was called a J. Bernard Minkoff.

After he finished, Mr. Minkoff capped the pen and leaned back in his chair. Mrs. Andrews gathered up the legal documents.

"Do you know anything about guns, Mrs. Andrews?" Mr. Minkoff asked, staring at the door of his office.

"I don't, but my husband does." She tapped the papers on Mr. Minkoff's desk so that they aligned. "Why? Are you in the market for a gun?"

"You could say that," Mr. Minkoff said, putting his fingers together so that they formed a steeple and placing the tip of the steeple underneath his chin. His intertwined fingers created an anatomical Gaudi. "Does your husband like to hunt, Mrs. Andrews?"

"He loves to hunt, Mr. Minkoff. And fish. He prefers fishing over hunting, though, any day of the week." She blinked. "He's leaving for a fishing trip very soon, with our son."

"And where are they going, Mrs. Andrews?"

"To Alberta," she said, and then she snapped her fingers, correcting herself. "Pardon me, I meant Ontario. His family has a cabin up there."

"Your husband is from Canada?"

"He was born here but raised in Canada," she said. "Then he came back to the States and joined the army during the war. Then he got into advertising."

"What does he advertise, Mrs. Andrews?"

"Feminine products," Mrs. Andrews said, not wanting to tell Mr. Minkoff that her husband's specialty was tampons. It was more polite, and thus more feminine, to refer to such things as feminine products. "And he's done quite well at it. His firm on Madison Avenue raves about his work."

"And he loves to hunt?"

"Yes, he loves to hunt. And fish."

Mr. Minkoff peered at Mrs. Andrews. "Are you sure your husband's not from New Orleans?" Mr. Minkoff asked.

"Of course I'm sure," Mrs. Andrews said. "Why would you ask that, Mr. Minkoff?"

"It seems to me that we have too many people from New Orleans here in New York City," Mr. Minkoff said, exhaling loudly. His Peterson briar pipe, which he hadn't smoked in days, sat cradled in an ashtray to his right. "New Orleans seems to corrupt people. It corrupted my daughter. Did you know that she went to New Orleans?"

"No, I didn't know that," Mrs. Andrews said, feeling very uncomfortable and not knowing why she felt that way. "I hope that she enjoyed Mardi Gras."

"She didn't go there for Mardi Gras," Mr. Minkoff said sternly, looking at Mrs. Andrews with disapproval in his eyes. "She went there to study."

"Your daughter studied in New Orleans?"

"That's right," Mr. Minkoff said, nodding. Now Mrs. Andrews was getting the picture. Now she would be seeing the same things that he was seeing and making the same logical connections that he was making, dotting the Is, crossing the Ts, and learning what he was learning. "She studied at Tulane University. What do you think about that, Mrs. Andrews?"

"I'm sure it's a good school," Mrs. Andrews said. "I mean, it has to be, right? It's got such a good reputation."

"Oh, it has a reputation, all right," Mr. Minkoff said. He motioned for her to have a seat, something that she hesitantly did. "Am I making you nervous, Mrs. Andrews?"

"Not at all, Mr. Minkoff. I think I'm coming down with the chills. That's common for this time of year, you know."

"Of course, of course," Mr. Minkoff said, leaning back in his executive's chair and nodding, undoing the steeple that he had created. He drummed the fingers and thumbs of both hands on the arms of his chair. "I bet it's hard for people to get chilled in New Orleans, even at this time of year."

"Are you all right, Mr. Minkoff? Is something bothering you?"

"Do you like Laurel and Hardy films, Mrs. Andrews?" Before she could answer, he continued: "I used to. I used to enjoy them very much, especially when I was a boy."

"Oh, I suppose they're all right," Mrs. Andrews said. "I'm more partial to Abbot and Costello."

"Abbott and Costello? I've seen a few of their films. But Costello compares in no way to Oliver Hardy." Mr. Minkoff chuckled the way a man in an insane asylum chuckled, and Mrs. Andrews shifted uncomfortably in her chair. "Did you know that Oliver Hardy reads *The Consolation of Philosophy*? I bet you didn't know that, did you?"

"I don't know what that is, Mr. Minkoff. Should I?"

"We all should," Mr. Minkoff said, growling like an enraged Baptist minister in an Alabaman forest during a tent revival meeting. "Why, we need that book to shape our worldviews. Oliver Hardy told me that the other night, right at my dinner table."

"I didn't know that Oliver Hardy was your guest, Mr. Minkoff. I thought that he was dead. Why didn't you say anything about having a famous person at your house?"

"Because the cat brought him home," Mr. Minkoff said, now staring into space, more and more of the connections coming to him. "You see, I've been ashamed of the cat for so long. Sometimes I wish I had given up the cat for adoption. But Mrs. Minkoff wouldn't allow that, you see. She said that it was some sort of plan, that God meant it to be that way, and that we should be thankful for having the cat, even though I thought that I had done my best to prevent the cat from being conceived by using the best *masculine* product out there, or so the advertisers said." He sighed loudly. "Tell me, Mrs. Andrews, did your husband ever work with *masculine* products? If so, did he fail at his ventures? Is that why he now works with *feminine* products?"

Mrs. Andrews wasn't sure how to react. Mr. Minkoff wasn't making any sense whatsoever. Generally, when he spoke, he was direct, like an army general telling his underlings exactly what he wanted and expecting them to execute his commands without hesitation. She had never seen Mr. Minkoff so talkative before or heard him so accusatory in his tone.

"Did your husband ever work for Trojan?" Mr. Minkoff asked like a prosecutor sneaking up on the defense's best witness. "Did he, Mrs. Andrews?"

"No, not at all. He works at Gray Advertising. He's had the same account for years, and he's done wonders with it." She was on the verge of tears. "I don't know what this is all about, Mr. Minkoff, but I must tell you, I don't like it, and I feel very scared. That's right, I don't like it, and I feel very scared, and right now I want to go home to Long Island and be with my husband, John, when he gets home. I told him that I didn't want to work, but he said that we need the income so that we can continue to live in the Hamptons."

"The Hamptons are lovely," Mr. Minkoff said, forgetting, for a moment, the image of Ignatius's helping himself to a seventh helping of steaming mashed potatoes. "I'm glad that you live in the Hamptons. Oliver Hardy doesn't live there, you know. He lives in the Bronx with me, at my house."

Mrs. Andrews stood. "You're scaring me, Mr. Minkoff. I think I'm going to go home."

"Why, Mrs. Andrews? What's to be scared of? Oliver Hardy says that blind Fortuna is working her best for us all, all in due time."

Crying, Mrs. Andrews fled the office. Mr. Minkoff turned around in his executive's chair and peered out the window and down at the street below. He watched people, frowning when he saw some that he was sure were from New Orleans. He would have to speak that evening with Oliver Hardy and ask him if there was a surefire way to determine if someone was from New Orleans just by looking at him.

Six

Mrs. Reilly didn't like the Greyhound Scenicruiser in which she was riding. She didn't like the dour people on the bus. She didn't like the truculent, round-faced bus driver, a man who looked like a dirty Arab. And she didn't like Mr. Robichaux's continually putting his hand on her knee. She was beyond any natural ability to get impregnated, but, nonetheless, that one encounter with Mr. Reilly after the showing of *Red Dust* had made her wary of men, especially when she suspected what was on their minds.

"I wish you would stop that, Claude," Mrs. Reilly said, voice low, almost a hiss. "We ain't even married yet, and here you are acting like a Mardi Gras."

"I love you, Irene," Mr. Robichaux intoned solemnly. "And I want to show my love to you. What's wrong with that, sugar?"

"Just don't do it on my knee," Mrs. Reilly said. "You're as bad as Rex."

"Rex?" Mr. Robichaux felt the blood surging to his face because of his jealousy. "Who's that?"

"Ignatius's dead dog," she said, looking out the window of the Scenicruiser, which headed up a Tennessee highway. Night had fallen, and the Tennessee forests looked very foreboding, like the southwestern swamps of her native Louisiana but in a different way: the latter were more like home, the former, the ice forests of an evil witch. "When that Rex got in the mood, he'd hug my leg and go at it. Sometimes I got so mad, I told Ignatius, 'Boy, you don't do something with that dog, I'm gonna have him neutralized.' Ignatius, he didn't like that. He threatened to take me to the court if I had Rex neutralized." She sniffled, remembering Ignatius fondly. "I think we done him great wrong, Claude, I really do."

"You didn't neutralize him, so what's the great wrong?" Mr. Robichaux asked, blinking his dull eyes. "Rex lived a long life, didn't he, Irene?"

"I wasn't talking about Rex, you dodo. I was talking about Ignatius."

"You neutralized Ignatius!" Mr. Robichaux barked, and several people, who had been reading newspapers, magazines, or books by overhead lights, or dozing, turned their attention to Mrs. Reilly and Mr. Robichaux.

She elbowed him hard, and Mr. Robichaux gasped, wincing and holding his side.

"That hurt," Mr. Robichaux said slowly and softly in protest. "Why you do that for, Irene?"

"Because you drawing us too much attention," Mrs. Reilly said. "Do you think I would neutralize my own boy, you dodo?"

"Well, you was going to send him to Charity," Mr. Robichaux replied earnestly. "I mean, that's close to neutralizing him, I guess. You know, come to think about it, maybe you should have neutralized Ignatius. He probably wouldn't be causin' the trouble he's been causin', Irene. Like one of my neighbors, Mr. Santini, who had him a tufty-headed organ-grinder monkey name of Francis."

"Was he that little man used to walk around downtown with his monkey and that big black mustache?"

"Francis didn't have a big black mustache, but Mr. Santini, he sure did."

"Of course no monkey is going to have a mustache, Claude," Mrs. Reilly said, and she felt like smacking Mr. Robichaux upside his head. "I meant that little Italian man."

"Yeah, that little dago had a big black mustache, all right."

Mrs. Reilly sighed. "So what's your point, Claude?"

"Oh, right. Well, Francis was a good monkey until he turned about five or six, and then he became a holy terror, believe you me. See, he had gone into pooberty, and he got to tearin' up things around the Santini home and terrorizing everyone and everything, including Mrs. Santini, who used to set a plate at the table for Francis. She told Mr. Santini, 'You better do something with that monkey, Mr. Santini, or I am leaving you once for all.'"

"He must've got rit of Mrs. Santini, because I saw him working that monkey on the street corners."

"No, not at all," Mr. Robichaux said quite gravely. "He took it to heart, of course."

"Of course Mr. Santini took it to heart. That monkey was his lifeblood. Why wouldn't he take it to heart?"

"I was talking about Francis," Mr. Robichaux said. "I suspect he knew what was coming. See, he tried to reform his ways before Mr. Santini took him to the vet's."

"And how would a monkey do that, you dodo?" Mrs. Reilly asked, feeling herself becoming more irritable. She was tired of all this talk about little Italian men and their little organ-grinder monkeys. She wanted her boy, that was all. And that was more than enough for her to deal with. "Monkeys ain't people, Claude."

"Francis was. Wore hisself that nice little suit with shiny buttons and a nice cap. Kinda looked like one of those bellboys at the Roosevelt."

"Can you just come to the end of the story, Claude?"

"Mr. Santini, well, he had Francis neutralized because even though Francis tried, Francis couldn't reform hisself. Francis sure did calm down after being neutralized, though. He didn't throw plates no more, and Mrs. Santini didn't have to worry about Francis trying to do his thing on her leg or playing with hisself in front of her friends when they came over for coffee."

"That's disgusting, Claude." Mrs. Reilly made a face. "Why are you telling me these things?"

"Because if you had neutralized Ignatius, you probably wouldn't be in the mess you're in now, Irene. He'd probably be at home, working a good job and not tearing up things the way Francis did."

"Ignatius ain't no monkey, Claude." She held up a hand before he could answer. "And he didn't tear up no things, except, well, the Night of Joy and Mr. Levy's pants company. I don't want to hear no more nonsense about monkeys and things that need to be neutralized."

"It was just a thought."

"Let it go, Claude. I'm gonna get me some sleep. Why don't you take a nap, too?"

"All right, Irene, I will."

Mr. Robichaux snapped off the overhead lights, and, for a few moments, Mrs. Reilly kept her eyes closed and pretended to sleep. Then she opened her eyes and looked over at Mr. Robichaux, whose eyes were closed, and then looked out the window.

The bus was progressing up the winding highway, and because there was no light pollution, she was able to see the Tennessee forests, which resembled black ink painted jaggedly on a deep-purple canvas. They didn't get nights like these in New Orleans, that was for sure, where the light pollution kept the stars at bay. Mrs. Reilly sighed, wondering what was happening with her boy. She hoped that he was doing well. Myrna's momma, that strange woman, had said that Ignatius had become rabid. Mrs. Reilly was sure that the woman was crazy. Ignatius was many things, but he was not rabid, and he certainly was not Orthodox rabid, whatever that meant. Or did that woman say Orthodox rabbit? Mrs. Reilly frowned. Perhaps she had misunderstood the strange woman. Those people out east sure sounded like the Irish Channel people back home, but one thing was for sure, those people in

New York City had to be crazy if they believed in anything like Orthodox rabbits, whatever those were.

Mrs. Reilly's eyelids felt heavier. She didn't want to sleep; she wanted to think about Ignatius and the good times that they had had together. When she found him, she would bring him home, safe and sound. Crazy or not, Ignatius was her boy.

II

Dr. Talc, who had lectured earlier that day at Johns Hopkins, smiled as his train sped northward to New York City. The recent debacle in New Orleans had almost undone his career, with the head of his department at Tulane insisting that he, Dr. Talc, take a much needed sabbatical. An old colleague of Dr. Talc's, Dr. Gertrude, had just received full tenure at Johns Hopkins and had invited her old friend for a visit, which turned into an opportunity for Dr. Talc to lecture on volitional solecisms in Melville.

Of course, before the lecture he consulted his many notes on how to make the proper delivery, when to laugh during his presentation, and he made it a point to tell a joke that he had heard between a Tulane colleague and a visiting professor from Oxford.

Though Dr. Talc didn't understand the joke (no matter how many times he told it to himself), the professors and students attending his lecture, however, had a hearty laugh, several of them afterwards congratulating Dr. Talc on his quite dry, and quite subtle, wit.

Dr. Talc frowned. He was no longer daydreaming, and the train was speeding past houses and buildings that, while brilliant in color—many of the houses were yellow or red or green—nonetheless looked dreary because it was winter.

He blinked, and a phantasm of Ignatius J. Reilly and Myrna Minkoff came into Dr. Talc's mind. They were sitting in his classroom and mocking him, taunting him, leering at him. Dr. Talc shuddered. He closed his eyes, doing his best to will away the phantasm, which he was able to replace successfully with a phantasm of how he thought midtown Manhattan would appear, Dr. Talc never having visited New York City before.

"Sir?" a deep-voiced man asked.

Dr. Talc opened his wearied eyes. A Negro porter asked Dr. Talc if he would like another cup of tea, to which Dr. Talc replied that he would. After the porter went to get the tea, Dr. Talc looked at the landscape speeding by. New Orleans was far, far behind him. Something better, he knew and sensed, was on the horizon.

"Ignatius J. Reilly," Dr. Talc said, grimacing and shaking his head, "you are probably in an insane asylum where you belong."

The thought of Ignatius J. Reilly's being in an insane asylum caused Dr. Talc to giggle. And then to giggle more. And more. And more, like a schoolgirl whose best friend had just shared the world's darkest, dirtiest, most scandalous secret.

"You all right, friend?"

Dr. Talc stopped giggling. A man wearing a gray flannel suit was staring questioningly at Dr. Talc. Dr. Talc blushed. He didn't want the other passenger to think that he, Dr. Talc, was insane or had issues.

"Oh, I was thinking about a joke that I heard."

"I like jokes. Why don't you tell it to me?"

So Dr. Talc told the stranger the joke that he, Dr. Talc, had told during the lecture, and then the stranger was laughing loudly and slapping his knee and telling Dr. Talc that, indeed, the joke was a good one.

Dr. Talc, however, wished that he understood the joke.

The train sped northward, and the Negro porter brought Dr. Talc his cup of tea.

III

It was morning, and Ignatius was sitting in a wooden chair among others that formed a circle in a wooden-floored room.

To Ignatius's right sat Myrna, to his left, Ralph and Miss Kitty. Ralph was holding Miss Kitty close to his mouth and whispering sweet nothings to her. Miss Kitty giggled like a schoolgirl. Ignatius sighed. He had agreed to go to the group therapy group so that he could get out of work.

Dr. Ingloss, who was seated at the twelve o'clock position of the circle, and who had been speaking for the past twenty minutes or so, cleared his voice and continued: "Perverse sexual acts, without being dependent upon perversion, often come under our observation. This is especially true with reference to sexual acts between persons of the same sex, particularly in pederasty." Dr. Ingloss fixed his beady eyes on Ignatius. "Here sexual paresthesia is not necessarily at work, but hyperesthesia is, with physical or psychical impossibility for natural sexual satisfaction."

"And where is this leading, sirrah?" Ignatius said. "To me this sounds like nothing but gibberish, the psychobabble of the modern shaman who, while pretending to understand the cost of the psyche, knows absolutely nothing about the value of the soul. So what is your point?"

"The point is this," Dr. Ingloss replied sternly, holding up a finger, indicating that he did not want to be interrupted. "Thus we find homosexual intercourse in impotent masturbators or debauchees."

Ignatius's face crimsoned. "And, dear Dr. Quack Ingloss, can you define your terms? Have you even defined the problem, let alone the solution?"

"Ah, I have the solution," Dr. Ingloss said. "There is an immediate return to normal sexual intercourse as soon as the obstacles to it are removed. Very frequently the cause of such temporary aberration is masturbation in youthful individuals like yourself, Ignatius."

"Oh, my God!"

"It's good that you're getting angry, Ignatius," Myrna said. "This shows that the repressed thoughts and emotions are coming out."

"Myrna knows what she's talking about," Mrs. Murray said. "By the way, Myrna, Fred gave me the crabs."

"I have an easy cure for that," Myrna said. "Speak to me after our group therapy group session is over."

"Oh, my God!" Ignatius said, and he wished that he had stayed at the Charlie Chan Chinese Fortune Cookie Company. At least there he could lock the door to his office and lie on his desk, which creaked from his immense weight. "Is everyone here a deviant?"

"We are here to help you, Ignatius," Dr. Ingloss said. "You do want to be helped, don't you? After all, Myrna has told us all. You must, of course, be an inveterate masturbator, like our friend Ralph."

"If anyone is an onanist, it is you, sirrah," Ignatius said angrily. "I accuse you of onanism of the worst variety, namely, the mental. Your words are those of the quack, the charlatan, the mountebank. Do you realize that in a proper civilization you would be hanged, and rightly so?"

"Ah, but I would still maintain my optimism," said Dr. Ingloss. "You see, Ignatius, your hostilities are arising from your lack of sexual-psycho energy. Though you have not admitted it, I believe that you have developed a habit of chronic masturbation—a very pernicious habit, mind you, in circumstances like yours—and that this pernicious habit has contaminated, if not exhausted, the source of all noble and ideal sentiments, which, in and of themselves, arise from a normally developing sexual instinct."

Ignatius swooned. Ralph whispered something to Miss Kitty, and Miss Kitty told Ralph to behave himself. Leonard, arms crossed, rolled his eyes.

"Such a practice despoils the unfolding bud of perfume and beauty and leaves behind only the coarse animal desire for sexual satisfaction, Ignatius. If an individual like you, thus deprived, reaches the age of physical maturity, there is a wanting in him. The glow of sensual sensibility wanes, and the inclination towards the opposite is weakened."

"How dare you!" Ignatius bellowed, unable to contain himself. "Such effrontery! Do you not realize, sirrah, that I am vice president of the most esteemed Charlie Chan Chinese Fortune Cookie Company!"

Dr. Ingloss shook his head sympathetically and continued: "This character defect then influences the morals, the character, fancy, feeling, and instinct of the youthful masturbator, male or female, in an unfavorable manner, even causing, under certain circumstances, the desire for the opposite sex to sink to *nil*, so that masturbation is preferred to the natural mode of satisfaction."

"More asinine hogwash and gibbon gibberish," Ignatius said, and he turned to Myrna. "And you have been spending months with this fool? And you believe what this pseudo-Germanic idiot says?"

"Dr. Ingloss is a pioneer in psycho-sexual research," Myrna replied in protest, and she placed a hand on Ignatius's knee, a hand that he quickly brushed away. "He's here to help you, Ignatius. I'm here to help you." She motioned at the group. "We're all here to help you."

"I'm certainly here to help you," said the hand Miss Kitty in her high-pitched voice. "In fact, if you need a hand—"

"That is enough, Miss Kitty," Dr. Ingloss said to Miss Kitty. "It seems, Ignatius, that you have, quite inadvertently of course, turned yourself into a homosexual who is in denial of his current sexuality."

"Again, I say, how dare you!" Ignatius hollered. "You know absolutely nothing about my psyche or my worldview. Were you to understand, you would be on your knees in St. Patrick's Cathedral this very moment, begging a most wrathful God for His mercy for your outlandish, and quite heretical, worldview."

"I was like you and thought that Dr. Ingloss was crazy at first, Ignatius," said Mrs. Murray sympathetically. "But he got me straightened out, all right. I came to understand that I was sexually frustrated and that I repressed this frustration as a means of getting back at the late Mr. Murray, God rest his soul. Well, now that I'm on track, my sex life is going along wonderfully, even though my companion, Fred, is an ex-con from Sing Sing who just gave me the crabs."

"I can't believe that I'm hearing such outrageous, arabesque comments!" Ignatius bellowed. He stood, gesticulating the way he had gesticulated at Levy Pants during his failed coup. "Do any of you, including this man and his talking hand, understand the depravity to which you've sunk? Don't you see the foolishness of all this? What happens when Freud and Jung and Adler are no longer current but passé? Then to whom shall you turn? Another quack like this so-called doctor, or will it be a mystic, perhaps a Marxist pretending to be a Protestant minister who causes his devotees to commit suicide in some Third World jungle?"

Dr. Ingloss looked sad. He shook his sad-faced head sadly and jotted in his moleskin notebook.

"Ah, you're writing about my so-called rant," Ignatius said, pointing an accusing finger at Dr. Ingloss. "I'll have you know, sirrah, that this is not a rant, it is a jeremiad against this corrupt and corrupting age. I'll have you know that when proper theology and geometry return, there are going to be Nuremberg-style trials for the likes of you, with your ballet not occurring at Spandau, sirrah, but in Central Park!"

"This could be a sense of pseudo penis envy," Dr. Ingloss said, wagging his Wagnerian head.

Ignatius turned to Myrna. "How can you stomach this tripe?"

"Freud's the one who led us into the world that we needed to enter," Myrna said, "but he didn't go far enough, according to Dr. Ingloss. And neither did Jung. And neither did Reich, who was on the right path, right, Dr. Ingloss?"

Dr. Ingloss smiled. "As I like to say, Reich was on the 'Reich' path."

"You haven't experienced life until you've had a full-body orgasm," Mrs. Murray said to Ignatius. "It's like the whole cosmos opens up to you, and you enter a nirvana, let me tell you."

"You've been reading too many of Myrna Minkoff's missives," Ignatius said to the woman of Irish descent. "Everything to her can be cured by an orgasm, in whatever form the stimulation is administered." Ignatius shuddered. "And to think that I came here to speak about proper theology and geometry."

"You've returned to your old nasty self," Myrna said to Ignatius. "Something told me that I shouldn't have gone down to New Orleans to rescue you."

"Please, go on," Dr. Ingloss said.

"Please do," said Miss Kitty in her high-pitched voice. "Please, we want to know your thoughts and opinions about the subject at hand, Myrna."

"I thought that I could finally save someone," Myrna said to her group therapy group. "So I figured that I would go down to New Orleans and rescue Ignatius. He got nasty a few times on the way to New York City, but I thought these were just minor relapses."

Ignatius, fearing that he was going to lose his residence at the Minkoff manse, feigned a smile.

"Your Renault was a bit cramped," Ignatius said. "You will have to give me that."

"Yes, I'll give you that, but you were also playing the backseat driver all the way, telling me all the time to slow down so that your valve wouldn't seal," Myrna said. She looked at the members of her group therapy group one by one, and then at Dr. Ingloss, and then at Ignatius. "And when I tried to help you in those motel rooms, you claimed that you were too sick to perform. That's why I had to do it with those three sailors behind that barn in North Carolina."

Leonard rolled his eyes.

"I thought that they were three lumberjacks," Ignatius said.

"They could've been," Myrna said. "Anyway, if it wasn't a crab shack, it should've been called a crab shack."

"You did get them treated, didn't you?" Dr. Ingloss said.

"Of course," Myrna said. "Do you honestly believe that I'm that disgusting?"

Ignatius looked down at an imaginary watch on his thick wrist. "Well," he said, "it looks as if our time is up. We've made wonderful progress. To those of you who care to read about weightier matters, please obtain a copy of Boethius's *The Consolation of Philosophy* and begin reading it immediately. Negate that. Do not read the book, study it. Negate that. Do not study the book, imbibe it. Make it a part of your soul as I have made it a part of mine. Learn that you are ultimately doomed, and come to accept your fate." He looked at Myrna. "Meanwhile, too, work on your sexuality and perhaps look into taking a yoga course at the New School or some ashram run by a Hindu yogi, preferably an ascetic not given to certain proclivities. Perhaps your *ida* and *pingala* will unite with your *kundalini*, or whatever it is, and you'll experience the orgasmic wonders of the universe. If not, you can settle back down into reality and come to terms with blind Fortuna."

"And what about those of us who aren't readers?" Miss Kitty asked. "What kind of hand can you lend us?"

"Then obtain the latest Batman comics from your news vendor," Ignatius said to Miss Kitty. "His morality, at least, is the morality that you'll need to survive Gotham."

"I like the parts about the yoga and orgasms," Myrna said, "but I'm finding that other stuff a bit too fishy, Ignatius."

"I find myself a bit fishy too," Mrs. Murray said, "after a good orgasm."

"Ah, we must discuss that this next session," Dr. Ingloss said, jotting a note.

"Agreed!" Ignatius said heartily, desiring to exit the group therapy group.

Dr. Ingloss handed a stack of mimeographed notes to Mrs. Murray, who took one copy and passed the stack to Ralph and Miss Kitty. Ignatius didn't understand why the session was continuing.

"What do you make of these notes, Miss Kitty?" Ralph asked his hand.

"I have to give a hand to Dr. Ingloss," Miss Kitty replied. "If I could, I would applaud this scientific genius."

Ignatius, in his rage, snatched the papers and shook them at Dr. Ingloss.

"If anyone, my dear sirrah, is a dunce, it is you!" Ignatius said to the psychologist. "If the theory of psychological projection is true, then I suggest that you are, indeed, projecting your own sexual perversities upon us all!"

Ignoring Ignatius, Dr. Ingloss cleared his throat and read: "This degree of homosexuality is attained when a person exercises an aphrodisiac effect over another person of the same sex who reciprocates the sexual feeling. Character and instinct, however, still correspond with the sex of the individual. He feels himself in the active role. He recognizes his impulse towards his own sex as an aberration and finally seeks aid.

"With episodic improvement of the neurosis, at first even normal sexual feelings may reappear and assert themselves—"

"Pseudoscientific tripe, sirrah—"

"If, in cases of antipathic sexual instinct thus developed, no restoration occurs, then deep and lasting transformations of the psychical personality may occur. The process completing itself in this way may be designated eviration. The patient undergoes a deep change of character, particularly in his feeling and inclinations, which thus become those of a female. After this, he also feels himself to be a woman during the sexual act, has desire only for passive sexual indulgence, and, under certain circumstances, sinks to the level of a prostitute. In this condition of deep and more lasting psycho-sexual transformation, the individual is similar to the congenital homosexual of high grade. The possibility of a restoration of the previous mental and sexual personality seems, in such a case, precluded."

Dr. Ingloss lowered his paper and looked at Ignatius. "I believe that we have described you to a T," the psychologist said. "Now, tell me about your mother."

"My dear mother is none of your damnable business," Ignatius said. "My mother, like all of us, has the stain of original sin. It is through the likes of Boethius, Augustine, and others that we come to an understanding of how we are to deal with this taint. Your way, of course, is by saying that we are all suffering from sexual neuroses. Your true desire is not to save me but to bed this minx, Myrna Minkoff!"

Ignatius thrust an accusing finger at Dr. Ingloss, who blinked.

"So?" Dr. Ingloss said.

"So?" Ignatius blustered. "So, isn't this hypocritical of you?"

"I am only doing what the likes of Alfred Kinsey and others have done, Ignatius. If I can cure neuroses by engaging in sexual congress with my patients, so be it."

"Ah, but you yourself were speaking about sexual aberration," Ignatius said. "To cure this, do you then engage in such aberration?"

"Of course not, Ignatius. You seem, in your hysteria, to say that you want to have sexual congress with me. Of course, this cannot be. Your case is certainly one of acquired sexual passions, given that your sexual feeling was originally directed towards the female sex. Such passions became neurasthenic through masturbation."

"I do not know how much more of this nonsense I can take," Ignatius said, and he tossed aside the stack of mimeographed notes, which slowly crested one way, then the other, as they made their descent to the floor. "I can assure you, I have no sexual attraction to the same sex, sirrah, and certainly not to you!"

"The result of this emasculation is that the passive role and even more passive pederasty become desirable," Dr. Ingloss said, continuing as if he were an automaton. "And this urge extends its influence to the character, which becomes more interested in feminine pastimes, and the masturbator even resorts to makeup and other titivation in order to revive his fading charms and to make 'conquests.'"

"I have had no need to make conquests," Ignatius said imperiously. "I have no such need because I have nothing to prove, at least in that arena of this circus. Might I suggest that we turn to Boethius and the ancients for enlightenment?"

"The foregoing facts concerning acquired antipathic sexual instinct and feminization find an interesting confirmation in the following ethnological data.

"Herodotus already describes a peculiar disease that frequently affected the Scythians. The disease consisted of this: that men became effeminate in character, put on female garments, did the work of women, used menstrual rags, and even became effeminate in appearance. As an explanation of this insanity of the Scythians, Herodotus relates the myth that the goddess Venus, angered by the plundering of the temple at Ascalon by the Scythians, had made women of these plunderers and their posterity.

"Hippocrates, not believing in supernatural diseases, nonetheless recognized that impotence was here a causative factor, and explained it, though incorrectly, as due to the custom of the Scythians to have themselves bled behind the ears in order to cure disease induced by constant horseback riding. He thought that the veins were of great importance in the preservation of the sexual powers and that when they were severed, impotence was induced. Since the Scythians considered their impotence due to divine punishment and thus incurable, they put on the clothing of females and lived as women among women.

"It is worthy of note that, according to Klaproth and Chomsky, even at this present time, impotence is very frequent among the Tartars, as a result of riding unsaddled horses. The same is observed among the Apaches and Navajos of the United States, who ride excessively, scarcely ever going on foot, and are remarkable for their small genitals and mild libido and virility. Many others recognize the fact that excessive riding may be injurious to the sexual organs."

"I do not ride horses," said Ignatius. "And, to be as crass as you are, Dr. Ingloss, in regard to the size of one's pudenda, I refer you to Dr. Talc of Tulane University in New Orleans, Louisiana. I am sure that you two could commiserate on your assets, or lack thereof."

"You don't have to be so hostile about it," Myrna said. "Dr. Ingloss is just trying to help you."

"We're all trying to help you," Mrs. Murray said, "and once you have a full-body orgasm, you'll never have another mental problem again."

"The group therapy group is here for us all, Ignatius," said Ralph to Ignatius, and then Ralph said to his left hand, "Isn't it, Miss Kitty?"

"Of course it is," Miss Kitty replied. "We're not here to handicap you, Ignatius, we're here to lend you a hand so that you can be liberated from your troubles."

Leonard rolled his eyes.

Ignatius shook his head in disbelief, and his blue-yellow eyes crossed in anger. "Not one of you has heard a single word of what I have said," Ignatius said. "What on earth am I going to do with you? I see that my time here is being wasted, so I shall leave. Myrna, are you coming with me? I'm sure that your mother would like to have you home for dinner."

"Please don't go," Miss Kitty said. "If only there was a handbook to which we could refer."

"We tried a handbook, remember?" Ralph asked Miss Kitty. "And you said that it wasn't doing the trick."

"I don't want to talk about our sex life right now," replied Miss Kitty. "On the other hand, I don't want to discuss it later, either."

"You never want to discuss our sex life," Ralph complained. "Every time I bring it up, you find a convenient way to change the subject."

"You would be the first one to know if I wasn't having an orgasm," Miss Kitty said. "At least you've got to hand that to me."

Ignatius trembled. "Blind Fortuna, why have you spun me into this cycle!"

He picked up his heavy green winter coat and donned his green hunting cap, the flaps of which stuck out at odd angles. The room suddenly felt hot—too hot—and strangely, he wanted to get outside into the bitter cold, which, though he detested it, beckoned to him with its sirens' call. Then the room began spinning, and Ignatius felt his pyloric valve seal, and then Mandelbrot phosphenes danced in front of his blue-yellow eyes, which crossed as he fainted.

Ignatius jolted awake at his desk because of the nightmare, the worst expergefactor that he had ever experienced. (This expergefactor, however, did not compare with the uhtceares that he had experienced after the Night of Joy episode. He had stayed in bed so long that the staddle in the center of the bed looked as if it had become a permanent feature.) Ignatius wiped his forehead with one of the many paper napkins on his desk, which was cluttered with empty Chinese food containers and legal pads.

What had happened? Ah, of course. He had grubbled through the contents of a desk drawer, looking for loose change before copying, quite slowly, two lines of Boethius. And then he had daydreamed about his old room in New Orleans. Then he had fallen asleep as he thought about Myrna and her group therapy group, with which he had become well acquainted through her graphic descriptions of the sessions.

The office door burst open, and Myrna entered, shaking her head angrily.

"I can't keep going on like this," she said, pacing, throwing up her hands in exasperation. "This has been the most frustrating period of my life. I haven't achieved a full-body orgasm yet, and the Chinese workers don't understand what I'm saying, even though I've taken the revolutionary name Ho Ree Chit. I thought that one of them was going to rape me after I lifted up my skirt. I need to see Dr. Ingloss and my group therapy group."

"Oh, my God!" Ignatius said. "Do not mention Dr. Ingloss or your group therapy group ever again!"

"But Ignatius, besides starting a revolution and overturning the Western world, I need to rescue you. Don't you want to be rescued?"

Ignatius wanted to holler at her to leave the office, but he knew better. Even though he had obtained this prestigious post at the Charlie Chan Chinese Fortune Cookie Company, he would not be paid until the following week. Thus, he was still in dire straits when it came to his housing situation. One slip of the tongue, one unjust *le mot juste*, and he would be out on the street. And being out on the street in New York City in the winter was not where he wanted to be.

He slammed his meaty fist onto his desk and rattled a glass jar that contained the sharpened pencils that he had been using to copy lines from Batman comic books and passages from *The Consolation of Philosophy*.

"Of course we will go to Dr. Ingloss!" Ignatius thundered. "All in due time! At the present, however, we must focus our energies on overthrowing these bourgeois exploiters of the Sino peasantry! Let us obarmate ourselves accordingly! After we have taken the Western world, then we will work on the issues of everyone's orgasms! Now, quit speaking as a rawgabbit, my dear minx, and get to it!"

"That's the revolutionary spirit that I was hoping to see!" Myrna said, pounding her fist on Ignatius's desk.

"Do be careful," Ignatius said. "You almost caused my glass of pencils to fall to the floor."

"I've got to get back to the line," Myrna said. "I need to show the workers that they are being unfairly exploited."

"Please close the door when you leave," Ignatius said.

She did, and Ignatius sighed. He felt thankful that Mrs. Minkoff had purchased the items that he was going to need for his project, namely, that of converting the citizenry of the United States, and then the citizenry of the remainder of the world, to proper theology and geometry.

And then he remembered the palimpsest. He opened a desk drawer and removed the parchment, which was ornamented in a delicate script. A very ornate fleur-de-lis acted as the first letter of the first line of the script, which was in Latin.

And he smiled. If the lines of script were iambic pentameter—and Ignatius believed that they were—this could be the very thing that he needed to bring about his revolution. He would save his nation, see a good, authoritarian king installed as rightful heir and ruler of the New World, and prove that proper theology and geometry were the true means of salvation.

And, of course, while doing these things, he would undo Myrna Minkoff.

Ignatius shoved aside legal pads and empty Chinese food containers and placed the palimpsest in the center of his desk.

It was time to begin translating.

IV

Magoohan stood erect in Sergeant Dumbrowski's office. Magoohan had donned a new outfit, that of a homosexual Barbary Coast pirate. Magoohan's costume came replete with a hot pink hat (cocked according to Sergeant Dumbrowski's specifications), a hot pink coat, a hot pink waistcoat, a cream-colored cravat (Sergeant Dumbrowski believed in variety, after all), hot pink breeches, cream-colored stockings (after all, something had to match the cream-colored cravat), and leather shoes painted a hot pink. Hot pink spatterdashes around Magoohan's calves and a hot pink spadroon at his side completed the getup.

But Magoohan found these things, oddly enough, tolerable. What was intolerable was the powder-white, bifurcated peruke that Sergeant Dumbrowski insisted that Magoohan wear, the peruke a hairpiece that the sergeant had doused liberally with anti-itch powder for jockstraps. ("On account we need to keep things authentic-like," Sergeant Dumbrowski had said.)

The two cops who had erroneously arrested Magoohan had blackened-and-blued Magoohan's eyes, loosened one of his incisors, and cracked three of his ribs. Even though Magoohan had been discharged from the hospital the previous day with a prescription for very potent painkillers, the beat cop still felt as though the Chinese army had spent an entire day marching over him.

Magoohan squirmed. He wondered if he was going to get another ass-reaming from Sergeant Dumbrowski. You could never tell with that Polack. He could be nice and smiling one minute—chatting with you about the Yankees, his favorite sports team—and then he could turn on you like an enraged alligator.

Sergeant Dumbrowski's office, through which ran several pipes near the ceiling, felt too hot, almost like a sticky, late August day. The sergeant, who had eusuchian features, particularly his eyes and his malevolent smile, closed the police report that the two cops had filed and shook his head once again. Sergeant Dumbrowski reeked of Old Spice, to which Magoohan was allergic.

"No wonder Scarletti wanted ya outta Baddery Pahk," Sergeant Dumbrowski said. "You are the stupidest, most friggin' incompetent asswipe who's evuh walked a beat in this precinct. You sure you ain't Polish, Magoohan?"

"No, sir," Magoohan answered sadly, unsure how to answer.

"Ya ask me, I'd say you was, even though that would be an insult to my people," Sergeant Dumbrowski said with a malevolent smile. "Only an idiot like you would get worked over by two of his own. Only an idiot like you would lose his badge. And only an idiot like you would let that suspicious queer get away."

"Yes, sir."

"Did I asks you to speak, Magoohan?"

"No, sir."

"Then shut your goddamn trap," Sergeant Dumbrowski said. "Now, how do you like your new uniform? You think you can find that suspicious queer for me now?"

Magoohan didn't answer.

"Goddamn, I just asked you a question!" Sergeant Dumbrowski hollered. "Ain't you gonna answer!"

"I didn't think you was wanting me to speak," Magoohan said.

"Well, I am now, you dumb mick. Now, you gonna find that suspicious queer or not, Magoohan? I'm losing my patience wid youse. The entire goddamn precinct is losing patience wid youse. I bet you even God is losing patience wid youse."

"I'm gonna get that queer, Sergeant Dumbrowski," Magoohan replied, and he felt unsteady in his hot pink pirate shoes, and the peruke that he was wearing was causing beads of anti-itch-powder-for-jockstraps-infused sweat to roll down into his eyes.

"You betta see to that!" Sergeant Dumbrowski said, jabbing a scaly finger at Magoohan. "And I goddamn mean it! Unastan!"

"Yes, sir, I unastan."

Sergeant Dumbrowski sighed. "Did I asks ya to speak, Magoohan?"

Magoohan pointed a trembling finger at his mouth, indicating that he didn't know how to answer the sergeant.

"Get the hell outta heh," Sergeant Dumbrowski said, waving a scaly hand at Magoohan. "I don't want to see ya ugly mug until you bring in that queer, unastan? And don't say a goddamn word. Just do it. And I don't kerr how long it takes ya. Just don't come back until you bring in that queer."

V

A morbidly obese waitress (Mrs. Reilly guessed that the waitress must have had an eighty-or-so-inch waist) waddled over with plates of food, and before Mr. Robichaux even tasted his mashed potatoes, he salted them heavily.

"Mr. Reilly used to say that was a sign of a fool," Mrs. Reilly said, picking up a fork and digging into her coleslaw, which most people ate after the main course—in her case, a small steak cooked rare—but Mrs. Reilly liked to eat her coleslaw first.

"I don't know what you mean," Mr. Robichaux said, eating a mouthful of potatoes that were overly salted. He grimaced and forced himself to swallow.

"Just that," Mrs. Reilly said. "You put too much salt on them potatoes, didn't you? Mr. Reilly, why, when he ate mashed potatoes, he tasted them first before salting them." She looked out the restaurant's plate glass window that ran the length of the building. A light snow was falling in North Carolina, and, for a brief moment, she thought about Christmas. She felt like crying but decided that she had to be strong. She continued with her chiding of Mr. Robichaux: "You just eating them potatoes to prove your point, ain't you, Claude?"

"I like salt," Mr. Robichaux said, and now he felt more defensive than he had ever felt with Mrs. Reilly. Was this the way she was going to be when they were married? What happened to the sweet little woman with the maroon hair, the woman wearing the bowling shoes? Perhaps it was just her concern for her boy that was causing her to act this way. "The saltier the better. They say salt's good for the blood."

"Who's they?"

"Doctors and such," Mr. Robichaux said. "Those kind of folk."

"I wonder if they serve muscatel here," Mrs. Reilly said. "I hadn't had me a good shot of muscatel in the two days we been traveling."

"I'll find out, Irene."

Mr. Robichaux motioned at the morbidly obese waitress, whose milk-gallon-sized breasts threatened to spill out of her top. Mr. Robichaux asked what kind of alcohol they served, and the woman shook her head, saying that the county was dry, but if they went to the next county, they could get whatever they wanted to drink. Mr. Robichaux thanked her, and the waitress waddled off.

"Figures," Mrs. Reilly said. "I need me a shot of muscatel, and I can't even get that."

"Next stop, I'll get you a beer. How does that sound, Irene?"

"If I can't get me any muscatel, beer will have to do, I guess."

They ate in silence, and after Mrs. Reilly finished her meal, she belched softly and covered her mouth with her small fist. The snow was falling harder now, and she wondered how much longer it would be before she and Mr. Robichaux reached New York City. They were supposed to have been there that afternoon, but because of snowstorms in Tennessee, their bus was behind schedule.

"Are the Jews communiss?" Mrs. Reilly asked Mr. Robichaux out of the blue.

He blinked. "Lots of 'em are, Irene, but I don't think all of 'em are. Why?"

"Myrna's momma said that Ignatius done become a Jew," Mrs. Reilly said, shaking her head. "It wasn't enough he had to become a revolutionary and almost destroy Mr. Levy's pants factory. It wasn't enough that he had to dress up like a Mardi Gras and go out and get attacked by a bird at the Night of Joy. Now he's a Jew, a wandering Jew, and he's causing trouble again."

"You shoulda had that boy in the Boy Scouts," Mr. Robichaux said. "They keep a boy from turning into a communiss, let me tell you."

"Ignatius is too old for the Boy Scouts."

"I know, Irene. I was just speaking about the past. If he had belonged in the past, maybe he wouldna become a Jew communiss."

"I didn't say he was a communiss," Mrs. Reilly said, irritated. "I said I think Ignatius become a Jew." She thought about it for a moment and then smiled. "And now I think I understand why."

"Why, Irene?"

"Why else, Claude? Ignatius is going to marry Myrna. He's going to settle down and raise hisself some children. You know, maybe Ignatius's running off was the best thing that happened."

"Well, if it was, why don't we head back to New Orleans?" Mr. Robichaux asked, blinking. "My arthur-i-tis don't like this cold weather."

"We have to get us to New York City to make sure." Mrs. Reilly wanted a glass of muscatel very desperately. "I need to make sure that my boy is fine. If he is, why, he can stay in New York City and marry Myrna and have a good life if he wants to. Of course, if it was up to me, I'd have him come back to New Orleans. He and Myrna could live in his old room before they went out and found themselves a good home."

"I got plenty in the Ninth Ward," Mr. Robichaux said enthusiastically. "Good for a young couple like Ignatius and his wife to start a family in."

"You think you could cut Ignatius a deal?" Mrs. Reilly asked.

"What do you mean?"

"Lower the rent, what do you think I mean?" She sighed. "Ignatius don't make himself a lot of money. If he and Myrna come back, why, they'll have to start from what little they have."

"There ain't too many Jews in New Orleans, though. And from what I heard, they can't drive to church. They have to walk."

"Ignatius needs to walk. He needs to lose weight. And I don't think they call it church."

"What do they call it, Irene?"

"School, I think," Mrs. Reilly replied. "At least it sounds like school. Stool, I think. Something like that."

"But they suppose to live close to the Jew church, or whatever it is, ain't they?" Mr. Robichaux asked. "And they don't like to walk too far, from what I heard."

Mrs. Reilly frowned. "You know, I never heard Myrna once talk about going to any Jewish stool. I bet Ignatius is just pretending to be a Jew so that her folks is happy. That's probably the case."

Mr. Robichaux reached across the table and put his weathered hand on Mrs. Reilly's hand. She quickly whipped her hand away. Mr. Robichaux felt hurt.

"I thought you was my sweetie, Irene."

"Your hand is as cold as the devil himself," Mrs. Reilly answered, shuddering. "I need me a glass of muscatel. It figures that this place would be dry."

Mr. Robichaux frowned. Was she, by chance, a secret communist? Was she luring him to New York City so that the communists could do him in?

"When I find my boy, I'm gonna bring him back home where he belongs, if he ain't gonna marry Myrna," Mrs. Reilly said tearfully. "Santa ain't going to like it, and you probably ain't going to like it either, Claude. But if you want to marry me, really marry me, you're going to have to accept Ignatius as he is."

"Sure thing, Irene," Mr. Robichaux said, and he sipped his coffee and yawned. This bus trip was wearing him out. He hoped that it would soon be over.

"I think I'm going to have me some cherry pie," Mrs. Reilly said. She looked around for the waitress. "Now, where is that gargy-gantuan woman?"

Seven

Miss Ping knocked on Ignatius's office door. Ignatius, who was doodling images of medieval musicians on a legal pad upon which he had been translating the palimpsest (of the two hundred or so lines, he had managed to translate only three), was thankful that Myrna had taken the day off so that she could attend her group therapy group. He bade Miss Ping to enter.

"More-uh tea for ah-you, Mr. Lei-ly," she said, carrying a tray on which sat a teapot, from whose spout wisps of steam curled into the air.

"You were supposed to have had that here ten minutes ago," Ignatius said when she placed the tray atop his desk. "I need you to call me a cab, Miss Ping. I have urgent business."

"Business-uh?" Miss Ping said, her eyes crossing. "Cab-uh?"

"Yes, call me a cab, Miss Ping. I have urgent business with a very important client of the Charlie Chan Chinese Fortune Cookie Company."

"Call-er you-uh a cab-uh?" a puzzled Miss Ping asked.

"Yes, call me a cab, Miss Ping," Ignatius said impatiently. "How many times do I have to ask you?"

"You are-uh a cab-uh, Mr. Lei-ly." She blushed, cupped her hands to her mouth, and laughed her phocine laugh. "I think-er I make-er another-uh joke-er. Many-er people uh-tell me I should-er go on-uh stage. They-uh say I am-er the new-er Lenny-uh Bluce."

"Never mind," Ignatius said, picking up a telephone receiver. "I'll take care of this myself. You can leave now, Miss Ping."

Giggling like a schoolgirl, Miss Ping exited the office, closing the office door gently behind her.

Five minutes later, Ignatius, who was waiting in the front office, heard the honk of a cab. Ignatius wrapped his muffler tighter around his neck and pulled his green hunting cap tight onto his head. When he stepped outside, an icy sheet of wind cut his face and caused his eyes to water.

"I wonder how Batman ever survived this Gotham nonsense," Ignatius said, slowly descending well-salted steps, holding on to a rail with a death grip because he was afraid that he might fall. "When I am finally out of this mess, I am going back to New Orleans, where it is at least safe and civilized."

The cab driver, a Greek, snapped gum and asked Ignatius where he wanted to go.

"Wherever they film that filth called *The Ed Sullivan Show*," Ignatius said. "I have an urgent business matter with Mr. Sullivan. Get me there quickly, but do not make unwarranted haste. I do not believe that my pyloric valve can take any additional strain this day."

"I don't unastan half what you sayin'," the Greek said, pulling the cab away from the curb and out onto the icy street. "You ask me, you crazy. Ed Sullivan, he ain't gonna see no bum like you."

"How dare you, you impertinent immigrant miscreant!" Ignatius bellowed. "I'll have you know, sirrah, that I am an executive with the Charlie Chan Chinese Fortune Cookie Company!"

"You?" The cab driver shook his head in derision. "You ain't no chink. And you ain't no executive."

"Oh, I'm not?" Ignatius said, removing one of his business cards (which came from Miss Ping by way of Mrs. Wang by way of Mr. Pong) from a coat pocket and handing the smudged card to the Greek, who took it. "Take a look at that, sirrah."

The driver snapped gum, looked at the card, and raised an eyebrow.

"Says you're a VP." The driver shrugged and stuck his hand out, offering Ignatius the card, which Ignatius snatched. "Sorry, mister. You look like a goddamn bum to me."

"I am not a bum."

"What business you got with Ed Sullivan?"

"Quite frankly, that is none of *your* business. Since we're being so nosy, tell me, sirrah, do you spend your free time peeping into the windows of unsuspecting women?"

The Greek shrugged. "Who the hell don't?"

Ignatius sighed. A child ran into the street, and the Greek braked, causing the cab to skid. Ignatius yelled and threw up his arms to shield himself. The Greek raised a middle finger at the child, cussed under his breath, and drove around the child. Soon the cab departed Chinatown, cut across several streets, and headed to Broadway.

Forty minutes after he had departed the Charlie Chan Chinese Fortune Cookie Company, Ignatius was standing in front of the Ed Sullivan Theater. He pounded loudly on a front door, and a wizened little man who was nearing his nineties, and who had a mop in hand, opened the door.

"Yeah?" the man said loudly, leaning his good ear, which had a large hearing aid in it, towards Ignatius.

"I'm here to see Mr. Sullivan," Ignatius said, shivering. "It's an urgent business matter."

"He ain't here." The old man turned his head and peered up at Ignatius. "What kinda business a bum like you got with Ed Sullivan?"

"That is the second time today that I have been accused of being a vagabond," Ignatius said impudently. "And I do not appreciate it. Now, can you treat your betters better, or I am going to have to see to it that they use the iron maiden on you, sirrah?"

"He ain't here."

"Obviously he's somewhere," Ignatius said. "Do you know where he is?"

"What?" the old man said, turning his good, near-deaf ear towards Ignatius.

"Do you know where Mr. Sullivan is!" Ignatius hollered.

"Lounge around da corner." The old man pointed, giving in because he wanted to get back to his mopping.

"Excellent," Ignatius said. "I thank you for your time, kind sir."

"Whatever, you goddamn bum. Now get outta here, and leave me alone."

The old man locked the door to the theater. Shivering, Ignatius hurried away.

At a corner he saw Gray's, a hot dog emporium, and he smelled his favorite smell, namely, the smell of freshly boiled hot dogs. His mouth watered because of the smell, and the smell reminded him of Mr. Clyde's foot-longs. Ignatius scurried across a street, almost getting hit by a cab, and entered the establishment, in which there was a standing-room-only crowd.

Steam encased the windows of the establishment, and businessmen eating hot dogs like gentlemen stood next to junkies eating hot dogs like wolves. Ignatius stood in a queue, which quickly dwindled as he neared the counter.

A bored order-taker scratched his oily, pimply nose and asked Ignatius what he would have. Ignatius scanned the menu.

"Come on, I ain't got all day," the order-taker said, snapping. "What're you waitin' for, mac? Christmas?"

"Just a moment," Ignatius said angrily. "Remember, I am the customer here."

"You won't be, you keep holdin' up the line, mac," the order-taker said. "We got more people comin' in. You either order or get to the back of the line."

"Two of your best hot dogs," Ignatius said, placing two quarters onto the counter.

"What two, mac? You gotta be more specific."

"Just give me two of your plain hot dogs, you buffoon," Ignatius answered haughtily. "As always, I must do everything."

The order-taker took Ignatius's quarters, barked out the order to frenzied men who slaved over overly heated bun bins that scorched the hand upon touch and who slaved over vats holding paramecia-like hot dogs, and motioned for Ignatius to step aside so that the next customer could approach the counter.

When Ignatius's order was ready, Ignatius greedily snatched the two hot dogs out of the order-taker's hands and scurried over to a counter where condiments were lined in a row. Ignatius doled out several heapings of sauerkraut and squirted several squirts of mustard onto his first hot dog.

He fed it lovingly into his maw, devouring the hot dog one lovely inch at a time. It was like taking in twelve inches of paradise all at once, Ignatius mused, vaguely remembering that line from somewhere. After he finished his first hot dog, he prepared his second hot dog in the same manner in which he had prepared his first, and he devoured his second hot dog as he had his first, one delightful inch at a time.

Ignatius was picking crumbs out of his mustache when he noticed that a neighboring man was watching and smiling.

"You find it amusing to watch others partake of their prandial pleasures?" Ignatius asked, eructating loudly, covering his mouth with a fist. "From where I originate, that is considered very rude. Of course, what could one expect in a place like Gotham?"

"You're out of this world," the man said, studying Ignatius. "You're like a character out of a picaresque novel."

"Oh? And what would someone like you know about books?"

"Because I'm an editor," the man said, and he handed Ignatius a business card, upon which stood out the embossed name B. I. GLOBETROTTER.

Ignatius placed the card into one of his coat pockets and eructated. Ed Sullivan was no longer on Ignatius's mind. Now Ignatius was intrigued by this man, B. I. Globetrotter. Perhaps this man could be of great use. After all, Ignatius mused, he had brought several manuscripts with him from New Orleans. An editor, if used strategically and cleverly, might be able to create a book about Ignatius's worldview, a real page-turner in an age lacking proper theology and geometry.

"You all right?" Globetrotter asked, cocking his head, peering at Ignatius. "You look a little green under the gills."

"It's my pyloric valve," Ignatius said. "Ever since I fled New Orleans, my valve's been acting up. Sometimes I wonder if I'm going to need surgery."

"Fled New Orleans? Why did you flee New Orleans?"

Ignatius introduced himself and proceeded to tell the man the entire story, from the Greyhound Scenicruiser that took him to Baton Rouge to the street in the French Quarter where the Wreck of the Plymouth occurred, from Levy Pants and the failed revolution there all the way to the debacle at the Night of Joy. When Ignatius mentioned Darlene's cockatoo, Globetrotter chortled.

"You're full of you know what," Globetrotter said, playfully punching Ignatius in the arm. "Who would ever believe such a story?"

"But it's true," Ignatius said. "These things actually happened. And subsequently, because of these things, I had to flee New Orleans. You see, my mother was going to put me into a charity insane asylum. In fact, these things are so true that no one would probably believe them unless they appeared in a novel."

Globetrotter laughed. He laughed so hard that his eyes watered, and he shook his head, his face crimsoning. Even though he covered his mouth with his hand, others in the hot dog emporium, including a disgruntled cop, were looking, wondering what in the hell was going on.

"That's insane," Globetrotter said, finally calming down. "I can't imagine someone's trying to take that story and make a novel out of it. Sure, the episodes would be hilarious, but ultimately there would be no point."

"What do you mean there would be no point?" Ignatius said, speaking in a stentorian basso profundo. "Of course there would be a point. That wonton Fortuna was having her way with me, spinning me through a vicious cycle."

"Is that the woman who wanted to retire and who kept falling asleep?"

"No, no," Ignatius said, shaking his head. "Even though you might see yourself as a learned man, you are not a learned man if you do not know who Fortuna is. Have you heard of *The Consolation of Philosophy?*"

"Just from what you told me during this conversation," Globetrotter answered. "Look, that's a funny-as-hell story. But the thing is, it wouldn't make a great novel."

"And why not, sir?" answered an indignant Ignatius.

"Because of the lack of character motivation," Globetrotter answered. "You see, fiction dictates that whenever we have what we call a novel, a short story, or a play, there's got to be something, a thing, that motivates the primary character—the protagonist, in other words—to achieve his goal.

"For instance, in *Moby Dick*, the goal is the destruction of the great white whale. In *Huckleberry Finn*, the goal is essentially the obtainment of freedom, as seen in the rescue of the runaway slave Jim."

"But my story has plenty of action," Ignatius said in protest. "Why can't you, of all people, see that?"

"But it's not true action, at least not in the fictional sense," Globetrotter replied. "You see, instead of acting and attempting to reach your overall goal, you reacted to each situation, often mindlessly, it seems, without putting any due thought or due consideration into your words or actions. For instance, did you honestly believe that you were going to overthrow the management at Levy Pants? Weren't you aware that you if committed acts of violence against anyone, you probably would have ended up on felony charges?"

"But Myrna—"

"Right, right, Myrna Minkoff. Always trying to outdo her because she somehow upsets that oh-so-pure, oh-so-sensitive worldview of yours. Even that motivation is completely lacking. I doubt few, if any people, would have gone to the extremes that you did, Mr. Reilly, in attempting to impress a young Jewish vixen." Globetrotter coughed and covered his mouth with a silk handkerchief. "Where was your critical thinking? Where was your proprioception? Why didn't you analyze the situation closely, Mr. Reilly, and figure out what it was that you needed to do? And why didn't you struggle against the odds? Had you failed, well, perhaps, your story would be more along the lines of a tragedy as opposed to a comedy, which is very difficult to write. On the other hand, your adventures would probably win you a Pulitzer Prize, given the absurdity of our universe." He paused, giving his next point very serious consideration. "But I can think of something far more unbelievable than your adventures, Mr. Reilly."

"Oh, and what would that be?" Ignatius asked contemptuously.

"Someone's writing a parody of the events that *might* occur subsequent to your New Orleans adventures." The editor shuddered. "Mind you, just merely writing about subsequent events would mean that the new work was a sequel. But to write about events that *might* occur subsequent to your New Orleans adventures—and to use these new events to parody your New Orleans adventures—would therefore mean that the new work was a parody. I couldn't imagine anything more dreadful, though. Actually, there is. The potentially heated or negative responses to such a parody, especially in the legal realm, in which there would be no genuine case against the author for a number of reasons that a well-written foreword to the parody would enumerate. Ah, the potentially heated responses and negative reviews! Those I would find quite puzzling."

"You jackanapes," Ignatius said, jabbing a meaty finger at the book editor. "Do you know who I am?"

"To me and to everyone else, you look like a slob who gets himself into hilarious messes," Globetrotter said. "Am I supposed to see something else?"

Ignatius removed one of his business cards from a coat pocket and handed the card to Globetrotter, who studied the card.

"A VP at a fortune cookie company? Is this another one of your ploys, Mr. Reilly?"

"I do not have any 'ploys,' Globetrotter, and yes, I am vice president of a very prestigious fortune cookie company in the heart of what is colloquially known as Chinatown," Ignatius said imperiously. "A Mr. Pong hired me because he sees me as the new Confucius, something, according to Mr. Pong, that is much needed. And I heartily agree. We live in a decadent age, Globetrotter, one lacking proper theology and geometry. My life's mission is to impart the proper worldview unto our age and to rescue our age from the errors of the Renaissance and the Enlightenment."

"You can't be serious," Globetrotter said, absentmindedly putting Ignatius's business card into a coat pocket.

"I am very serious indeed, sirrah," Ignatius replied. "I am crafting fortune cookies that are, at this very moment, being disseminated around the world. Why, at this very moment, I'm sure that some Mancunian housewife and her proletarian husband are eating Chinese takeout as a way to celebrate one of their anniversaries. And I am sure, at this very moment, that one of them is reading one of the fortunes that I composed.

"And I am sure that my fortunes are being read in Poughkeepsie, and in Topeka, and in Denver, and in Salt Lake City, and in Los Angeles, and in San Diego, and in San Francisco, and in Portland, and in Seattle, and in Miami, and in Little Rock, and in my beloved New Orleans. My gospel of proper theology and geometry is spreading, Globetrotter. Oh, I'm sure that you have quite a few bestsellers in your stable of writers. And I am sure that these bestsellers are making you and your *haute bourgeoisie* publishing firm ample amounts of money. Nonetheless, you are not speaking the truth. At least I am."

Globetrotter raised his finger and was about to speak when Ignatius raised his paw, interrupting the editor. "It is not the bestsellers of our age, sirrah, that affect the necessary change that society needs. Are you aware of that horrid bestselling author Octave Thanet? That was the pseudonym of Alice French, a poseur. Thanet outsold Dickens several times over, but, nonetheless, it was Dickens who had the day.

"Likewise, sirrah, with me. My movement is slow at this time, like a turtle poking its head out of its shell. But mind you, in due time, my movement is going to become free and slip through the crack and touch and influence each and every thing that comes into its path, from the highest of society's highs to the lowest of society's lows. Mark my words, sirrah. I have not yet begun to fight."

Ignatius eructated, covering his mouth with a fist. Nick the Nose bumped into Ignatius, who scowled at the diminutive man. Nick the Nose feigned a smile and helped himself to his hot dog.

"All the best to you," the editor said, donning his fedora. "If you ever decide to write your memoirs, please contact me. I'm not promising that I'll publish them, but perhaps we can work on them together. And, at the least, I could provide you encouragement of some sort." He tipped his hat. "A fond adieu, Mr. Reilly. It's been a great pleasure to meet you, and yet, it feels as if I've known you for quite some time."

Globetrotter offered his hand to Ignatius. Ignatius didn't want to shake it but went ahead and did so anyway. The editor's handshake felt very strong, causing Ignatius to wince and grunt. Globetrotter released his grip, tipped his fedora, and turned and disappeared into the noonday crowd that had flooded Gray's.

Nick the Nose slapped Ignatius's bicep with the back of a grimy hand.

"What?" Ignatius growled.

"How about passing me the mustud, buddy?"

Ignatius picked up the mustard bottle and thrust it at the diminutive man, who doused his foot-long hot dog with the yellow liquid.

"Amazing stuff," Nick the Nose said, sniffling and wiping his nose with a sleeve of his seedy topcoat. "We met before?"

"I think not," said Ignatius, nonetheless sensing that he had seen the small man somewhere. "I do not care to have any further discourse with someone like you. You remind me of a shrimp of an undercover detective in New Orleans, a cretin whose aunt was far worse than her moronic nephew." Ignatius pushed his way through the crowd. "Part the way. I have an urgent meeting with Ed Sullivan."

The operative wiped a window with a sleeve of his seedy topcoat and watched the heavyset, bundled man trudge his way to Broadway. The man made a lonely, buffoon-like figure. For some reason, perhaps because he was so tired, Nick the Nose wanted to cry.

"I need ta gid hobe," Henley said, hot dog in hand, huffing, methamphetamine flowing through his veins and arteries to keep him going. "I need to ged bad to my boodiful wibe."

"I don't unastan a word yer sayin'. We godda eat, so you bedda eat, Ids."

"Ids nod Ids. Ids Henley."

Nick the Nose shrugged and took a bite of his hot dog.

II

Mrs. Minkoff combed Grandmother Horowitz's hair in Grandmother Horowitz's bedroom. Soundly asleep, Grandmother Horowitz was sitting in a chair. Myrna sat down on the edge of Grandmother Horowitz's bed and watched her mother comb the grandmother's once-all-black-but-now-quite-white hair.

"Guess what she told me today," Mrs. Minkoff, who was standing behind the chair, said to Myrna.

"That she wants her own place?"

"Close," Mrs. Minkoff said, and she turned Grandmother Horowitz's head to the side. The old woman snored lightly and smacked her lips. "She says that she wants a man."

"Good for her," Myrna said. "I think she should have one. After all, she's a woman, and she has her sexual needs."

"It's a specific man, Myrna."

"Did she grab Dad's crotch again?"

"No, nothing like that," Mrs. Minkoff said, disappointed, wishing that it had been that. "She's chasing after Ivan."

"You mean Ignatius."

"Who?"

"Ignatius, our guest, Mom!"

"And I've been calling him Ivan all this time?" Mrs. Minkoff's eyes crossed in bewilderment. "Why didn't he say anything?"

"He has been," Myrna answered, lying on the bed, whose sheets Mrs. Minkoff had changed earlier that day. The bed smelled like an aromatic Turkish bath bathed in indigos and silvers, foreboding, yet inviting and hospitable. "And I've been telling you over and over again, it's not Ivan or Isaiah or Ichabod, it's Ignatius."

"That doesn't sound like a Jewish name, Myrna. That's the kind of name a Catholic boy would have."

"That's because Ignatius was raised a Catholic," Myrna said, "in a horrible, sexually repressive environment. If I hadn't rescued him when I did, what would have become of him? His hysterical mother and her Nazi boyfriend would have put Ignatius into a Gestapo holding cell."

Mrs. Minkoff tsk-tsked. "And she sounded so nice."

"Who sounded so nice?" Myrna frowned, not liking what she hearing.

"Nothing," Mrs. Minkoff said, suddenly realizing her mistake and knowing that she could never undo it. "I was thinking of Mrs. Berenstein."

"What does she have to do with Ignatius?" Myrna stood. "You weren't thinking of Mrs. Berenstein. You spoke with Mrs. Reilly, didn't you? You called her house in New Orleans and told her where Ignatius was, didn't you?"

"I didn't call Ivan's mother, Myrna."

"You snitched on Ignatius, didn't you, Mom?"

"It wasn't like that, Myrna," Myrna's mother replied. Grandmother Horowitz snorted and then farted softly. Mrs. Minkoff made a face. "She called here."

"How did she get the number?"

"I don't know how Mrs. Feinstein got the number. You'd have to ask her."

"Who's Mrs. Feinstein? I've never heard of her, Mom."

"Ivan's mother, who else?"

"It's Ignatius, and his last name isn't Feinstein," Myrna said, and now she was beginning to understand why her father had been so frustrated all those years. "His last name's Reilly. And Mrs. Reilly, his mother, is on her way up here, isn't she?"

"You mustn't tell Ivan," Mrs. Minkoff replied, rueful. "She misses her boy. She wants the best for him. She wants him to be the best rabbi that he can possibly be."

"Mrs. Reilly told you that?"

"I think she did." Mrs. Minkoff stopped her combing of Grandmother Horowitz's hair and looked up at the ceiling. "She said something about his doing good up here."

"I don't believe a word of that, Mom," Myrna said. "You know, for a while, I thought you had changed. I thought you were no longer like Dad and that you had broken out of your repressive shell. But the more I see you, the more I see that you are really nothing more than a bourgeois hack."

"I'm afraid I don't know what that is, Myrna."

"It means, Mother dearest, that you are an average house-wife with a lower-than-average intelligence who spends her days living a lower-than-average existence while the whole world is out there, waiting to be saved." Myrna, unconsciously, had crossed her arms. "You live on behalf of a man who has little or no use for women. Don't you remember what I read to you from Betty Friedan? Didn't any of those words sink into your skull?"

Mrs. Minkoff chuckled. "Of course I remember what you read to me. It was lovely poetry."

"Betty Friedan is not a poet!" Myrna screamed. "She is a feminist! Like me, she is doing her best to free the women and men of this world from the phallic patriarchy that is attempting to destroy us all!"

Grandmother Horowitz shuddered awake.

"Someone say something about a schlong?" the elderly woman asked. "I was dreaming about a schlong, I think. At first I thought it was a Hebrew National hot dog, but then I saw that it was attached to Mr. Klein, who used to own the photo lab near Yonkers." She blinked. "He had quite a schlong!"

"Mother!" Mrs. Minkoff said. "How many times I have asked you not to speak about those things?"

"See!" Myrna said, thrusting an accusing finger at her mother. "Your bourgeois pretensions are showing themselves once again. At least Grandmother Horowitz wants to talk about something real."

"Oh, it was real, all right," Grandmother Horowitz said, cackling. "You never felt something as real as that schlong."

"Mother!" Mrs. Minkoff said.

"See," Myrna said, "you're acting like a bourgeois housewife with middle-class moral conventions. In plenty of African tribes, sex is openly discussed among members of the tribe, even among family members. What do you think about that?"

"I don't know what to think," Mrs. Minkoff said, nearly on the verge of tears. "This is all so confusing. Mother acts up, and so do you. And Bernard has been acting stranger and stranger each day. He doesn't even watch Walter Cronkite anymore but goes to his study and stares at the wall or watches Laurel and Hardy." Now Mrs. Minkoff was crying. "Are you satisfied now, Myrna? How could you? How could you do this to your own mother?"

"You are not going to put a guilt trip on me," Myrna said, and now Grandmother Horowitz was lying on her stomach on the bed, hand underneath her. "I am breaking this chain of this Jewish guilt trip. Your mother may have done that to you—"

"Whatever she does, she does to herself—"

"But I am not going to live that way, Mom." Myrna felt as if she were speaking in front of the NAACP a year before, when she had declared that she was no longer an overly privileged white Jewess but a proud Negress and that she was going to fight for the rights of all Negroes, for which she received a pelting of raisins. "I am going to be a part of this world, the real world, and that real world is populated with sex. I see that you're cringing when I use that word. Sex! Sex! Sex! What do you think of that, Mom!"

"I can't believe that you treat your own mother this way," Mrs. Minkoff said, sitting down in a plush chair and blowing her nose into a tissue that she took from a box on a nightstand. "Ivan doesn't treat his mother this way, and he's a convert who's an outstanding Orthodox rabbi. Does Ivan know that you talk about such things, Myrna? Does he?"

"It's Ignatius, not Ivan," Myrna said. "And he was raised a Catholic."

"That's what makes it even more meaningful," Mrs. Minkoff said, wiping away the tears. "Ivan converted from his native faith to ours. As God says, 'Thou shalt love the convert.'"

"You are impossible, Mom!"

Myrna stormed out of the room. Grandmother Horowitz groaned in pleasure, and Mrs. Minkoff ruefully shook her head.

Mrs. Minkoff knew that she needed to speak to Ivan. He would know what to do. He would have the answers. After all, he was a rabbi, wasn't he?

III

Grenadine sighed, shook his head, and slapped his forehead.

"This is not working," the owner of the Stone Carver Inn said. "You are not keeping up with the beat, girls. You are not working as a team, girls. You are not showing the requisite enthusiasm that our queens require, girls. Frank, please stop the record. Frank, please stop the goddamn record now!"

A very harried and much wearied Frank removed a stylus that was following a groove on a vinyl disc. El Lobo Macho, Guapo, and Chico, who were dressed in Carmen Miranda-like drag, were standing onstage, wobbling unsteadily in very high heels. El Lobo Macho, who was in the middle, scowled at Grenadine.

"Don't you give me that look, sister," Grenadine said, walking away from the table at which he had been sitting and wagging a long thin finger at the gang leader. "We've been over this before. You three are not rehearsing as hard as you should be."

"We here every day, *puto*," El Lobo Macho said. "And you say we not practicing?"

"I meant the practice that you should be doing *after* you leave the Stone Carver Inn," Grenadine said, and he bit one of his green fingernails, trying his best not to throw a hissy fit. He had already thrown two hissy fits that day, and a psychologist had told him that it was probably better if he, Grenadine, had no more than three hissy fits a day. If he, Grenadine, were going to have a hissy fit, he was going to have it over something more drastic, like, say, the destruction of his establishment. "Why aren't you practicing at night as you've been instructed? Why aren't you getting used to those high heels?"

"You think we can walk around like this without getting our throats cut, man?" Guapo asked condescendingly. "Man, we go around in our neighborhood dressed like this, they gonna kill us, man."

Giacomo stood next to Grenadine. "He's right, boss," said the janitor, who was wearing the Wayfarer sunglasses and who reeked of freshly smoked marijuana. "They go out dressed like that, they gonna get whacked."

"Then just take your cornucopias, dresses, and high heels with you in suitcases," Grenadine replied, shaking his head because he had to explain the simplest of things to the simplest of minds. "Choose a place where you can rehearse in private and then practice, practice, practice until you have it all down."

"That song must go," El Lobo Macho said.

"What's wrong with 'Guantanamera'?" Grenadine asked defensively. "After all, it's a lovely Latin folksong made popular by

Pete Seeger and other folksingers. Me, I think it's the right opening song, not too fast, not too slow. The song allows us to build up the tension to something more lively."

"Is not a Puerto Rican song," El Lobo Macho said. "Is a Cuban song. And Cubans not the same as Puerto Ricans. We better than Cubans."

"I'm sure that they say that they're better than you."

"We not communists," El Lobo Macho said, his face crimsoning.

"Yeah, we are not communists," Chico said.

El Lobo Macho shoved Chico, who tottered in his high heels. "I just say that, *maricón*," the gang leader said testily.

"My apologies," Chico said, adjusting a yellow bra strap.

"Girls, now is not the time for bickering," Grenadine said, holding out his hands imploringly. "Our debut is Sunday evening. We must get this show on the road."

"I thought the show was gonna be here, boss," Giacomo said. "That being the case, how about I bring in Miss Maggie and my congas and show you what I can do?"

"Get back to dry-mopping," Grenadine replied testily to Giacomo. To the others Grenadine said: "I was speaking metaphorically, of course. Obviously, we're not going on the road—at least not yet. But if this act becomes a smash, we'll do as many queer cabarets as we can around the country. Before you know it, there will be a chain of Stone Carver Inns across the nation."

Giacomo frowned and started to dry-mop the floor. "You have to see my act to believe it, boss. There ain't nothing like it on the face of this earth."

"Your act would probably symbolize the collapse of my establishment," Grenadine said. "And I'm not fond of snakes, unless they're tucked away in the crotch of a pair of nice tight pants." Grenadine cleared his throat. "Now, girls, let's take it from the top. Remember, girls, it's rhythm, rhythm, rhythm! Maestro, the recording, please."

Frank, who had been deftly drying freshly washed beer mugs, tossed a damp bar towel aside, wiped his hands on his black pants, and turned on the record player. He placed the stylus onto the record, and on the speakers there came a loud hiss and then the opening lines of a tinny Japanese-issued rendition of "Guantanamera." El Lobo Macho took his place in the middle of the three men, who wrapped their arms around each other's shoulders and swayed with the music.

"Better, much better," said Grenadine, who returned to his table and lit a long thin cigarette. "That's the spirit, girls."

Then the male singer sang the opening lines of the song, and the three Puerto Ricans unwrapped their arms from around each other and made hula-like movements with their arms and hips. Unfortunately, El Lobo Macho, who was still unsteady on his ruby-colored high heels, tripped when he was accidentally bumped by Guapo. Cussing in Spanish, the gang leader fell onto Chico, who yelped as the two collapsed onto the stage, followed by Guapo.

"Horrid, horrid, horrid!" Grenadine squealed, jumping up and down and stamping his feet, allowing himself to throw his third hissy fit for the day. "How many times I have told you girls to watch your spacing! Spacing, spacing, spacing! It's all about spacing!"

"I thought you said it was all about rhythm, boss," Giacomo said, nearing Grenadine. "If it's about rhythm, you should hear my congas."

"You know where you can stick your congas!" Grenadine aspirated angrily. "Now get back to dry-mopping!" Grenadine clapped his hands. "Girls, Frank, from the top!"

· Eight

Desiring a change of pace that morning and dejected that he had not found Ed Sullivan, and hoping that he might, perchance, meet kindred spirits who would help him implement his grand, magnificent plan, Ignatius took a cab to Greenwich Village. There he picked up a copy of that day's edition of the *New York Times* from a blind newspaper vendor redolent of a recently smoked cigar.

The air tasted metallically bitter and bitterly cold, and Ignatius, who was not getting acclimated to the New York City winter, felt a tear forming at a corner of his eye. He missed New Orleans, a city that had an aura unlike any other city, a city that easily could have been placed on an island in the Caribbean. He missed his miserable mother, who probably that very moment was sitting at the oilcloth-covered kitchen table and drinking bottles of muscatel and mooning over that miserable Claude *roué*. Ignatius missed his old bedroom, whose odor was that of used tea bags and whose floor was littered with his Big Chief tablets. He missed the mighty Mississippi, and he missed Constantinople Street. He even missed his next-door neighbor Miss Annie, that hateful harridan.

Ignatius sighed and told himself that he wasn't crying; indeed, the tear had formed because of the biting cold air. He shuddered. How savage Gotham could be. Rather, how savage Gotham *was*.

Tucking the newspaper under his arm, he lumbered down pavement, which had been heavily salted to prevent anyone's slipping. People moved about the street, a few people tossing bags of garbage into garbage bins so overloaded that they looked as if they might explode. Overhead, a loud jet made its descent. A woman at a corner waved at a cab, which sped past her, and the woman raised her middle finger and muttered what the cab driver could do with it. A billboard screamed BOWERY BREW BEATS ALL!

Ignatius sniffed, and a newly arrived scent tickled his nostrils: a pleasing combination of freshly peeled oranges and baked bread and brewing coffee. Ignatius salivated, and, turning a corner, happened upon the New Dominican Bakery, the front window of which displayed breads, donuts, pies, turnovers, and phalerate cakes, some of the cakes for birthdays, some for anniversaries, some for the upcoming Christmas celebration. Behind the counter a barista dispensed coffee and donuts to gray, winter-worn people, who sniffled and coughed while numerous bakers toiled at stainless steel tables as the bakers massaged, slapped, and pinched mountains and hills and heaps of gray dough.

Ignatius grubbled in his pants pocket and scooped out a handful of change that he had pilfered from a drawer in Miss Ping's desk. His paw held a half dollar, several quarters, plenty of dimes, a few nickels, and three pennies. Ah, yes, he had more than enough for a hearty breakfast before he began his morning's onerous work—namely, reviewing the ad that he had placed in the *New York Times*.

Ignatius entered the bakery, and a pleasant heat, similar to what he had had in his old bedroom, enveloped him. He smiled, closed the door and, loose change in his ursine paw, trudged towards the counter and waved the rolled-up newspaper to grab the barista's attention.

"Your best tea, preferably an orange pekoe, my dear woman," Ignatius said magnanimously to the barista, whose aubergine beehive hairdo and forest-green eye shadow contrasted sharply and obnoxiously one against the other. Instead of focusing on her lack of proper theology and geometry, however, Ignatius's eyes fixed themselves on a gleaming glass case in front of him, a case that displayed the bakery's finest wares, all fresh from having been created that very morning. "And a baker's dozen of those very large sugar donuts, my dear woman."

The woman snapped gum. "A goddamn baker's what?"

"Why, don't you know what a baker's dozen is?" Ignatius asked, dumbfounded. "In times of yore, my dear woman, bakers would add an extra donut so that the king would always be ensured of having at least twelve donuts, should the baker have made an error in his arithmetic. Otherwise, the king, in his rage, might cut off the baker's head."

And with that, Ignatius made a slicing motion with his rolled-up copy of the *New York Times*, causing the startled barista to jump back.

"Goddamn, watch that!" the barista said brassily, eyes wide in shock and indignation. "You almost hit me with that goddamn thing!"

"There some sort of problem, Velma?" asked one of the bakers, a bald man whose graying face had deep furrows and who had stopped pinching and poking and prodding the gray lump of dough in front of him. "This guy busting your chops or somethin'? He is, I'll bust his goddamn chops or somethin'."

"No one need bust anything," Ignatius replied royally. "I was merely emphasizing a point, my kind sir and my dear woman. To reiterate my order: I will have a large orange pekoe tea, along with thirteen of those very fine, and very large, sugar donuts."

"I can charge you the regular goddamn price for the goddamn dozen," the barista said, snapping gum, "but you're going to have to pay for the thirteenth goddamn donut like it was a goddamn single. You want a goddamn slice of goddamn lemon with that goddamn hot tea?"

"Most indubitably," Ignatius replied.

"Goddamn, does that mean yes or no?" the barista asked, getting impatient with what she considered to be a fat slob jerk jerking her around.

"It means a most certain and hearty yes," Ignatius said, impatient with what he considered to be an uneducated virago.

The woman told him the goddamn amount, Ignatius counted out the goddamn change and gave her a goddamn nickel for a goddamn tip, and the woman poured goddamn boiling water into a goddamn large black mug, into which she dropped a goddamn orange pekoe tea bag and a goddamn slice of goddamn lemon. After she gathered the goddamn thirteen donuts and goddamn handed them to Ignatius, she goddamn motioned him aside so that she could help the next goddamn customer.

Ignatius surveyed tables, half of which were full, and noticed an amused man. The man, unlike Ignatius, was dressed finely, in a suit becoming a student of, say, Columbia University. The man smiled at Ignatius, jotted in a notebook, and then closed the notebook. He motioned for Ignatius to have a seat at the table at which he, the man, was sitting.

Ignatius warily approached the table, and the man continued to smile.

"You seem most amused," Ignatius said to the man, "as if you had stumbled upon some creature from your past who was supplying you with vast amounts of humor."

"You can't be real," the man said in an accent that was smooth and soft, an accent that Ignatius recognized instantly.

"I am, indeed, very much real," Ignatius said, sitting down, and he took a bite of a sugar donut, which was as large as his ursine paw and almost as warm. Ignatius savored the taste of the sugary dough as he masticated it. If there were a heaven, it tasted like freshly baked sugar donuts. "One wonders if you, sir, are real."

"Very much so," the man said, and he cocked his head to his right, studying Ignatius. "You're from New Orleans, aren't you?"

"Just as you are," Ignatius said, having finished his second donut and starting on his third. "Perhaps you were attracted to me because you recognized within me a propinquity. It is not every day that one runs into a fellow expatriate from our beloved city."

"No, there aren't too many people from New Orleans who are here in New York City," the man said, beside whose elbow was a flier advertising an all-night dance at the Roseland Ballroom. "By the way, I'm Ken."

"Ken?" Ignatius sipped his hot orange pekoe tea. "Ken? That sounds like the name that one would give a doll, his female counterpart being, I suppose, a temptress named Barbie."

"Actually, it's John Kennedy Toole, but I go by Ken," Toole said. "Which university did you attend?"

"What other, but the noblest university of the Deep South, where some semblance of proper theology and geometry once prevailed," Ignatius replied, finishing his sixth donut. "Tulane. I earned my bachelor's and master's there and contributed many papers to the library. Of course, nowadays librarians and others expect work to be typewritten, but when things were sane, when things were intelligent, when things were at their highest in civilization, the handwritten word ruled as king. Alas, those times are long gone."

Ignatius eructated loudly. He sipped his tea and studied the man who was sitting across from him.

Toole leaned back in his chair. "Interesting. I myself am a graduate of Tulane, by the way. What exactly do you mean by proper theology and geometry? Oh, I don't know your name."

"My name is Ignatius J. Reilly," Ignatius answered solemnly, and he started on his eighth donut. "You, however, may call me

Mr. Reilly, given that I am the vice president of one of the most prestigious firms in Gotham."

"You're kidding me," Toole said, chuckling. "You, a vice president? Where? Of what?"

Ignatius scowled. "Are you mocking me, sirrah? I believe that you are. I'll have you know that I am the vice president of a company that manufactures the finest of Oriental victuals, a company without whose presence, I'm afraid, the purveyors of Oriental cuisine in this country—nay, in the entire free world—would find themselves living in the gutters of their respective communities, whether Gotham, our beloved New Orleans, or even the infamous Seattle.

"And, as vice president of this establishment, it is my duty to ensure that I create the most economical, most pithy of sayings that are sent along with the delicacies produced by this one-of-a-kind company. To wit, sirrah, I spread proper theology and geometry through the simplest of devices, the Chinese fortune cookie. It is Asian on the outside but thoroughly Western on the inside. And, lest you ask again, by proper theology and geometry I speak of the theology and geometry of the medieval world, a world wherein worthy kings ruled and in which the peasantry knew its place. Theologically, this was a world of the Ancient Church and Her sacred creeds, best seen in saints like Benedict, that beloved protector of Europe, and Hroswitha, of course.

"As for things geometrical, suffice to say that medieval architecture shows us how we should live in our environment. We can easily see this by comparing Gotham to, say, a village of fifteenth-century England. Gotham, as you know, has an endless series of skyscrapers. They maunder here and there, seemingly with no purpose but to house industries with which we could all do without, to wit, insurance industries, brokerage firms, and last and certainly not least in terms of abominations, the offices of lawyers, those horrid creatures who enjoy the trappings of modernity by retarding our progress towards the past. Is any of this making sense, Mr. Toole?"

Toole had opened his notebook and was hurriedly scrawling notes, writing as quickly as a receptionist writing in shorthand while listening to a Dictaphone tape of her gravelly voiced boss.

"Amazing," Toole said, shaking his head in amazement. "This is absolutely amazing. Whoever would have thought that I would run into someone like you, Ignatius?"

"Mr. Reilly," Ignatius replied sternly, correcting his apt but wayward pupil. "I'm glad to see that you are taking notes. If only others would take notes and live by these ideals, then we wouldn't be in the mess that we're in, with men working themselves senseless for no objective reasons and pimply faced teenagers rotting their brains out by watching Frankie Valli and the Four Seasons on one of those horrid, innumerable dance shows that plague our once-great nation."

Toole chuckled.

"I do not consider this to be humorous," Ignatius said, and he finished the thirteenth donut. "Changing the worldviews of modern man is a very taxing experience."

"Oh?" Toole said, looking up from his notebook.

"Are you a journalist?"

"No, a grad student at Columbia University."

"Ah, all the better," Ignatius said heartily, and he quaffed his orange pekoe tea. "Excellent. While I was hoping for coverage in the *Times*, having my words appear in the annals of your seemingly worthy institution might be of more importance, in the perspective of the historical long run as opposed to the ephemeral present, which is the only thing that the *Times* and other sundry rags like it have to offer. Suffice to say—are you getting all this down?"

"As much as I can get," Toole said, scrawling furiously. "What adventures have you had?"

"Several," Ignatius replied judiciously, and in no particular order he thought about the fleeing of New Orleans, the hospital, Mr. Levy's appearance at the house on Constantinople Street, the many restless days and nights that he, Ignatius, spent in his room with his rubber glove, his collapse in front of the Scenicruiser in front of the Night of Joy, the bird that attacked him, the party at that sodomite's apartment, the aborted coup at Levy Pants, the accident with the Plymouth that started it all—or, rather, nearly started it all, it all having really, really started that afternoon in front of the D. H. Holmes, when that diminutive patrolman Mancuso had harassed him, Ignatius J. Reilly.

"Well?" Toole asked.

Ignatius started with the Greyhound Scenicruiser and the journey to Baton Rouge. Toole, who scribbled away, bit his tongue, doing his best not to burst out laughing. Ignatius, reliving the past, paid no attention to Toole's contorting facial expressions but instead told the story, seeing it now as his, Ignatius's, own journey into Dante's Inferno.

"That's a very astute comparison," Toole said, and he leaned back in his chair and forced himself to hold back the laughter that was dying to exit his belly. "It's a wonder that you didn't run into Kerberos in the bayous."

"Given that I was entering the so-called redneck area of Louisiana, it's a wonder that I didn't," Ignatius said. "I have heard tell that the resident rubes, when not poaching, brew a moonshine nearly as potent as that concocted in Tennessee. And I have heard tell that these rednecks breed monstrous creatures to protect the stills that are hidden in the bayous. It wouldn't surprise me, given the inbreeding that these wantons are given to, if they somehow wouldn't come up with a three-headed dog."

Toole cleared his throat. He had something here. Definitely. Something very powerful. No one would ever believe this story, could believe this story. What Toole had heard was uncanny. It was unfathomable. The story had to be told. He would tell the story as soon as he obtained his degree at Columbia. He would go back to New Orleans and finish this tale. In fact, he might even pay a visit to Ignatius's mother to ensure that the facts were correct. This, Toole told himself, might be on par with A. J. Liebling's *The Earl of Louisiana*. But what if no one believed the story? What then? Perhaps something like this would make an excellent novel. No one would know the difference, would they? Someone had to tell this story, after all. This story couldn't go to waste.

"Mr. Toole?" Ignatius said indignantly, interrupting Toole's daydreaming.

"Sorry, I was in deep thought," Toole said. "Do you happen to know a professor named Robert Byrne? They call him Bobby Byrne. He teaches at what is now called the University of Southwestern Louisiana."

"And why would I know this man?" Ignatius asked indolently, and his belly growled, not from hunger, but from being satiated by the thirteen donuts that he had just eaten. He was thirsty, however, and wanted another hot orange pekoe tea. "Is he a medievalist? Would he be sympathetic to me and my worldview?"

"Very much so," Toole said. "He's a lot like you. In fact, you both share the same physical characteristics and dress very much the same. He was my colleague, and we used to discuss Boethius quite a bit."

"Ah, then you are familiar with *The Consolation of Philosophy*," Ignatius said. "That book defines my worldview. After I get the proper worldview instilled into the people of this nation, nay, into the people of this world, I intend to send a copy of this book to the president. After he reads it, I'm sure that he'll do the correct thing and step down from office and allow a just and noble monarch to rule."

"Do you honestly believe that you can do this?" Toole asked. "Things are what they are, to paraphrase Lenny Bruce."

"You are not the only one who has mentioned that so-called comedian," Ignatius said in contempt. "My secretary, Miss Ping, compares herself to him, though she is not in the leastways humorous, either in this age or in the age to come."

Toole looked at his watch. "I need to keep an eye on the time. I was here today in the Village in search of antiquated books. I need to get to Hunter."

"Hunter? I thought that you said that you were a student at Columbia."

"I am," Toole said, "but I teach at Hunter. You should see my students. Most of them are beatnik liberal Jewish girls who see a white supremacist behind every flat tire."

Ignatius frowned. "Why, that sounds like my very own Myrna minx."

"Who?"

"Myrna Minkoff, with whose family I am staying in the Bronx."

"I'm going to get another coffee before I go. Would you care for another tea?"

"Very much so, Mr. Toole."

Toole returned a minute later and offered Ignatius the tea, which Ignatius took without thanking his benefactor.

"You and Bob sure do bear a strong resemblance," Toole said. "It's just uncanny. If someone were to ask me, I would say that you two were brothers."

"I am an only child," Ignatius said, sipping his tea, which tasted pleasantly of orange, spices, and honey. "I believe that my dear mother could have only one child."

"Same as mine. I think she knocked herself down, something that allowed her to knock herself up."

Ignatius grimaced. "For someone from New Orleans, you seem to lack the finer graces in life, Mr. Toole. For a moment, I thought you were one for proper theology and geometry. Now I believe that your claim of being a citizen of New Orleans might be a dubious charge."

"I don't mean to offend you or your dubiety," Toole said. He frowned. "New York City has had a strange effect on me. Part of me wants to remain who I am, that is, a scholar from New Orleans who'll eventually get a professorship at an elite private school, perhaps one of the Little Ivies like Hamilton or Bowdoin.

"Another part of me, however, wants to be rich. And famous. I want to be a well-known author. Perhaps in this universe I will be."

"You make it sound as if you believe in the possibility of alternative realities belonging to the realm of parody," Ignatius said.

"I don't know," Toole replied, shrugging. "Somehow I feel as if I shouldn't be here."

"If you weren't here, then where would you be?" Ignatius enquired.

"Probably drafted and living on some Caribbean army base, where I'd be teaching Spanish-speaking recruits how to speak English." He paused, then took a sip of his coffee. "That's one scenario, I suppose, among many others."

"The desire for riches and the desire for fame are deceitful," Ignatius said. "If I were you, I'd finish your degree at Columbia and then go back to New Orleans. You might be able to get a teaching post at Tulane, our old alma mater. Should I be able to go back to New Orleans, I'll be sure to visit your office. I am generally not one for collaboration, but we might be able to work together on a tome upon which I have been working for a number of years."

"What's it about?"

"The fall of Western civilization, especially from our nation's perspective," Ignatius replied quite seriously. "It is a work that I have been striving to complete for years. Unfortunately, blind Fortuna in her wanton ways has prevented me from doing so."

"When you did have the time to work on it, how much time did you spend a day?" Toole asked. It sounded as if he were speaking in his, Ignatius's voice, something that unnerved Ignatius. Toole cleared his throat and continued in his own voice. "If you were writing a thousand words a day—"

"I approach that almost every day," Ignatius said, "when I am working in my Big Chief tablets. However, these are journal entries. For my other projects, I might, on average, get ten words a week if I am fortunate enough. You see, not only is this treatise a labor of love, it is a trying labor, one that no one else on this earth can accomplish, I'm afraid."

"So what are you doing here in New York City, Mr. Reilly?"

So Ignatius started with the trip from New Orleans to New York City, and Myrna's failed attempts to seduce him, and the crashing of the china cabinet at the Minkoff estate, and his job at the Charlie Chan Chinese Fortune Cookie Company, and his recent venturing to find Ed Sullivan, only to be waylaid by an intellectual saboteur at an indoor hot dog stand. And then the placing of the ad in the *New York Times* to find musically inclined compatriots to help him, Ignatius, with his campaign for proper theology and geometry.

After Ignatius finished, Toole shook his head slowly in empathy.

"And now you're in New York City," Toole said as a statement, rather than as a question. "You have quite a story."

"You have no idea," Ignatius said, "of the torments that I've had to endure since arriving in Gotham. The lecherous Myrna Minkoff desires to take my virginity. Mrs. Minkoff cannot remember my name and believes that I am an Orthodox rabbi. Only Mr. Minkoff seems to understand me. Well, and Grandmother Horowitz, when she's not sleeping or talking about the size of bananas in Italian markets."

"How does Mr. Minkoff show you that he understands you?" Toole asked zestfully.

"He just does," Ignatius replied yearningly.

"Sounds as if he's afraid of you," Toole replied xenophobically.

"He might be, given that New York City is actually more provincial than it is cosmopolitan," Ignatius replied warily.

"Do you honestly believe that, Mr. Reilly?" Toole asked vexingly.

"I've been here long enough to see that Gotham is not as cosmopolitan as it would like to appear," Ignatius said universally.

"Actually, I'm seeing your point," Toole said topographically.

"It is, indeed, true," Ignatius replied sadly.

"Sometimes I wonder if cities like New Orleans will go the way of New York City and lose their soul," Toole added ruefully.

"You can't possibly mean that?" Ignatius asked questioningly.

"Everything's blending into one, thanks to television and other electronic media," Toole answered persistently.

"That might change, once my appearance on *The Ed Sullivan Show* sparks the very things needed to change the worldviews of the American citizenry," Ignatius said optimistically.

"I'm not sure if I believe that," Toole said negatively.

"You don't believe that I am capable of doing this undertaking?" Ignatius asked myopically.

"No, I'm not sure that you are going to appear on *The Ed Sullivan Show*, and if, indeed, you are, that you're going to be able to pull off what you're attempting to pull off, given that the medium is the message, and the message is the medium, with my not being so sure that your message is ready for anyone's medium or your medium ready for anyone's message," Toole replied laconically.

"I see that you doubt my attempts, but I wonder if you are not being an ass," said Ignatius kinesthetically.

"I'm not being an ass, and I'm not being a fool," Toole said jestingly.

"Indeed," Ignatius said insolently.

"You think so?" asked Toole haughtily.

"Why else would I say it?" Ignatius said gratingly.

"Look, let's stop before we get into a deep debate or heated argument," Toole said festively.

"You of all people should understand my intentions and that my intentions are meant for the best," Ignatius said existentially.

"I maintain that even if we are nearing the last hour, you won't be able to change this world, Mr. Reilly," said Toole dogmatically.

"We shall see about that," said Ignatius crazily.

"We shall," replied Toole benignly.

"'I'm amazed that a man of your intellectual stature cannot believe that my mission is going to be a success," Ignatius said amazedly.

"If that's true, then why haven't you changed the worldviews of everyone already?"

"Ah, I might not have changed the worldviews of everyone, but I have changed the worldview of one man, to wit, Mr. Minkoff."

"How do you know that you've changed his worldview?" Toole asked.

"He stares at the walls as he listens to me," Ignatius said. "At first, I thought he was entering a sort of catatonic state but then surmised later on that he was taking in each and every word that I said. I intend to give him a copy of *The Consolation of Philosophy* so that he can further engrain the proper worldview into his psyche." Ignatius eructated loudly, unable to control himself. People at other tables looked over, momentarily annoyed, and then returned to the conversations that they were having. "Eventually, I believe, he will convert Madam Minkoff and Grandmother Horowitz. And they, in turn, will influence the minx, who will abandon her slatternly, tawdry ways and become a redeemed woman, if such a thing were possible."

"Like Mary Magdalene," Toole said.

"Exactly," Ignatius said, pounding his fist on the tabletop, causing it, saucers, cups, spoons, and a sugar container to rattle. "And because of her need to evangelize a cause, no matter what that cause is, she will spread the worldview of medievalism instead of spreading her legs. Before you know it, the world will be full of right-minded people, and the world will finally be sane, though, because of the fall of man, there will be the requisite consequential misery that man *qua* man must suffer."

Toole chuckled and shook his head.

"You find this amusing, do you?" Ignatius asked, his hands and forehead becoming hot.

"You're like Don Quixote," Toole replied, "and your friend Myrna Minkoff is your Sancho Panza. You're taking on some very big windmills, Mr. Reilly. Do you honestly believe that you stand a chance?"

"Of course I stand a chance," Ignatius said. His huge pink tongue reached down into the bottom of his mug and tagged the remainder of honey. "*We* have a chance. More and more of *us* are coming out of the woodwork, Mr. Toole. You'll see. The patration of our work is at hand, I being the thumb upon which all others are dependent. We'll eventually remake this world into what it should be, with the help of Fortuna and many prayers to the saints, especially Hroswitha."

Toole sipped his coffee. This strange fat man really was like Don Quixote and Oliver Hardy rolled up into one. Throw in a heavy salting (or peppering, as it were) of Bobby Byrne, and you had the makings of a comical character unlike any anyone had ever seen.

"Now, tell me about this band—"

"We will be a troupe, not a band," Ignatius said abruptly, holding up an ursine paw, its palm facing Toole, as if Ignatius were telling Toole to speak to the paw. "This troupe will not be like those monstrosities one sees on those so-called teen programs. We will be troubadours, balladeers, and singers of great songs of yore, minstrels who will undo the aural contamination perpetuated by the likes of the Four Seasons, Frankie Avalon, and Annette Funicello, among other Italians."

"At least she has a great set of legs," Toole said. "And her breasts are large. That said, I prefer the recently deceased Marilyn Monroe."

Ignatius shook his head, sighing sadly. "And I thought that you were one of us, Mr. Toole. I thought that if anyone would understand my medievalist worldview and the need for proper theology and geometry, it would be you."

"Oh, I more than understand where you're coming from," Toole said. "My mother is overly domineering, and my father is slowly but surely becoming insane with the onset of senile dementia. And he's paranoid, to boot. Sometimes when I'm alone in my room, pondering the words of John Lyly or another Renaissance writer, and working through their tropes and attempting to figure out how they crafted their works, I wonder if I'm going to go insane, too. Insanity, you see, runs in my family, not only on the Toole side but on my mother's side, the Ducoing. Sometimes I fear that I am going to fall prey to the very things that tormented my relatives."

For the first time in his life, Ignatius felt something like compassion. Perhaps he and this John Kennedy Toole had more in common than he, Ignatius, wanted to admit. Still, however, this was not a time for compassion. This was a time for contemplation, and after contemplation, a time for action. The minx, after all, had to pay for what she had done. This entailed, of course, the undoing and subsequent redoing of her family. And if all was going according to plan (and now it seemed as if blind Fortuna were finally smiling down upon him), he, Ignatius J. Reilly, would soon have his very just, very justified, and very sought-for revenge, not only on her but on the world.

"You gonna order any more goddamn things?" the barista said, now standing at the table, snapping gum, looking highly annoyed. "Because if you goddamn ain't, you gotta leave, according to the goddamn police." She pointed with her thumb at a sign on a wall: NO ORDERS MEANS YOU MUST LEAVE. "It's our goddamn police, you see. Too many goddamn smelly bums wanna come in here and just goddamn sit and goddamn talk to themselves or goddamn jack off. Me, I'd let them goddamn do it, but on account the goddamn management don't like it, I have to follow the goddamn police."

"I do believe that you mean policy," Ignatius said superciliously. "Or should I say, 'goddamn' policy?"

"Whatevuh, ya fat goddamn bum."

Toole checked his watch. "Really, I must be going, Ignatius. Excuse me, Mr. Reilly."

Out on the sidewalk, Ignatius found himself not wanting to shake parting hands with Toole. It wasn't so much that Ignatius hated human touch—he did, indeed, hate human touch—but that he and Toole were somehow grafted together, for whatever reason, and that parting, for whatever reason, might cause one or the other, or both, to die.

As the youthful, erudite scholar turned and headed away, perantique tomes in hand, a chilled and chilling winter wind whipped through the intersection where Ignatius stood and sliced into him, cutting him to the marrow. He shuddered, never feeling so abandoned, never feeling so alone.

Ignatius farted loudly, but the wind drowned out the sound of his flatulence, and he looked for a cab to hail.

II

A late afternoon sun hung white over a New Jersey landfill, and Henley wanted to sleep. And sleep and sleep and sleep. And, if need be, sleep forever. He had never had it so bad. If only he had never joined Skull and Bones. If only he had followed his father's footsteps and stayed in Boston, working for his family's law firm, which had been in existence almost two hundred years.

He and Nick the Nose had been in the dump for two hours. Henley thought about a poem by Thomas Hardy. Henley didn't remember the title of the poem, but the poem was bleak and spoke of a white sun, just like the one that he was experiencing now. And Henley, who tossed aside a dented Campbell's chicken noodle soup can, understood what Hardy meant when he spoke of neutral tones.

But now was not the time to think about Thomas Hardy, Henley knew. Now was the time to think about finding the palimpsest. Each hour, each minute, each second grew more and more sacred. If his superiors weren't able to start the takeover on time, Henley knew that his home would no longer be in Santa Barbara but in a fifty-five-gallon drum at the bottom of the icy Hudson.

Had his pneumonia not prevented him from smelling the garbage, Henley would have smelled the sweet odor of rotten cantaloupe rinds and the rancid, foot-like odor of stale coffee grounds. He rubbed his crimsoned nose with his forearm and sniffled. His eyes watered, and for a moment he thought about his beautiful wife. She was probably sitting in a chaise lounge at the pool and sunning herself and enjoying a mojito. The thought of alcohol caused his mouth to water, and Henley retrieved a silver flask, a college graduation present that he had received from his father, and uncapped it. Henley took two large gulps of Russian vodka.

Nick the Nose studied a few grapefruit rinds, then tossed them aside. Henley picked up a sodden grocery sack, turned it upside down, and emptied its contents. He knelt, and, as quickly as he could, he foraged through the garbage in search of the lost palimpsest.

"It's gotta be heh," Nick the Nose said, pressing a nostril with a thumb and sending a stream of hot air down the other nostril, causing a small wad of yellow snot to shoot into the garbage. "It's gotta be heh, you ask me, Ids."

"Not askin' you," Henley said. "And id idn't Ids, id's Henley."

"What I been sayin' all along," Nick the Nose replied, shaking his head.

"Keeb loogin."

And look they did, going through empty milk cartons, soiled diapers, oily newspapers, rotten fish heads, crimsoned tampons, moldy potato peels, clumpy cat litter, and other detritus and debris. Henley then saw an empty wine bottle from the corner of his eye. But it wasn't the wine bottle that interested him; it was what was lying underneath the wine bottle: a stained sheet of brown paper bearing ornate Latinate script.

"I dink I found id," Henley said. The wind whipped hard around hills and mountains of garbage, and the operative's eyes watered in response. "I dink dis might be id."

Nick the Nose, who was hugging himself with both arms, hurried over.

Henley pointed a trembling, gloved finger at the wine bottle. A front page of the *Wall Street Journal* blew onto the bottle and then blew away. Henley knelt, knees aching from the exertion, and flipped the wine bottle aside and snatched what appeared to be the palimpsest before another icy wind blew.

"Now I kin go back to Sanna Baba," Henley said, imagining the welcoming swimming pool and his welcoming wife and the welcoming sun. "Now I kin be back wid my wide."

"It's wide here, you want wide," Nick the Nose said, holding out his arms to indicate the wide expanse of the dump. "Don't know why you want wide."

"No, no, no. Wide. My wide. I'b goin' back to my wide."

"Ids, I think we need to get you home. You goin' crazy out here."

"I'b goin' crazy cuz of you," Henley said.

A gust of sharp wind whipped around a mountain of garbage. Henley hugged the thing that looked like the palimpsest so that the wind couldn't steal the paper from him.

Henley chuckled. "A'most god avay."

"You gotta learn to talk right," Nick the Nose said.

"Oh, shud up."

Another wind blew, and this time, as if orchestrated by a malevolent deity or by the writer of this parody, the icy blast struck Henley in the face. Henley's eyes closed in response, and he instinctively let go of the paper that resembled the palimpsest so that he could cover his nose and mouth when he sneezed.

"Shit!" Nick the Nose screamed. "Holy shit! It's takin' off again!"

Henley, whose eyes were now open, watched in horror as the wind whipped the faux palimpsest upward. For a split second, Henley thought that he saw clouds twisting into the face of a maniacal Oliver Hardy, his lips twisted in demented glee.

III

Myrna, who was sitting directly across from Dr. Ingloss in the group therapy group session, was wearing a shortened peasant's skirt, which Dr. Ingloss loved with a passion. The skirt revealed her shapely thighs. What's more, whenever she crossed and uncrossed her legs, Myrna revealed that she was not wearing any panties. Dr. Ingloss had crossed his legs in response, the third and much smaller of his legs standing like a soldier erect.

"Now where were we?" the psychologist asked, squirming in exquisite torture.

Mrs. Murray shook her head. "Myrna keeps talking about her orgasm problems. I'm tired of hearing about them."

"The whole point of this group is to help each other," Myrna said in protest.

Ralph held up Miss Kitty.

"Does Miss Kitty have anything to say?" Dr. Ingloss asked.

"I don't know," Ralph replied, looking at Dr. Ingloss and then at Miss Kitty. "Do you have anything to say, Miss Kitty?"

"I have to hand it to you, Ralph, you really gave me some wonderful multiples this morning," Miss Kitty said.

Mrs. Murray rolled her eyes. "And I thought the Irish was crazy."

"That's petty and bourgeois," Myrna said, and she patted Rastajaq's thigh. Rastajaq, whom Myrna had brought to that session and who was wearing his black balaclava, camouflage fatigues, and spit-polished jump boots, stared at the ceiling and muttered to himself. "Isn't it all about sexual repression, Dr. Ingloss? Wasn't it Reich who said something like that?"

"Reich was right," Dr. Ingloss said, nodding, hoping that Myrna would uncross her legs so that he could see the treasure that he so desperately craved. As if in response to his unspoken desire, Myrna crossed and then uncrossed her legs, giving him a brief glimpse of her treasure. His voice rose an octave. "Of course"— and now he cleared his throat so that his voice would lower—"we do need to keep in mind that society is not quite ready for what we here at the Ingloss Institute for Psycho-Sexual Research offer."

"I doubt it will ever be ready," said Leonard, who had been giving serious consideration to leaving the group. "Aren't we just wasting our time?"

"Not at all," Dr. Ingloss said, feeling as if he were traipsing in a minefield. "We are not wasting our time. As a group, we have progressed considerably. At first, we must admit, we were uncomfortable with one another. Now we are at a point where we can open up with each other."

"If that's true, then why are you squirming?" Miss Kitty asked Dr. Ingloss. "Why are your hands holding that notebook to cover up your lap that way?"

"I'm hiding nothing, Miss Kitty. Now please be a good hand."

"You're thinking about a handy snatch, that's what you're thinking about," Miss Kitty said in an accusatory tone. "And I know whose."

"Please, Miss Kitty," the psychologist said, "don't be a rude hand."

"I'm just telling it handily, like Lenny Bruce," Miss Kitty said.

"If you don't be quiet, Miss Kitty, I'm going to rap you with my ruler," the disgruntled psychologist said, glowering at Miss Kitty.

"All hands below deck." And Ralph opened his left hand and put it into his left pants pocket and stared morosely at a far wall, now that Miss Kitty was no longer with them.

"I'm tired of going without multiple orgasms," Myrna said, continuing from where she had left off. "More and more, men aren't lasting that long. They aren't able to keep up with me. And I'm getting tired of it."

"You ask me, you're now acting like a slut," Mrs. Murray said. "First it was getting Ignatius into bed, and now you've moved on to multiple orgasms and multiple partners."

Myrna's eyes crossed. "That sounds like an anti-Semitic remark, Mrs. Murray."

"If I wanted to be anti-Semitic, I would call you a kike."

"Aha!" Myrna yelled, thrusting an accusatory finger at Mrs. Murray. "You just called me a kike! You are an anti-Semite!"

"I didn't call you a kike," Mrs. Murray said. "And I'm not anti-Semitic, I'm anti-slut. And I have a cure for what ails you."

"Oh, yeah? What's that?"

"Come down to the shop where I used to work," the retired Irishwoman said, "and let me sew that goddamn thing shut for you."

The two women rushed at each other, claws drawn, and screeched like alley cats caught in a turf war. Dr. Ingloss hugged

Mrs. Murray from behind, and Ralph, with the aid of Miss Kitty, put Myrna into a headlock. Mrs. Murray screamed.

Myrna bit Miss Kitty, a technique that Myrna had learned in a rape prevention class taught at the New School. Ralph screamed and hopped about, nursing the wounded Miss Kitty.

Dr. Ingloss spoke first with Mrs. Murray, then with Myrna, assuaging their feelings and doing his best to bring equanimity to the group. Leonard shook his head and rolled his eyes.

"Are you all right, Miss Kitty?" Ralph asked Miss Kitty. "What did she do to you?"

"It's a hand, not a person," Myrna said, taking her seat, breathing heavily, not only from exertion but because she found the encounter with Miss Kitty oddly stimulating. "It doesn't talk, and it isn't alive, and it doesn't know anything about orgasms, regardless of what it said a few moments ago."

"Speak to me, Miss Kitty," Ralph said.

"I survived," Miss Kitty replied in her high-pitched voice. "Please keep her away from me, Ralph. She's a handful. You know that I'm the only hand who ever really loved you."

"I know that, Miss Kitty."

"Kiss me, you fool," Miss Kitty said. "Kiss me as you've never kissed another hand."

"Of course, Miss Kitty."

Ralph kissed Miss Kitty on her painted lips. Dr. Ingloss frowned, fearful that Ralph had reverted.

"That's disgusting," Mrs. Murray said. "Maybe I shoulda attacked you, Ralph."

"Leave us alone," Miss Kitty said. And then the hand said to Ralph, "Kiss me like I'm the most important hand in the world."

"You got it, Miss Kitty."

Mrs. Murray stood and said that she had had enough. She bundled herself up, gathered her things, and exited, followed by Leonard. Ralph and Miss Kitty continued their make-out session.

Myrna stood, as did Rastajaq, who continued to stare at the ceiling and mutter.

"Are you off, too?" Dr. Ingloss said, hoping that he could get her alone.

"Ignatius needs me," she said, putting on her coat. "And I need to get that revolution going. Those Chinese peasants need to understand how they're being exploited. And oh, before I forget, Mrs. Reilly called. She knows where Ignatius is. I keep forgetting to tell Ignatius." Rastajaq mumbled, and Myrna took his hand. "I'll give you a report later, Dr. Ingloss, and keep you updated about those things and any progress that I might make with the multiple orgasms."

She kissed Dr. Ingloss on the forehead, and Dr. Ingloss felt like grabbing her ample breasts, throwing her face-first over a chair, and having his way with her from behind.

Instead, he cleared his throat and feigned a smile. "That's a lovely idea," he said. "Please give Ignatius my regards."

IV

Ignatius farted and leaned back in bed, the sheets of which Mrs. Minkoff had changed earlier that day. The sheets smelled of a fresh spring day, and Ignatius thought about his mother and wondered how she was doing. At the fortune cookie factory earlier that day, he had been tempted to call their house on Constantinople Street but had ultimately decided against it. Fortuna was giving him another chance. He must not ruin that chance. Soon, very soon, he would reveal to the minx what she truly was. And he would put the Minkoff family on the right track. And his worldview would start a fire that encircled the globe, once he got his chance to appear on television.

Ignatius flipped open his Big Chief tablet after retrieving it from underneath the sagging bed. With a freshly sharpened pencil, he began to write.

November 10, 1918

The War to End All Wars is almost over, dear, gentle, and kind reader. Your Doughboy Dave is now a Dagwood who continues his onerous work at the Charlie Chan Chinese Fortune Cookie Company, with my making decisions that are affecting millions of lives, if not the course of the entire world. Suffice to say, I see one day a blending of the East and the West, the meeting of the *Analects* of Confucius with the *Dialogues* of Plato and the philosophy of Aristotle and the aphorisms of Marcus Aurelius and the work of my own beloved Boethius. I am fusing that bond with a passion. My hour of glory is at hand. Yet at the same time, I must be mindful of the details of my life and all that these details entail. (In New Orleans, my dear, gentle, and kind reader, I made the mistake of not being mindful of the small, needful things. My mind, as it were, was on the big picture but not on the execution of that big picture. Now, not only do I have the big picture clearly in mind, I have the *details* of that big picture clearly in mind. My day, my victory, my worldview, is at hand. Beware, O cruel world: Fortuna will have you know that Ignatius J. Reilly is about!)

That cast aside, I must detail the various sundries goings-on at the Charlie Chan Chinese Fortune Cookie Company.

Mr. Pong, for instance, continues to read (with tears of joy in his eyes) the fortunes that I am composing. He insists that someday I will have to go to Hong Kong. Though I do not speak Chinese (Mandarin or Cantonese), I believe that the endeavor of learning to speak and write Chinese will be more difficult than when I began to learn classical Japanese, on a lark that the ancient and noble culture of Japan would provide insight into the wanton hedonism of the twentieth century. Perhaps I shall go to Hong Kong after my televised victory. Of course, because of my exertions, I might need a year or two of rest. If not here, *chez* Minkoff, then perhaps the Algonquin Hotel. I have heard tell that this is where the so-called literary set of New York City makes its humble abode. We shall see.

Miss Ping, in her diablerie, continues to make jokes that I do not understand. If, indeed, they can be called jokes. Perhaps it is her Chinese sensibility; after all, our cultures *are* vastly different; hence, our worldviews are different and not compatible. It is my hope that Miss Ping will someday learn what true humor is; first, of course, she must become acquainted with the writings of Boethius and, perhaps, the late Romans. And, should she desire something humorous to read, then I can lead her to Chaucer's tales.

Myrna continues her fellow traveler's work on the coolies in the factory. Of course, as vice president of the Charlie Chan Chinese Fortune Cookie Company, I will brook only so much dissent. That is, I will allow Myrna minx to have one small demonstration, no more than ten minutes long. And then it's a clap of the hands and back to work for everyone, as it should be. (I still dislike Western-style capitalism intensely. Nonetheless, it will be paying the bills, and soon I shall be able to purchase another lute and a new trumpet.)

Mr. Minkoff was strangely happy at the dining room table this evening. In fact, he encouraged me to continue with what he called my "comedy routine," but which, I told him in stern correction, was properly termed a jeremiad for our age. (Grandmother Horowitz, for whatever reason, could not keep her hand off my leg. And she was groaning incessantly, much to the consternation of Madam Minkoff—bless her simple soul and her simple mind—who commanded Grandmother Horowitz to be silent, something that Grandmother Horowitz eventually did, not out of obeisance but because she fell asleep, as she often does, at the dining room table.)

In previous times, Mr. Minkoff's volcanic temper might have erupted. This time, however, he listened pleasantly and, after I finished, said that was the finest speech that he had ever heard Oliver Hardy give. Oliver Hardy? Perhaps Mr. Minkoff had been drinking earlier that day. This is a gentile season, but, nonetheless, I am sure that Jews and Jewesses do drink during these holidays to keep up with the festive spirits of their gentile neighbors and friends. Madam Minkoff, however, asked Mr. Minkoff if he was "fine." ("Oh, yes, I am very fine indeed," Mr. Minkoff said. "Deliverance is soon at hand." "What on earth do you mean, Bernard?" "Oh, you'll soon find out.") I take these words as good omens that Mr. Minkoff's business interests have taken a turn for the better. While I might have failed in my endeavors to help Gus Levy, my endeavors with the Minkoffs, especially Mr. Minkoff, seem to be working. The onset of his new personality occurred with the inadvertent destruction of his late mother's china cabinet and its sacred contents. I believe that this unfortunate incident—to which I erroneously tied Madam Minkoff, the real culprit being, of course, Grandmother Horowitz—has caused Mr. Minkoff to take a Boethian worldview. He has come to realize the futility of it all, especially modernity and the quest for material possessions that, in this sickened and psychologized society, mean "success." I give an unqualified and enthusiastic hip, hip, hooray for Mr. Minkoff!

I have had numerous responses to the advertisement that I placed in the *New York Times*. Unfortunately, a left-handed Negro guitar player, while versatile, had little understanding of the nuances of my worldview, as did a young man named Tork, a Greenwich Village folk musician who, I estimate, has absolutely no future as either a musician or as a television personality. (And I'm afraid that the left-handed Negro guitar player does not have much of a future either, seemingly talented as he is.) Mr. Pong, by the way, has wholeheartedly agreed to this venture, saying that I may do, or have, whatever I need to complete my work. I, of course, wholeheartedly concur with him. Miss Ping has scheduled auditions, which begin promptly at 11:00 a.m. Given the immensity of Gotham, and given its numerous artisans, artists, and craftsmen, I believe that I shall have the clichéd cream of the crop at my artistic disposal. Unfortunately, I have not had much time to translate that ancient parchment that I discovered in the alley. Perhaps there shall be time for that later; as it is, I must focus my energies on my upcoming television appearance, which I intend to garner very soon.

Your working man is tired and will sign off for the evening. The armistice, from what I hear, is almost at hand. It is nearing the eleventh hour, nay, the twelfth, and our delivery is most assured.

Dagwood

V

Mr. Minkoff ascended subway steps. Whistling, he skipped towards his restaurant supply business. The air smelled of freshly washed laundry, and Mr. Minkoff smiled, pleased with the scent. If anything, it was the one thing that reminded him of his halcyon youth, when things always and seemingly went well, and when there was never a worry in the world, except for the time when he almost strangled himself to death at that yoyo contest in Central Park. Mr. Minkoff had never thanked the meandering *mohel* for his help. Looking up at a white sky, Mr. Minkoff gave silent thanks to the circumciser, who was probably long dead.

For a moment or two, Mr. Minkoff stood on a street corner, contemplating the path upon which life had taken him.

A woman frowned at him, indicating that he should step aside. Mr. Minkoff flashed a Stan Laurel smile at the woman, stepped aside for her, and exhaled a plume of carbon dioxide into the wintery air, this plume being replaced by another as Mr. Minkoff continued his calm, controlled breathing. Then he walked.

When he was a boy, Mr. Minkoff had intended to become a lawyer. Lawyers, he had once believed, were the real men of power. They made the laws that everyone had to follow. And if you were a clever enough lawyer, you could make it as a clever enough politician in this dog-eat-dog world. Mr. Minkoff's father, however, had insisted that he, J. Bernard Minkoff, come work in the restaurant supply business after he graduated from high school. Being an obedient and dutiful son, Mr. Minkoff had done just that.

And being an obedient and dutiful son, Mr. Minkoff had become highly resentful of his father. For several years, Mr. Minkoff had had nightmares about killing his father by means of strangulation or the straight razor. Even after Mr. Minkoff the Senior had passed, Mr. Minkoff the Junior had the nightmares, the father appearing and asking, "Why, Bernard? Why did you do it? Why did you murder me? Why didn't you get that shipment sent off to Harbinger's Restaurant in Ashland, Wisconsin, on time?" And after each nightmare, Mr. Minkoff the Junior awoke terrified, drenched in sweat, wondering when the nightmares would end. Unfortunately for him, the nightmares ended after Grandmother Horowitz moved in, and extremely terrifying nightmares about his wizened mother-in-law replaced those of his long-deceased father.

But Ollie changed all that, that was for sure.

Mr. Minkoff smiled as he continued his way down the side-walk. The nightmares had vanished, thanks to Ollie. Yep, all thanks to Ollie, who pretended to be a medieval scholar from New Orleans.

Mr. Minkoff had had several dreams about Ollie: Ollie lec-turing him on the need for having a worldview that had the proper theological and geometrical dimensions, Ollie lectur-ing him about the dangers of not using a reliable condom to prevent the birth of the cat that kept dragging things into the house, Ollie playing medieval ballads on an off-tune lute, in a singing voice that proved that while there might not be a choir in heaven, there certainly was the wailing of damned souls in hell.

Mr. Minkoff had felt distress because of these dreams, but then things changed.

In his dreams, Mr. Minkoff turned the tables on Ollie.

In the earliest dreams, Mr. Minkoff sprayed Ollie with selt-zer bottles or smacked Ollie in the face with cherry cream pies. Those dreams had amused Mr. Minkoff so much that he chuck-led in his sleep, unaware that his wife would often awaken and turn to study her husband.

But seltzer bottles and cherry cream pies were soon replaced with boxing gloves. In a later dream, Mr. Minkoff went fifteen rounds with Ollie and defeated Ollie in the fifteenth round with a right jab-right jab-left hook-right cross combination that knocked Ollie flat on his fat behind. There were literal stars floating above Ollie's head as he stared at the ceiling, his eyes crossing as Ollie uttered unintelligible things about Greyhound Scenicruisers and cockatoos. Unfortunately, the round girls had been Myrna and Grandmother Horowitz, both wearing green velveteen bikinis, Grandmother Horowitz's breasts sagging so low that they almost reached the mat.

But then the dreams had turned from those of boxing to those of wrestling, and in one dream Mr. Minkoff-Stan Laurel put Ignatius J. Reilly-Oliver Hardy into a Bulgarian headlock and twisted and twisted and twisted until Ignatius J. Reilly-Oliver Hardy's neck snapped like a dried chicken bone. Though the crowd booed Mr. Minkoff-Stan Laurel, he raised his hands in victory and taunted the crowd, declaring that he was the best, that Ollie would no longer torture him, that he, Stan Laurel, was now a solo act and that they could catch his next film at the nearest Loews.

At work (while Mrs. Andrews hurried in and of his office with orders to confirm or dropped off receipts for him to sign or poured his coffee), Mr. Minkoff often leaned back in his chair and pondered the previous evening's dreams. He no longer felt angry. He no longer felt weak. If anything, he felt empowered. Hadn't his daughter, the cat, talked of empowerment? Empowerment for women, empowerment for epileptic Negro banjo players, empowerment for oppressed Chinese workers. Empowerment for these people, yes, she had certainly spoken of their empowerment. But never empowerment for J. Bernard Minkoff. Well, he, J. Bernard Minkoff, he, Stan Laurel, was now empowered.

A cold wind awakened Mr. Minkoff from his daydream. His ungloved hands felt cold, and he knew that he had a mission to complete. So instead of heading up a street that led to his restaurant supply business, he headed down the street.

He cupped his hands and blew hot air into them. When he was younger, he had hated the cold, but now he enjoyed it. To be cold was to be alive. It revitalized the soul, as Ollie might have said. And, as if to echo Mr. Minkoff's newfound sentiment about the cold, a harsh wind blew and whirled snowflakes around his head and around the heads of other pedestrians: white symphonies interplaying one among another in this winter wonderland.

He stopped at the first pawn shop that he encountered. Integuments of ice and snow, remnants of the last major storm, adorned the pawnshop's awning. Icicles broke, and the stiricide caused Mr. Minkoff to step under the awning. There, he studied the wares and bric-a-brac in the pawnshop's windows: a dusty violin, two guitars, worn-out mechanic's boots, what looked like a broken chainsaw, false teeth. No, no, this pawnshop would not do, Mr. Minkoff told himself, and he hurried on.

Mr. Minkoff walked a few paces until he arrived at the next pawnshop. Watches, wedding rings, engagement rings, pearl necklaces, pendants, cufflinks, and other jewelry, some of very high value, some of very low value, ornamented racks in the windows. This place seemed to be a cut above the other pawnshop, but from the looks of it, this pawnshop dealt mostly, if not exclusively, in the aforementioned items. Not satisfied, Mr. Minkoff shook his head, shrugged his shoulders against a biting wind, and walked to the next pawnshop, which was at an intersection busy with traffic, pedestrian and auto.

He liked the sign above the awning: SCRINOPSKI'S PAWN AND LOAN. The neon lettering of the sign glowed incarnadine, something that Mr. Minkoff took as a good omen. Unlike the previous two pawnshops, this one seemed to specialize in items that would be of particular interest to a man: a male mannequin dressed in cold-water waders stood in a front window, a fly fishing pole in hand, the mannequin looking as if it might be fishing serenely in the Catskills. Shotguns adorned another part of the huge window display, which led to a glass front door that was partially steamed but that had enough clear pane to show Mr. Minkoff that this pawnshop contained the very thing that he was seeking. Delighted, feeling a *joie de vivre* that he had not felt in years, Mr. Minkoff opened the partially steamed glass door and stepped inside, the warmth of the pawnshop comforting him as a bell affixed to the glass door announced his arrival.

"May I help you?" a man's gravelly voice asked from a back room. The man appeared, and his refined, Noachian face, which would have made for a fine portrait by John Singer Sargent, was attached to a refined head on which perched a fine black yarmulke. The pawnbroker's shiny, shaggy, gray hair hung on his forehead and down the back of his neck, and his gray *payot* stuck out as if they were a cat's whiskers. He was wearing a blue *tallith* that had many *tzitzith*. And he was carrying a dusty ledger, and his gentle, gray, peaceful eyes reminded Mr. Minkoff of his childhood rabbi, Rabbi Shlomo Shapiro, who had gone to prison for tax evasion. "See anything that you fancy, sir?"

"Ah, you're observant, aren't you?" Mr. Minkoff asked.

The pawnbroker placed the heavy ledger next to an antique cash register. "If you're asking me if I'm an Orthodox Jew, yes, I am."

"I myself am Jewish," said Mr. Minkoff in his best Boy Scout-earnest voice.

The pawnbroker wanted to ask, "Well, then why aren't you wearing a yarmulke?" Instead, however, the pawnbroker, wanting to be polite so that he could get a sale, replied, "Well, it's good to make your acquaintance, sir. Obviously you've chosen my pawnshop for a special reason."

"That's right," Mr. Minkoff replied. "I'm here for a special reason. I need something special for a special person."

"Oh? Special person? Is this a gift for your son? A nephew? A grandson? Is this for a bar mitzvah? If this special person is an outdoorsman, you've come to the right place, sir."

"No, this is for an ex-partner of mine," Mr. Minkoff said, and he surveyed shotguns and rifles hanging in locked racks on the walls, and then his eyes wandered down to the numerous pistols, standard and semiautomatic, displayed in polished glass cases that ran throughout the pawnshop. "A business partner. We used to be a real team. People said that we were real comedians, even though Ollie did treat me poorly, and I got the brunt of his abuse."

The pawnbroker Scrinopski frowned. Something was wrong with this prospective customer. In fact, something was desperately wrong with this man. The pawnbroker touched his prayer shawl, behind which was hidden a 1911 .45 semiautomatic.

"And what exactly do you want to get for Ollie?" the pawnbroker asked hesitatingly.

"I think that Ollie deserves a revolver, don't you?" Mr. Minkoff said.

Scrinopski warily eyed Mr. Minkoff. Why did he, Scrinopski, get all the crazies? Things were bad enough with the *schwarzes*. Now the pawnbroker had to deal with this Jew who, at the minimum, had suffered a nervous breakdown, and, at the maximum, had gone entirely insane.

Scrinopski decided that it would be best to get rid of this would-be customer. "Why not go to one of the shops up the street? I'm sure that you could find your friend Ollie a good suit at a very reasonable price."

Mr. Minkoff knew that the pawnbroker was being condescending. Furthermore, Mr. Minkoff knew that the pawnbroker thought that he, Mr. Minkoff, was insane. Mr. Minkoff didn't like being considered insane. Mr. Minkoff didn't like being condescended to, either. Mr. Minkoff wasn't going to play the game.

"No, Ollie doesn't need a good suit," Mr. Minkoff said. "He has his own clothes that he says are correct according to his proper theology and geometry. No, no suit for Ollie. Ollie is going to need protection."

"From whom?" the pawnbroker asked suspiciously, taking a step back, wishing that Solomon, his brother, was not sick at home but there at the pawnshop to help deal with this crazy Jew.

"From any attackers, that's who," Mr. Minkoff explained. "He's going to be a very famous man. He'll have fans, and he'll have fanatics. It's the latter who worry me."

"Oh?"

"You see, Ollie is a very special person," Mr. Minkoff said. "I want to ensure that nothing bad happens to him. Mind you, he doesn't need an arsenal, he just needs something small that can get the job done quickly and at a very short distance. Something that can be concealed very easily and something that doesn't have more than five bullets."

"Five bullets? Why five bullets?"

"Oh, it has nothing to do with my family, if that's what you're getting at," Mr. Minkoff said, laughing, doing his best to sound genuine. He smiled a Cheshire Cat smile, a smile big enough, in fact, for two Cheshire Cats. "Yes, there are five of us, me included. Yes, five of us, indeed. Me, my wife, Miriam, my daughter the cat, the virginal Grandmother Horowitz, and Ollie."

The pawnbroker let out a long, slow exhale. "Have you been drinking this morning, sir?"

"Not me!" Mr. Minkoff shouted. "I'm a teetotaler, leastways in the mornings!"

"You're not on any sort of medication at this time?" the pawnbroker asked, studying Mr. Minkoff very carefully. "Any drugs?"

"If you weren't an observant Jew, I would be very offended by that question," Mr. Minkoff said. "Do I look like one who's on the catbird seat? Do I look as though I'm coked to the gills? Do you believe that I sit in one of those jazz juke joints and smoke marijuana and listen to poetry about men singing in tune, 'Ullalume, ullalume, an astronaut should stay on the moon'? Do I look like some Puerto Rican kid who hangs out on an alley fire escape and who sticks needles into his arms?"

"No, sir, you look like a very respectable businessman, from what I can tell," Scrinopski the pawnbroker said, wishing that he had not opened the pawnshop that day. Perhaps it was best to play along with this crazy. Perhaps he, the pawnbroker, could get rid of the crazy soon enough, while turning a profit and ensuring that this crazy wouldn't, and couldn't, hurt anyone. "In fact, you look like a very upstanding citizen. You are a credit to our people, sir."

"Why, thank you," Mr. Minkoff replied, genuinely pleased and touched by the compliment. "I've always prided myself on being an upstanding citizen. That's why I was such a devotee of Walter Cronkite. Do you watch him?" And before the pawnbroker could answer, Mr. Minkoff pointed at a police-issue .38 in a display case. "That's the one. That's the one Ollie should have."

The pawnbroker bit a corner of his mouth. "Interesting that you chose that one."

"Oh? Why?"

"It's a five-shot revolver," Scrinopski said, and he did his best to keep his hands and fingers from trembling, but the harder he tried, the more his hands and fingers trembled. "It belonged to a cop from Greenwich Village who's now retired and living in Los Angeles. But that's beside the point."

"I'd like to see it," Mr. Minkoff said.

The pawnbroker exhaled and unlocked the display case, reached into the display case, and removed the revolver, around the trigger guard of which hung a small price tag.

Scrinopski the pawnbroker handed the revolver to Mr. Minkoff, who lovingly stroked his cheek against the weapon the way a cat rubbed its cheek against a leg of the cat's owner.

"Beautiful," Mr. Minkoff said. "Absolutely beautiful."

"You seem to like that one."

"Yes, I do." Mr. Minkoff looked around. "Do you sell bullets?"

"Yes, I do," Scrinopski the pawnbroker said, and he gently took the gun away from Mr. Minkoff's hands and placed the gun back into the display case, which the pawnbroker locked. "I assume that you want to purchase this revolver?"

"That's the one," Mr. Minkoff said energetically. "Yep, a present for Ollie. And, oh, I'll need a holster, too."

"I have it and the bullets in a back room," the pawnbroker said. "I'll be right back."

"Please, take your time. I have all the time in the world. Ollie has all the time in the world. The cat has all the time in the world. My wife has all the time in the world. Grandmother Horowitz has all the time in the world. We all have all the time in the world."

"Just a moment, please."

In a neatly arranged back room, Scrinopski paused. Was he doing the right thing? This customer was completely *meshugge*, that was for sure. Absolutely *meshugge*. From the looks of him, possibly *meshugge* for the rest of his life. But if he, Scrinopski, didn't sell this crazy Jew a pistol, somebody else would, like that pesky Lieberman across the street. And Lieberman wouldn't care, would he? No, he wouldn't; Lieberman would want a sale, and that was that. Of course he, Scrinopski, wanted a sale, too. Very much so. But he knew that he also wanted to be responsible. What to do, what to do?

Then Scrinopski saw the answer. He opened a box of .38 blanks and then emptied a box of .38 hollow-point rounds. The pawnbroker then poured the blanks into the box that had contained the hollow-point rounds. The kook didn't know a thing about guns; that Scrinopski knew. Delighted, he took the box containing the .38 blanks and a leather holster and went back to the display case, against which a smiling Mr. Minkoff leaned, waiting patiently.

Mr. Minkoff used cash to pay for the revolver, the holster, and the box of blanks, items that he then placed into the pockets of his coat. He knew that for the rest of the morning, while he was alone in his office, he would be doing dry-fire practice.

"Great doing business with you," Mr. Minkoff said, tipping his Cossack cap at the pawnbroker after the business transaction was completed.

"I hope that Ollie enjoys his present," Scrinopski the pawnbroker said with not much enthusiasm.

"Oh, he's going to love it," Mr. Minkoff said. "And so are the others."

And with that, Mr. Minkoff skipped off to the front door, and Scrinopski the pawnbroker sighed, shook his head ruefully, and silently recited a Kaddish.

• *Nine*

Dejected, his dejection compounded by his anger at not being able to find Ed Sullivan, Ignatius trudged angrily up Broadway. A cab had brought him there from Chinatown.

Because of the cold air and his expanded girth, Ignatius breathed stertorously, and he wondered how long he could stay in the cold. That morning wasn't going as planned. He needed to find Ed Sullivan as soon as possible. The mission could not be delayed any further.

"Wanna have some fun, mister?" a woman with a black bee-hive hairdo asked. She was leaning against a post box, and her heavy faux-fur coat provided protection for her ample chest, and fishnet stocks encased her shapely legs, and high heels ensconced her feet, and her calves tensed whenever she shifted from one cold foot to the other.

"I do not have the time for fun," Ignatius said. "Pray tell, do you know where I can find Ed Sullivan?"

"That a joke, like asking how do you get to Carnegie Hall?" The woman's irides twisted up and then to her left.

"This is very urgent," Ignatius said. "I must find Ed Sullivan."

"Who doesn't wanna find Ed Sullivan, sweetheart?"

"I have a mission that must be done immediately."

"I think I might've done a missionary position or two recently," the woman said, surmising that Ignatius wasn't an undercover cop. "Thought one of them was a fag trying to prove to himself that he wasn't. What a lazy lay he was."

"Lazy lay? What exactly does that mean?"

"You kidding me?" the woman said. "You kidding me, right?"

"I jest not, madam," Ignatius said, and he shivered. "I've tried his theater, but Fortuna hasn't spun the right cycle for me by opening the door. If you could point me in the direction of where he might be, I would be greatly obliged."

"Hell if I know," the woman said, angry and irritated because she was tired and cold and hadn't had a customer in two hours. "You want to find someone, you do it on your own dime, pal."

"Such rudeness," Ignatius said, "especially from a trull."

"I ain't no troll," the woman said. "I'm a sophisticate. I almost graduated from high school, and I almost qualify for welfare. I'm on the verge of respectability. That's probably more than what they can say about you, you fat slob."

"I myself have never had to stoop to receive the services of the state," Ignatius replied nobly. "Fortuna, even when she has treated me in the most depraved of ways, has seen to it that I have a some sort of roof, no matter how quaint, no matter how grand."

"Fortuna? Is that that black bitch with the big hair and the big hips?"

Ignatius grimaced. "For someone who's such a 'sophisticate,' you know so little, trull."

"I told you, mister, I ain't no goddamn troll. You think I live under a bridge or something? You keep it up, I'll have my pimp, who also happens to be my boyfriend, work you over."

"I am not one for violence," Ignatius said, and now he surveyed his surroundings, looking for a place where he might get the warmth that he so desperately needed. "Ah, what do we have here?"

Across the street was a restaurant-bar, and because the wind was whipping thousands upon thousands of snowflakes, Ignatius couldn't make out the restaurant-bar's name.

Ignatius reached into his coat pocket and withdrew a small bottle of brandy that he had pilfered from Mr. Minkoff's bar. Ignatius uncapped the bottle, took a large swig, and recapped the bottle. A pleasant warmth spread over his face, and his sinuses cleared.

"What's that you're drinking, pal?"

"Brandy," Ignatius replied absentmindedly, and he put the bottle back into his coat pocket. "I must get to that oasis, so therefore I shan't be engaging in any more molrowing."

"Before you do that, gimme a swig of that brandy," the prostitute said. "I'm freezing out here."

"You want a drink, you do it on your own dime, trull," Ignatius said, and he trudged towards an intersection. "I am not a bartender at the Night of Joy!"

"Gimme a drink, mister! I mean it!"

Ignatius waved a mitten-encased paw at her and huffed and puffed as he made his way.

"You come back here and give me a drink of that whiskey!"

"It's brandy!" Ignatius replied. "And you are not going to get a single drop!"

"Asshole!"

"Trull!"

"Asshole, asshole, asshole!"

"Trull, trull, trull!"

Though he was barely able to see it, the light across the street changed to green. Ignatius stepped into an intersection, its snow grayed and blackened from heavy traffic.

Something hard struck the back of his head, and he grunted, almost pitching face-forward into the intersection. Then another object hit him, this time in the leg. He turned to see the prostitute. She was hurriedly making snowballs and pitching them the way a star Yankees pitcher threw baseballs at a batter: with deadly accuracy and speed.

"Stop that!" Ignatius yelled, and he moaned as a snowball caught him on the side of his head. "You idiot, what do you think you're doing!"

"Gimme that brandy or else!" the weatherly frustrated prostitute screeched, packing another snowball, which she threw at Ignatius, hitting him full force in the chest. "You gimme that brandy or else!"

"Help!" Ignatius screamed in the middle of the intersection, as honking cars and blaring cabs did their best not to hit him. "Help! Help! A trull is trying to kill me! Help!"

Regardless of Ignatius's protests, the assault continued. As soon as the prostitute finished packing a snowball, she threw it at Ignatius, who was doing his best to dodge the assault but with no success. A snowball struck his heavy thigh, another struck his paw, another almost knocked off his green hunting cap, another struck him in the nose, and yet another nailed him dead-center in the groin, almost hard enough to knock the remaining wind out of him.

Ignatius bellowed, flailed his arms, and did his best to make his way across the snow-impacted intersection. An enraged cab driver, whose vehicle's wheels spun, raised a middle finger at Ignatius.

The volume of the snowballs and the magnitude of their impact on Ignatius increased exponentially. Exhausted, Ignatius removed the bottle of brandy from his coat pocket and threw it in a parabolic arc in the general direction of the prostitute, who dropped a highly compacted snowball and, with eager hands, reached for, and caught, the bottle of brandy.

Drivers honked horns at the two. Ignatius stepped onto the other side of Broadway. He looked up at the bleak sky and wished that he had not mentioned Fortuna.

Ignatius removed his mittens and brushed away the remainder of a snowball that encrusted his black mustache. Now that he was standing in front of the restaurant-bar, he could see, through patches in the steamed front window, a bartender behind a bar and a lone figure at the bar. The restaurant-bar looked warm and inviting, and Ignatius grunted as his tree-trunk-like legs did their best to get him inside.

Warm air, like the warm air in the folds and in the pockets and in the seams of the many layers of his winter clothing, enveloped him. It almost felt as if he were back home, and Ignatius thought about his halcyon days on Constantinople Street.

The bartender was wiping a highly polished mahogany counter with a fulgent towel. At the bar sat a man with his back to Ignatius, and cigarette smoke spiraled around the man's head. Next to the man's left elbow rested five empty martini glasses.

The bartender gave Ignatius a questioning look. "We don't serve your kind here. You want spare change, you go to the corner."

"I, sirrah, am not a vagrant," Ignatius replied pompously. "I'll have you know that I am the vice president of the Charlie Chan Chinese Fortune Cookie Company in what is famously, or infamously, known as Chinatown. I am in this part of Gotham in search of television's preeminent host."

"You must mean me," the man said, and he turned, facing Ignatius, who now recognized not only the voice but the avuncular face. "I'm Ed Sullivan. What's up with that getup, kid?"

"He's a bum," the bartender said, and he tossed the towel aside and put his hands on his waist. He had been a professional boxer turned professional wrestler, and he had not had a good fight in eighty-two days. "Didn't I tell you to get out of here, you bum?"

Ignatius searched for his business cards and brought out not only a handful of his business cards but wads of Christmas candy wrappers. He stepped forward and handed a card to Ed Sullivan and a card to the bartender.

"'Ignatius J. Reilly,'" Ed Sullivan read aloud. "'Esquire. Philosopher, Poet, Historian, Troubadour, and Scholar of Boethius.'" Ed Sullivan squinted. "The print underneath that is too small to read."

"'Vice President of the Charlie Chan Chinese Fortune Cookie Company,'" the bartender quoted. "And beneath that are the symbols you see on those chink restaurants. You ask me, anyone could have a card like that made up." The bartender harrumphed. "Philosophy, poetry, history, and troublemaking, that's what you're all about, pal."

"Easy, Lloyd," Ed Sullivan said in Ignatius's defense. "I think our boy here's a genius. You are a genius, aren't you, my boy?"

"Mr. Sullivan," Ignatius began, "let me say—"

"I think you've had too much, Mr. Sullivan," Lloyd the bartender said. "And I think you have your dry-martini glasses on. You remember what happened last time when that fat-assed drag queen came in here chasing that poodle, don't you?"

Ed Sullivan grimaced. "Vaguely, Lloyd. You know how bad my memory is."

Ignatius sat on a stool next to Ed Sullivan's. "Mr. Sullivan, I'm here to help you."

"Help me?" Ed Sullivan asked, and he snubbed out the Chesterfield that he had been smoking. The extinguished cigarette emitted an acrid odor. "How is a boy like you going to help me, kid?"

"I'm going to reinvigorate your show," Ignatius said.

"Are you saying that my show is lousy?" Ed Sullivan asked suspiciously. "Say, Steve Allen didn't send you here, did he? Is this some sort of Steve Allen prank or something?"

"I take deep offense at that," Ignatius retorted. "Compared to you, Steve Allen is a mere pissant in the sea of television waves. You, sir, are the agonarch of television. Your show is regnant above all others. Even now, in your apotheosis, you are appearing in your sartorial splendor, as if you were ascending to heaven itself."

Ed Sullivan lit another Chesterfield and motioned at Lloyd to make another dry martini.

"I don't understand all those fancy words, kid, but I get the feeling that you're flattering me. Please go on. I'm all ears."

And Ed Sullivan wiggled his ears, and Lloyd laughed as he shook the dry martini before pouring it into a martini glass, the bartender adding a speared green olive as the last bit of his fancywork. He placed the dry martini in front of Ed Sullivan, who sipped it and smiled.

"You make the best dry martinis in the world, Lloyd," Ed Sullivan said. "No one can make them like you."

"And what will you have?" Lloyd, who had decided to show some civility to Ignatius, asked.

"Brandy," Ignatius replied. "A trull across the street assaulted me with a barrage of snowballs when she discovered that I had brandy on me. I barely made it here alive. Unfortunately, she got my bottle of brandy, but fortunately, I was not accosted after that."

"How are you going to help me, kid?" Ed Sullivan said, exhaling bluish-blackish smoke. "I have to admit, some of the acts have been lame lately. Jugglers who can't juggle, comedians who are telling yesterday's jokes, animal acts like that one with that goddamn monkey that pretended he could add."

"I saw that," Ignatius said, "and I found it deplorable that that simian would have the audacity to attempt to dupe you."

"You're a poet and all that jazz," said Ed Sullivan in his alcoholic haze. "And you make fortune cookies. So, how are you going to help me? What can you do to jazz up my show?"

"I play the lute," Ignatius said, "and I sing songs of yore. I believe, as you probably believe, in a world that once existed and that exceeds our own in terms of proper theology and geometry."

"Go on, kid, I'm all ears," Ed Sullivan said, but this time he didn't wiggle his ears but instead took another sip of his dry martini and another deep drag off his Chesterfield. "You mean that your thing is about family values and family entertainment?"

"In a manner of speaking, yes," Ignatius said. "When civilization is strong, the Church is strong. And when the Church is strong, proper theology and geometry are strong. And when proper theology and geometry are strong, well, then entertainment, for want of better wording, is strong."

"You think your act could turn back the tide against the goddamn lack of morals in this day and age?" Ed Sullivan said. "I like the idea, kid. Truth be told, I hated Elvis when he came out. I thought that he was a moral degenerate. Did you know that I had to have his pants adjusted? It was his cock. It looked like he was hanging a sausage in his crotch. And they wanted me to show that. Can you believe that, kid?"

"Elvis should be the least of our concerns," Ignatius replied. "I'm more concerned about the likes of Frankie Valli and his ilk and those forename boy wonders like Dion and so forth. Most of them seem to be Italian, and I am convinced that the Mafia might be behind all this moral depravity infecting our once-noble country."

"Those are fancy words," Ed Sullivan said. "Are you sure you aren't a doctor, kid?"

"I am a doctor of the soul, not of the body," Ignatius replied. "I am a phylactologist contra this age."

"Now, what about this dog act you were talking about?"

"Not a dog act, a musical act, if you will," Ignatius said. "Perhaps I should show you the lyrics."

Ignatius handed the palimpsest to Ed Sullivan, who put on his reading glasses and read, his lips moving while his eyes scanned the lines of text.

"I don't understand a word of it," Ed Sullivan said. "Does it have a beat?"

"That's iambic pentameter," Ignatius said. "I've yet to complete the translation, in fact, I've translated only four lines, but it starts off with a rhyming pattern, as if the thing were a Petrarchan sonnet. Then the pattern ceases, and blank verse emerges. It's avant-garde before avant-garde was invented. In the right hands, specifically mine, a lute accompaniment would provide the necessary background. Of course, I shall need musicians to accompany me, and for that I placed an advertisement in the *New York Times*."

"If this is hot, I need you on my show this Sunday," Ed Sullivan said excitedly. "Why, if we don't act on this now, this might fade. A new teenage king might arise in the next week or so."

"I agree, this is a matter of dire urgency," Ignatius said, truly and wholeheartedly agreeing with Ed Sullivan. "That settles it, I shall appear on your show this Sunday, and I shall have the appropriate lute accompaniment for this lyrical masterpiece, along with troubadours to help me with my musical presentation."

Because of his alcoholic haze, Ed Sullivan handed Ignatius the palimpsest absentmindedly.

"What about your singers?" Ed Sullivan asked. "Do you think you have enough time?"

"Many noble feats and accomplishments have occurred within very short amounts of time," Ignatius said. "I agree, time is of the utmost. We must act, and we must act now, if we are to save our nation."

Ed Sullivan slammed his fist onto the highly polished mahogany counter, and Lloyd, who had been counting dollar bills at a cash register, looked disapprovingly over his shoulder at the television host and the larger-than-life character.

"To Sunday's show!" Ed Sullivan said, holding up his dry martini.

Ignatius raised his brandy glass and tapped the martini glass. "To Sunday's show, Mr. Sullivan. You shan't be disappointed. After Sunday's show, neither you, nor Gotham, nor this state, nor this country, nor this world is ever going to be the same. I can promise you that."

"I'll take you at your word, kid," the television host said, greedily downing the remainder of his drink.

"I prefer to be called Mr. Reilly," Ignatius intoned solemnly. "Ignatius J. Reilly."

"That's the name of your act?" Lloyd asked, wiping his hands with a freshly laundered bar towel. "I thought it would've been Johnny and the Moondogs or some bullshit like that, considering how deep it is in here."

Ignatius scowled at the bartender. "Does this conversation concern you, sirrah? Mr. Sullivan and I are executives of the highest order in our respective fields. You, on the other hand, are a lowly bartender."

"Could be," Lloyd said, shrugging, turning his back on the two and attending to matters that pertained to the maintenance of the restaurant-bar. "Time and the devil will tell, right?"

"He's a good boy, Lloyd," Ed Sullivan said, and he lit another Chesterfield and then belched loudly, a belch that impressed Ignatius and of which Ignatius heartily approved. "Now, what's your name again, and what's the name of this fabulous act of yours?"

"I'm Ignatius J. Reilly," Ignatius said. Name of the act? Of course there had to be the name of the act. The Troubadours? Ignatius and the Crusaders? The Boethians? No, no, no, none of those would do.

"Well?" Ed Sullivan asked.

Ignatius panicked, not wanting to lose this grand opportunity to have his revenge on Myrna and the Minkoffs (now that would make a good name for a contemporary pop band, wouldn't it?), Santa Battaglia, Claude Robichaux, Officer Mancuso and the entire New Orleans Police Department, those wanton homosexual derelicts in the French Quarter (especially that horrid Dorian Greene and those three equally offensive lesbians), Dr. Talc, the faculty in Baton Rouge, all Greyhound Scenicruiser drivers and enthusiasts, and any others who had offended him, Ignatius J. Reilly.

Then Ignatius saw the words that he needed. He saw them clearly and plainly among the beer, liquor, and liqueur advertisements on the wall: BOWERY BREW BEATS ALL!

"We're the Beat-Alls," Ignatius said.

"The Beetles?" Ed Sullivan frowned. "Who would go for a band named after bugs?"

"No, not the Beetles, the Beat-Alls," Ignatius said, and he uncapped one of his Charlie Chan Chinese Fortune Cookie Company pens and scrawled BEAT-ALLS on a napkin. "Like that. That is the name of the act, which will, of course, be plebicolar."

"Pubes? I thought you said you had a decent act."

"Appealing to the common man," Ignatius said.

"Ah, that's swell, kid."

Ed Sullivan picked up the napkin and peered at it, holding it at arm's length so that he could read it. "The Beat-Alls. You beat all. I like that sound of that, kid."

"Mr. Reilly," Ignatius said, correcting the television host. "But since we're being informal, you may call me Ignatius, and I'll call you Ed."

"I like being called Ed," Ed Sullivan said in his alcoholic stupor, "especially when I'm around good friends like you." He belched, and his face paled and then returned to its normal coloring. "Now, about this coming Sunday. You must be there."

"And I shall be there, Fortuna willing," Ignatius said energetically.

"Who's Fortuna?" Ed Sullivan asked. "Is she part of the act?"

"No, she's more of a mover of things," Ignatius said, attempting to find a way to explain the medieval concept of Fortuna and Fortuna's Wheel to the television host. "If you have to picture her, see her as a woman who spins a wheel that determines our fates, oftentimes in the most ludicrous of ways. Many refer to her, in the vernacular, as Dame Fortune."

"She sounds like one crazy dame, Ignatius. I could have a wildly dressed woman and a shouting audience, and every time she spins the wheel, someone wins or loses."

"That's a good way of seeing it, at least in terms that someone like you could understand," Ignatius replied.

"She's like Carmen Miranda," Ed Sullivan said, and he chuckled. "Don't tell anyone, but I almost laid Carmen Miranda."

"Don't worry, Ed. Your secrets are safe with me."

Ed Sullivan punched Ignatius's triceps lightly. "That's what I like about you, Ignatius. You're a swell kid. Let me write something on my card so that they'll let you backstage on Sunday."

After Ed Sullivan handed Ignatius the business card, Ed Sullivan stood, bobbing on his feet like a punch-drunk former contender. He donned his bowler and heavy winter coat and tipped his hat at Lloyd the bartender, who was leaning against a railing, his tongue and lips working a toothpick that moved from one corner of his mouth to the other.

"Have a wonderful afternoon," Lloyd the bartender said. "And please tell the missus that I said hello."

"Will do, Lloyd," Ed Sullivan said, belching loudly, stumbling to the door. "Now to brave these harsh winds and get back to those goddamn writers. You wouldn't believe some of the bullshit that they're putting out these days."

Ignatius motioned at Lloyd, who glumly and slowly pushed himself from his perch.

"Yes?" the bartender asked, his tone of voice showing that he was irritated by Ignatius's presence.

"Another brandy," Ignatius said, and, as Lloyd was getting ready to pour another brandy, Ignatius held up a finger. "No, make that a cognac. This is a special occasion, after all."

"Special occasion?" Lloyd said, putting away the bottle of brandy among the other liquor bottles, the light behind them endowing the bottles with hues of indigos and silvers. "You're the bullshitter, not the bullfighter, pal. There ain't no way that you're going to be on that show."

"Mr. Sullivan wants me on that show, and on his show I shall be because it is *his* show, after all," Ignatius said. "Now, pour that cognac, sirrah. I have other urgent business. Besides writing new verses for fortune cookies, I must obtain my troubadours."

"You're full of shit," Lloyd the bartender said, pouring cognac sloppily into a new glass, which he slid down the mahogany counter at Ignatius.

"For that you are not getting a tip," Ignatius said.

"I don't want a tip. In fact, I don't want your money. Consider the drinks on the house. Just finish your cognac, and get the hell outta here."

"In due time," Ignatius said, and he began jotting notes on a paper napkin.

The bartender shook his head and turned on a television set, which broadcast an early news program. One of the clips showed a group of retired Minnesotans flooding the lobby of the Hotel Claridge, and another clip showed a bewildered Mrs. Reilly and a dour Mr. Robichaux disembarking a Greyhound Scenicruiser at a Manhattan terminal.

Ignatius looked at the bartender and held up the pen just as scenes of tourists skating at ice rinks appeared on the television set.

"Would you happen to have a pen that I could use, most noble sirrah?" Ignatius asked.

"If I give it to you, will you get the hell outta here?"

"I must compose one more line of my speech, and I am done. I plan to use it for my introduction on Mr. Sullivan's show. Perhaps I should write a quatrain."

"Whatever the hell a quadrille is," Lloyd the bartender said, throwing a ballpoint pen at Ignatius.

Ignatius went back to work, and the image on the television screen reverted to a scowling Mr. Robichaux waving his large hand angrily at the camera.

II

Not liking the stares that he was getting from other pedestrians, Magoohan wandered towards W. Eighth Street. He reasoned that he was getting the stares because he was wearing green, purple, and gold tights and a Venetian mask. He thought that he had seen the little queer and his dignified-looking friend, but when Magoohan rounded a corner and accosted the couple, he discovered that it was an elderly cancer-riddled woman and her oncologist.

Grenadine was leaning against the jamb of the door of his establishment and smoking a long thin cigarette in an ivory holder. Magoohan rounded the corner, and Grenadine chuckled loudly.

"Whad's so funny?" Magoohan said, stopping, placing his hands on his waist. "Ain't you never seen a perv fairy before?"

"You can't be real," the owner of the tavern said, tapping the cigarette holder, causing cigarette ash to descend like snowflakes. "You just cannot be real, my dear."

"Well, I am real." Magoohan thrust out his chest. "I'm a perv fairy, and I'm looking for some action. Are you lookin' for some action, big boy?"

Grenadine giggled. "You can't be serious."

"Serious as the friggin' heart attack that killed my dear mother," Magoohan said, inching slowly towards Grenadine. "You looking for rough trade, fellow queer?"

"Where on earth did you get those lines?" Grenadine shook his head and then tilted it, the tavern owner studying the fireplug of a man and wondering if the man's lower apparatus matched in size the symbolic representation made by the proboscis of the Venetian mask. "At the local precinct? Or some cop television show like *Dragnet?* Please don't tell me that you got them from *Dragnet. Dragnet* is such a turgid, turgid show."

"I don't watch no *Dragnet,*" Magoohan said. "And I don't work at no precinct. I'm a fairy perv, like you, lookin' to get my rocks off." Magoohan feigned a smile. "How about we go into that back alley dere, sweetie, and see what kind of fun we can have?"

Grenadine shook his head. "No, thank you. One, you're not my type. Two, I don't have time for such nonsense. And three, I'm busy working on the show of shows, a show that is going to cause a sensation not only in Greenwich Village but in New York City. Nay, the show of shows that will be the shot heard round the world for my people."

"People? What are you talkin' about?"

"Who else?" Grenadine asked, taking a long drag off the cigarette and holding the smoke for an extended moment before exhaling. "My fellow queers, 'fairy pervs' as you call them. We're tired, you know, of being hassled by the police, spat on by the media establishment, relegated to the lowest ranks of society, marginalized as if we were the shameful dregs that never belonged, and tormented by bullies. I tell you, a revolution is brewing in this country, a revolution that's been building for centuries, and the time is right for this revolution to break forth, either here, at the Stone Carver Inn, or somewhere else in the Village. And this revolution will happen, and it's going to happen, with or without you or me. Speaking for myself"—and Grenadine took another long drag—"I'd like to be a part of the revolution."

Magoohan did his best not to frown. He didn't like the sound of this. It sounded like a communist plot, that's what it sounded like. The commies were doing their best to overturn things. They overturned the art world, according to the police commissioner, but as far as Magoohan was concerned, that was all right because art was for fairies anyway. Real men liked sports like baseball and football, and real men spent their evenings at home, watching television and drinking beer as their wives washed that evening's dishes or ironed the clothes that the husbands would wear the next day.

"Tell me more about this 'show of shows,'" Magoohan said, inching closer. "I got to hear more."

"It's going to blow the lid off the entire world," Grenadine said, exhaling smoke and giggling. "It's going to be the hottest revue ever. Neither you nor New York City nor anyone else in this world has seen the likes of it. It's going to blow everyone away, and then some."

Magoohan eyed Grenadine suspiciously. "You saying dat dis involves oral sex?"

"I'm saying that you're attempting to reframe my words, you undercover *dick*," Grenadine said, and he tapped his cigarette holder; gray ash descended to pedestrian-blackened snow. "That's what I'm saying. And I'm saying that as an undercover *dick*, you're a very lame one."

"I could take that in one of two ways," Magoohan said, doing his best to keep his Irish temper under control. "And you better mean cop when you say I'm a dick."

"Ah, but I thought that you said you were a 'perv fairy' and a 'fairy perv,'" replied Grenadine, who was now enjoying the game. "So which one is it, big boy? Are you an undercover *dick* in that ridiculous outfit, or are you some 'fairy perv' or 'perv fairy' looking for some dick in this area of the Village?"

"I'm a fairy perv, you perv fairy," Magoohan said, and he knew that he was going to relish the beating that he was going to give to this perv fairy once he, Magoohan, got this perv fairy into the confines of one of the holding cells back at the jail. "And I want you to give it to me."

"In one way or in two ways?" Grenadine asked, chuckling. He took another drag off his cigarette, which was quickly nearing its end. He exhaled a large cloud of exhaust into Magoohan's Venetian mask. "Or are you just into oral?"

"Whaddaya mean by that?" Magoohan asked testily. "I don't understand what you mean."

"You really are a loser, aren't you?" Grenadine shook his head. "Let me guess. You were working another precinct and screwed up royally, so now you've been assigned to the Village, where you're supposed to harass us. Isn't that true? Of course, you probably have the time to do that, given that you're not a married man."

"So what if I ain't married? A perv fairy ain't going to be married, is he?"

"If, indeed, you are a 'perv fairy,'" Grenadine replied haughtily. "No, no, you're a beat cop who screwed up somewhere, somehow. Your desk sergeant was tired of you, so he assigned you here to the Village. You're working with Dumbrowski, that despicable Polack who does his best to torment my people. And now he has you here, in the Village, running about in these ridiculous outfits. My dear, if you were indeed one of us, you would at least have enough sense to be coordinated in terms of your colors, if not in your mannerisms."

Magoohan's jaw muscles clenched. The beat cop felt a rage that he had never felt before.

"Obviously, you want to arrest me," Grenadine said, "but you know better. First, there is no violation, though you would probably claim that I had solicited you or resisted a false arrest. However, I do have witnesses."

And Grenadine motioned at the front window, from which Giacomo and Frank were watching.

"They would testify against you, for starters," Grenadine said. "Second, I would sue your department, and after the litigation was over, I would sue you personally. Mind you, I'm fully aware that I would probably lose in the court system, which is rigged and has been rigged from the get-go by the powers that be, always deciding in their favor.

"Nevertheless, your name would get in the papers, especially those delicious New York City tabloids, and many would begin to wonder if—no, make that suspect—that you were one of us. Your fellow beat cops would talk behind your back, and your neighbors would whisper one to another whenever you came and went. You know it, and I know it. And that's where I have you."

Magoohan's hands were trembling because of his rage. He wanted to wrap his stubby fingers around the perv fairy's trachea. And after the trachea was crushed, Magoohan wanted to keep squeezing until the perv fairy's eyeballs popped out of their sockets. And after the eyeballs popped out of their sockets, Magoohan wanted to keep squeezing until the perv fairy's head popped off.

Grenadine, who knew that Magoohan was enraged but could do nothing about his rage, chuckled.

"So, if you're going to bust me, you'll have to come to the show," Grenadine said, tapping his cigarette with a delicate finger, its nail a glossy green that contrasted sharply with the blacks, whites, and grays of that winter. "Otherwise, why don't you do us all a favor and go do something to yourself that's anatomically impossible?"

"You just wait," Magoohan said, thrusting a trembling index finger at Grenadine. "You just wait, smartass. I'm gonna take you down, and I'm gonna to take you down hard."

"At least you're not threatening to go down on me hard," the owner of the Stone Carver Inn said. "Then again, that might not be such a bad idea."

"What's yer name?" Magoohan said, whipping out his pad and a pen. "And yer address, what is it? And what's yer phone number?"

"And I haven't even agreed to go out on a date with you," Grenadine said. "My, we are forward, aren't we?"

"You gonna answer me or not?"

"I don't give my personal information to brutes."

"Give it—"

"I can't—and *won't*—say another word." Grenadine took a final drag off the cigarette, removed it from its holder, and dropped the cigarette onto the snowy ground, which resembled abstract chiaroscuros that Jackson Pollock could have created. The long thin cigarette extinguished with a long low hiss. "You'll have to come see the show. And bring along a few of your police buddies."

"I told ya, I ain't no cop."

"Right, and I'm not a queen, at least not Mary Queen of Scots," Grenadine said, chuckling.

"Yer askin' for trouble, pal."

"Actually, I'm asking for two dollars a head," Grenadine answered, turning, heading into his establishment. "Have a wonderful time, Officer. I hope you catch what you deserve, namely, a case of the crabs." The front door of the Stone Carver Inn closed behind a cackling Grenadine.

Magoohan made a face. Goddamn fairy. He, Paddy Magoohan, would take care of that goddamn fairy. If it was the last thing that he, Paddy Magoohan, ever did, he would get that goddamn fairy and put that goddamn fairy into his goddamn place.

Magoohan scrawled, in his uglyography, information from a poster advertising the Las Tres Amigas show.

III

Mrs. Reilly and Mr. Robichaux emerged from a cab that had stopped in front of the Colonial Revival house on Valentine Avenue in the Bedford Park area of the Bronx. Mr. Robichaux paid the cab driver, a belligerent Bulgarian who uttered Gypsy curses under his breath because Mr. Robichaux failed to pay a tip.

The cab sped off, and Mr. Robichaux hunched his shoulders against the bitter cold. Mr. Robichaux, like Mrs. Reilly, was freezing, and even though they were wearing the heaviest winter clothing that they could find in their respective homes in New Orleans, the many layers weren't enough to repel the cold that wanted so desperately to pierce Mrs. Reilly and Mr. Robichaux to the marrow.

"It's a wonder Ignatius ain't froze to death," Mrs. Reilly said. She removed a smudged envelope from her purse and then looked up at the house and squinted. "Same address as on this here envelope, Claude. This must be where Ignatius has been staying."

"Don't look like the house of a communiss," Mr. Robichaux said. He held out his arm, which Mrs. Reilly took, and he gingerly led the way to salted steps ascending to the front door of the Minkoff estate. "Looks like the house of a rich man."

"From what Ignatius told me a long time ago, Myrna's papa has done right well in the corrupt gentile world," Mrs. Reilly said, doing her best to remember Ignatius's exact words. "I don't know what that means, but it must mean that Mr. Minkoff done right well for hisself."

"Looks that way," Mr. Robichaux said, and slowly but surely, the two ascended the steps until Mrs. Reilly and Mr. Robichaux stood at the front door.

Mrs. Reilly pushed the doorbell, which chimed a pleasant four-ring chime. There was the sound of someone in the foyer, and Mr. Robichaux saw a huge eye appear in the front door's spyglass.

"We're not buying anything," Mrs. Minkoff said from the other side of the door. "And if you're not selling anything, we're not converting to any religion, especially the Jehovah's Witnesses. My husband, Bernard, says that we're quite content being Jews, though he hasn't said that lately."

"I'm Mrs. Reilly," Mrs. Reilly said.

"Who?"

"Mrs. Reilly from New Orleans," Mrs. Reilly said, irritated. "I called the other week."

"You did? Were you trying to sell something?"

"I called about Ignatius," Mrs. Reilly said.

"Who?"

Mrs. Minkoff's being purblind, along with its being cold, irritated Mrs. Reilly.

"Ignatius, my boy. He done run off to New York City with your Myrna."

"You must be Igor's mother!"

"You mean Ignatius's momma."

The front door opened, and Mrs. Minkoff smiled at the two.

"You must be frozen solid," Mrs. Minkoff said, motioning for them to enter. "It's a pleasure to meet the mother of the world's foremost Talmud scholar, Mrs. Fierstein."

"It's Mrs. Reilly, and I don't know what you mean, but Ignatius graduated smart from college," Mrs. Reilly said, stepping into the foyer, followed by Mr. Robichaux, and Mrs. Minkoff closed the front door behind them. "This here is my finance, Claude Robichaux."

Mr. Robichaux made a small polite bow, and Mrs. Minkoff beamed, then frowned.

"Something wrong?" Mrs. Reilly asked.

"You don't look Jewish, Mrs. Fierstein. And neither does your fiancé, Mr. Rothman."

"We ain't Jewish, we's Catholics," Mrs. Reilly said.

"Of course, Mrs. Fierstein. I need to keep reminding myself that Igor is a convert."

Mrs. Reilly stamped her bowling-shoe-encased feet on a mat, and Mr. Robichaux stamped his overly large feet a bit too harshly.

"Would you care for tea or coffee?" Mrs. Minkoff asked, leading the way to the living room.

"Will it turn us into communiss?" Mr. Robichaux asked.

Mrs. Reilly elbowed Mr. Robichaux in the ribs, and he grunted.

"Hush up, you dodo," Mrs. Reilly said in a low hiss. "We got to be polite. We got to make a good impression."

In the living room, Mrs. Reilly and Mr. Robichaux sat down on the sofa.

"I believe I heard you say that you wanted coffee," Mrs. Minkoff said. "Lucky for us, I have a pot brewing. Isn't that convenient?"

She smiled at Mrs. Reilly and Mr. Robichaux, and then Mrs. Minkoff said that she would be back in a few minutes. After she was gone, Mr. Robichaux motioned at a spot on the floor; the now-destroyed china cabinet, the heirloom that Mr. Minkoff's late dear mother had bequeathed to Mr. Minkoff, had left a rectangular-shaped intaglio.

"Christ Amight," Mr. Robichaux said, doing his best to keep his voice low. "I bet you she moved a trunk of pamphlets, maybe even bomb-making stuff that the communiss use in this city."

"Didn't I tell you to hush up, you dodo?"

"I tell you, Irene, New York City is the bed of the communiss," Mr. Robichaux said solemnly. He put a hand to his mouth and whispered. "For all we know, could've been a trunk holdin' the body of Ignatius."

"Claude, sometimes I'm a wonder what I'm gonna do with you," Mrs. Reilly said. "They didn't put Ignatius in a box. Besides, Ignatius wouldn't fit in something that small."

"You don't know what these communiss capable of," Mr. Robichaux said.

Mrs. Reilly felt her temper about to erupt like a volcano. She wanted to smack Mr. Robichaux upside his head the way that she had smacked Ignatius upside his.

Before Mrs. Reilly could do that, however, Mrs. Minkoff came into the living room, a silver tray in her hands. She placed three elegant china cups down onto a coffee table (upon which Ignatius had rested his ursine feet while he watched television and imbibed innumerable soft drinks) and then poured coffee for Mrs. Reilly and for Mr. Robichaux. Mrs. Minkoff then placed a small carafe of heavy whipping cream and a sugar bowl beside the two cups, and, with a flourish of a hand, said they could have their coffee any way that they pleased.

"Better let me drink first," Mr. Robichaux whispered to Mrs. Reilly, "leastways in case she's trying to poison us."

"Would you hush up, Claude?"

Mrs. Minkoff sat down in Mr. Minkoff's recliner and sipped her coffee, which she drank black. Mrs. Reilly added healthy doses of heavy whipping cream and sugar to her coffee, and Mr. Robichaux, like Mrs. Minkoff, drank his coffee black, reasoning that if she had poisoned anything, it was the cream or the sugar or both and not the coffee, seeing that she was drinking it. Then again, his little mind reasoned, she could have made two pots of coffee and poisoned the one intended for her gentile victims.

"Now I remember your call," Mrs. Minkoff said. "I didn't tell Igor about your visit. I'm sure that he'll be surprised."

"Don't seem that he's here," Mrs. Reilly said. "When do you expect him back, hon?"

"Sometime this evening," Mrs. Minkoff said. "He's been coming home earlier from work because he says that he needs the right ambiance if he's going to create his masterpiece, and the factory doesn't have the right ambiance for him."

"Ambulance?" Mrs. Reilly asked, eyes crossing. "Ignatius been sick? Don't let him fool you, hon. I know Ignatius, and he plays games with people. You can't trust him. He plays sick to shirk work and his responsibilities."

"I'm not sure we're talking about the same person," Mrs. Minkoff said in protest. "Igor is a very hardworking young man. He's absolutely changed everyone's life here for the better. Me, well, I now know how godawful our culture really is. And Mother, well, Mother has calmed down considerably, though she still needs more work. And Myrna has work, and she's not talking about overthrowing the government or running off with some

Negro boy. And my husband, Bernard, is doing much better. I thought he was going crazy, but Igor spoke harshly to Bernard the way a rabbi should, and Bernard took it to heart. Igor's a wonderful rabbi."

"Rabid?" Mrs. Minkoff said. "Ignatius ain't rabid."

"He's also a fine scholar, Mrs. Fierstein," Mrs. Minkoff said, "and I'm sure that he's going to get his own congregation very soon. What with his working as a vice president of that factory and this great project of his and his studies, it's a wonder that he finds the time to sleep. But find time he does."

"You said that Ignatius was *working*?" Mrs. Reilly asked. "First time I thought I wasn't hearing you correct. Second time I thought I wasn't hearing you correct. Third time I still wonder if I'm hearing you correct."

There was a loud moan of pleasure from Grandmother Horowitz's bedroom, which was adjacent to the living room. Mrs. Minkoff blushed.

"Never mind that," she said to Mrs. Reilly and Mr. Robichaux. "Mother's watching a special program."

"Sounds like a special program, all right," Mr. Robichaux said, and there was another loud moan from Grandmother Horowitz's room.

"Ignatius don't believe in work," Mrs. Reilly said. "Never has. After he graduated, he worked at a library, but they fired him. And wherever he's been, he's managed to destroy something."

"Well, something did happen," Mrs. Minkoff began, and there was another loud moan, and Mrs. Minkoff grimaced. "Igor fainted in the living room after he and I discussed his marrying Myrna, and Bernard's late mother's china cabinet fell over, and everything in it was destroyed. Bernard was devastated, of course, because it was the last physical reminder he had of his mother. And that's when I thought that he was going crazy, until Igor straightened him out. Bernard's not talking about guns any longer, and he's not watching Laurel and Hardy but has returned to his favorite, Walter Cronkite. He couldn't be happier."

"Walter Cronkite's a communiss," Mr. Robichaux said, believing that if the coffee had been poisoned, it would have done the trick by then. "You can't trust the media, Mrs. Minkoff."

"That's exactly what Igor says, Mr. Rothman. Were you Igor's rabbi?"

"His what?" Mr. Robichaux said.

"Claude's my finance," Mrs. Reilly said. "After we get married, he's gonna be Ignatius's step-papa."

"Isn't that sweet?" Mrs. Minkoff said because the thought did, indeed, sound sweet, but she was not sure, nonetheless, why the thought sounded sweet.

There was another loud moan. Mrs. Minkoff rued ever having allowed Myrna to speak to Grandmother Horowitz about female needs.

"Some kind of show," Mr. Robichaux said. "They say the Jews the ones not only behind the communiss but behind the pornography, too."

Mrs. Reilly pointed at a print on a far wall. "What's that a picture of, hon?"

"Oh, that," Mrs. Minkoff said. "That's a Picasso print that one of Bernard's customers gave to Bernard for Christmas last year."

And as Mrs. Minkoff started to provide further information about the print, Mrs. Reilly lifted a bowling-shoe-encased foot and brought the heel down hard on top of Mr. Robichaux's shoe. Mr. Robichaux yelled and spat out his coffee, and Mrs. Minkoff stared at the man, who whimpered and nursed his wounded foot.

"I'm so sorry," Mrs. Minkoff said. "I didn't think that the coffee was that hot."

"It's his sciati-ticky," Mrs. Reilly said. "It acts up in the cold."

"That's horrible," Mrs. Minkoff said. "Is there anything that I can do to help?"

"Just tell us where my boy is, Mrs. Minkoff."

"I can call the factory and tell Igor that you're here, Mrs. Fierstein."

"No, it's best, hon, that we surprise Ignatius."

"I'm sure that he would find that quite delightful, Mrs. Fierstein. Oh, I almost forgot. Myrna mentioned that she and Igor might be going to that institute where she gets therapy. You probably want to go there first. Let me get the addresses for you."

"And would you mind callin' a cab for us, hon?"

"Not at all, Mrs. Fierstein. I'll do anything for the mother of the world's foremost Talmud scholar."

And Mrs. Minkoff went to get the addresses and to call a cab for Mrs. Reilly and Mr. Robichaux.

Mr. Robichaux winced, still nursing his foot. "Wished you wouldna have done that, sweetie."

"I wouldna, 'cept you was rude," Mrs. Reilly said, and there was a long piercing moan from Grandmother Horowitz's room. "Now, you mind your manners, and I'll mind my foot!"

Ten

Ignatius shook his head in disgust. None of the people who were auditioning had read the ad thoroughly, or, if they had, they had not fully understood what he was seeking.

"And what makes you think that I was seeking a poodle act?" Ignatius asked a small, nervous woman standing in front of his desk. "I specifically said that I was looking for a performer who could play a medieval instrument like the lute or even something like the French horn."

"But Charlot is a *French* poodle," the woman said, holding up her miniature black poodle, which snarled at Ignatius. "Doesn't that count?"

"No, it does not," Ignatius replied haughtily. "While your poodle is descended from a noble breed, and while he certainly dances the quadrille very well—for a poodle, that is—he is, nonetheless, not what I am seeking. Now, if he could recite the noble words of Boethius or those of Chaucer, then perhaps I could use his services."

"Charlot can talk," the woman said, her voice and eyes and facial expression pleading with Ignatius for a second chance. "He can count to four. Come, Charlot, count to four for the nice man."

But the poodle, which detested Ignatius, snarled and bared its teeth. Ignatius frowned, shook his head, and sighed. He rose slowly from his desk, using his ursine paws to help push himself up. Too many rich meals, courtesy of Mrs. Minkoff and of Miss Ping, had caused his girth to expand by two or so inches.

"Don't call us, we'll call you," Ignatius said, motioning the way to the door of his office, doing his best to be polite but wanting more than anything to drop-kick the woman and her dog across a football field. "I do appreciate your coming in, Mrs. Turner. I wish you all the best with your poodle. May he learn from the great Boethius and come to accept proper theology and geometry."

The woman scowled, the dog snarled, and as the woman and her dog exited, Miss Ping brought in the next applicants, a young woman, no more than nineteen, if that, dressed in yellow medieval garb, and her companion, a young man who resembled her and who was dressed entirely in black medieval garb. Ignatius raised an eyebrow. These two seemed to have promise.

"And who are you?" Ignatius asked, and, after he closed the office door, he used his paws to wheelbarrow his huge girth over to his desk, where he sat down. "Have you read the ad thoroughly? Do you understand its contents in their entirety? Do you understand that this is a very urgent matter? Do you understand that I am not accepting just anyone for this mission? After all, the worldviews of millions are at stake if I do not intervene."

"We read it, man," the young man said, and he had red, puffy, leporine eyes, as if he had stayed up all night, and Ignatius noticed that the young man had a peculiar odor, like burnt twitch weed. "We get the medieval thing, man, and we think that we can do the gig, man."

"What is it with this *man* business?" Ignatius said. "You're speaking like one of those insufferable beatnik lickspittles who hang around coffee houses all day and all night and who bat bongos and scribble scatological, silly poetry that no one in his right mind could possibly understand. In fact, if anyone understands this so-called Beat poetry, I say that he has gone mad and lost his mind and is no longer part of a great generation."

"Heavy, man," the young man said, removing a pack of cigarettes from somewhere deep inside his shirt. "Mind if I smoke, man?"

"Mind if I have flatulence?" Ignatius said, his blue-yellow eyes crossing in consternation.

"Doesn't bother me, man," the young man replied, and he lit his cigarette.

"Put that out immediately!" Ignatius thundered. To the young woman, he said, "You haven't said one word. But before you do, pray tell, what are your names?"

"I'm Laye, and this is my twin brother, Sidney," she replied.

"It's Sid, not Sidney, man," Sid said.

Laye rolled her eyes and smirked. "Pardon him, sir, but he's always talked like this."

"Even when he was a child?"

Laye nodded. "Our mom doesn't understand it, either."

"What about your father?"

"We don't know who he is, man," said Sid sadly. "Our mom said that it was some strange guy from the Deep South, maybe a Black Irish guy, who wrote funny books but was afraid that the government was after him, man."

"Interesting," Ignatius said, stroking his chin. He motioned at the cases that they had in their hands. "What kind of instruments are those? I might be able to tolerate a classical guitar or two, seeing that I am slightly enamored with the tinkling of Andrés Segovia, but if they're electric instruments, that will never do."

"I play the lute," Laye said, and she opened her case and removed the instrument, which had intricate carvings on the body and shiny strings. "And I play the harpsichord, too."

Ignatius raised both eyebrows in delight and in surprise. "The harpsichord? I believe that we are possibly on to the right start."

Sid opened his case and removed an acoustic bass guitar. Ignatius bit his lower lip and shook his head.

"No, no, no, that will never do," Ignatius said. "If, perhaps, we were going to play for a group of Hawaiians, your ukulele might do the trick. But we are not playing for Hawaiians, we are playing for a worldwide audience. Besides, I consider the ukulele an abomination, one that's one step below the tinny banjo."

"It's a bass, man," said Sid as he stroked the neck of the instrument salaciously. "It provides the heavy beat you're gonna need, man."

"What exactly is this worldview thing?" Laye asked, putting the strap of the lute over her left shoulder and tuning her instrument. "We're not sure what you mean by that."

"My worldview is the one of correct and proper theology and geometry," Ignatius replied. "Civilization reached its apogee in the medieval period, when just kings and queens ruled and each person knew his proper place within society. Society then, I'll have you know, not only had the best in Christendom, as found in the patristic teachings and practices of the Church, but the best in pagan antiquity from both the Greek world and the Roman world. The latter, fortunately, provided us with the writings of the great philosopher Boethius, whose seminal work *The Consolation of Philosophy* provided the necessary philosophical worldview for the inhabitants of the medieval world.

"Unfortunately, the Renaissance arose. While many in our day and age see it as necessary, the Renaissance was an assault against all that was properly theological and properly geometrical. Whereas the individual learned his proper place in medieval society, in the Renaissance world, the cult of personality took over. People began to believe that reason was the chief arbiter of things."

Laye made a face, showing that she didn't understand. "What's wrong with reason? Weren't they more or less living by blind faith during the medieval period?"

"What's wrong with reason?" Ignatius said mockingly. "What's wrong with reason is this: it's completely, totally unreasonable."

"Heavy, man." Sid smiled.

"Do you mind if I continue?" Ignatius said, and his stomach grumbled, and he craved a foot-long hot dog. "After the Renaissance, we then have the Enlightenment, which, unfortunately, has led to our current state of affairs. To paraphrase Chesterton, when a man has lost everything but his reason, he has nothing left but his madness. And that is what our modern world now has: complete, utter madness. Do you realize how utterly insane it is for everyone to believe, and to follow, Madison Avenue? Do you realize how utterly banal and vapid and vacuous the modern world has become, thanks to shows like *American Bandstand*? Do you realize how utterly short and meaningless modern life is, where a new teenage idol can be crowned, and is crowned, at each and every moment of the day?"

"I like that last line, man," said Sid. "I think it would make a great line in a great song, man."

"I think it would, too," Laye said. "How about something like this? 'Charleston was once the rage, uh-huh, history has turned the page, uh-huh, the miniskirt is the current thing, uh-huh, teenybopper is our newborn king, uh-huh.'"

Hands covering his ears, eyes shut tightly, lips twisting into a grimace, Ignatius shook his head.

"Stop, stop, stop!" he bellowed. "This is exactly the thing that I am combatting this very moment! And what on earth is a miniskirt! Is that an accoutrement, like a sporran, that a Scotsman wears!"

The intercom buzzed, and Miss Ping's voice crackled on the line. "Are-uh you-uh in need-er of-er assistance-uh, Mr. Lei-ly?"

Ignatius pushed a button. "If I need anything, Miss Ping, I will let you know! Never interrupt me ever again!"

"You are-er in the-uh middle-uh of-er a busy-er meeting-er," Miss Ping said, and she laughed her phocine laugh. "Sorry-uh, but-uh I am-er joking again. People-uh say-er I am-uh so-uh funny—"

Ignatius pushed a button on the intercom, cutting her off.

"Now where were we?" Ignatius said, returning his attention to the fraternal twins standing in front of him.

"You didn't like the song we came up with, man," Sid said sadly. He turned to Laye. "We could do our own gig, man, and probably become a great act and when things broke up, man, you'd probably become a diva, man."

"Man, man, man," Ignatius said. "Worthless apposition. And worthless ideas that you are bandying about, Sir Sid."

Sir Sid beamed. "Sir Sid, man. I like the sound of that, man."

"I'm not going to be called Sir Laye," Laye said petulantly, "if that's the idea."

"You're Lady Laye," Ignatius said to her, and he leaned back in his reinforced office chair, which groaned.

"So, you have a song ready, man?"

"I do indeed," Ignatius said, and he stood and removed the palimpsest from his shirt pocket. "The great and mysterious Fortuna, popularly known as Dame Fortune, brought this to me. It is written in Latin, and I have transcribed the words into beautiful medieval English. I've done my research, but I cannot determine who the author is. And, alas, this beautiful work does not even have a title. Therefore, I am calling this song 'A Canticle for Ignatius J. Reilly,' or, perhaps even better, 'A Canticle for Ignatius.' What do you think of the proposed titles?"

"Heavy, man," a heavy-eyed Sir Sid said sleepily. "I think I asked, but you mind if I smoke, man?"

"I do mind, and I do not want you to ask me that question ever again," Ignatius said. He folded the palimpsest tenderly and placed it into his shirt pocket.

"Is there a name for our group?" Lady Laye asked.

"Originally I thought that we should be called the Troubadours or Ignatius J. Reilly and Company," Ignatius said. "Each name has its own merits, of course. The former hearkens to the days of yore, when knights were bold and certain things, as that bawdy rhyme goes, had not been invented. The latter is more modern, akin to an acting troupe working at a playhouse, say, somewhere in a place like Pasadena.

"But ultimately, after much thought, I knew that these names would never do. I knew that my band of troubadours would need to be named something that would catch the attention of the harried housewife, the overworked salesman, the pimply teenager. And the name came to me, in an instant, when I was speaking to the great Ed Sullivan himself."

"You know Ed Sullivan?" Lady Laye asked.

"We are well acquainted," Ignatius replied. "Like me, he is an old soul in a new world. O brave, new world! Alas, not even the Bard himself would be prepared for times like ours."

"What's the name of our band, man?" Sir Sid said.

Ignatius cleared his throat, and, using his hands as if spelling the name on a marquee, said, "The Beat-Alls."

Lady Laye frowned. "The Beetles? Why are you naming your band after bugs?"

"Not Beetles," Ignatius protested, "Beat-Alls! We are the Beat-Alls! We are going to *beat all* who are out there!"

"I get it, man," Sir Sid said. "It's like we're the end all of beat-all, man."

"You are very correct, Sir Sid, at least this time," Ignatius said with passion, gesticulating to paint a picture of what was to come. "Can you imagine how we'll take over the world! The teenagers will scream wildly because of us and abandon the likes of Frankie Valli and other high-pitched Italian singers! Some, like right-wing Calvinistic preachers in the Deep South, might consider us a menace! Or perhaps a rival band might form, attempting to outdo us!"

"What would be the name of this rival band, man?"

"Something like the Railing Storms," Ignatius said after giving the question serious thought. "The newspapers will probably ask inane questions, to wit, would you rather your sister date a Beat-All or a Railing Storm? The controversies, comparisons, contrasts, adjuncts, species, and so forth, I can assure you, will be far too innumerous."

"What kind of gig is this?" Lady Laye said. "Folk or rock or country?"

"The answer is D, none of the above," Ignatius said. "We are minstrels of the present, hearkening to the music of the past. In other words, we are going far into the past, around the time of Chaucer."

"Sounds like folk music to me, man," Sir Sid said. "You dig Pete Seeger, man? Or that new cat, Bobby Dylan, man? His songs aren't good like Seeger's, but at least he has a decent voice, man."

"I wish that you would quit this *man* business," Ignatius said. "Now, if you'll play your instruments and give me a taste of what you can do, I'll sit here and consider if you are worthy to appear with me on *The Ed Sullivan Show*."

Lady Laye played her well-tempered lute, singing "Greensleeves" while Sir Sid played his acoustic bass.

"We shall have to work on that ukulele," Ignatius said after they were done, "but otherwise, I think you two will do. Now, if you'll please return here at three, we shall have our first rehearsal."

Lady Laye and Sir Sid said that they would return, and, after they left the office, Ignatius locked the door, sat down at his desk, and ate an entire bag of potato chips. Then he fell into a deep sleep, in which he dreamed of screaming, green-sleeved teenagers in the audience of *The Ed Sullivan Show*, and all the green-sleeved Minkoffs (including the beloved, green-sleeved Grandmother Horowitz) were in attendance, and a green-sleeved Rex ran up a verdant acclivity that could be dreamed only in a dream.

II

Myrna adjusted her peasant's skirt. She had wanted to purchase a shirt and a pair of pants, the type Chairman Mao wore, but the secondhand shop down the street from the fortune cookie company didn't have any her size. So, she settled for her peasant's clothing, hoping that the workers would be empathetic with her nonetheless.

From a window overlooking the innards of the fortune cookie company, she watched an intricate network of machines, all humming and chugging and moving fortune cookies along conveyor belts. The Chinese workers moved their fine hands swiftly and deftly, like small rodents handling gems.

Myrna glowed with pride. First there would be the liberation of Chinatown. Then there would be the liberation of Little Italy. And then the rest of Manhattan, the entirety of Brooklyn, Yonkers, the Bronx, and eventually Westchester County. And eventually the revolution would spread far beyond New York City and wind its way up the coast, through Providence and Boston and into Bangor, and spread its way down into Pennsylvania and across into Ohio. Soon the Midwest, with its sheep-slaughtering winds, would be taken, and then the Southwest, with its spicy Mexican dishes, would be taken, and then the Pacific Northwest, with its quiet, antisocial people, would be taken. Myrna nodded in appreciation. She was saving everyone, including Ignatius.

Miss Ping appeared, holding in both hands a tray supporting a pot of steaming orange pekoe tea and Ignatius's heavily stained mug.

"You must-er be uh-gathering information-er for-uh Mr. Lei-ly," Miss Ping said. She blushed and giggled. "So-uh sorry. I do-uh not-er mean-uh to make-er jokes so-uh early-uh an hour-er."

"You're a regular Lenny Bruce," Myrna replied, and she would be glad to get rid of Miss Ping and Mr. Pong and Mrs. Wang. No longer would they be allowed to exploit the defenseless workers of the Charlie Chan Chinese Fortune Cookie Company. "I might as well give you a fair warning, Miss Ping."

"Warming-uh?" Miss Ping's eyes crossed. "Why-uh do-er I need-er a warming-uh? Is it-er not-uh hot-er enough in here-uh?"

"*Warning*," Myrna said, gritting her teeth, ensuring that she enunciated the word clearly and revolutionarily. "Soon the workers are going to be up here, running things, and you and that tyrant Mr. Pong and that sharpie Mrs. Wang are going to be down there, working those machines."

"No," Miss Ping said. She shook her head defiantly to emphasize her emphatic no, her pigtails turning in defiance, too. "I now-uh work-er for Mr. Lei-ly and only Mr. Lei-ly."

"Ignatius just thinks that he's a vice president," Myrna said. "It's all a sexual delusion, of course. His office is a symbol for phallic narcissism. I'm not sure entirely what that means, but Dr. Ingloss said it, so it must mean something significant."

Miss Ping blinked. "In-gros? Phal-rick? I do not-er know-uh these words-uh."

"That's because bourgeois exploiters like you don't have to know big words," Myrna replied, and she felt revolutionary anger boiling up from the depths of her vagina and into her stomach and into her breasts and into her throat and all the way into the interior of her thick skull. "You force others to do the dirty work for you." Myrna made a face of contempt at Miss Ping. "You're a minion's minion, and because you refuse to join the revolution and thereby redeem yourself, you persist in being entirely evil. It wouldn't surprise me, too, if you turned out to be anti-Semitic."

Miss Ping's small mind was doing its best to figure out what Myrna was talking about. After a moment or two of consideration, Miss Ping concluded that Myrna was talking about the upcoming Chinese New Year. Miss Ping smiled.

"So obsequious, aren't we?" Myrna said haughtily. "If I were as shallow as you, I'd be smug, too."

"I am-uh glad that you-er mention-uh the lions-er," Miss Ping said. "The Charlie-uh Chan-er Chinese-er Fortune-uh Cookie-uh Company-er always uh-supplies lions-uh for the parade-er." Miss Ping bowed. "Now-uh if you-uh please excuse-uh. I must take-er Mr. Lei-ly his-uh tea-uh."

"You don't understand," Myrna, who was following after Miss Ping, said. "I didn't say lions, I said minions. You're just a minion of another minion in the grand scheme of things. If only your Chinese heritage and your proud Chinese breasts would see that."

"Plenty of-uh lions!" Miss Ping exclaimed. "Yes, we will-uh have-er plenty of-uh lions!"

Myrna turned away in frustration and strutted to the door that opened to the stairs descending to the innards of the factory. Before she opened the door, she adjusted her peasant's blouse and her peasant's skirt. Even though the area was warm, Myrna's breasts felt very cold, like ice, and her nipples had stiffened because of that. Myrna told herself that they were soldiers erect, ready to do battle for the sake of the revolution, and, if necessary, to die for it.

And with that, Myrna opened the door and stepped out onto the stairs.

The noises from below—whistles and grindings and churnings—deafened anything within their proximity. Myrna winced and told herself that no matter what, she was not going to back out. She boldly went down the two flights of stairs.

Myrna strode to relay boxes and pushed a button on a relay box affixed to a conveyor belt overladen with fortune cookies that needed to be wrapped. The conveyor belt slowed. Delicate-handed workers looked at Myrna, who removed a People's Republic of China flag from between her ample, braless breasts and who waved the flag as if she were signaling the start of a drag race.

She leaped onto a stainless steel table, and her peasant's skirt rode too far up her legs, thereby revealing her panty-less crotch.

"Comrades, our time has come! Comrades, we are going to overthrow the reactionary Mr. Pong! Comrades, the revolution is now!"

The workers, not speaking or understanding a word of English, blinked. A man standing next to the relay box looked at his colleague.

"Is it lunchtime?" the first man asked in Cantonese.

The second man shrugged and replied in Cantonese: "I thought lunchtime was in an hour. And why is that white devil waving a communist flag?"

"I believe that she is a ward of our noble, highly esteemed vice president," the first man said. "She is said to be deeply disturbed. It is probably cheaper to keep her here, among the workers, than to send her to Bellevue, just as the rich white devils send their insane children to public universities instead of getting the children the help that they so desperately need."

"She looks like a matador I saw on television." The second man scratched the side of his pug nose with a stubby finger. "Someday I hope to travel to Spain, you know."

The first man grimaced. "Now she is raising her voice and waving the flag frantically. Now she has tossed aside the flag. Now I cannot believe what I am seeing!"

Indeed, not only could he not believe what he was seeing, but neither could his colleagues, who were watching in utter amazement as Myrna pressed her breasts together, looking as if she were working an old-time squeezebox in a Western film.

"Liberty, eternity, and frugality!" Myrna yelled at the workers. "I believe that's what they were yelling during the French Revolution, or something like that! Anyway, our breasts, especially those belonging to the women, who are more oppressed than you men, even though you are oppressed, are angry! Our breasts are angry, and our breasts, at which the exploitative capitalist piglets on Wall Street suckle, are demanding justice! Justice, justice, justice! That is what our angry breasts are demanding! Justice!"

The second man scratched his head, whose hair was thinning at the top. "I think that she wants us to work faster, as if we are not working fast enough."

"That is probably what she means by her otherwise obscene gesture," the first man said. "Her motions mimic, I believe, the motion of the dough machine as it forges the fortune cookies."

Myrna squeezed her breasts harder, doing her best to communicate her revolutionary message. "The piglets are suckling at our breasts, and our children are going hungry in the tenements because we are barely able to afford rent—well, not me, I live with my reactionary father in the Bronx, and that's a far worse fate than yours, I can tell you, because at least you have your own homes— but anyway, we are all oppressed, and I'm tired of writing letters to editors and sending off manuscripts only to see my work rejected because of the so-called spelling errors and typos and ink stains!"

"I do not understand a word of what she is saying," the first man said, and he reached for the relay box. "We must get back to work if we are to meet our quota."

Myrna, seeing him reach for the relay box, thrust a finger at him.

"You are no longer a slave, comrade!" Myrna shouted. "You will never have to work on this line ever again! If anyone will have to, it will be Mr. Pong and his reactionary investors in this sweatshop!"

And with that, Myrna ripped off her peasant's blouse and revealed her bare breasts.

"I will lead the way, like the bare-breasted woman in that painting that I thought was a reactionary work until a docent told me what it was all about!" Myrna yelled, pointing her finger at the door at the top of the stairs. "This is the way to freedom, comrades!"

The first man's face paled, and he became nauseated, not because of his seeing Myrna's now-exposed breasts, but from smelling their odor, which was similar to the rendling of garlicy cheese. The second man had fainted and fallen over the stilled conveyor belt.

Myrna, who believed that the spirit of revolutionary fervor had overtaken the workers, leaped from the stainless steel table onto the factory floor. Two women rushed over with a white sheet to cover her.

"You are very offensive in more ways than one," the first woman said warily in Cantonese to Myrna. "And you need a bath. I thought that you white devils knew the value of hygiene."

"You are wasting your words," the second woman said to her colleague. "She is insane. She is like the many white devils and black devils and brown devils who live in the streets. We must get her wrapped up as tightly as possible. We must summon our noble vice president immediately after we have subdued her."

"We must all expose ourselves for the sake of the revolution!" Myrna yelled at the women, believing that they had brought the white sheet as a flag of victory. Myrna tore the white sheet out of their hands and waved it about.

"I shall lead the way with this in hand," Myrna said. "Libertine, equality, and maternity! This is our motto, comrades!"

The two women grabbed the white sheet, and, aided by the first man, wrapped up Myrna in it, as if they were wrapping a mummy prior to its burial. Myrna squealed in delight, believing that the workers were engaging proactively in the revolution.

It wasn't until she couldn't move that she knew that something was amiss. "Let me go!" Myrna yelled. "What do you think you're doing!"

"I am not sure," said the first man in Cantonese to another, "but I believe that this makeshift straightjacket ought to hold her for a while."

"We should contact our noble vice president," the two women said simultaneously in Cantonese.

Ignatius, who was sleeping peacefully in his chair, startled awake to an extremely loud buzz on his intercom. Miss Ping told Ignatius that he was needed because of an issue with Myrna and then giggled and apologized for being jocular. Ignatius's ears rang because of the loudness of Miss Ping's voice.

"I am not to be disturbed," Ignatius said, and he snorted in contempt. "First, quit your insolent giggling. You are not a little schoolgirl but the secretary to the most important, the most integral component of this company. And second, tell the factory workers to do whatever they want to do with my factotum, Miss Ping."

"Your-uh fat-uh what-uh, Mr. Lei-ly?"

"My *editorial assistant!*" Ignatius hissed like a testy cottonmouth awakened from its deep slumber on a bank of the Mississippi River. "Tell them that they can do whatever they want with Myrna minx! Now if you'll excuse me, Miss Ping, I must get back to the urgent matters at hand! The Charlie Chan Chinese Fortune Cookie Company is on the verge of falling into a deep abyss from which this company might never emerge if I do not apply my ample business acumen to the numerous problems that are plaguing us! In other words, my dear woman, I am not to be disturbed!"

Ignatius reached into a bowl of unwrapped fortune cookies, cracked one open, and crumpled the fortune into a tiny ball, which he tossed at an overflowing litter basket. He shoved the fortune cookie halves into his gaping maw, chewing the halves loudly and licking the crumbs from the whiskers of his black mustache. He leaned back in his chair, closed his eyes, and hoped that he would dream of his long-dead Rex.

The first man put down an in-company telephone receiver.

"According to Miss Ping, we are to discard her fat ass," the first man said in Cantonese to the other workers. "We are to take her to the top of the building, where we are to drop her into the garbage below."

"Are you sure?" a woman asked in Cantonese.

"That is what Miss Ping said that our noble, highly esteemed vice president said to do," the first man replied somberly. "Ours is not to reason why, ours is but to do or die."

"How true," the woman said. "Your words would make a noble fortune indeed."

The others nodded in agreement.

Then a handful of the men and women dragged a bound and screaming Myrna to the delivery elevator.

Instead of having a pleasant dream about Rex, Ignatius was instead having a nightmare about his mother and Claude Robichaux and Santa Battaglia, all three nude, all three engaged in wanton sexual acts. He awoke when he heard Myrna scream but attributed his sudden awakening to the nightmare.

He took a deep breath, exhaled slowly, and told himself that he would have to take things much, much easier.

III

Giacomo entered the Stone Carver Inn, hoping that the maroon-haired woman and the elderly man who had just left the tavern found the boy whom they were seeking. Grenadine asked Giacomo if he had disposed of a bagful of empty Bowery Brew beer bottles appropriately and accordingly, and Giacomo replied in the affirmative. Grenadine then told Giacomo to check for a delivery from Japan. Giacomo nodded.

Grenadine, who was thankful that those two irritating creatures were no longer in his establishment, returned his attention to the small stage. He shook his head. He was not pleased. He was not pleased with the new decorations, and he was not pleased with the way rehearsals were going with Las Tres Amigas. And he was not pleased with Frank. Frank was refusing to wear a tuxedo that he, Grenadine, had purchased.

"I tell you, Grenadine, you're making the biggest mistake of your life," Frank said, and he held up the tuxedo. "I can't wear this goddamn thing. How could you ever expect me to wear this goddamn thing? Where's your common sense, Grenadine?"

"That's a lovely tuxedo," Grenadine said, swiveling on his bar stool. "I myself would wear it, but I already have clothes that I've been dying to wear."

Frank studied the hot pink tuxedo and its matching hot pink tie and its matching hot pink cummerbund, the latter two items affixed to a clothes hanger from which the hot pink tuxedo hung. He placed the clothing onto the shiny mahogany counter, as if the clothing were somehow contaminated, and wiped his hands on his damp bartender's apron.

"You ask me, you should sell this joint," Frank said. "I gotta bad feeling, Grenadine, about this whole thing, like I been tellin' ya all along."

"Ever since I've known you, it's been nothing but bad feelings, my dear. If it isn't a torn anterior cruciate ligament or a corn or a bunion, it's your elbows or some respiratory infection. Speaking of which, have you ever considered giving up smoking? If you did that, my dear, you'd probably ache half as much and be a quarter of your usual bitchy self."

Frank grimaced, and his hands, as if they had minds of their own, clenched into tight fists. Had Grenadine been anyone else, Frank would have struck. But he, Frank, needed the work. He had a wife and three kids. They were dependent on him. What was he going to do?

"And I tell you, Grenadine, those three clowns aren't getting any better. You ask me, they're deliberately gettin' worse."

Grenadine was studying the far green wall. "Judy Garland."

"What? Who?" Frank said, making a face. "Have you heard a word of what I said, Grenadine?"

"Judy Garland," Grenadine said, and he smiled and studied the barren green wall. "A portrait of Judy Garland would just be so lovely there, wouldn't it?"

Frank shook his head. "I shoulda listened to my Uncle Louie. He told me to go to trade school. I coulda been a bricklayer or a mechanic or a printer, anything but a goddamn bartender." He tossed a moist towel to the side and felt like crying. Family or no family, he couldn't take the humiliation any longer. "I ain't gonna wear it, Grenadine."

Grenadine, who was envisioning a lush portrait of Judy Garland—perhaps something painted in the style of David or, perhaps, one of the Pre-Raphaelites—wasn't paying attention either to Frank or to Frank's protestations.

"You know how those Chinese restaurants have those three gods?" Grenadine asked, continuing to study the barren green wall.

"Yeah, three chinks all lined up in a row, with an orange or an apple in front of them like some sort of goddamn offering," Frank said, not realizing that Grenadine had been speaking rhetorically. "Fook, Luke, and Duke, I think that's what the chinks call 'em. Missus and I haven't eaten chink in a long time, so I'm not much up on it."

"She shall be the goddess of our good fortune," Grenadine said, deciding that the style of the portrait would be that of John

Singer Sargent. "Find me a good portraitist, Frank. This is the most urgent project we have."

Suitcases in hand, Las Tres Amigas emerged from the back, El Lobo Macho in the lead. El Lobo Macho didn't know it, but he was still wearing hot pink lipstick.

"We want pay," the gang leader said in a high-pitched voice, and then, noticing how his compatriots stared at him, changed his pitch. "We men. We hardworking men. We deserve pay of hardworking men."

"You get a cut from the box," Grenadine said. "Now, we have practice tomorrow at three. No more being late and no more excuses, girls."

El Lobo Macho cussed in Spanish. After this was over, he, El Lobo Macho, was going to put Grenadine's *bicho* and *cojones* into a jar of isopropyl alcohol, signifying El Lobo Macho's complete and total victory over *la putería*.

Just then the door to the tavern slammed opened, and Henley and Nick the Nose stumbled in, both having blackened eyes and bruised faces that they had received courtesy of the members of a men's Bible study group in Harlem. Henley leaned against a heavy wooden post, his breathing stertorous, and Nick the Nose crossed his arms and shook in his seedy topcoat because of the winter cold refusing to leave the marrow of his bones.

"May I help you?" Grenadine said, sauntering over to the two. "The door doesn't open for two more hours. If you're here to collect for charity, well, my dears, I gave at the office, and then some."

Henley hacked into his handkerchief, hacking heapings of hot phlegmy hash. After the beating, he saw the wind carry the faux palimpsest to the south and across Central Park. In Greenwich Village, he and Nick the Nose saw a woman sporting maroon hair and wearing bowling shoes pick up the faux palimpsest. On foot, Henley and Nick the Nose tailed her and her elderly companion before the maroon-haired woman and her elderly companion entered a cab. Hailing their own cab, Henley and Nick the Nose followed the cab in which the woman and the man were riding, Henley sensing that he had seen or met the woman somewhere before.

Because of the past few days, Henley wasn't in the mood for much of anything. Henley wasn't in the mood for Negro attendees at a men's Bible study group in Harlem, Henley wasn't in the mood for meddling Irish cops like the one dressed as Robin Hood, and Henley certainly wasn't in the mood for some cheeky pain-in-the-ass fag in a cheeky pain-in-the-ass fag joint in a cheeky pain-in-the-ass fag area of lower Manhattan.

"Wherb arb dey?" Henley asked, gasping, methamphetamine coursing through him, his lungs aching for the clean ocean air of Santa Barbara, where his beautiful wife was lying by their beautiful pool and tanning her beautiful legs.

"I'm sorry, but I don't understand a single word of what you're saying, you poor thing," Grenadine said, taking compassion on the man, who looked to Grenadine like a freshly arrived immigrant not prepared for this brutal winter in New York City. To Nick the Nose, Grenadine said, "Is your friend from one of those obscure Germanic countries like Lichtenstein?"

"He's from Cal-cal-cal-cali-fornia," Nick the Nose replied, teeth chattering, reminding Grenadine of the comedian Charlie Callas. "He ain't-ain't-ain't used to the cold out-out-out heh."

"And from the looks of it, neither are you," Grenadine said. "Why aren't you wearing heavier coats?"

"Da paber," Henley said, wiping his nose with his silk handkerchief, which he pocketed after taking a deep breath, doing his best not to choke on a catch that was in his throat. "I sawb dem. Da paber."

"I don't know what kind of idiom or dialect they use in California, but it's hideous," Grenadine said, and he shuddered after thinking briefly about his own upbringing in Kansas City.

"If America is going the way of California, as one of our futurist friends has said, then we are, indeed, in very deep trouble."

Henley staggered over to the bar, where he sat down on a green leatherette stool.

"Cobbee," Henley said, pointing at a pot of freshly brewed coffee. "Gimme cobbee."

Frank, who was having a harder time than Grenadine understanding Henley, nonetheless knew that Henley wanted coffee, so Frank poured Henley a cup and then Nick the Nose a cup. Henley sipped the scalding brew, which gave him the warmth that his body so desperately craved.

Meanwhile, El Lobo Macho, Guapo, and Chico surrounded Grenadine.

"Our mamas need to pay rent," El Lobo Macho said. "You say we make big money if we dress like *mujeres*. So we dress like *mujeres*. But we do not have money."

"What don't you understand!" Grenadine said, tossing up his hands in exasperation. "This is a commission-only gig. You get paid *after* you do a show, *not before*!"

Giacomo appeared, wearing the Wayfarer sunglasses and carrying a set of congas. Miss Maggie, his boa constrictor, hung loosely around his neck. Grenadine shrieked when he saw the snake and jumped behind a post.

"I wanna be part of the act, boss," Giacomo said. "My ma thinks that I have a future beyond dry-mopping. I love dry-mopping, but if I could play congas for a living, I would do that instead."

"Get that hideous thing out of here!" Grenadine yelled at his janitor. "Where on earth did you get it!"

"This?" Giacomo replied, holding up the set of congas. "I got 'em after saving my money for two years, boss. Why you acting so afraid? You never seen congas or something?"

Henley took another sip of his coffee, which felt nice and hot as it went down his sore throat. He sniffled. Find those people, he told himself, get the paper, and then get the hell out of there, even if it meant killing those people and anyone else, including Nick the Nose.

Henley looked at Giacomo and said in a very raspy voice, "Wherb arb dey? Wherb da paber, youb stubid fag kib?"

Giacomo adjusted his sunglasses, stared at Henley, and refused to answer.

"You unastan?" Henley asked, reaching into a pocket of his pea coat, feeling his black .38. "Dey hab a slib of paber."

"We need money, *puto*," El Lobo Macho said to Grenadine as the gang leader jabbed a finger in Grenadine's chest.

Henley removed the .38 from his pocket, waved the weapon menacingly, and, with his other hand, ran a finger across the phoenigm of his philtrum. Then he motioned at Nick the Nose.

"A heist!" Grenadine squealed. "We're being robbed! Frank, call your dago cousins and have them come down here at once!"

"Ya better pay attention," Nick the Nose said, gesticulating, no longer stuttering because the coffee had warmed him. "Now, we some people come in heh, and we want dis goddamn paper dat dey have so that we can like overturn dis goddamn government and the rest of dis goddamn world."

Irritated by Nick the Nose's indiscretion, Henley side-kicked Nick the Nose in the shin, the side-kick a technique that Henley had learned in the OSS.

"Whad you do dat for!" Nick the Nose hollered, holding his shin while he hopped around on the other foot. "I'm on yer side, Ids!"

"Id idn't Ids," Henley said.

Henley scowled at Grenadine, at Giacomo, at Las Tres Amigas, and at Frank, who was reaching underneath the cash register.

Henley aimed the pistol at Frank. "You bad up, wob, or I blobe yer hed ob."

Frank slowly raised his hands and backed away. Grenadine wiped a tear from his eye.

"I can't believe that I'm being robbed," the owner of the Stone Carver Inn said.

"We ain't robbing youse," Nick the Nose said. "We saw a woman come in heh with dis retard guy she's wid. The woman sounds like she's from Brooklyn, and the retard guy sounds like he comes from the Deep South. Retard guy can't keep his hands off the woman, and the woman can't stand him putting his hands on her. Now, sound familiar?"

Frank cleared his throat. "The slow guy kept accusing everyone of being a communist. You ask me, he and that woman are inbreds, like in one of them plays written by a Central Park South queer."

Grenadine glowered. Frank shrugged and gave Grenadine an apologetic look.

"They show you da paper?" Nick the Nose asked. "You have it?"

"They didn't say nothin' about no paper," Giacomo said. For a moment he thought about jumping Henley but thought the better of it, sensing that Henley, even though he was ill, was a desperate, trapped rat. "They said they was looking for a cat named Ignatius."

"Idnatius?" Henley said, and he wheezed. "Who dob hell ib Idnatius?"

"She said it was her son," Grenadine said, and he sighed, closed his eyes, and pinched the bridge of his nose. "I didn't get the whole story, my dears, but it seems that he was an insane student who had studied at Tulane and who escaped some sort of mental institution, thanks to his communist girlfriend who lives somewhere in New York City." Grenadine opened his eyes. "A Jewish woman, the mother of this young communist girlfriend, supposedly gave the mother and her companion the directions to a hangout where the communist girlfriend goes, an institute of some sort here in the Village. The woman and her companion were searching for the hangout."

Henley motioned at Nick the Nose to continue with the questions.

"So, you didn't see da paper?" Nick the Nose said. "Okay, you have any idea where dese inbreds are? We didn't like see dem leave heh."

Grenadine shook his head. "Not a clue, my dear. I didn't get their names. It's clear that the slow man's done menial labor all his life, and he did mention something about getting back to his rental properties and getting away from all the 'communiss' in New York City. The woman elbowed him, and he grunted, and before I knew it, the two had mistakenly exited by way of the back door. I assume that they crossed onto the next street and are meandering who knows where."

"Where dey from?"

Grenadine shrugged in frustration and sighed in resignation. "As you said, the woman sounded as if she were from Brooklyn, and the man sounded as if he were from the Deep South. Oh, yes, I learned that they were engaged. For all I know, they could be from Mobile, Alabama, Waycross, Georgia, or Houston, Texas. I'm from the Midwest myself, and I never ventured to the Deep South, save for one excursion to New Orleans, where I went for Mardi Gras."

Henley looked at Grenadine and then at Las Tres Amigas, who weren't saying a word. Henley nodded at Nick the Nose. Nick the Nose backed up, as did Henley, who kept the .38 trained in the general direction of Grenadine and the others.

"Nod a word," Henley mustered from his tortured throat, the pain so searing that it brought tears to the corners of his winter-wind-whipped eyes. "Nod one goddamn word."

Grenadine and the others nodded. Nick the Nose and Henley, walking backwards, exited the Stone Carver Inn. A whoosh of cold air filled the tavern, causing Grenadine's skin to goose-pimple even more.

"Christ, I almost lost my establishment," a tearful Grenadine said.

"We want our money," El Lobo Macho said, now that Henley and Nick the Nose were gone. "Now, where is *el dinero, puto?*"

IV

Magoohan was sitting in a stall in a men's subway restroom, waiting for Nick the Nose. Magoohan was wearing a black trench coat, flesh-colored tights, black combat boots, and sunglasses, and was attempting to look like an exhibitionist.

Magoohan had seen Henley and Nick the Nose leave the Stone Carver Inn and had followed them to the subway station and overheard the smaller of the two say that he needed to take a dump. Believing that this was his chance, Magoohan had rushed into the second of two stalls in the men's restroom and waited for Nick the Nose to enter the first stall.

What Magoohan didn't know was that in his, the operative's, haste, Nick the Nose had entered the unoccupied women's restroom and was taking care of his business there.

Magoohan began to lose patience. Where was that suspicious queer? He had sounded so desperate to use the men's room.

Giacomo, who was on his way home to Spanish Harlem but who needed to use the restroom, entered the other stall, dropped his pants, and sat down on a cold porcelain seat. It had been a long day, especially because of the two creeps who had almost caused the boss to have a heart attack. Giacomo wanted nothing more than to toke the marijuana that he had purchased the previous evening from his Jamaican dealer.

Magoohan slid his boot into Giacomo's stall. Giacomo, who couldn't help but notice the boot, nudged the boot to get it to go away.

"You a perv fairy, too?" Magoohan asked. "I am so hot. I need it right now, big boy. I need it good and hard."

"I just want your foot outta my stall," Giacomo replied. "You wanna play footsie, go do it someplace else."

Crap, it wasn't that suspicious character! Magoohan reasoned with himself. It was late, he was tired, and if he kept wearing get-ups like the one that he was now wearing, he was going to catch pneumonia and die. And he didn't want to die. The way to prevent that was to take someone, guilty or not, in.

Magoohan rose from the porcelain seat upon which he had been sitting and stepped out of the stall. He faced Giacomo's stall.

"Yer under arrest," Magoohan said, holding out his badge and a pair of handcuffs.

"What for?" Giacomo asked, evacuating his bowels loudly.

"For soliciting, you perv fairy," Magoohan said. "Ya touched my foot."

"Cuz you placed your foot in my stall," Giacomo said, wiping. "I touched your foot so that you'd take it away."

"Only faggots use the subway toilets, pal."

"That must make you a faggot, too," Giacomo replied, wiping more, ensuring that he was bone-dry clean.

"Ya comin' along peaceful, or do I have to make this hard?" an enraged Magoohan asked.

"Sounds like you want it hard," Giacomo said, standing, buttoning, zipping up.

"Get outta there right now, you fairy perv faggot!"

Giacomo flushed the toilet and slammed open the door to the stall, which, because Magoohan was wearing sunglasses, Magoohan didn't see in time. The door struck him hard in the face, and Magoohan grunted as he became an airgonaut, and he dropped his handcuffs and his badge, which skittered on the concrete floor. Magoohan struck the restroom wall hard with his back, thereby knocking the wind out of him and causing him to slump to his knees. Gasping, Magoohan reached out for Giacomo, who jumped aside, washed his hands quickly, and bolted from the restroom.

Magoohan groaned. A suspicious person, a suspicious person, his badge for a suspicious person!

• *Eleven*

It was late afternoon at the Charlie Chan Chinese Fortune Cookie Company. The klaxon had rung a few minutes earlier, indicating the end of the shift. Workers emerged from the front entrance of the factory, and the workers proceeded home slowly because of the brutally hard day. Neither the cold winter air nor the steel-blue gloaming added anything negative to their moods, which were already dour. The workers were exhausted. They wanted to go home, they wanted to drain bowls of Campbell's chicken noodle soup, they wanted to sleep in warm beds.

Ignatius, who had copied three lines of Boethius and a line or two from a Batman comic book as his day's work, was leaning forward at his desk, thankful that Myrna was still at the doctor's because of her inauspicious fall into the garbage. Ignatius, Lady Laye, and Sir Sid had been practicing one hour for their appearance that coming Sunday on *The Ed Sullivan Show.*

"You are not singing it correctly," a scowling Ignatius said to Lady Laye, and he shook his head in disgust. "Perhaps it is because of your Yankee accent. Do you think, perchance, that you could do your best to imitate the bland Midwestern?"

"I don't understand this crap," Lady Laye said, studying a mimeographed translation of the palimpsest. "'Whan' this and 'whan' that. What the hell is that supposed to mean?"

"It's our introduction," Ignatius said testily, and he stood and began to pace as best as he could in the cramped office. "These are the immortal words of this immortal, anonymous bard. Many call Shakespeare the Bard. That is a positive statement, of course, but in comparison, Chaucer, who is another bard, becomes the Greater Bard. But he is not the greatest bard. Nay, we must take it to the superlative. The anonymous writer of these lines, he is the Greatest Bard."

"Whatever," Lady Laye said in exasperation. "As long as I'm getting paid, I'll sing whatever shit you want me to, Ignatius."

Sir Sid belched and plucked an out-of-tune string on his acoustic bass. "Hey, you have any more fortune cookies, man? I've got cotton mouth and the munchies at the same time, man."

"Munchies?" Ignatius asked. "Ah, yes, of course, a repast. While I do not understand or agree with many of the unintelligible things that you say, Sir Sid, I do agree that we need to take a quick break. Is anyone up for a hot dog?"

"Sure, man."

"I really think that we need to get back to work," Lady Laye said in protest. "I mean, the show's this Sunday, and we don't even have our act together."

"Rome was not built in a day," Ignatius replied haughtily. "And haste makes waste. We need our energy, especially me, after a long day's work."

Lady Laye eyed him suspiciously. "What exactly is it that you do all day, Ignatius?"

"I'll have you know that the work that I do here at the Charlie Chan Chinese Fortune Cookie Company is the hardest, most brutal work that any mortal man could ever endure," Ignatius pontificated. "I'll have you know that I am striving, under the blessings of blind Fortuna, to deliver modern man from the errors of his evil ways and his evil worldviews."

"We gonna eat or not, man?" Sir Sid asked. "We eat, or I'm going out to smoke another joint, man."

"We'll continue this discussion later, should we need to," Ignatius said to Lady Laye.

Then he held up a finger, indicating that he wanted silence. He used the intercom to call Miss Ping and ordered five foot-long hot dogs—three for himself and one apiece for Lady Laye and Sir Sid—and three large soft drinks.

Sir Sid cracked open a fortune cookie, tossed the fortune aside, and wolfed down the halves.

"These taste kinda funny, man," Sir Sid said. "They puttin' sawdust in these things or somethin', man?"

Ignatius raised an eyebrow. "Pray tell, what could possibly be wrong with those fortune cookies? I assure that you that the Charlie Chan Chinese Fortune Cookie Company produces the finest fortune cookies in the world."

"Practice," Lady Laye whined. "We need to practice, guys!"

"In due time," Ignatius said, "in due time."

A few minutes passed, and Miss Ping brought in their order of hot dogs and soft drinks (and almost caused Ignatius to spit out his soft drink when she said, laughing her phocine laugh, "Me-uh Chi-uh-nese, me-uh play-er joke, me-uh go-uh pee-pee in your Coke!"). After Ignatius's shock wore off, and after Ignatius scolded Miss Ping, Ignatius downed his three foot-longs one right after the other, like a ravenous grizzly feasting on rainbow trout. Not only did the hot dogs taste extremely pleasant, but the liberal spreading of mustard and ketchup and relish on each hot dog did, too.

"Are we gonna get back to practice or not?" Lady Laye said, wiping her full, incarnadine lips with a paper napkin. "I don't think that we're going to be ready, Ignatius."

"We are going to be ready," Ignatius said. "If worse comes to worst, we'll improvise."

"I like to improvise, man," Sir Sid said. "We can make it like a jam session, man."

"Indeed we could," Ignatius said. "That's the spirit, Sir Sid. You should take a few lessons from him, Lady Laye."

"Come on, guys, we need to practice. I mean it."

A cab stopped in front of the Charlie Chan Chinese Fortune Cookie Company. Mr. Robichaux paid the concupiscent Chinese driver, and Mrs. Reilly studied the factory of which her son was vice president.

"We finally got here," Mrs. Reilly said, "after all them wrong turns with them other chinks. Now, you keep quiet about them communiss. It's a wonder that one chink didn't shoot you in the leg, Claude. You let me do the talking here."

"Whatever you say, sweetie," Mr. Robichaux said, wanting to get back on Mrs. Reilly's good side.

At the receptionist desk, Miss Ping slaved over ledgers, Mrs. Wang being gone, having gone to Hong Kong. The door opened, and Mrs. Reilly entered, followed by Mr. Robichaux.

"May-er I-uh help-er you?" Miss Ping asked the two.

"Mrs. Minkoff said that Ignatius and Myrna might be here," Mrs. Reilly said to a blinking Miss Ping, Mrs. Reilly grateful that the office felt warm as she dusted off the New York City winter from the sleeves of her coat. "I need to see Ignatius."

Miss Ping blinked. "You-er are-uh here-uh for job-uh?"

"No, I'm here to see Ignatius, my boy," Mrs. Reilly said. "Before we left the Minkoff house, Mrs. Minkoff said that he said that he's the vice president of this chink company. I don't know if I can believe that, honey. You have to watch Ignatius. He can be mean, and he can be sly, let me tell you."

"You-er are-uh Mr. Lei-ly's mother-uh?"

"Yes, I'm his momma," Mrs. Reilly said. "Now, where is that boy?"

"It is-er such-er honor to meet-er the mother-uh of-uh the most high-ree esteemed-uh poet-er and philosophy-uh," Miss Ping said quite sincerely to Mrs. Reilly. "You must-er be-uh very proud-uh. He is-er like-uh Confucius. I am-uh Miss-er Ping, by-er the way."

"Is that what he's calling himself now?" Mrs. Reilly asked, perplexed. "It's not Confucius, it's Ignatius, and he's not a Confucius, he's more like a confusion. Me and Mr. Reilly didn't give him no chink name. He's named after that feller what done established the Jeserits."

Miss Ping frowned. "Are you-uh sure this is-er your-uh son?"

"Has anything real bad happened here?" Mrs. Reilly asked, looking around.

"Not at-er all. Thanks-uh to Ignatius-er J. Lei-ly, our sales-er have-er increased-uh velly much."

"That's not the Ignatius J. Reilly that I know," Mrs. Reilly said, "and there can't be two Ignatius J. Reillys. The Ignatius J. Reilly I know don't know how to make anything good for no one."

Mrs. Reilly felt weak, and so she braced herself with a hand on the receptionist desk before sitting down in a chair that Mr. Robichaux pulled up for her. What if Ignatius had had an identical twin, unbeknown to her? Two of him? Was it possible? Why, she'd probably be in her grave that very moment, if that were true. Mrs. Reilly shuddered in horror at the thought of there being two Ignatius J. Reillys.

"He's my boy," Mrs. Reilly said imploringly to Miss Ping, "and I love him dear, but he don't belong here in New York City. He needs to go back to New Orleans, where he can get the help he needs."

"Pray-er tell-uh, what kind-er help?"

"He's crazy," Mrs. Reilly said, and her mouth watered for a sip of muscatel. "Been crazy ever since he got him that master's at Tulane. Maybe even before. All he wanted to do was watch television and shout at dancing teenagers just having a good time, and when he wasn't doing that, why, he was up in his room and writing the craziest, weirdest stuff in those Big Chief tablets of his.

"Now, you didn't realize it, hon, but when you hired Ignatius, you hired something akin to the devil himself. Ignatius knows how to manipulate people to get what he wants. I didn't realize that fully until after Ignatius done fled New Orleans with that Myrna Minkoff girl."

"Ah, Miss-er Minkoffed, yes. She is-er what-uh Mr. Lei-ly call his-uh fat-sclotum."

"His fat scrotum?" Mrs. Reilly asked, eyes crossing, not believing what she had just heard.

"I am-uh not-er fanciful with the English-er language-uh, woman-er who-uh claim-uh to be-uh Mrs. Lei-ly. I am-uh Hong Kong woman. Because of-uh that, I am a very-uh funny-er."

"You let me see my boy. I'm tired of being bounced around from one place to the other. If it ain't Mrs. Minkoff acting goofy, it's people like you, who should know better."

"Unfortunately, Mr. Lei-ly is not avay-rable," Miss Ping said. "He is-uh seeking to change-er the world-er-views."

"I don't believe a word of it," Mrs. Reilly said. "And why can't you learn to talk right? We have a chink in our neighborhood named Wong Duk Dong. He's in the restaurant business like you, Miss Ping-Pong Ball, and he talks perfect good English. So does his brother, Jack Duk Dong, the chink what runs the laundry. Now, where's that Ignatius!"

In the office, the intercom buzzed, indicating that Miss Ping was calling.

Ignatius pushed a button on the intercom to answer Miss Ping's call. "What is it, you incorrigible vixen of the Orient? Do you desire a raise? If so, the answer is a flat-out no."

"Two-uh people are-er here to see-uh you," Miss Ping said on the static-filled line.

"Ah, the FBI agents," Ignatius said, and he smiled. Ignatius had contacted the FBI earlier that morning and told an agent that he, Ignatius, was going to change worldviews; if the FBI wanted to get in on the act, now was the time. "Please tell them that I shall be ready to see them in an hour or two, after practice is over and after I've had a chance to nap."

"Ignatius!" Mrs. Reilly screamed into the intercom. "Ignatius, is that you! Are you doing to this company what you did to Levy Pants, boy! Ignatius, you come out here—"

Ignatius pushed a button and immediately cut off Mrs. Reilly and Mrs. Reilly's screaming. His face blanched. In fact, his entire body blanched. Flummoxed, he jumped up from his chair and scurried around his office, looking for a means of escape. Sir Sid had fallen asleep, his long chin resting on his narrow chest, and Lady Laye made a face of disapproval at Ignatius.

"We gonna practice or not, Ignatius? Like I said, I want everything to be perfect—"

"You must get me out of here!" Ignatius bellowed. "I don't want to go to Bellevue or to Mandeville or to any other asylum! Such places would do irreparable damage to my already fragile psyche! Do you understand, they are here for me! They are here, here, here!"

"Who are here for you?" Lady Laye asked. "And for what? What are you talking about, Ignatius?"

"My mother and her McCarthyite," Ignatius said, and he cracked open his office door and peered out into the narrow hallway. He heard Mrs. Reilly argue with Miss Ping. Ignatius closed the door, snapped the lock into place, and looked frantically around the small office. "They attempted to put me away when a sodomite revolution failed in the French Quarter, thanks to the machinations of that trickster Fortuna. Unfortunately, one of my earlier attempts, a campaign for Moorish dignity, failed, too. No one understood what I was attempting to do for the modern world, not in the slightest, not even my mother and her neo-Klansman."

"Your mom and her what?"

"Her fiancé, a John Bircher," Ignatius said, moving one way, then the other, in the cramped office. "He believes that there's a communist underneath everyone's bed. I daresay that if he gets a flat tire, he blames a fellow traveler for it."

"The only way out is the only way in," Lady Laye said. "I hear them coming."

And Ignatius heard the hurried footsteps of his irate mother. He could never forget her gait or how her feet sounded whenever she walked in her bowling shoes.

The door rattled, and the doorknob twisted one way, then the other, clearly showing someone's determination to get into the office.

"Ignatius, you open up this door! I mean it, boy! Claude and me come up here to take you back to New Orleans!"

The door handle rattled in the hands of the contumacious Mrs. Reilly. Miss Ping said something, and Mrs. Reilly snapped something unintelligible, and Ignatius thought he heard Mr. Robichaux call Miss Ping a communist.

Sir Sid snorted awake. "Whoa, man, I was dreaming of this huge joint, man—"

"We don't have time to talk about juke joints and jazz dives," Ignatius said, and he eyed the window and then looked at boxes of discarded burlap sacks. "A rope! We need to make a rope! My safety with a rope! The window! You must lower me from the window!"

Ignatius tore burlap sacks and began knotting them together, and was helped by Lady Laye, who was able to knot more of them together than Ignatius. The door rattled, as if an enraged demon were attempting to get in. Sir Sid smacked his lips, yawned, and fell back into a deep sleep.

"Ignatius, boy, you open up! You hear me! You open this door!"

"Can you imagine what they will attempt to do to me?" Ignatius said, hands shaking so badly that he couldn't complete the knot upon which he was working. Lady Laye took over and knotted the shredded burlap with a sailor's knot and tugged hard at her handiwork to ensure that the knot would hold. "They'll put me in a straightjacket and lock me up in a padded room, as they do all the dissidents in that horrid Soviet Union. They'll prod me with questions and poke me with innuendoes and insinuate that my antiquarian but true worldview is a sure sign of closeted homosexuality. I am sure that they would persecute any other with the same worldview by assuming that his propriety could only mean that he was a closeted homosexual, without perhaps taking into consideration that he might have been a celibate or chosen celibacy as a means of enhancing his creativeness, or simply because he did not care for the touch of human flesh."

Ignatius heard Myrna's calling out in the hallway.

"Ignatius, your reactionary mother and her equally reactionary lover are here for you!" Myrna yelled. "Sorry, but in my revolutionary haste, I forgot to tell you that Mom spilled the beans to your mom! You've got to get out of here! The doctor says I'm okay, by the way! I'm not going to sue because Mr. Pong has given me a raise and is going to allow me to lecture the workers on Mao, even though I'm afraid the glass ceiling is still there for me!"

"Would you please shut up for once, you doxy!" Ignatius yelled in extreme frustration and in extreme fear.

"Ignatius, boy, you open up this door!"

On the other side of the door, Myrna and Miss Ping did their best to pull Mrs. Reilly away from the door. She refused to release her death grip on the doorknob, which she twisted one way, then the other, the way that she wanted to twist Ignatius's neck.

"You and your fascist friend aren't taking Ignatius anywhere!" Myrna said, attempting to place herself between Mrs. Reilly and the office door. "He's safe for once!"

"I shoulda knowed a girl like you would do something like this to Ignatius!" Mrs. Reilly said. "Claude, help me with this door!"

Myrna wedged her way in, and now she had her back against the door and forced Mrs. Reilly to release her grip on the doorknob.

"You a communiss?" Mr. Robichaux asked Myrna. "You sound like a communiss."

"I'm Ignatius's liberator!" Myrna said. "I'm helping him to escape the confines of his mind through his sexuality! Once he gives me his virginity, he'll be liberated for life!"

"You not only a communiss, you a deviated prevert," Mr. Robichaux said, and he placed his huge hands on Myrna's shoulders in an attempt to move her aside.

"Rape!" Myrna screamed at the top of her lungs. "Someone, please help me! Rape! Rape! Rape!"

In the office, Ignatius slowed his breathing so that he would not hyperventilate. "It seems as if that right-wing pundit of the Klan is assaulting my factotum."

"Rape! Rape! Rape!" came through the office door.

"You stop that, girl!" Mrs. Reilly, who was held back by Miss Ping, shouted. "Claude ain't trying to rape you, he's just trying to get you out of the way so that we can take Ignatius home!"

Ignatius turned from the door. Lady Laye knotted the last knot. Sir Sid rolled a marijuana cigarette. Ignatius rubbed his hands nervously, like a first-time surgeon preparing for the most delicate of hernia operations.

"Done," Lady Laye said. "Sid, come on. Help me tie this to the desk."

"Let me finish my joint first, man," Sir Sid said, and he ran his tongue along the paper and then twisted the ends of the marijuana cigarette.

"We don't have the time for this!" Ignatius said. "We must ensure my escape! Don't just sit there smoking your twitch weed!"

"Yeah, all right, man," Sir Sid sibilated sleepily. "What do you need me to do, man?"

"Over here, Sid," Lady Laye said, indicating the leg of Ignatius's desk closest to the window.

In the hallway, Mrs. Reilly thrust a finger into Myrna's face. "We ain't joking, Myrna. You get out of the way! Ignatius needs to get home to New Orleans!"

"So that you can put him in a reactionary insane asylum!" Myrna yelled.

"Perhaps-uh we have-er tea-uh and talk-er this over," Miss Ping interjected. "I make-er jokes and make-er everyone so happy-er happy."

"Get your hands off of me!" Myrna snarled at Mr. Robichaux, who was still doing his best to unbrace her from the doorframe. "Not only are you a reactionary fascist, you're probably a repressed homosexual who's attacking me to prove his virility!"

"Christ Amight, you communiss so stubborn," Mr. Robichaux said, and even though he had worked as a railroad brakeman for the Illinois Central for over five decades, and even though he had developed the grip of a gorilla, thanks to the many stuck railroad switches he had thrown and the many hand brakes that he had tightened, he could not budge Myrna.

"If only Dr. Ingloss was here!" Myrna yelled at Mrs. Reilly. "He'd set you straight! Then you'd see the great harm that you've done to Ignatius!"

"We come to make things right!" Mrs. Reilly said, doing her best to help Mr. Robichaux remove Myrna from the doorframe. "Now you get out of the way, girl!"

In the office, Lady Laye and Sir Sid tied the end of the jury-rigged burlap rope to the heavy leg of Ignatius's desk. Ignatius, meanwhile, attempted to pry open the window. The dusty frame refused to budge even one thousandth of a millimeter. Ignatius tried again, his face crimsoning because of his physical exertion, drops of sweat rolling down his forehead and into his blue and yellow eyes.

"It's no use!" Ignatius said, gasping and eyes stinging as he slumped down into his chair. "I'm doomed!"

"Rape! Help, me! Rape!"

Miss Ping said something that was inaudible to those in the office, and Mr. Robichaux bellowed that he did not eat what communists ate.

"Move out of the way," Lady Laye said to Ignatius.

Lady Laye picked up Ignatius's copy of *The Consolation of Philosophy*, which she threw at the window, which shattered into several shards that tumbled through the air like broken icicles.

In front of the office door, Mrs. Reilly swooned. "Ignatius done jumped out the window to his death! Look at what you done, Myrna Minkoff!"

Mr. Robichaux pried harder at Myrna, who then remembered a trick that she had learned in a jiu-jitsu manual written for anarchists. She removed her hands from the doorframe in which she had been bracing herself, placed her hands on Mr. Robichaux's shoulders, and drove her knee up into his groin.

Mr. Robichaux's eyes crossed, and he gasped, his knees instinctively locking as his weathered, spotted, knotty hands covered his groin. He staggered back a step, his eyes rolled up into his head, and he slumped unconscious to the floor.

In the office, Lady Laye cleared away broken glass and covered the lower edge of the window frame with a heavy blanket with which Ignatius had covered himself during his many naps.

"I've changed my mind," Ignatius said. He took a step back, and his heart pounded like a timpani in one of Beethoven's symphonies. "If blind Fortuna wants to lead me away, let her do so safely."

"Your message, man," Sir Sid said, and he grabbed one of Ignatius's arms and led Ignatius to the window. "We gotta get your message out there, man, and we gotta get you outta here, man."

In the hallway, Mrs. Reilly attempted to box Myrna's ears. Miss Ping, who had studied the praying mantis style of kung fu at a kwoon in Hong Kong, grabbed Mrs. Reilly's wrist, twisted Mrs. Reilly's arm to the side, and then twisted Mrs. Reilly's arm up into her back. Mrs. Reilly screamed, not in pain but in surprise. Mr. Robichaux, who was slowly coming to, groaned and rolled on the floor. Myrna pounded on the office door.

"Ignatius, hurry! Get out of here!"

Lady Laye and Sir Sid did their best to get Ignatius feet-first out the window. Ignatius's hefty ass, which had gained considerable girth, got stuck. Ignatius fluttered his legs as if he were swimming a fifty-yard dash.

"You're going to kill me!" Ignatius bellowed like an ox. "I am now convinced that you two are a part of a conspiracy, if there is one!"

"Hang on," Lady Laye said, and she formed a lasso with the makeshift rope.

She looped the lasso around the chest of a protesting Ignatius, his hands grasping at anything within reach. Lady Laye tightened the lasso around Ignatius's chest and nodded at Sir Sid.

"Whatever you do, hang on to the rope," Lady Laye said to Ignatius, and she grunted because the liberation of Ignatius was like an extremely difficult parturition, only done in reverse. "We're almost there."

Myrna yelled loudly and continued her pounding on the door. Mrs. Reilly was yelling at Miss Ping, threatening to have the police arrest her for assaulting a white woman.

Sir Sid chuckled. "This is wild, like a Laurel and Hardy comedy, man."

"No time for joking," Lady Laye replied to him. "Come on, Sid, push!"

And with one huge, final shove, the two pushed Ignatius out the window. He descended so quickly that he didn't have time to scream. His descent caused the desk to rush towards the window, Lady Laye and Sir Sid hopping out of the way before the desk pinned them against the wall.

In the alley, the makeshift rope snapped tight around Ignatius's chest when the rope extended to its full length. Ignatius grunted, and his pyloric valve sealed. He glanced below, seeing that he was dangling roughly six feet above an open garbage container filled with soft packaging materials.

Meanwhile, the palimpsest, which he had put into a back pants pocket, slipped out of the pocket and descended towards an open window in a lower part of the factory where workers and machines mixed fortune cookie ingredients.

Looking up, Ignatius saw that he had descended about twelve feet. He swung smoothly, like a grandfather clock's pendulum. Having trouble breathing, he grabbed the burlap sack rope and braced his ursine feet against an ice-slickened alley wall. His feet gave way, and Ignatius slammed against the wall and cried out loudly for help.

In the office, the burlap rope was starting to give because of Ignatius's heft. Lady Laye leaned her head out the window.

"It's about to give, Ignatius, but you should be okay!" Lady Laye yelled. "Don't worry, you don't have too far to fall!"

"Oh, my God, I don't want to die!" Ignatius hollered. "I would rather be sent to that charity hospital than to suffer this horrid fate! Do bring me back into the office!"

Sir Sid poked his sick-looking face out the window. "No way, man. It would be like hoisting up a bull elephant, man. Seriously, you gotta consider losing some weight, man. They say that television makes you look heavier than you really are, man. Ever consider doing the Jack LaLanne thing, man?"

Miss Ping led Mrs. Reilly down the hallway, Mrs. Reilly's arm still pinned painlessly to her back. Mr. Robichaux reached out for Myrna, who jumped to the side and who fumbled nervously with keys as she attempted to unlock the office door.

She slammed shut the office door behind her, almost crushing the outstretched fingers of Mr. Robichaux, who had enough sense, even in his delirium, to whip his fingers out of the way.

"Communiss," Mr. Robichaux groaned. "You all a bunch of communiss."

Myrna locked the door and, turning and seeing Lady Laye and Sir Sid at the window, rushed over.

"He's about to give, man," Sir Sid said to Myrna. "It's like watching an episode of *The Twilight Zone* or something, man. You ever seen anything like it, man?"

Just as Myrna poked her head out the window to see if what Sir Sid had said was true, the makeshift burlap rope popped loudly. Ignatius yelled like Oliver Hardy, Ignatius's fall cushioned by the soft packaging materials, which gave way until Ignatius's body was less than one thousandth of a millimeter away from the bottom of the garbage container.

Ignatius looked up at the wintry sky, turned his head, and vomited into the packaging materials. And then he fainted.

"We've got to help him," Myrna said. "He's almost cured of his repression. If he dies now, it will be too late."

"We have to go out through the hallway," Lady Laye said. "What are we going to do about that creep out there?"

"Never mind him," Myrna said. "I'll take care of that fascist once for all."

Myrna unlocked the office door, opened it, and raised her peasant's skirt to show Mr. Robichaux her treasure. Mr. Robichaux gasped, not having seen a woman's nether regions in years, and passed out from the shock.

Myrna raced down the hallway, followed by Lady Laye and Sir Sid, the three passing an office into which Miss Ping had taken Mrs. Reilly.

"They say-er I am-uh the new-er Lenny-uh Bluce," Miss Ping said, still applying the armlock to Mrs. Reilly. "You like-er funny-uh jokes?"

• *Twelve*

Giacomo was sitting on a barstool, elbow resting on the bar, hand cupping his chin. He felt bored, like a gray gargoyle atop a medieval church, and sighed.

Nearby Grenadine adjusted the gilded frame of a Judy Garland portrait, took a step back and tutted, and stepped forward. He adjusted the gilded frame again and shook his head. It was so difficult to get Judy Garland right. It was a wonder she was ever able to appear in all those films and musical productions and television shows. It must have taken her hours to get prepared. And here he was, attempting to do her portrait justice.

Giacomo sighed loudly. Grenadine looked over his shoulder at his janitor.

"What's the matter, Giacomo? Boyfriend dump you? Not enough marijuana to get you through the weekend? Still angry that I won't let you perform?"

"I wanna be part of the act this Sunday, boss," Giacomo said thuggishly as he took a sip of soda water through a twelve-inch straw. He leaned back on the barstool, his buttocks expertly working the stool so that he stayed perfectly balanced, his gluteal muscles contracting and releasing. "Life's gotta mean more than dry-mopping a floor."

"It does mean more than that," Grenadine said, making another adjustment to his beloved portrait of Judy Garland. "It also includes folding dish towels, cleaning our bar's counter, sterilizing our glasses, ensuring that the bar is properly stocked for Frank, and wet-mopping the bathrooms. I hate to say it, Giacomo, but you are the worst janitor that I ever hired."

"I do the best dry-mopping in the city, boss," Giacomo said in protest. "Who else you gonna find that dry-mops like me?"

"That's the problem, my dear," Grenadine, the owner of the fine establishment, said, and now he stepped back to admire the masterpiece. It looked perfect. Perhaps, he thought, he should use a mason's level to see if the picture was perfectly flush. Well, that could wait for later. "Dry-mopping is the only thing that you do."

"I want something more outta life, boss."

"Like what? A new car? A room of your own so that you can live apart from that dreadful thing that you call your mother?"

"I want to be in da act, boss." He paused. "Or else."

Grenadine raised a green-tinted eyebrow. "Beg your pardon, my dear boy? Did you just threaten me?"

"I was just tryin' to grab ya attention, boss. I wanna be in da act. I want to be as big as your girlfriend there."

"*You* want to be as big as Judy Garland?" Grenadine asked. "I don't think you understand what you're saying, my little thuggish friend."

"I got talent," Giacomo responded raspingly. "Plenty of talent. You need me to do an act for you, boss. I mean it. Me and my snake, Miss Maggie, we could do it."

"Don't mention that horrid thing," Grenadine said in protest, making a face, shuddering in disgust. "You know how I feel about those dreadful things."

"You hate 'em as much as you hate my ma?" Giacomo asked.

"Almost," Grenadine said. "Your mother is such a beast. It's a wonder that they didn't sterilize her after she was born."

"Look," Giacomo said, standing, catching the barstool before it fell over and clattered on the floor. "Whenever I'm playing the congas, I can get Miss Maggie to move to the beat. Played 'em an hour last night, and it was like I was a snake charmer, boss. My ma, she said that I should take the road on the show or at least audition for Ed Sullivan."

Grenadine wrinkled his nose. "That's show on the road. And, of course, she would say something like that. Ed Sullivan is so, so…." The word escaped him, then came to him. "Ah, yes…*bourgeois*…That's it."

"I don't care what country he come from," Giacomo said. "My ma's family come from the old country, and look at the success they had."

"Indeed. They're the best 'dry-moppers' in the city."

"More than that, boss. We good dishwashers, too. And barbacks. Me, I'm the first one that ever made janitor."

"Two hundred or so years and your descendants will have evolved into common street sweepers," Grenadine said, looking around his establishment for other things that needed to get done. "Be satisfied with what you have, Giacomo. Believe you me, without my help, you would end up staying forever in that horrible tenement with your mother and living on welfare for the remainder of your pitiful life."

"You believe that, boss, then why you keep me? Why you have me around?"

Grenadine gave Giacomo's questions serious consideration. "Those are excellent questions, my mentally challenged friend. Probably because you're going to be used in a *deus ex machina* ending of some sort."

"A what?" Giacomo asked, so confused that his eyes crossed.

"An ending whereby things, the consequents, fall into their so-called proper places without there being the proper antecedents," Grenadine said philosophically. "Imagine, if you will, a picaresque novel wherein a picaro destroys everything with which he comes into contact because of his lack of proprioception, with everything, nonetheless, falling magically into place at the end. That would be a *deus ex machina* type of work."

"I think I understand," Giacomo replied. "Yer sayin' that da guy would have to be the cause of all the things for it to be a real novel."

"That's right," Grenadine replied heartily in agreement. "Now, get back to work."

Giacomo blinked and went back to dry-mopping the floor. Frank came in from the alley, the veins in his forearms and biceps bulging because of a heavy crate of champagne that he was carrying. He set the crate on the edge of the shiny bar, and, with a foot, he opened a small refrigerator underneath the shiny bar. The crate tilted precariously one way, then the other, and a squealing Grenadine rushed over and caught the crate before it crashed onto the floor.

"Do be careful!" Grenadine screamed. "I paid a fortune for that champagne! And I intend to get a fortune back from it! Now, how many more crates do you have! Get Giacomo to help you if you can't do the job yourself!"

Frank wanted to tell Grenadine, who had been acting like an arrogant, petulant sissy all week long, where he could stick his champagne. Instead, Frank replied that it was the last crate and quickly put bottles of champagne, one right after the other, into the small refrigerator, which he closed with his foot.

"Done with the champagne," the bartender said, wiping his hands on his apron, "but we have a large crate to open."

"It's arrived!" Grenadine exclaimed, hopping up and down. "It's arrived, it's arrived, it's arrived!"

"What's arrived?" Giacomo said, and Grenadine removed the Wayfarer sunglasses that Giacomo had donned, folded them shut, and hung them in the V of the janitor's T-shirt. "Something for my act, boss?"

"No, no, you fool," Grenadine said, heading towards the back office, with Giacomo and Frank in tow. "Something much, much better. This is something that I've always dreamed about having."

In the back room stood a seven-foot-tall wooden crate, THIS SIDE UP, along with kanji, stenciled in several places on the crate. At Grenadine's urging, Frank and Giacomo took crowbars and began digging at the lid of the crate. The sound of splintering wood and a banana-like smell filled the air, and Grenadine clapped his hands in expectation. Giacomo and Frank removed armfuls of packing straw from the crate. With Frank on one side of the crate and Giacomo on the other, the two reached into the crate and, with herculean effort, removed the precious object, a fully clothed, six-foot-eight robot that looked like a stupid, blond-haired lumberjack ready to begin a day's hard work.

Frank and Giacomo stepped back, looking up in awe at the mute creature. Grenadine grinned.

"What's it for?" Frank asked after a few moments. "What the hell is this thing supposed to do?"

"This is Rex, our robot stud," Grenadine said, and he stepped forward and placed his hand on the robot's jeans-encased crotch. The robot's teratoid appendage hung there, ready to spring to rigid attention upon command. Smiling, Grenadine squeezed the mechanical phallus, and then Grenadine stepped back, admiring the creature, which had been manufactured in Japan and shipped from there.

"I've always wanted to have a novelty in my establishment," Grenadine continued, "a novelty that will give the queens plenty to talk about after the show is over."

Frank rubbed the stubble on his unshaved chin. "You know, you should have consulted me, Grenadine. I think I got an idea that might've made you a lot of money."

"What's your idea, Frank?" asked Grenadine, who was slightly peeved at the bartender for insinuating that he, Grenadine, could have chosen a better novelty.

"How about a mechanical bull?" Frank said, eyes wide. "See, this—"

"A mechanical bull? And what would we use it for, my dear bartender? Artificial insemination of our clientele?"

"No, no, no," Frank said, his Sicilian blood beginning to boil. "Not for anything kinky like that. For riding, like at a rodeo. You get people up on the mechanical bull, and they see how long they can ride the thing before getting thrown off. Hell, you could have different speeds and all—"

"That's the most ridiculous thing I've ever heard of," Grenadine said, shaking his head. "Where do you come up with these idiotic notions, Frank? Who would ever want to ride a mechanical bull? *Real* bulls are bad enough, let alone mechanical ones. Besides, can you imagine the droppings?"

"It would be mechanical," Frank answered in protest and in exasperation, wondering why he, a straight man, had ever taken a job in a queer joint. "Which means it ain't gonna shit."

Grenadine ignored Frank. The owner of the Stone Carver Inn studied his new acquisition. The instructions explained how to plug in the robot and said that the on-off switch was at the base of the robot's back. After plugging in the robot, Grenadine reached behind it and flipped the on-off switch up. The robot's patina-colored irides lit up, and its teratoid phallus rose visibly in its pants.

"Hi, I'm Rex the Robot!" the robot said. "I'm at your service!"

Grenadine chuckled and turned off the robot. The mechanical phallus lowered in the loose jeans. "Can you imagine what a sensation this thing is going to make?"

Frank shook his head. "Like I said, I don't have good feelings about none of this, Grenadine. You ask me, this is a black swan."

"Black swan? What on earth do you mean, Frank?"

"I mean that there are too many converging forces," Frank said. "Like everything's coming together at once. I can't put my finger on it. It's like we're puppets on a stage, doing the bidding for some puppet master. And all of this is going to lead to disaster—"

"If we don't take care of this faster," Giacomo said. "Like that rhyme? I like rhyme. And rhythm. If you'd let me clap my congas, boss, you'd see how great a clapper of congas I really was, just because."

"Enough, you two!" Grenadine said, his mood momentarily acrasial. "Move Rex to the back of the office. After Las Tres Amigas appear, we'll introduce Rex. Those who want his services will have to pay a dollar a pop."

Frank and Giacomo wrestled with the deadweight robot. Grenadine decided that instead of doing additional work on the portrait of Judy Garland, he would instead go and work on the hems of the dresses that Las Tres Amigas would wear that Sunday evening. That night, after all, was going to be the night of nights.

II

Dr. Talc shuddered awake in his room at the Hotel Claridge. He had been dreaming about *The Ed Sullivan Show*. In the dream, he was onstage, and he had just told the joke that he had heard at Tulane and that he had often repeated since then, though he still did not understand the joke.

The audience laughed heartily, and Dr. Talc bowed in deep and utter appreciation until he saw Ignatius J. Reilly and Myrna Minkoff in the front row, the two pointing and laughing. And soon the entire audience was pointing and laughing, too.

"Historiaster!" Ignatius yelled, standing, thrusting an accusing finger at Dr. Talc. "I, Zorro, accuse of you corrupting our youth and of having puny pudenda!"

And then Dr. Talc understood why everyone was laughing at him: his black tuxedo trousers, silk boxers, and garters had fallen to his ankles. And, indeed, the world could see his puny pudenda.

Dr. Talc shook his head as he remembered the note that he had received from Ignatius. How on earth did he, Ignatius J. Reilly, ever know that he, Dr. Talc, had very small genitalia?

III

An ingredients mixer at the Charlie Chan Chinese Fortune Cookie Company found the palimpsest that had fallen out of Ignatius's pocket. This worker, like the others in the factory, originated from Hong Kong, but unlike many of the workers, this worker had attended a missionary Catholic school and had learned a smattering of Latin. Studying the palimpsest, the worker rightly assumed that it was a recipe.

The mixer picked up an in-company telephone receiver and dialed Miss Ping's number. She would know what to do.

IV

Mrs. Reilly shook her head sadly. Mr. Robichaux, who was sitting across from her at a small table in a coffee shop in the Hotel Claridge, sipped his coffee and wished that the coffee shop had chicory. Even though the coffee shop didn't have chicory, the coffee shop did have the pleasant scent of vanilla, one of Mr. Robichaux's favorite scents. And, fortunately for Mrs. Reilly and Mr. Robichaux, the hotel had adjoining rooms for them.

Mrs. Reilly sighed. Ignatius had managed to escape, and when Mrs. Reilly called the Minkoff house, Mrs. Minkoff said that Ignatius and Myrna weren't anywhere to be found. Now what was she, Mrs. Reilly, going to do? What to do, what to do, what to do?

"I figure this is a good hotel," Mr. Robichaux said, hoping that the lively atmosphere of the coffee shop would enliven Mrs. Reilly. "And seeing that you like the picture shows at the Prytania, well, maybe you'd like one of these fancy theater productions."

"Where did I go wrong, Claude?" Mrs. Reilly asked, sniffling, putting a tissue to her reddened eyes. "I did all I could for that boy. Me and Mr. Reilly raised him right, and the sisters at his school said he was such a darling angel."

"When do you figure things might've gone wrong?" Mr. Robichaux said, and then he regretted his asking the question, having forgotten that his intention was to get his beloved fiancée's mind on something else besides her wayward son. "I saw signs for a show called *Who's Afraid of the Big Bad Virginie Woof?* Sounds like a real charmer to me, 'specially if it's set in Virginie. The thing's probably about hunting in the Blue Ridge Mountains. I was stationed in Virginie before going to France in 1918, you know."

"That don't make sense, Claude," Mrs. Reilly said. "One moment you're asking questions about Ignatius, the next you're talking about some kiddie play about woofs." She shook her head. "I think I know what happened to make things go wrong with Ignatius. It wadn't me. It was them public schools. Ignatius started goin' downhill after he entered them public schools. After Mr. Reilly died, we couldn't afford the Catholics no more. At least Ignatius was able to go to college, where he graduated smart."

"Ignatius is probably safe and sound," Mr. Robichaux said, hoping that she would cheer up. "You ask me, I was wrong. That Myrna Minkoff ain't no communiss, just a beatnik. Since she ain't a communiss, Ignatius is probably just hanging around characters like you'd find in the French Quarter."

With his mentioning the French Quarter, Mrs. Reilly wailed, causing the coffee shop's patrons to turn and look inquisitively at Mrs. Reilly and Mr. Robichaux, many of the customers giving Mr. Robichaux a mean look because they believed that he had just said something cruel to the frail-looking, maroon-haired woman wearing several layers of winter clothing and out-of-place bowling shoes.

"Ignatius a Mardi Gras!" she said. "The shame of it all! And now he's going to be a Mardi Gras in the French Quarter in New York City!"

"I don't think they's a French Quarter here," Mr. Robichaux said quite seriously, frowning, the deep furrows in his brow deepening. "Seems that a lot of Irish settled here and a lot of Polacks and Jews, too. They might be a Irish Quarter or a Polack Quarter or a Jew Quarter. Maybe where that communiss girl has gone is the Jew Quarter."

"You just said she wasn't a communiss!" Mrs. Reilly said, and now she wailed again. "Now Ignatius is in danger because he's with that communiss Myrna!"

A cetacean woman sitting at a nearby table arose and, smiling, approached the small table at which Mrs. Reilly and Mr. Robichaux were sitting. The woman offered Mrs. Reilly a fresh, lavender-scented tissue, given that the tissues Mrs. Reilly clutched in her small hands were soaked through with tears.

"I just hate to see anyone hurting, you betcha," the woman said in a hurdy-gurdy Minnesotan accent common to that state's Scandinavian descendants. "Is there anything that I can do to help you, honey?"

"We's fine," Mr. Robichaux said, wanting the woman, whom he considered a pest, to go away. "You sound like you ain't from around these parts."

"Yah, sure, I could say the same of you," the cetacean woman said, not picking up on the hostility that Mr. Robichaux was exhibiting. "And no, neither my fiancé nor I are from these parts. We're from Shakopee, Minnesota, you betcha. We're here for the Noble Order of the Sons of St. Olaf convention. It's all retirees, you know. We generally have our Christmas parties in Minneapolis, but this year, Per Nielsen, our president, wanted to have this year's party in New York City."

"Never heard of the Noble Order of the Sons of St. Olaf," Mr. Robichaux said. "I'm a member of the Knights of Columbus, the American Legion, St. Odo of Cluny Holy Name Society, and the AAA. Them's American organizations. Olaf's Russian, ain't it? You a communiss?"

"Hush up, Claude," Mrs. Reilly said, sniffing and wiping her eyes with the tissue that the cetacean woman had just given to Mrs. Reilly. "Never mind him, babe. And thank you so much for the tissue. You a angel in a city of demons."

The cetacean woman put her hand on Mrs. Reilly's shoulder, and Mrs. Reilly flinched instinctively because of Miss Ping's having applied an arm lock earlier that day.

"Oh, I didn't mean to hurt you if I did, you betcha," the woman with the hurdy-gurdy accent said. "I had surgery on my shoulder last year, and I know how painful that can be. Well, I don't know if you're part of a group, but you're more than welcome to join us. We're having a free buffet in an hour. Yah, sure, please come be our guests."

"We don't eat communiss food," Mr. Robichaux said, peering meanly at the woman. "We eat American food."

The woman from Minnesota chuckled, believing that Mr. Robichaux was being playful.

"I'm Marge Margold, by the way," the cetacean woman said, extending her hand to Mrs. Reilly, who shook it. "And who might you be?"

"I'm Irene Reilly," Mrs. Reilly said. "And this here's my finance, Claude Robichaux. We're from New Orleans, and I came up here to find my boy, Ignatius, and he, he, he—"

Mrs. Reilly broke down, unable to go on. Mr. Robichaux stood.

"She's had a hard day," the retired brakeman said to the Minnesotan. "She needs a rest."

"Please remember the free buffet, Claude," Mrs. Margold said, turning. "Yah, sure, I hope to see you two in an hour or so, you betcha."

After taking a long hot bath followed by a short cool nap, Mrs. Reilly discovered that she was ready for dinner. After changing into her best dress, one that she had purchased at D. H. Holmes before this whole mess with Ignatius had started, and after putting on her bowling shoes, she knocked on a door that separated her room from Mr. Robichaux's. Minutes later, she and Mr. Robichaux stood in an elevator with two members of the Noble Order of the Sons of St. Olaf, a morbidly obese man and a morbidly obese woman who had strange Minnesotan accents like Mrs. Reilly's benefactor. The elevator sped the four down to the main floor of the Hotel Claridge.

The ballroom radiated with Christmas decorations and other holiday paraphernalia. Touched by the thought of Christmas and by Ignatius's absence, Mrs. Reilly dabbed at her eyes with a piece of toilet tissue torn from a ball that she had taken from her hotel bathroom, Mrs. Margold's gift of tissue having been flushed down the toilet. Mrs. Reilly and Mr. Robichaux sat down at a table.

"You all right?" Mr. Robichaux asked. "Don't worry, it's free, so you don't have to cry about it, Irene."

"I know it's free, Claude," Mrs. Reilly replied. "I ain't crying because of that. I'm crying because it's almost Christmas. I'm crying because I miss my boy. I'm crying because I want us all to be safe and sound and back in New Orleans, where at least if things is crazy, they ain't strange."

"I hear you," Mr. Robichaux said, looking around the room at the elderly Minnesotans, who were busily and loudly gabbing one with another in their strange hurdy-gurdy accents. He caught snippets of conversations about ice fishing, ice skating, ice hockey, ice curling, and ice manufacturing. He shuddered. New York City was cold enough, but Minnesota sounded like a veritable frozen-over hell. "Our home might be a bit crazy at times, but it sure ain't strange."

"You can say that again, Claude."

"Our home—"

"I didn't mean for you to repeat it, dodo," Mrs. Reilly said, and she looked across the ballroom at the buffet line. She thought that she smelled smoked salmon and cream cheese, and her mouth watered. "Lordy, look who's here."

Mrs. Margold appeared with a big-boned man who had blondish-grayish hair and the dour expression of the terminally angry.

"Ole, this is—what was your name again, honey?" Mrs. Margold asked Mrs. Reilly.

"Irene Reilly," Mrs. Reilly said, pointing at herself. Then pointing at Mr. Robichaux: "And this here is Claude Robichaux, my finance."

"This is my fiancé, Ole Anderson."

Mr. Robichaux rose to shake hands with the terminally angry man, who, according to Mr. Robichaux's estimation, might have worked for a railroad. "Pleasure, I think. You a retired brakeman?"

"Postman, pal," the man replied in a hurdy-gurdy accent. "I worked for a living."

Mr. Robichaux felt the blood rising up his chicken-skinned neck and squeezed Mr. Anderson's hand tighter, causing Mr. Anderson to wince.

Mr. Anderson, in turn, attempted to squeeze harder. The two men stood there, grimacing, their arms tensed, both attempting to get the other to give.

"My, they do seem to like each other quite a bit, you betcha," Mrs. Margold said, taking a seat next to her newfound friend. "Why don't we go get ourselves something to eat? You do like fish, don't you? Yah, sure, please tell me that you do. I couldn't live without it, you betcha. Why, I'm from the Land of Ten Thousand Lakes, after all!"

In the hotel lobby, Henley and Nick the Nose studied passersby, the majority of them members of the Noble Order of the Sons of St. Olaf. Henley and Nick the Nose had found Mrs. Reilly and Mr. Robichaux in Greenwich Village and had followed them to the Charlie Chan Chinese Fortune Cookie Company, from which, fifteen minutes or so later, three kids emerged and ran into an alley. Five minutes or so after that, Mrs. Reilly, nursing her arm, and Mr. Robichaux, cradling his crotch, exited the factory and hailed a cab, which took them to the Hotel Claridge, in the lobby of which Henley and Nick the Nose lost sight of the two.

"Look at all these old bastuds," Nick the Nose said. "You'd think that Miami had moved up to New York City or sumpin."

Many of the men in the Noble Order of the Sons of St. Olaf smoked rank cigars. The noxious odors irritated Henley's already sensitive nose and rheumy eyes and pneumonia-infected lungs. Henley hacked into his silk handkerchief, which he wadded up and put into a pocket of his pea coat, and looked around.

"Fuhgid 'em," Henley said. "You see da cob?"

"I don't see no cobs," Nick the Nose replied. "No cobs, corn or otherwise, Ids."

Henley shoved Nick the Nose. "Nod a cob, you sombidtch," Henley said, "but da cob. Dad redhead cob!"

"Ah, gotcha, Ids," Nick the Nose said. "You mean that fat little redheaded mick bastud with the piggy eyes and the piggy nose. No, I ain't seen him around."

"Goob," Henley said, coughing, needing another fix of methamphetamine. "Led's go to da fromt ded."

In the ballroom, Mr. Robichaux and Mr. Anderson stopped their battle when Mr. Anderson excused himself, saying, in a cracking voice, that he needed to speak to Chester Rasmussen about an upcoming ice-fishing excursion on the Mississippi River. In reality, Mr. Anderson needed to rush to a restroom to soak his injured hand and to heal his wounded pride.

Mr. Robichaux, who knew that he had won the battle, and who took a retired brakeman's pride in having destroyed the retired postman, caught up with Mrs. Reilly in the buffet line. In front of Mrs. Reilly leaned Mrs. Margold, who speared meats, cheeses, fruits, vegetables, and gelatinous odds and ends with gleaming serving forks that resembled small silver tridents.

Mrs. Reilly studied the buffet foods very carefully, not sure which she should choose.

Mrs. Margold jabbed a serving fork at gelatinous mass. "That's haggis, Irene dear."

"Haggard?" Mrs. Reilly frowned. "I ain't never heard of such a thing. Does it make you tired, hon? If so, I'd better past it. This journey has been way too much for me already."

"Haggis, you betcha," Mrs. Margold said, chuckling at this simple, naïve woman from New Orleans. "It's a Scottish dish. It's not a traditional Scandinavian food, of course, but many of our members have come to love it, given that Mrs. MacDowell, who came from Denmark, was married to a man from Aberdeen, Scotland."

"And this man, he liked hay-giss?" Mrs. Reilly asked.

"To the point where it killed him, you betcha," Mrs. Margold said in her hurdy-gurdy accent. "Yah, sure, he stuffed himself with so much haggis that he died from the flatulence. In fact, if the Widow MacDowell hadn't opened the bedroom window, she would have gone to join Mr. MacDowell."

"I don't think I can take me any of that hay-giss," Mrs. Reilly said. She pointed at something that looked more familiar. "I think I'd like to try me some of that."

"Yah, sure, a splendid choice!" Mrs. Margold said, spearing haggis. "That's *rakfisk*, a traditional Scandinavian food. It's one of Ole's favorites, even though he says that it smells like a marinated dead cat. He says it'll make a man out of you, you betcha. You should try it, Claude."

Mr. Robichaux frowned, not sure if Mrs. Margold was being intentionally insulting. Regardless, he didn't like her, he didn't like her fiancé, Ole Anderson, and he didn't like the buffet foods, free of charge though they were.

"If they had real food, they'd have themselves some crawfish here," Mr. Robichaux said, turning up his nose at the repast. "And as for your beau, you might want to ask him how his hand is."

"Why on earth would I ask him about his hand?" Mrs. Margold asked, perplexed.

"Let's just say that he ain't ready for real food, the kind we have back home," Mr. Robichaux said.

Mrs. Reilly elbowed Mr. Robichaux and whispered, "What's got into you, Claude?"

"These Northern Yankees are pure dumb and pure mean," Mr. Robichaux whispered back to her.

"Well, I like Marge, and she's being a gracious hosteller, so you just keep it down." Now Mrs. Reilly addressed Mrs. Margold: "Hey, hon, do you think they have any muscatel?"

Henley and Nick the Nose stood in the entrance of the ballroom. Mr. Anderson walked by, cradling his crushed hand, his face contorted, Mr. Anderson unable to hide his wounded pride. Henley sniffled, and Nick the Nose scratched the edge of his nose with a craggy, grime-ridden fingernail.

"Look at all dis gray hair," Nick the Nose said. "Must be at least fifty shades of gray."

Henley scowled. "Jud find 'em."

Nick the Nose nodded and nudged past a Northern nurse named Nancy who nursed a woman named Natalie knitting in a Nantucket chair.

Henley went to the other side of the ballroom, away from the buffet line, and meandered among tables and studied the Northern, blondish-grayish-headed retirees, whose faces showed an open hostility towards a man who they thought might be crashing their holiday party.

Mrs. Reilly, Mr. Robichaux, and Mrs. Margold sat at their table. Mr. Anderson appeared with an overloaded plate in hand. He looked warily at his former prey, Mr. Robichaux.

"Happy holidays!" the cetacean Mrs. Margold said, raising a glass of cheap champagne. "I believe that this is going to be the best party ever, don't you, Ole?"

"Yes, the best party ever," Mr. Anderson replied sullenly.

"How's the hand?" Mr. Robichaux asked, smirking.

"Don't know what you're talking about, pal," Mr. Anderson said, cutting into a thick slice of honeyed, spiral-cut ham.

"Bet you don't," Mr. Robichaux said, and in a lower voice added, "you communiss."

Neither Mrs. Reilly nor Mrs. Margold nor Mr. Anderson heard the derogatory apposition.

Henley appeared at their table. The two couples didn't notice him, and Henley had a vague feeling that he knew Mrs. Reilly from somewhere. He studied her face, and then he thought about the Night of Joy in the French Quarter, when he had been doing that gig with Oswald. Hadn't she been sitting with an ill-dressed lug who had a greasy black mustache? Aha. Yes. Yes. Yes, it was her. It was her indeed.

Henley blinked and told himself that the woman and that lug were of the inconsequential past and that he had a job to do. He removed a fake badge from his coat pocket and flashed it in front of Mrs. Reilly's face, interrupting her forkful of her malodorous meal.

"Who are you?" Mrs. Reilly said, peering up at the man. "What do you want?"

"I'b Dedeckdiv Henley," Henley aspirated, sweat beading his flushed forehead. "Urgend madder."

"I knew they were troublemakers," Mr. Anderson said to his fiancée. "Didn't I tell you that? Didn't I tell you that we needed to stick to our own kind? Didn't I tell you not to invite them to the buffet, that they would only bring trouble? Didn't I tell you that? Huh, huh, huh—"

"Oh, shut up!" the cetacean Mrs. Margold wailed at Mr. Anderson, Mrs. Margold irritated by his rogitating. "You can be such a royal pain in the ass, Ole, you betcha!"

"You a po-lice?" Mrs. Reilly asked, bewildered at having her dinner interrupted. "Is this about my Ignatius?"

"No, this about da Charlie Chan Chinese Fortune Cookie Company," said Nick the Nose, who was now standing beside Henley. "You was there earlier today, wasn't you?"

Mrs. Reilly nodded, and Mr. Robichaux stood.

"Yes, Claude and me was there at the factory," Mrs. Reilly said, and she had a sinking feeling in her gut, a feeling that told her that Ignatius had done something terribly wrong. "I was looking for my boy, Ignatius, he works there—"

"Is anything wrong, Irene?" Mrs. Margold asked, placing a hand atop Mrs. Reilly's.

Henley coughed and motioned with a hand for Nick the Nose to continue.

"This is something dat we should like preferably discuss in private in the lobby of da hotel, if you get my drift," Nick the Nose said. "Please, if you would, follow me dis way, ma'am."

Mrs. Reilly shook her head. "I knew it was Ignatius. He done something to that chink fortune cookie company, didn't he?" Mrs. Reilly turned to Mrs. Margold. "Please excuse me, babe. This is an urgent matter regarding my boy, Ignatius. He caused a heap world of trouble down in New Orleans, and now he's up here with a female friend, and he's causing all sorts of problems in New York City."

"How terrible," Mrs. Margold said in genuine shock, and she covered her face with her hands.

"Figures," Mr. Anderson said, scowling.

Mrs. Reilly stood. "Let's go talk about what Ignatius done."

Mr. Robichaux started to follow, and Nick the Nose held out a grimy hand.

"This is a private mattuh," Nick the Nose said to Mr. Robichaux.

"Claude here's involved in this," Mrs. Reilly said. "If you have anything to say to me, you can say it in front of him."

"The friggin' hell I will," Nick the Nose said. "You stay heh, old man."

Mr. Robichaux sensed that there wasn't something quite right with this Detective Henley, and especially his little friend, whom Mr. Robichaux suspected of being a queer; the John Birch materials that Mr. Robichaux routinely pored over declared that communists, especially ones who were sexual deviants, often took on cop disguises to look like the nation's beloved G-men.

"Let's see that badge again," Mr. Robichaux said to Henley.

"Ya already seen da badge," Nick the Nose said, stepping between Henley and Mr. Robichaux. "Ya don't need to see id agin."

"You a communiss," Mr. Robichaux said.

Henley was starting to slump because his body was overwhelmed with pneumonia. And Nick the Nose's final nerve finally snapped.

"Where's dat goddamn piece of paper!" the diminutive operative screamed at Mrs. Reilly. "We saw you pick it up, lady! I bet you have it hid between those dry paps, don't ya, sweedheart!"

"What paper?" And Mrs. Reilly blinked, now remembering the paper that she had, indeed, picked up. "It looked like something Ignatius would like, so I put it—"

And before anyone could say anything or do anything, Nick the Nose stuck his grimy hands down the front of Mrs. Reilly's dress, his probing fingers searching for the missing faux palimpsest.

Mrs. Reilly screamed. Mrs. Margold screamed, too, at the little man's effrontery, and she leaped up and struck Nick the

Nose on his head with her purse, which was filled with snow globes and other heavy, touristy bric-a-brac that she had purchased at a kiosk near Central Park. Nick the Nose yelled in outrage and in pain, removed his hands from Mrs. Reilly's withered breasts, and covered his head as Mrs. Margold continued her assault.

"Communiss!" Mr. Robichaux shouted, and he swung at Henley, who, because of his weakened lungs, found it incredibly difficult to keep his hands up as the blows rained down upon him. "You all a bunch of communiss!"

Mr. Anderson now joined in, throwing a left hook at Nick the Nose, the blow falling short, causing Mr. Anderson to throw out his shoulder and yelp. Meanwhile, the other members of the Noble Order of the Sons of St. Olaf gave in in to a herd mentality and hit and spat and clawed and chewed and poked and gouged and scratched and kicked and pulled and screeched and cussed at Henley and Nick the Nose.

"Bastuds!" Nick the Nose shouted, swatting away an arthritic claw from his face. "Get away from me, youse bastuds!"

Henley, who couldn't run, barely kept ahead of the elderly people who came after him with walkers, canes, and other accoutrements for mobility. Nose bloodied, Nick the Nose stumbled out of the ballroom, falling onto parquet flooring, Henley following and tumbling over the seedy operative. Mrs. Reilly kicked Nick the Nose in the ass with the toe of a bowling shoe, causing him to bray. Henley hacked.

Hotel administrators wearing gray suits, along with bellboys wearing gray caps and gray long coats, ran to the ballroom after being alerted by a woman with blued hair. And instead of receiving a dinner of feeble punches and weak kicks from Mrs. Reilly and Mr. Robichaux and the Noble Order of the Sons of St. Olaf, Henley and Nick the Nose now received a dessert of brutal blows and steadfast stampings from the hotel personnel, who were enraged that the two men had assaulted elderly guests at the beloved Hotel Claridge.

Magoohan, who was dressed as Raggedy Ann and who had been tailing Nick the Nose and Henley all the way from Greenwich Village, stepped with handcuffs in hand out of the shadows. The hotel personnel, believing that Magoohan was in on the act, jumped him, and, against his protestations, gave him a harder beating than those they had administered to Henley and Nick the Nose, who managed to stumble and tumble into a hallway before finding a door labeled EXIT that allowed them to flee onto Broadway.

"I'm a friggin' cop, you freakin' idiots!" Magoohan shrieked. "Lemme show you my badge!"

"He's going to expose himself!" a front desk clerk yelled in a shrill voice. "Beat him to a purple pulp until he quits resisting!"

On Broadway, Henley leaned against a lamppost and wheezed, his face crimsoning. He closed his eyes, hoping that this nightmare would soon end and that, if it didn't, he would die a quick, peaceful death.

"Now what, Ids?" Nick the Nose asked.

Henley opened his eyes. And without saying a word, he slapped Nick the Nose.

• *Thirteen*

In a cab that they shared with Ignatius and Myrna, Sir Sid and Lady Laye led the way to an apartment that the fraternal twins shared in the Bowery. An extremely nervous and agitated Ignatius could barely walk up a set of brick stairs ascending to the second-floor apartment, and he trembled so hard that Sir Sid had to hold one ursine paw and Lady Laye the other, with Myrna shoving a near-deadweight Ignatius from behind. A wino on a stoop waved at Ignatius, and Ignatius, about to faint, closed his eyes and saw geometrical phosphenes of his long-dead Rex dancing down a declivity.

Twenty minutes later, Ignatius was sleeping on a secondhand sofa, his nervous strain having pushed him into a physically numbing exhaustion. Numerous blankets and sheets and quilts covered him, items that Sir Sid had heartily and happily heaped on the helpless and harried Beat-Alls headman. And now Sir Sid was in the sole bathroom of the two-bedroom apartment deficient of furnishings, and he smoked marijuana with a window cracked open so that the winter air carried out the quite fragrant, quite illegal odor. Myrna and Lady Laye, meanwhile, sat at a Formica table in the kitchen, where they sipped bitter and overly hot Folgers instant coffee.

"I figure that in a day or two Ignatius can leave this place and come back with me to the Bronx," Myrna said. "His reactionary mother and her Klansman boyfriend will probably go back to New Orleans and leave Ignatius alone, once they can't find him."

"How long have you known Ignatius, Myrna?"

"A few years, give or take one or two," Myrna said. "We took some of the same classes at Tulane, where I was studying sociology so that I could start a revolution in the Deep South. It's such a reactionary place, you know."

"I'm not much into politics," Lady Laye said. "I'm more into music. I believe that's where the real change is going to be this decade."

"I say it's going to be politics," Myrna said. "And sex. That's one of the reasons that I brought Ignatius up here."

"For sex?"

Myrna nodded. "He's still a virgin. Can you believe that? I think that these grandiose schemes of his are a way of expressing the sexual repression that he feels."

"You sound like a shrink," Lady Laye said, sipping her bitter coffee.

"I attend a group therapy group at the Ingloss Institute for Psycho-Sexual Research," Myrna said. "It's Dr. Ingloss's highly respected opinion that a lack of orgasmic energy is the major cause of social and political disorder in our time."

"We have a show on Sunday," Lady Laye said, very worried, and not interested in Myrna's sexual talk. "That's less than two days away. And we're not even ready."

"I wouldn't worry about it, Laye. Excuse me, Lady Laye. This is just another one of Ignatius's fantastical fantasies. It's his way of compensating for all those years that he lived in that cramped house on Constantinople Street in New Orleans, where he was living like a monk engaged in incestuous sex with his mother. In other words, this whole thing's bogus."

Lady Laye shook her head. "You have it all wrong, Myrna. It is real. Ignatius showed me the proof. Ed Sullivan really wants Ignatius on *The Ed Sullivan Show*."

Myrna exhaled, flabbergasted. "You can't be serious! That reactionary wants Ignatius Reilly to appear on television!"

"I'm very serious. And yeah, Ed Sullivan wants Ignatius. Ignatius met Ed Sullivan in a bar. Ed Sullivan was very impressed with what he saw in Ignatius and said that Ignatius needed to appear on the show."

"And it's this Sunday?"

"It is," Lady Laye said. "And Ignatius plans to start his own revolution."

"You mean it?" Myrna asked, hoping against all hope that what she was hearing was true. "Ignatius plans to start something big?"

"Didn't you know about the ad that he placed in the *Times*? He said that he was seeking revolutionary musicians to start a revolutionary new musical group to revolt against the rabid establishment and its reactionary pretensions."

"I can't believe it," Myrna said, tears coming to her eyes. "I mean, I can believe it, and I want to believe it, but I find it hard to believe it. Ignatius is finally getting out of his shell. He wants to overthrow the government and lead us onto the correct path. And we're almost there. At first I thought he was lying to me. Once I get his virginity, he's going to be unstoppable."

Ignatius snorted in his sleep. He groaned loudly, and then he was snoring again at his previous pace.

Myrna continued: "And I thought that he was returning to his old nasty self. That wasn't it at all. He was doing espionage work. No wonder he was taking off so early from the factory. No wonder he was being so secretive. No wonder he made it seem like he wasn't changing. He was going out and seeking a means not only to overthrow the Charlie Chan Chinese Fortune Cookie Company but the entire US government. And I was about to kick him out of my dad's house."

She slapped her forehead and closed her eyes and wished that she hadn't struck herself so hard.

"And he has this weird song that he translated from some strange, leathery paper," Lady Laye said. "I read the so-called song several times. I think that the thing Ignatius translated is a recipe, even though Ignatius says it's a song like 'Scarborough Fair.' The thing says that whoever eats of the things written therein is going to invert the world and turn the whole world into a gay orgy or something like that."

"What does happiness have to do with the revolution?" Myrna asked. "We can be happy after the revolution. I haven't slept with him, and so I don't know how good he is in bed, but the new boyfriend in my life, Rastajaq, says that no one can be happy until the revolution occurs and the new utopia arrives."

"Is he an African guy who wears a funny face mask and hangs around diners in the Village and talks to himself?" Lady Laye asked.

"That's him. Why? You dated him?"

"No, I ran away from him. What the hell else would I do?"

"Anyway," Myrna said, wanting to change the subject, "what are we going to do about Ignatius right *now*?"

"He can stay here," Lady Laye said. "The way he complains about everything, I'm not sure that he'll like it here. But at least he'll be safe. And like you said, after this blows over, Ignatius can go back to the Bronx with you. Besides, we need to do some serious practicing, and that fortune cookie company was way too much of a distraction for him."

"I might as well stay, too," Myrna said, "since I'm on the run like Ignatius."

Myrna finished her bitter coffee, and when she wasn't looking, Lady Laye made a face of disapproval.

II

Mrs. Reilly was lying in the bed in her hotel room. She had been crying nonstop for the past two hours. She had spoken to a police sergeant named Scarletti, who complained that he had been transferred unjustly from the Battery Park Precinct and who said that she could file a report the next day before rudely hanging up on her.

Mr. Robichaux was in the other room and was fretting because Mrs. Reilly had said that she wanted to be alone.

Mrs. Reilly sat up in bed, turned on a light on a nightstand, and picked up a telephone receiver. She dialed O for the hotel operator, who, upon hearing Mrs. Reilly's request, called a Manhattan operator who, in turn, called the telephone number that Mrs. Reilly requested.

A few moments passed, and then there was the sound of a ringing telephone several hundred miles away. Mrs. Reilly heard someone's fumbling with a telephone receiver and then heard her best friend, Santa Battaglia, scream at one of her grandchildren, Rodney; Santa threatened to knock his teeth down his throat if he didn't stop teasing Charmaine, his older sister.

"Hello?" Santa said.

"It's me, babe," Mrs. Reilly said ruefully, sniffling, wiping her eyes with a tissue. "How you doin'?"

"Irene! Irene! How you been, hon!" And then Mrs. Reilly heard Santa cover the telephone receiver with a hand and then heard a child's screaming, which was followed by Santa's screaming, which was followed by the Doppler-effect-like wailing of a child.

"Back," Santa said. "Angelo told me you went to New York City with your sweetie. You eloped, huh, kid? I bet you having the time of your life there, ain't you? You taking pictures? Is Claude a good provider in more ways than one?"

"Santa, please," Mrs. Reilly said, sighing, unhappy with the snoopy questions. "Claude and me ain't married yet, and we ain't staying in the same room. I guess Angelo didn't tell you the whole story, or he don't understand all that I told him before Claude and me left New Orleans."

"What? Not married? You shacked up with that old man?"

"I came up here to find Ignatius," Mrs. Reilly said. "I woulda tolt you, but you probably woulda tried to stop me from coming up here."

"Ignatius is in New York City, babe? What kinda craziness is that boy doing up there?"

"Ignatius done ran up here with his girlfriend, Myrna Minkoff, and Myrna's momma done told me that Ignatius was living with them and pretending to be a wandering Orthodox rabid. And on top of that, Ignatius somehow got him a good job at a chink fortune cookie factory. And when me and Claude went to the factory to get him, Myrna showed up, and she and two beatniks helped Ignatius to escape. We can't find hide nor hair of him anywhere, and the police ain't willing to help, and Myrna's momma said they ain't come back to the home in the Bronchitis. I been calling and calling and calling every hour, and she says they still no sign of Ignatius or Myrna. I think my boy done run off with that communiss girl and them beatniks to Russia!"

And now Mrs. Reilly began to wail, and Mr. Robichaux knocked on the door adjoining the two rooms, and Mrs. Reilly told the retired Illinois Central brakeman that she was on the telephone. Mr. Robichaux grumbled something and then audibly said that if she needed him, she knew where to look.

"Aww, I'm so sorry to hear that, sweetie," Santa said, truly sorry for Mrs. Reilly but not sorry at all that Ignatius had escaped. "You need to forget that boy, Irene. If he can manage to get to New York City and get him a job with the chinks, he's able to take care of hisself. Them chinks don't like to hire white people or Negroes or anyone not of their own race. Just take a look at those Duk Dong brothers, they don't hire nobody who's not a chink. Ask Angelo. He tried to get him a summer job at that chink laundry one time."

"But Ignatius is my boy," Mrs. Reilly said, and she thought back to the previous Christmas Eve. Ignatius had been watching television—a Doris Day film whose title she didn't remember—when she asked him if he wanted to attend midnight mass with her. He replied that he would do so when the modern Church truly reformed and repented of the ways in which it had treated him and Rex. The memory was too much for Mrs. Reilly, and she wept, shaking her head, wondering where she had gone wrong with Ignatius.

"There, there, babe," Santa said. "You and Claude, you come back home to New Orleans where you all belong. Ignatius might buckle up and become a real man on his own. When he does, then you can see him. This is tearing you apart, Irene, and I hate to see that. You need to let Ignatius go. I learnt that from a Jew woman what has a new television show. She studied psychology through the mail, and she's helped a lot of women, especially older women like us. She seems right smart, and she says that if something don't work out, you have to let it go and find a good vibrating board that can help relieve the tension. Do what that Jew woman says you should do, Irene. Come back to New Orleans."

"All right, Santa," Mrs. Reilly said, and her breathing was becoming normal, and she felt slightly cheered. "I'll listen to you and that Jew woman. Me and Claude, we'll head back first chance we get. I wanna do me some sightseeing while me and Claude is up here—"

"You want to find Ignatius, that's what you want to do," Santa said, doing her best to control her temper. "Ain't you heard a word of what that Jew woman said, Irene? You got to let this go."

"I'll call you later, Santa."

"Where you staying, babe?"

"Goodnight, Santa."

And Mrs. Reilly hung up the telephone.

She sighed, got out of bed, and started to get dressed. If her boy was still out there, she was going to do all that she could to find him, Jew woman on television or not.

III

While Mrs. Reilly and Mr. Robichaux cruised around Manhattan in a cab that Saturday morning, Ignatius, covered by many blankets and sheets and quilts, slept a deep, deep sleep on the secondhand sofa. Lady Laye pestered Ignatius to get up to practice, but Ignatius mumbled that they would have to improvise Sunday night's show. Lady Laye frowned, and Sir Sid went to the fire escape to smoke marijuana.

Myrna, meanwhile, retreated to a Bowery café, where she telephoned her mother and father's house. Mr. Minkoff answered, and Myrna asked if Mrs. Reilly and Mr. Robichaux had been at the house. Mr. Minkoff replied that they hadn't. Myrna told Mr. Minkoff that Ignatius was slated to appear the next evening on *The Ed Sullivan Show* and that Mr. Minkoff had to ensure that neither Mrs. Reilly nor Mr. Robichaux found out about the appearance. Mr. Minkoff exclaimed loudly and said that he wanted her and Ignatius to get home as soon as possible. Mr. Minkoff said that he had something special to give to them. Myrna said that they would be there that Sunday afternoon, after she was sure that the coast was clear. Mr. Minkoff said that before he gave her and Ignatius the surprise, he, Mr. Minkoff, would take everyone out to dinner at a nice Italian restaurant.

"Remember, you must be here Sunday afternoon," Mr. Minkoff said, tittering. "You promised, remember? Remember, I have something special for all of us, especially you and Ollie."

"It's Ignatius, Dad, not Ollie. You're getting as bad as Mom. And what's so special? What special thing did you get us, Dad?"

"Oh, you'll see," Mr. Minkoff replied, giggling. "Bye for now, you sly cat."

And Mr. Minkoff hung up. And Myrna, never having heard her father speak in such a manner, hung up the telephone receiver and saw a burly truck driver sizing her up. She went to introduce herself to her next pickup.

Ignatius slept all Saturday afternoon, too, while Mrs. Reilly, who fretted and twisted a tissue, and Mr. Robichaux, who grimaced each time the meter registered another penny, cruised through Central Park in the cab in which they had been riding all day. Lady Laye called the telephone number on the business card that Ed Sullivan had given to Ignatius and confirmed the slot of the Beat-Alls on Sunday's show, and the woman on the other end of the line told Lady Laye that the Beat-Alls would need to be at the Ed Sullivan Theater for the afternoon rehearsal. Fretting, Lady Laye, unable to awaken Ignatius, chewed her fingernails, and Sir Sid, having smoked several marijuana cigarettes, stuffed his face with stale popcorn that he had popped the previous week.

An unsatisfied, disappointed-by-the-truck-driver Myrna came to the apartment around two Sunday morning and slept on the floor next to the secondhand sofa on which Ignatius was sleeping. Ignatius awoke around ten and discovered that Myrna was up and drinking bitter coffee while Lady Laye was putting the finishing touches on her costume.

"We need to get moving, Ignatius," Lady Laye said, studying herself in a full-length Art Deco mirror, adjusting her red hood and smoothing her royal blue cotehardie. "We have a rehearsal at the Ed Sullivan Theater this afternoon. They probably won't even allow us on the show once they hear us at rehearsal."

"Reherdal, man?" said Sir Sid, who was lying on the floor, Sir Sid's eyes glassy and red.

Lady Laye sighed. "The shit that I go through." She shook her head. "Why the hell should I bother? You two haven't even practiced."

"I've had the worst shock imaginable to my nervous system, which needed to be shut down a day or two, much like those US Air Force supercomputers that are prone to overheating," Ignatius said, yawning, sitting up on the sofa. He was thirsty, and he was famished, and he wanted a good meal. "You cannot fathom the horrors of being chased across this nation by my brainwashed mother and her lothario of a fiancé. And as for rehearsal, improvisation and invention within the confines of strict structure are at the heart of the true medieval art, Lady Laye. In other words, Lady Laye, methinks thou dost worry too much."

"So cool, man," Sir Sid drawled, so stoned that he was seeing a sphere of nude, Ignatius-like cherubs hovering in an upper corner of the apartment. The cherubs played cornets and chased one another playfully.

"I remember you saying something like that," Lady Laye said. "But me, I like to be ready for things. I don't like winging it."

"Dad wants to treat us to dinner before you appear on *The Ed Sullivan Show*," Myrna said to Ignatius. "He said that he has something special for us, and I think it's money. I think he realizes what a reactionary he's been and wants to make it up to us, even though he sounded very weird."

"Define 'weird,'" Ignatius said, and he yawned and stretched his arms. His dreams of Rex had been pleasant dreams, dreams that, in terms of artistic styles, drifted and shifted from dark Rembrandt exteriors to light Vermeer interiors to starry Van Gogh dreamscapes. "Perhaps your father has finally and inexorably come around to the truth of how things are."

"But hc sounded so chirpy," Myrna said. "And that's what I don't like. That's not like him."

"True, optimism is the worst of all modern-day values, given the fall of man," replied Ignatius. "But perhaps his realizing that has raised his hopes for the time being, thus making him momentarily optimistic. As we learn in *Don Quixote*, life is not fun, but it can be funny, just as it can be momentarily joyful. You need not worry, minx. I am more than certain that your father will return to his dour self once the novelty wears off."

Sir Sid gurgled and giggled.

"Looks like we're going to need to take a cab," Lady Laye said. "I'd ask you to come along, Ignatius, but I'm going to have enough trouble as it is managing the instruments and my asshole twin brother."

And with that, she went downstairs to find a cab, and Myrna finished her bitter coffee and sighed. "We still haven't cured you," Myrna said.

"Cured?"

"Dealt with your virginity issues," she said. "I feel like a failure on that count. I thought about getting onto that sofa with you last night and seeing if you could perform. But I was too tired, and it wasn't because of Fred. He's another disappointment."

"Fred? That African who wears the balaclava?"

Sir Sid snored.

"No, that's Rastajaq. I gave up on Rastajaq yesterday after I met a truck driver named Fred," said Myrna. "I thought that if the revolution was about to begin, I might as well go to bed with a real revolutionary who would be a real proletarian, like a truck driver. Well, he might be a real proletarian, but he discovered that he's not a real stud. You should have seen the look on his face after it was over."

"Good heavens!" Ignatius said, wanting to get that look off her face, a look in which she stared as if into eternity, only to return to full consciousness with a libido that no man could ever possibly satiate. "Of course we shall deal with my virginity issues later. But for now we must stay focused on the revolution, and that means my going back to the Minkoff estate in the Bronx, where I need the accoutrements that your dear mother recently purchased for me. On top of that, I must review my notes in my Big Chief tablets before the Beat-Alls appear this evening on *The Ed Sullivan Show*."

"And that surprise from Dad. And he wants to take us to dinner before he gives us the surprise. I guess we'd better get going, Ignatius."

"Ah, lest I forget, the afternoon rehearsal—"

"We'll get it figured out, Ignatius."

Lady Laye entered the apartment with an enigmatic Eritrean cab driver, and Myrna promised Lady Laye that she, Myrna, would somehow get Ignatius to the Ed Sullivan Theater before that afternoon's rehearsal.

IV

Mr. Minkoff whistled loudly as he drove down Broadway. Ignatius was seated next to a very horny Myrna, who kept putting her hand on his knee and working her hand towards his crotch. Ignatius batted her hand away several times and held his tongue. Now was not the time to speak. The time to speak would be later, on the television show.

Mr. Minkoff sped into a parking lot and backed his Oldsmobile into a parking space and slammed the brakes. Ignatius groaned and felt as if he were about to vomit.

"Careful, Dad," Myrna said irritably. "What's the big idea?"

"Oh, I can't wait to get into that restaurant," Mr. Minkoff said happily, his smile big and toothy. "Italian food is great. Italian food is delicious. Italian food is a fine last meal."

"Last meal?" Mrs. Minkoff said. "What do you mean by that, Bernard?"

"Have you ever seen gangster films?" Mr. Minkoff said. "Well, generally, when someone gets whacked, it's done in an Italian restaurant."

Mr. Minkoff giggled. He put one hand, then the other, over his mouth. He was like an errant schoolboy who could not stop giggling because of a naughty joke that he had heard a fellow classmate tell about their teacher's derriere.

Mrs. Minkoff, who was staring at her husband, wondered if he had gone completely insane.

"Is there something you haven't told me, Bernard?" Mrs. Minkoff asked sincerely.

Mr. Minkoff stopped giggling and did his best to put on his normal, rather stern face. "And what would that be, Miriam?"

"Are you really Jewish?" Mrs. Minkoff asked. "Are you sure that you're Jewish? You look Jewish, but are you sure that you aren't descended from a line of Italian comics?"

"Why would you ask that, Miriam?" Mr. Minkoff suppressed a giggle.

"Because of your recent fascination with Laurel and Hardy," Mrs. Minkoff replied. "And because you're wearing an Italian suit, and I've never seen you wear an Italian suit. It's unsettling, Bernard, it really is. I believe you should seek Israel's counsel."

Mrs. Minkoff looked over her shoulder at Ignatius.

"Don't you think that Bernard should meet with one of your rabbinical teachers at the *yeshiva*?" Mrs. Minkoff asked him. "Would that help Bernard with whatever is bothering him?"

"Mom, please," Myrna said so loudly that she woke Grandmother Horowitz, who had been dozing soundly. "Enough of this reactionary talk already. What's going on with Dad has nothing to do with the spiritual, unless you're talking about the joys of tantric sex, which, I guess, could be considered spiritual if you're having multiple orgasms."

"Myrna, please, how many times—"

"Mom, Dad's repressed. He's stuffed his sexual repression so far down his throat that it's going down into his sexual organs and then coming back up and causing him to act this way. He doesn't need to see a rabbi, Dad needs to see Dr. Ingloss, and Dad needs to get laid."

"Enough!" Ignatius bellowed. "Do we need to hear about the sex lives of your parents? And you, Madam Minkoff, do you honestly believe that a rabbi could help your husband? Don't you people realize that in a mere two hours or so I shall be appearing on *The Ed Sullivan Show*? The worldviews of hundreds of thousands, nay, millions of Americans is at stake. I must partake heartily of hearty victuals if I am to maintain my strength for such a heartrending endeavor. Given that there are no hot dog vendors about at this hour, I suggest that we do what Mr. Minkoff has suggested—that is, get into that Italian restaurant and partake of this hearty Italian food of which he has so eloquently spoken—"

"You forgot to qualify that," Mr. Minkoff said, interrupting rudely. "And last. Last, last, last. Let us not forget that this is our *last* Italian meal." Mr. Minkoff covered his mouth and giggled.

Mrs. Minkoff didn't like the sound of what she had just heard. Mrs. Minkoff's face expressed worry. Grandmother Horowitz, on the other hand, smacked her dry lips and wondered where she was, and Ignatius did his best to get out of the Oldsmobile, Myrna shoving his ursine buttocks to get him through the door.

The exterior of the restaurant had a large, steam-covered plate glass window, upon which, in gilded lettering, appeared these words:

FALCONE'S
NEW YORK CITY'S FINEST RUSTIC ITALIAN CUISINE

The interior of the lobby was paneled oak, the walls covered with photographs of Frank Sinatra, Joe DiMaggio, Sophia Loren, Dean Martin, and other famous Italians. The air smelled pleasantly of garlic-laced spaghetti sauce and what to Ignatius smelled like freshly made hot vanilla pudding. His mouth watered, and his belly grumbled as he thought about bearing down into a plate of serpentine spaghetti and mountainous meatballs. This was no time for a prandicle, after all. Perhaps a fine red wine would help to wash things down, though he must not imbibe too much red wine. On second thought, he would have Dr Pepper. After all, he had to keep his wits about him. There was that evening's performance on *The Ed Sullivan Show* to consider, after all.

"This way," a man dressed impeccably in a tuxedo with a red cummerbund said, leading the way to a circular table in an alcove in the back of the restaurant. Ignatius sat by Myrna, who sat by Mrs. Minkoff, who sat by Grandmother Horowitz, who sat by Mr. Minkoff, who sat by Ignatius. The maître d' placed menus in front of each person and then hurried off to tend to other people waiting in the lobby. A white-shirted waiter appeared, poured glasses of chilled water for the Minkoff party, and, after wiping his large hands on his black pants, said that he would return soon to get their orders.

"I don't understand a single word of this nonsense," Grandmother Horowitz said, studying the menu. "Are you sure we aren't in a Chinese place? Or even Russian? You know how stupid these low-class Russian Jews are, don't you?"

"Mother, please," Mrs. Minkoff said, turning the menu right side up. "We're at an Italian restaurant. And please don't talk about Russian Jews. You've been doing that for years, and you know how sensitive Bernard is to that sort of talk."

Mr. Minkoff wasn't paying attention to what was being said but was, instead, whistling lines from *The Barber of Seville* and studying his menu.

"Mother didn't mean it," Mrs. Minkoff said to Mr. Minkoff.

Mr. Minkoff startled. "Oh, did someone say something? I was so engrossed with the menu that I wasn't paying attention."

"Mother was talking about those stupid Russian Jews," Mrs. Minkoff said. "But she really didn't mean it."

"That's all right," Mr. Minkoff said gleefully. "After tonight, no one is going to have to hear any more about stupid Russian Jews. Ever again. Or anything else for that matter."

"I'm glad that you feel that way, Bernard."

"So do I, Miriam." And Mr. Minkoff did his best to suppress a giggle.

The waiter came and took their orders. Ignatius selected the biggest plate of spaghetti that the restaurant served. In addition, Ignatius ordered a carafe of Dr Pepper.

Myrna attempted to start a conversation about a looming sexual revolution, but Ignatius changed the topic to his appearance that night on *The Ed Sullivan Show*. Myrna frowned, crossed her arms, and listened while Ignatius pontificated about the shortcomings of Ed Sullivan's audience. Myrna's sexual frustration and resentment grew deeper and deeper.

After the waiter placed their meals on the table, Mr. Minkoff bowed his head in prayer, giving audible thanks for the food and silent thanks for the five bullets that were in his snub-nosed revolver.

"You never seemed to be pious," Ignatius said to Mr. Minkoff. "Pray tell, why are you praying now, sirrah?"

"Pious is such a lovely word," Mrs. Minkoff said. "You are so pious, Israel."

"Gee, Ollie, I didn't think I did anything wrong," Mr. Minkoff said in his high-pitched imitation of Stan Laurel. Mr. Minkoff screwed up his face, as if he were about to cry.

"Why do you insist on calling me Ollie?" Ignatius said, eructating loudly from the Dr Pepper that he had just imbibed. Dr Pepper wasn't as good as Dr. Nut—nothing could be as good as that soft drink—but Dr Pepper came close. "If I'm Ollie, does that make you Stan?"

"Gee, Ollie, I don't know."

And Mr. Minkoff cried the way Stan Laurel cried after being bullied by Oliver Hardy. The patrons in the restaurant turned, and Mrs. Minkoff looked apologetically at them and then looked ruefully at her husband and placed her hand lovingly atop his as he continued to cry.

"I think we should go, Bernard," Mrs. Minkoff said. "Since I don't drive, I'll get us a cab. I'm sure that we can leave the car here. Or Myrna can use it to take Israel to the theater where he's going to preach his sermon."

"Mom, how many times—"

"No, I'm fine," Mr. Minkoff said, after imagining putting a fatal slug into Ignatius's thick skull. Mr. Minkoff feigned a smile and wiped his face with his cloth napkin. "How does everyone like my imitation? Don't you think that I do a good Stan Laurel?"

"I would say that it's a mediocre attempt at best," Ignatius intoned deeply. "But you should know, sirrah, that we have weightier matters than mere imitations of famous comics on our hands at this moment. We have the worldviews in this nation to change, and after that, the worldviews in the remainder of the world. Proper theology and geometry shall once again have their due rule over the minds of men."

"The worldviews, how could I ever forget!" Mr. Minkoff said, clapping his hands to add emphasis. "Of course, we must change the worldviews, Ollie."

"It's Ignatius," said Ignatius. "Methinks thou does jest too much, sirrah."

"I probably do," Mr. Minkoff said, and he took a gulp of red wine to steady his nerves. He was going to need them that evening, after all was said and done. "Well, that does that. Is everyone ready to go see *The Ed Sullivan Show*?"

"Only because Ignatius is appearing on it," Myrna said. "Otherwise, I have as much use for Ed Sullivan as I do Walter Cronkite."

"Please," Mrs. Minkoff said to her daughter, "not tonight, Myrna. Can you please just be normal tonight and radical Monday morning?"

"As if anything could be normal after the failed coup," Myrna said, smirking. "Life's never going to be the same."

"Coupé?" Grandmother Horowitz said. "I used to ride around in coupés with boys. Oh, the wonderful trains that we had."

"You mean the wonderful trains that you saw," Ignatius said. "I presume you went joyriding with young men and saw locomotives in the countryside or wherever you were driving."

"No, we didn't see trains, we *had* trains," Grandmother Horowitz said, leering at Ignatius and wondering if she would ever get a look at his package. "Ralph was the engine, and Ramon was the caboose—"

"Mother!" Mrs. Minkoff said. "Please! You're as bad as Myrna!"

"There is nothing wrong with sex and multiple partners and multiple orgasms!" Myrna said, and people at other tables looked at the table where Ignatius and the Minkoffs were sitting.

"This is not a time for a discussion of things slatternly," Ignatius intoned, his voice serious, somber, sonorous. "Please be aware that such discussions are not worthy of a refined eating establishment such as this one, albeit an Italian one."

"There you go again!" Myrna said, gesticulating. "You were faking it all along, weren't you, you *schnorrer*! You were just using me to get out of New Orleans, weren't you, when those reactionary, repressed fascists were getting ready to take you away to Mandeville!"

"Gee, Ollie, where's Mandeville?" Mr. Minkoff, who had been daydreaming about what he was going to do with his five bullets, asked Ignatius.

"Mandeville houses an institution for the so-called insane," Ignatius replied seriously to Mr. Minkoff's question. "It is where the state and the cruel institution known as psychiatry ruin the woof and warp of the souls of the damned for having worldviews that express a proper theology and geometry." To Myrna: "Actually, they were going to send me to a charity hospital."

"There you go again with your reactionary and anti-Semitic remarks," Myrna said. "It's bad enough that we can't talk about sex and multiple orgasms, but now you have to bring in that stuff."

Ignatius's face crimsoned. "And how, dear Myrna, were these remarks anti-Semitic? I can see where you might construe them as being 'reactionary,' given your own irrational, socialistic, and unsophisticated predilections."

"Theology is a *Catholic* concept," Myrna said, grinding her teeth, glowering at him. "And *Catholicism* is a reactionary faith that is inherently anti-Semitic. And so, because you keep mentioning theology, you keep being anti-Semitic."

"I didn't know that an Orthodox rabbi could be anti-Semitic," Mrs. Minkoff said to Ignatius. "Is that true, Israel?"

"My dear Madam Minkoff, anti-Catholicism is the anti-Semitism of the liberal," Ignatius said to the earnest but errant mother of Myrna. "Therefore, to be anti-Catholic is to be anti-Semitic. Your liberal daughter just made an anti-Catholic statement. Thus, and therefore, I charge your very own daughter, Myrna minx Minkoff, of being an anti-Semite!"

Mrs. Minkoff tilted her forehead at her daughter. "You of all people!" Mrs. Minkoff said angrily to Myrna. "After all our people have been through, how can you be an anti-Semite!"

"I am *not* an anti-Semite!" Myrna said, her anger exceeding her mother's. "Mom, I'm Jewish, so how could I be an anti-Semite, Mom!"

"That's very easy to explain," Ignatius interjected. "Judaism is a religion, not an ethnic distinction or a race. More properly and correctly said, you are a Hebrew who happened to be born of Jewish parents. Therefore, I can say that while you are of Hebraic descent, you are not Jewish, given that you do not regularly practice the religion but instead practice things contrary to the religion. As St. Paul says in Romans, not all of Israel is Israel."

Mrs. Minkoff was crying. "My own daughter, an anti-Semite—"

"Mom, please, don't be so reactionary, what you need is a good orgasm—"

"Please," Ignatius said, interrupting Myrna. "I believe that your father has something to say. I suppose Grandmother

Horowitz would have something to say, too, but she is now getting the sleep that she so desperately needs."

And, indeed, Grandmother Horowitz was sleeping, her forehead forward, as if she were in deep prayer. She snorted and smacked her lips.

Ignatius, Mrs. Minkoff, and Myrna looked expectantly at Mr. Minkoff, who had his right hand in his suit jacket, his fingers lovingly caressing the cold steel of the snub-nosed revolver in its leather holster. One shot for the bullying Ollie, one shot for the dingbat wife, one shot for the salacious cat, one shot for the horrid mother-in-law, and then one shot for himself, Stan Laurel. Then it would all be over. Ollie would no longer exist, and he, Stan Laurel, would forever know an unknowing, and unknown, bliss.

"Well?" Ignatius said impatiently.

Mr. Minkoff wanted to do the deed right then and there in the Italian restaurant. But why not stick to the original plan? Why not make a statement on the show? Why not show the world, on live television, that Ollie had not won?

Mr. Minkoff removed his hand from inside his suit jacket. "Nothing, nothing at all. Why don't we finish our dinner? After all, you must have your energy for tonight's show, when you change our worldviews once for all, Ignatius."

"I couldn't agree more," Ignatius replied heartily. He eructated loudly and placed a fist to his mouth and, with his other fist, pounded the dinner table. "Garçon! Garçon! We need more Dr Pepper, garçon!"

· *Fourteen*

The Minkoffs dropped off Ignatius, suitcase with accoutrements in hand, in front of the Ed Sullivan Theater, and after speaking with two ushers, Ignatius was ushered to a dressing room, where a nervous Lady Laye and a somnambulant Sir Sid were waiting.

"Where the hell have you been!" Lady Laye said, using her hands to emphasize her frustration. "You were supposed to be here for the afternoon rehearsal!"

"I was unfortunately delayed through no fault of my own," Ignatius replied dryly and drolly. "There's an august guest bed in the Minkoff estate that allows me, shall I say, to complete urgent meditations, after which I need an hour or two of rest."

"We about lost the gig," Lady Laye said, pacing, wondering how much more of this nerve-wracking stress she could take. "We would've lost it, but the Negro banjo player had a seizure."

"I must get ready then," Ignatius said, listening to the hustle and bustle outside the dressing room. "Now, if you will awaken somnambulist Sir Sid and beat a hasty exit, I shall change."

In front of the theater, the Minkoffs waited in a queue. Mr. Minkoff bared his teeth, which many around him, including his family, took as a smile.

"I'm surprised that you were able to get tickets, Dad," Myrna said, "especially on such short notice."

"Oh, I wouldn't miss seeing Ollie on this show for the whole wide world!" Mr. Minkoff said, covering his mouth with both hands and giggling. "Ollie must change everyone's worldviews the way that he's changed mine."

"Are you sure you're all right, Dad?" Myrna asked. "Have you been hanging out with Jehovah's Witnesses or something?"

"Oh, nothing like that," Mr. Minkoff replied. "Let's just say that I have five very good reasons for wanting to be here tonight."

And on Broadway, the cab in which Mrs. Reilly and Mr. Robichaux rode crept south, traffic in both directions congested because of the holiday festivities. Mrs. Reilly and Mr. Robichaux had just come from Harlem, where Mr. Robichaux thought Ignatius might have gone into hiding as a large Negro.

"They's the Ed Sullivan Theater," Mr. Robichaux said, pointing with a horny finger. "Look at all them folks. They's where they broadcast his show. I loved it when the Andrew Sisters was on it. Leastways I think it was them. You like them, sweetie?"

Mrs. Reilly sighed. "I don't know what I like, Claude. And I don't know where I went wrong. I think we should go home."

"That's what I was thinking." Then Mr. Robichaux squinted, not believing what he was seeing. "Christ Amight, it's that communiss girl!"

"You and your communiss, Claude—"

"Ignatius's girlfriend!" Mr. Robichaux said excitedly, pointing. "Look!"

And Mrs. Reilly looked, and, indeed, it was Myrna Minkoff, who was standing next to Mrs. Minkoff, who was speaking to a man whom Mrs. Reilly presumed was Mr. Minkoff, behind whom stooped an old woman who was reaching out to the crotch of a nineteen-year-old man who had his arm around his date.

"Stop this cab!" Mrs. Reilly screamed at the driver. "If Myrna is here, it means that Ignatius is here!"

And in a cab following the cab in which Mrs. Reilly and Mr. Robichaux were riding, Nick the Nose nudged Henley.

And following Henley and Nick the Nose's cab was Magoohan's cab.

In the dressing room, a makeup artist applied finishing touches to Ignatius's face.

"Of course, in this postmodern world, one must present oneself as what one idealizes, not as what one truly is," Ignatius said, looking into an actor's mirror and making a face to see how his makeup was holding up.

"That do it?" the woman said, snapping gum.

"Yes, that will 'do it,'" Ignatius replied haughtily. "You may now leave."

The makeup artist rolled her eyes and walked out of the dressing room before closing the door behind her.

Ignatius was about to study his notes in his Big Chief tablet when there was a knock on the door. Ignatius closed the tablet in exasperation.

"If you have an éclair or two on hand, then please enter," Ignatius said, studying his gargantuan face in the actor's mirror and twisting the ends of his thick black mustache. "Otherwise, go somewhere else. I am not to be disturbed."

The door opened, and Lady Laye and Sir Sid entered.

"Here's a tart," Lady Laye said, handing Ignatius a brown paper bag. "That's all that they had."

Ignatius sniffed the tart, which seemed more than a day old. The tart would have to do, he supposed, and so he sank his teeth into it and ate it the way a black bear heartily ate a freshly caught bass.

Ignatius then wiped his hands on his scarlet pantaloons, and pockets of warm air shifted in them. His belly growled, pleased with the tart but desiring more.

"We're on in ten minutes, man," Sir Sid said. "Man, I'm so nervous that my tongue's dry, no matter how much water I drink, man."

"Might I suggest, then," Ignatius suggested, "that you partake of one of those magical cigarettes of yours? They seem to calm your nerves in situations like these."

"Good idea, man," Sir Sid said, and he reached into his pocket, but Ignatius bellowed that he, Sir Sid, was not to smoke the magical cigarette in the dressing room but to do so in the back alley, for which Sir Sid took off.

"We've almost got the world in our hands," Lady Laye said. "Your wonderful worldview is about to change the modern world, as you like to say, Ignatius."

"Indubitably," Ignatius replied. "Now, if you'll leave, I will review my introductory speech before we go on the air."

"Sure thing, Ignatius."

Outside the theater, Henley and Nick the Nose attempted to force their way into the lobby while Mrs. Reilly and Mr. Robichaux entered the lobby. In the theater, an usher showed the Minkoff family to their front-row seats. A man with a chest that looked like a water barrel covered by a tight white dress shirt grumbled in protest as the Minkoffs crawled past him. Grandmother Horowitz leered and reached down for his crotch. Mrs. Minkoff snatched her mother's hand away before the older woman could cop a feel, and Myrna sat down. She blinked. She thought that she saw Dr. Talc on the other side of the theater and then shook her head in disbelief.

"A reactionary and mediocre professor from Tulane at this reactionary and mediocre hullabaloo called *The Ed Sullivan Show?*" she said.

"That's enough of that," Mrs. Minkoff said, wagging a finger at Myrna. "You knew we were coming here, young woman, to see Israel as he gives his exegesis."

"What?" Myrna said. "What are you talking about? This isn't a synagogue."

"Israel told me that fancy word," Mrs. Minkoff said. "And I don't know what it means, but I know that it's a serious word, and because it's a serious word, you are going to be serious, young woman."

"You can't be serious." Myrna rolled her eyes. "You still believe that Ignatius is a rabbi, don't you, Mom?"

"Not just a rabbi, an *Orthodox* rabbi," Mrs. Minkoff replied in utmost sincerity.

"I can't get through to you," Myrna said, throwing up her hands in exasperation. "How many times do I have to tell you, Mom? How many times? How many times? How many times? Ignatius isn't Jewish! He never was and probably never will be Jewish! And furthermore, rabbis don't give sermons or homilies or speeches on a reactionary television show like this one!"

"If that's true," Mrs. Minkoff said, leaning her forehead forward and knitting the ends of her eyebrows together, "then why is Israel so *pious?*"

"*Oi, vey,*" Myrna said, and she cussed in Yiddish before switching back to English. "If Ignatius is such a devout Jew, then why doesn't he wear a yarmulke, Mom? Can you tell me that? Do you have an answer for that one?"

"Israel doesn't need to wear a yarmulke," Mrs. Minkoff replied triumphantly. "He wears his green hunting cap. Green, you know, is a very sacred color."

"I can't believe you said that!" Myrna said. "I can't believe that you are so reactionary, Mom!"

The people around them had been listening in rapt attention, though Myrna and Mrs. Minkoff were oblivious to the stares and whispers. Grandmother Horowitz was wondering when the vaudeville show would begin, and Mr. Minkoff was replaying in his mind the last great scene that he and Ollie would ever do before their partnership was eternally dissolved.

"I don't want to hear another word," Mrs. Minkoff said sternly. "When Israel presents his sermon, we must be exceedingly reverent and *silent.*"

Myrna slapped her forehead, feeling the onset of a headache, which a good orgasm or two would dispel. Searching for a suitable man, she looked at the people around her.

Mr. Minkoff giggled.

Mrs. Minkoff nudged Mr. Minkoff. "Are you all right, Bernard?"

"Of course I'm all right," Mr. Minkoff said, and he caught himself before he began to speak like Stan Laurel. "Why wouldn't I be all right?"

"I thought that you were all right, but at dinner you began acting up again," Mrs. Minkoff said, feeling sad, wishing that her old Bernard would return. "And now you seem to be back to normal, except for that strange smile and your eyes."

"What's wrong with smiling?" Mr. Minkoff said, and the weight of the loaded gun in its holster felt comforting.

"There's nothing wrong with smiling," Mrs. Minkoff said, "but most of your life, you've never smiled. And your eyes."

"Oh, yes, I forgot all about them," Mr. Minkoff replied, continuing to stare at the stage the way a sociopathic dictator in Haiti might stare without blinking. "Mine eyes have seen the coming of the glory of the Lord, Miriam."

"That's the spirit," Mrs. Minkoff said, and she squeezed her husband's hand lovingly. "I knew that Israel would get to you."

"Oh, Ollie's got to me all right," Mr. Minkoff said, his voice rising a pitch or two. Then he spoke in his normal register and looked at his wife. "Everything's going to be all right after tonight. Ollie will be gone, and we won't have to worry ever again about what the cat drags in. In fact, after tonight, Miriam, we won't be worrying about anything. We're going to be in a different world, I promise you that."

"Oh, Bernard, thank you! Thank you, thank you, thank you!"

The people in the seats around the Minkoffs looked at Mr. Minkoff and Mrs. Minkoff. Mrs. Minkoff blushed and excused herself and squeezed her husband's hand in confirmation of his goodwill towards her, their family, Rabbi Israel, the audience, and the world at large.

Myrna looked at her mother. "Has Dad agreed to sleep with you now or something?"

"Myrna," Mrs. Minkoff said, ensuring that she kept her voice low, "that is no way to speak in such an elegant place as this. This is not one of your political meetings, young woman."

"Too much Walter Cronkite," Myrna said. "Dad has watched too much Walter Cronkite."

Grandmother Horowitz awoke from her nap. "Where is he?"

"Who?" Mrs. Minkoff asked.

"Farinelli," Grandmother Horowitz said, about to stick her hand up her dress before Mrs. Minkoff snatched away her mother's hand.

"Mother!" Mrs. Minkoff said. "Please, behave yourself."

A finger held up to his mouth, an usher with light-blond, thinning hair and elfin features stood next to the row.

"Hush, hush, hush," the effete usher said. "Our show, show, show is about to begin."

"I can't wait!" Mr. Minkoff said in his high-pitched imitation of Stan Laurel. "Ollie, where are you, Ollie! Ollie! Ollie! Ollie!"

"You are not all right, Bernard!" Mrs. Minkoff said in protest.

"Please, quiet, quiet, quiet!" the effete usher hissed.

Mrs. Minkoff frowned, and from the corner of her eye she watched Mr. Minkoff, who was smiling a smile big enough for two Cheshire Cats.

The lights in the theater dimmed, and Ed Sullivan, wearing an elegant dark suit, appeared onstage. The APPLAUSE lights came on, and the audience applauded, and Ed Sullivan clasped his hands together and nodded his head in acknowledgment of his audience's graciousness.

Behind the stage curtains, Ignatius studied hand lines, loading bridges, pipe weights, tension blocks, lock rails, and overhead sandbags. Stagehands hurried about, ensuring that everything was in place. Ignatius cleared his throat, satisfied that his speech and that that evening's performance by the Beat-Alls would forever change the worldviews held in his nation and eventually those in the entire world.

Grandmother Horowitz's head lolled to the side and rested on Mrs. Minkoff's shoulder. The wizened woman salivated and snored lightly.

"Ladies and gentlemen," Ed Sullivan said in his rich voice, "welcome to the show. As always, we have lots of great acts for you this evening. In fact, tonight I think we're going to have the biggest act that has ever been on this show."

The APPLAUSE lights came on again, and the audience clapped heartily. Ed Sullivan smiled at a television camera.

"Now, you haven't heard of these young people, but I recently discovered them here in the heart of Manhattan. Their leader, a virtuous young man, is going to be, as far as I can tell, the new Elvis Presley."

The APPLAUSE lights came on again. Many teenage girls, having heard Ed Sullivan say Elvis Presley's name, believed that Elvis was going to perform, and so they began screaming in joy and calling out Elvis's name.

Ed Sullivan, who was amused, held out his hands, indicating that the teenagers should become silent. When one of them didn't, an usher appeared and told her sternly that if she didn't shut her trap, he would throw her out onto the street.

"Elvis has left the building," Ed Sullivan said, unsure why he had said those exact words and wondering if they would somehow become a viral meme. *Elvis has left the building. The words* had such meaning, such deep impact. "No, there is a greater one than Elvis here this evening, ladies and gentlemen, boys and girls—"

"We want Elvis!" the young woman who had been told to shut up yelled. "Elvis, Elvis, Elvis!"

There was the sound of someone's muttering loudly behind the stage curtains, and Myrna distinctly heard Ignatius say, "Such effrontery! Such audacity!"

Two ushers dragged the protesting teenager from the auditorium. Through the stage curtains, Ignatius told Ed Sullivan to continue with the introduction.

"Generally, ladies and gentlemen, I introduce the act and afterwards have a word or two with the performers," Ed Sullivan said to his audience and to the television cameras in front of him. "But this evening, we're going to break tradition, and I'm going to have a few words with a young man who says that he is going to change your world with his music."

The stage curtains parted, revealing Ignatius standing in front of a microphone, lute in hand. Besides scarlet pantaloons, he was wearing a royal purple cotehardie, Moroccan leather chausses whose toes pointed upward, and his green hunting cap, its flaps pulled up and buttoned, thereby exposing thatches of his black hair and his two signal-indicator ears.

Behind Ignatius stood Lady Laye and Sir Sid. Feeling very nervous, Lady Laye stood in front of her harpsichord. Sir Sid, who had smoked marijuana, felt relaxed as he tuned the fourth and thickest string of his acoustic bass.

The audience stared in rapt attention. Mrs. Minkoff smiled, Grandmother Horowitz snored lightly, and Mr. Minkoff stared at Ignatius, Mr. Minkoff moving his lips, speaking to himself in his high-pitched, Stan Laurel-like voice. In the theater lobby, Mrs. Reilly argued with a burly usher, Mrs. Reilly demanding that she and Mr. Robichaux be allowed to enter the theater as

Mr. Robichaux accused the burly usher of being a communist. Outside the theater, Nick the Nose argued with a demure usher, Nick the Nose demanding that he and Henley, who could no longer speak, be allowed to enter the lobby.

A costumed Magoohan hid in shadows, watching Henley and Nick the Nose.

Onstage, Ed Sullivan grinned and extended his hand to Ignatius, who refused to shake it. A few people in the audience laughed nervously, and a man in the front row loudly cleared his throat.

"Who knows where that thing has been," Ignatius said indignantly to the world-famous television host. "After all, you've spent the day cavorting with jugglers, contortionists, and animal handlers, who, I'm afraid, are living very unsavory lives."

"Well," Ed Sullivan replied, lowering his hand, deeply offended at Ignatius's rudeness but nonetheless smiling. The television host hoped that he could steer Ignatius in another direction. "So, you're the Beat-Alls?"

"Who else would we be?" Ignatius said haughtily. He plucked an arpeggio on his freshly tuned lute, and the glissando wafted sonorously into the air. "We are the Beat-Alls, and I, Ignatius J. Reilly, am the leader of this noble band of troubadours." Ignatius gave Ed Sullivan a very serious, very stern look. "By the way, you said in your introduction that we were here to change the world. You must define your terms more carefully, sirrah. We cannot change, transmute, or alter in any way the fundamental essence of the universe. Were you versed in philosophical enquiry and proper theology and geometry, you would have said that we were here to change the worldviews of your audience, something, sirrah, that we are here to do indeed."

Ed Sullivan chuckled somewhat ruefully. "You're obviously very educated, Mr. Reilly."

"Of course," Ignatius replied, "I am educated, unlike you and these morons inhabiting the rows before us."

The audience gasped, except for the three Minkoffs (Mrs. Minkoff continued to smile mindlessly, and Myrna was wondering if she was going to get laid that night, and Mr. Minkoff screwed up his face up so that he resembled a crying Stan Laurel). Grandmother Horowitz had stopped snoring and was dreaming of the grocer Farinelli and Farinelli's shop and a sign above Farinelli's head that read TWELVE INCHES OF TUBE STEAK PARADISE HERE!

"I like your style, kid," Ed Sullivan said, laughing. "Not only are you the leader of the newest, most sensational act in the industry, you're the newest comedic hipster!"

And now the audience, believing that it had been a joke all along, laughed uproariously. Ignatius made a sour face, and the audience laughed harder. A viewer in Pueblo, Colorado, laughed so hard that he spewed coffee onto his television tray, thereby ruining a Yankee pot roast dinner that his diligent wife had diligently prepared for him.

"My words seem to amuse you and these sybarites," Ignatius said, raising an eyebrow superciliously.

"Oh, you have a way with words, all right," Ed Sullivan said, and he was beginning to feel a tad bit uneasy, uncertain of what was about to happen or where Ignatius was going to go with this. "Mind telling us where you learned all those fancy words, Mr. Reilly?"

"When I was very young, I was educated in the best private school in New Orleans," Ignatius replied. "Mind you, this was not an ordinary private school but a Catholic school of the old order, where one not only gets a true education but learns the morals and the dogmas of the Church. I attended this school until I was ten years old or so, when blind Fortuna spun me into a cycle where I was forced to attend public schools. Fortunately, however, after the death of my paternal grandmother, I was able to continue my education at Tulane University, which, at one time, was an earnest and worthwhile institution until it hired the likes of Dr. Talc, a great pretender, a monster of a fraud who has bamboozled the Tulane intelligentsia, among others, with his faux scholarship. But Talc, mind you, never got beyond my own dubiety or my all-seeing eye."

The audience laughed, and Dr. Talc, who was laughing with the audience, even though he did not understand why he was laughing, sank down into his chair and did his best to make himself appear as small as possible.

"And when did you form the Beat-Alls?" Ed Sullivan asked, wondering who Dr. Talc was and if he, Ed Sullivan, was now somehow liable for a slander lawsuit.

"Within the past week or so," Ignatius replied. "I've been very busy these past two months, thanks to an unfortunate incident that occurred in the French Quarter with my mother's Plymouth, but an incident that has, according to blind Fortuna's whims and desires, brought me here to this stage. Ours is a nascent group, nay, more than a nascent group, a nascent movement, and now that my duties as the vice president of the Charlie Chan Chinese Fortune Cookie Company are not so strenuous, I have been able to spend time formulating a plan to bring about a Boethian worldview, in short, a means to get rid of that failed god called democracy and to act as a herald for a worthy monarch, one enamored with proper theology and geometry."

Had anyone else said these words, the audience would have rushed the stage and torn him limb from limb. But because Ignatius had said these words, and had said them so imperiously, the people who were watching took it as part of his act. In fact, a television critic who was watching and jotting notes described Ignatius in a humorous way as the best of Don Rickles meeting the worst in Mort Sahl.

"Fancy words and old-time music," Ed Sullivan—who had not understood one word of what Ignatius had been saying—said. "What a novelty act you have!"

"Of course, to an unworthy mongoloid esquire like you, we are a novelty act," Ignatius said, and the audience howled with laughter and clapped loudly in appreciation of what they considered to be Ignatius's biting comedy routine. Ignatius's eyes crossed in frustration. "And the people who compose your audience are a bunch of idiotic mongoloids."

The audience laughed harder, and Ed Sullivan, who didn't understand why Ignatius was acting the way that he was acting, feigned a grin. This kid was supposed to be a class act, wasn't he? If so, then why was he acting so rudely? Was this part of the Beat-Alls's gimmick?

Miss Ping, who was watching the show with her extended family, none of whom spoke English, laughed her phocine laugh and pointed.

"Mr. Lei-ly is-er uh-new Lenny-uh Bluce!" she said.

Onstage, Ignatius made a face, and the audience laughed harder.

"Now, most of the idiots here and elsewhere have never heard of Anicius Manlius Severinus Boethius," Ignatius said, and another round of laughter broke out. "He wrote my favorite book, which shaped my worldview. The work is titled *The Consolation of Philosophy*, and I suggest that the people who are watching this frivolous television production first watch my performance this evening and then turn off their television sets for good. Never watch this show again, or any other television show, for that matter, and be sure to purchase copies of this book first thing tomorrow morning. Boethius suffered for modern man, and we must show our appreciation by taking up his worldview and refusing to idolize the idolatrous idea of having a so-called successful life."

A blue-haired elderly woman in the front row was laughing so hard that her dentures shot out of her mouth. This caused the people in the front row to howl even harder with laughter, and

Ignatius, believing that they were mocking him, his words, and Boethius, scowled and thrust his finger at the toothless woman.

"How dare you, you elderly trull!" Ignatius yelled at the woman, who had scooped up her dentures and was doing her best to reinsert them into her maw. "That, dear audience, is the insolence of the modern world. Were this a sane and rational world, that woman would be punished by the strappado!"

Ed Sullivan, who was grinning the way a monkey grinned when threatened, clapped his hands together. "And now that you're finished with your opening salvo," the television host said, "I'm sure that the audience is anxious to hear the wonderful song that you're about to play for us. Ladies and gentlemen, the Beat-Alls—"

"I am not finished, sirrah!" Ignatius screamed. "Do not interrupt me ever again!"

And the audience howled harder, and the people who were watching in Duluth were howling, as were the people who were watching in Topeka, Amarillo, Phoenix, Seattle, and the rest of the country. Even Miss Annie in New Orleans was howling with laughter.

"I like your style," Ed Sullivan—who didn't like either Ignatius or Ignatius's style—said. "The good thing about novelty acts is that you can combine music and comedy, don't you think, everyone?"

The audience clapped. Ignatius shook his head haughtily, and the audience laughed.

"You addlebrained moron, of course you would say something like that," Ignatius said, and he stared into a camera, his lips and cheeks—in fact, his entire being—shaking because of a passion that was overwhelming him. "The members of your audience, like you, are a bunch of simpleminded idiots who find satisfaction in working day jobs that barely allow them to survive the horrors of the modern world and who spend their evenings in front of color television sets and who allow their minds to rot from the vacuous content that the likes of you shove into their skulls."

"You see here!" Ed Sullivan said, unable any longer to control his temper and wondering if he should have imbibed another dry martini or two before that night's show. "My show is the show of shows! It brings the American people the entertainment they desperately need and deserve!"

"You call has-been jugglers and unfunny comedians 'entertainment' that the people of America 'desperately need and deserve'? You, sirrah, are a self-aggrandizing charlatan! You are a mountebank! You are a Dr. Caligari! But I am not your somnambulist! I have to come liberate you and your audience!"

"Sounds like a communist to me!" a man in the audience shouted, and backstage, circus animals grew restless and paced their cages and made noises that showed their displeasure at the goings-on onstage.

"I am not a fellow traveler," said Ignatius, shaking a fist. "I understand the depravity of this age, and I have had the misfortune of being born into it, and I have come to liberate you."

A few people in the audience laughed uneasily, not knowing if this was a gag being played by Ed Sullivan or if what had just been said was said in bad taste. Robotically, Mr. Minkoff rose from his seat and stuck his right hand inside his suit jacket.

Mrs. Minkoff tugged at his suit jacket. "Bernard, where are you going? You're going to miss Israel's sermon."

"I'm not going to miss anything," Mr. Minkoff replied, his eyes fixed on Ignatius, who was continuing his banter with Ed Sullivan, whose face, by this time, had crimsoned in rage. "I can assure you of that, my dear."

Myrna rolled her eyes. "He's been watching too much Walter Cronkite. It's bound to lead to sexual repression, which in turns leads to a deep frustration and dissatisfaction with life."

"Oh, you won't have to worry about life any longer," Mr. Minkoff said.

He forced his way past complaining people until he was in an aisle, where he strode towards the stage. An usher took Mr. Minkoff by his elbow and attempted to escort him back to his seat, but Mr. Minkoff shoved the usher, who tumbled backwards into an obese woman who reeked of lavender.

The obese woman yelped, and several ushers rushed towards Mr. Minkoff, who kept his right hand inside his suit jacket, his eyes fixed on Ignatius.

Onstage, Ed Sullivan, who told himself that after that night's show he was going to drink himself blind, put a hand on his brow to shade his eyes from stage lighting so that he could see what was going on in the audience.

"Is there some sort of trouble?" Ed Sullivan asked.

"Of course there's trouble," Ignatius said pompously. "You idiot, haven't you listened to a word that I've been saying? The Boethian Revolution is at hand! The worldviews of those in our nation and in our world must change if this planet is to be saved!"

But Ed Sullivan wasn't paying attention to Ignatius. A gaffer stood at the side of the stage and motioned with his hands. Ed Sullivan didn't understand what the gaffer was attempting to communicate.

"And now, if you'll leave the stage," Ignatius intoned deeply to Ed Sullivan.

"Ladies and gentlemen," the television host, who was looking at a television camera, said, "we must cut to a commercial break."

Illuminated stage signs indicated that a commercial break was underway. Mr. Minkoff punched an usher in the face and knocked him back into other ushers, who fell like a row of dominos. With a newfound energy fueling his mission, Mr. Minkoff leaped onstage and strode towards Ignatius and Ed Sullivan, who were not paying attention to the crazed figure heading their way because of the heated argument that they were having.

"Commercial break!" Ignatius screamed. "The Beat-Alls were about to perform a song that would become *the* number one hit in America! No one has ever heard anything like it!"

Ed Sullivan thrust a trembling finger at his antagonist. "You get this straight, and you get this straight now!" Ed Sullivan said, shaking with rage. "You said that you were some sort of fun novelty act! Well, all you've done since you've got here is insult me and my audience! And I, Ed Sullivan, am not going to take it from the likes of you!"

"Do you realize, sirrah, to whom you are speaking!" Ignatius replied, and now, like Ed Sullivan, Ignatius was enraged. "I am not only the leader of the troubadour band the Beat-Alls, I happen to be the vice president of the Charlie Chan Chinese Fortune Cookie Company, an earnest establishment in what is known colloquially as Chinatown! Now, if you will leave the stage and get those horrid modern contraptions known as television cameras turned on, I and the Beat-Alls will proceed to change the worldviews of you and your audience!"

A girl Friday rushed at Mr. Minkoff, who knelt and stuck out his leg, tripping his would-be assailant. Mr. Minkoff removed the snub-nosed .38 from its holster.

"Ollie!" Mr. Minkoff cried in his high-pitched, Stan Laurel-like voice while Mr. Minkoff knelt into a shooting position. "Ollie, oh, Ollie!"

"Ollie must be a stagehand," Ignatius said to Lady Laye. "It seems—"

Before Ignatius could say another word, Mr. Minkoff squeezed off a round. People screamed, and a toothless and clawless lion ran about its cage and clawed at the bars and roared, and a tufted capuchin dressed like a bellboy screeched and broke free from its Italian handler.

Ignatius turned and saw Mr. Minkoff aim the .38. Mr. Minkoff pulled the trigger a second time. The blank exploded when the firing pin came into contact with the rim of the round, and more people screamed. Ignatius bellowed, believing that he had been hit.

"Why aren't you dead, Ollie?" Mr. Minkoff said in his Stan Laurel-like voice. He stood and examined the pistols' smoking barrel. "Oh, Ollie, Ollie, Ollie, I've royally screwed up again!"

In the commotion of people running around the theater and into the lobby, Dr. Talc found himself pushed onstage. Mr. Minkoff aimed and pulled the trigger of the .38 twice. The blanks exploded one right after the other.

"He tried to kill me!" Ignatius squealed, gesticulating wildly and turning in circles. "Me, of all people! Me, who delivered him from his pathetic worldview to a worldview more in tune with the ways of his people! Me, who saved his family from destruction!"

Ed Sullivan, who was watching the melee from stage left, unscrewed the cap on a silver flask (a Christmas present from Walter Cronkite the previous year) and downed the contents of the silver flask, Russian vodka that he, Ed Sullivan, had obtained from a Moldovan smuggler. The burning liquid gave Ed Sullivan the madman-like strength that he needed, and he rushed into the melee and pushed aside an acrobat and kicked at a top-hatted French poodle that snapped at Ed Sullivan's heels.

"Calm down, Ignatius!" a now-onstage Myrna said, putting her hands on Ignatius's shoulders. "Now you see what sexual repression does! Now you see the evils of this great evil!"

"Get me out of here!" Ignatius yelled, searching for a way of escape.

Mr. Minkoff aimed at Ignatius and pulled the trigger. The fifth blank exploded.

"It's too late for Dad! He probably hasn't had a good orgasm in years, and now you see the results!"

Mr. Minkoff and stagehands now wrestled on the stage floor.

Dr. Talc attempted to remember the rules that his mother had taught him when he was in kindergarten and had almost been hit by automobiles and trucks because he didn't know how to cross busy intersections. But in his panic, the rules wouldn't come to his mind, and Dr. Talc found himself wandering aimlessly around the stage and unsure what to do. A giraffe ran past him, and a bull elephant trumpeted. Stagehands attempted to grab loose animals. The escaped tufted capuchin bit a stagehand's ear, severing it the way an enraged boxer might sever the ear of his opponent, and then leaped at Dr. Talc, who raised his arms in defense.

The tufted capuchin landed in Dr. Talc's arms, as if the monkey were Dr. Talc's new bride and Dr. Talc were taking his new bride across the threshold of their honeymoon suite. Dr. Talc yelled and spun like a whirling dervish, and the tufted capuchin clawed at him and snapped loose one of Dr. Talc's suspenders, and Dr. Talc's baggy pants sagged to the side. Dr. Talc felt a cold draft on his thigh, and he attempted to grab the monkey, which was crawling over Dr. Talc's shoulder. Dr. Talc pulled, and the tufted capuchin shrieked in anger and fought harder to escape Dr. Talc's grasp. Dr. Talc's other suspender gave, and Dr. Talc felt his trousers tumble to the stage floor.

Then the tufted capuchin, heading headfirst down Dr. Talc's back, stuck its paws inside Dr. Talc's silk boxers. The monkey's paws felt cold, and Dr. Talc screamed. The tufted capuchin continued its descent into Dr. Talc's underwear, and Dr. Talc leaped and hopped out of his baggy trousers, which were kicked aside by a woman fleeing a growling black bear.

"It's Dr. Talc!" Myrna said, pointing at the professor, whose ass looked as if it were sprouting a tail. "That reactionary! He's the one who's behind all of this!"

And Ignatius's eyes, which followed the direction in which Myrna was pointing, saw that the man was, indeed, Dr. Talc. What tricks was Fortuna playing now? What vicious cycle was she spinning him, Ignatius Reilly, into? Why did she have to pull the rug out from under his, Ignatius Reilly's, feet? When would this all end? Wasn't New Orleans enough to satiate her?

Meanwhile, a stagehand, who was huffing and puffing, straddled Mr. Minkoff, who was on his stomach, his hands covering the back of his neck because the stagehand was pummeling Mr. Minkoff's head.

"Ollie, oh, Ollie!" Mr. Minkoff yelled in his Stan Laurel-like voice. "Where are you, Ollie!"

"I'll tell you where he is," the stagehand said, face red with rage. "Ollie's here, and he's going to pound the living snot outta youse for destroying Mr. Sullivan's show, you sonofabitch!"

"That's my husband you're attacking, you brute!" Mrs. Minkoff yelled, attempting to shove the stagehand off her husband and to keep others at bay. "If you want to pick on someone, why don't you go after a wolf! I saw one running around here somewhere!"

On the other side of the stage, Dr. Talc was still hopping about. The tufted capuchin slid down Dr. Talc's legs, the monkey taking with him Dr. Talc's silk boxers, thereby exposing Dr. Talc's highly underdeveloped genitalia.

A cross-eyed woman, a script editor, screamed when she saw Dr. Talc's assets, or lack thereof. Dr. Talc covered his prepubescent-like crotch, his underwear and the tufted capuchin tangled around his ankles. The Tulane professor fainted, and the monkey ran off into the dark bowels of the backstage and waved Dr. Talc's torn underwear as if it were a trophy won in battle.

Myrna grabbed Ignatius's right arm, Lady Laye, his left.

"Come on," Myrna said, pulling one way.

"This way," Lady Laye said, pulling the other.

Ignatius struggled to break free of their grips. "My pyloric valve is about to seal, I can hardly breathe, and the stage is spinning! You both are about to drive me mad!"

"This way, man," Sir Sid said, pointing at the backstage. "There's got to be an exit somewhere back there, man."

Ignatius did his best to keep up with the three. Mrs. Reilly was now onstage and pushing her way through a throng of stage-hands and loose animals and doing her best to get to Ignatius.

"Ignatius!" she called out. "Ignatius! Ignatius! Boy, don't you pretend that you don't hear me! Ignatius!"

"Oh, my God!" Ignatius said on seeing Mrs. Reilly, with Mr. Robichaux following close behind her. "What are they doing here!"

"They've come to take you back to New Orleans!" Myrna said, reappearing, taking Ignatius by his paw. "They've come to take you back to Mandeville or some charity hospital, where those reactionary redneck psychiatrists can do their thing to you!"

"Never!" Ignatius bellowed. "I shall never enter such an institution! The thought of it is patently absurd!"

"Then follow us!" Myrna said.

And Ignatius did.

An usher prevented Mrs. Reilly from proceeding.

"You don't understand!" Mrs. Reilly said. "Ignatius is my boy! I need to get him back to New Orleans! He's crazy and needs help!"

Meanwhile, the toothless and clawless lion chased Ed Sullivan across the stage, and the tufted capuchin, which was now hanging about in the overhead rigging, clapped its paws in glee and chittered.

"We can't allow anyone onstage till we get everything under control," the usher said in a heavy Bronx accent to Mrs. Reilly. "Till then, you gonna have to stay back."

"Communiss," Mr. Robichaux said to the man, Mr. Robichaux squinting like a simian. "You all nothin' but a bunch of communiss."

"Oh, hush up, Claude," Mrs. Reilly said.

Henley grabbed Mrs. Reilly's arm, and she screamed, and Nick the Nose pointed his .38 at her face.

"Bitch," Nick the Nose said, "we know you have dat goddamn paper, you bitch. Now, we ain't foolin' around—"

A one-pound sandbag dropped by the tufted capuchin cold-cocked Nick the Nose. Henley attempted to flee, but the toothless and clawless lion leaped on him. Magoohan, dressed as Little Red Riding Hood, slapped handcuffs onto the unconscious Nick the Nose.

Lady Laye, Sir Sid, Myrna, and Ignatius, in that order, fled the theater through a back door.

Meanwhile, as the chaos continued, cops led Mr. Minkoff, Henley, and Nick the Nose to a paddy wagon in front of the Ed Sullivan Theater. Mrs. Minkoff and Grandmother Horowitz followed the arrestees, Mrs. Minkoff shaking her head sadly.

"You all right, lady?" Magoohan, who was walking near them, said.

Mrs. Minkoff glowered at the beat cop. "You arrested my husband, Little Red Riding Hood. Do you think that I'm all right?"

"Had to arrest 'im," Magoohan said, carrying a picnic basket, imagining what Sergeant Dumbrowski would say when he heard of the three arrests that he, Magoohan, had made that evening, even though Magoohan had left his precinct. "He was tryin' ta kill one of da performers."

"Israel is not a performer, he's a rabbi," Mrs. Minkoff said petulantly. "An *Orthodox* rabbi. I believe that this whole thing was part of Israel's sermon. He believes that Gotham is inherently corrupt and that the only thing not corrupt in Gotham is Batman. At least he has a hardcore morality, according to Israel."

Grandmother Horowitz stared at Magoohan's crotch. "Looks like you're packing something there, little fellow."

"Got my police-issue revolver on me," Magoohan said. "She's a beaut."

"Thought it would be more like a he," Grandmother Horowitz said salaciously, and she reached for his crotch.

Mrs. Minkoff slapped away Grandmother Horowitz's hand.

"Stop that, Mother," Mrs. Minkoff said. To Magoohan she said apologetically: "Pardon her. Sometimes she acts just like a kid."

Magoohan, not understanding what Mrs. Minkoff was talking about, shrugged.

Mrs. Minkoff flagged a cab, and she and Grandmother Horowitz went to the Colonial Revival house in the Bronx.

Mrs. Reilly and Mr. Robichaux were now standing in front of the theater. The winter winds felt cold and fierce, and even though her fiancé was standing beside her on a crowded street in the heart of Manhattan, Mrs. Reilly had never felt so alone.

"We'd better get back home, I guess," Mr. Robichaux said, and he looked at Broadway and at its revelers and at its Christmas lights and at its traffic congestion and at its piles of exhaust-stained snow that lined its curbs. "We just have to wait till Ignatius comes to his senses and comes back on his own."

Mrs. Reilly sighed in resignation. She nodded, and Mr. Robichaux took her hand. He waved for a cab, hoping that he and Mrs. Reilly would soon be out of that horrible, communist-infested city.

• *Fifteen*

In Greenwich Village, two beat cops headed down W. Eighth Street. One nodded at the Stone Carver Inn, which had a long line of motley arrayed homosexuals and lesbians waiting to enter.

"We oughtta close that place," the younger of the two, a rookie beat cop, said. "Looks like goddamn Mardi Gras. Before you know it, these queers are going to take over the world."

"Close that place?" his comrade, a veteran beat cop, said, and he wanted to be home, watching the news and drinking shots of rye. "You gotta be kidding me. Sarge would have our asses. That place is paying off his retirement home in Jersey."

"What are you talking about?"

The older cop scowled. "The take, man, the take. Sergeant Dumbrowski makes thousands of dollars off that fairy joint. You think he wants that money to end?"

"No." The rookie cop thought a moment. "But ain't that illegal? Ain't that what they call bribery or extortion or graft or something?"

"Who cares what's legal?" the veteran cop said. "You really think I give a damn about what's right or wrong? You do, you need to reconsider why you became a cop, my friend. We ain't here to protect and serve, we're here to be protected and served."

The rookie cop grinned. "I never looked at it that way."

"You should," the veteran cop said, and now he withdrew his truncheon from its slot on his heavy utility belt. "That said, let's go take a look and see what we can get for ourselves. Who knows, we might be able to shake down a few queers and dykes and get us an easy hundred or so."

The two cops bullied their way into the Stone Carver Inn. Many of the men and women muttered oaths and curses against the two cops, but the two cops were oblivious to the muttering because of the loudness and festiveness of the place.

It took a moment for their eyes to adjust to the dim lighting, but when their eyes did adjust, the two cops saw a bare-chested, barefoot, dungarees-wearing Giacomo, a boa constrictor wrapped around Giacomo's neck as if the snake were an *haute couture* fashion item. Giacomo raised an eyebrow at the veteran cop, who scowled and shook his head.

"Goddamn queers," the veteran cop said with disdain. "Completely worthless. Hitler had the right idea about 'em."

"I don't like Hitler," the rookie cop said. "He killed two uh my uncles."

"I was speaking metaphysically," the veteran cop said. "I fought the sonofabitch during the war. You think I like Hitler? Hell, no. I just like what he did to a few people, what we should've done, you ask me, if we was to remain a free country. Get rid of the queers, get rid of the niggers, and get rid of the spics, in that order."

"Hey!"

"Hey, what?" the veteran cop asked suspiciously.

"My wife's Puerto Rican," the rookie cop said. "She's a good woman. Not all PRs are bad. Just get rid of the bad PRs, the bad Negroes, and the bad queers, and you and me are in agreement."

"Yeah, right," the veteran cop said, not sure now how to view his partner, a white man married to a Puerto Rican. What would happen next? Whites marrying blacks? Then men marrying men and women marrying women? The veteran cop shuddered at the thought.

A small East Indian man, barely five feet tall and dressed as Carmen Miranda, held out a silver bowl containing Charlie Chan fortune cookies. The veteran cop waved away the East Indian with a dismissive hand, but the rookie cop reached into the bowl and removed a fortune cookie.

"I'd put that back if I was you," the veteran cop said. "You never know what these queers put into things. Some say that they put stuff in food to turn people queer."

"I heard about that," the rookie cop replied, "but these are wrapped, and I recognize them. They're Charlie Chan. My wife and me eat 'em whenever we get chink."

"Oh?" the veteran cop said, and he motioned at the small East Indian man dressed as Carmen Miranda to return, and the small East Indian man did. The veteran cop picked up a fortune cookie and studied it. "Wonder why they're giving out fortune cookies in here. This ain't a chink joint."

"No, it ain't a chink joint, but maybe this is part of the new act," the rookie cop said, and he looked around at the motley arrayed crowd, which resembled the people he had seen in a television program about New Orleans. "You never know."

The rookie cop popped the fortune cookie's wrapper, cracked open the cookie, and, with the delicate tips of his thumb and index finger, pulled out the small slip of paper from the fortune cookie. He caught a pleasant and delicate scent of chocolate, and his mouth watered because chocolate was his favorite flavor. The slip said that his lucky numbers were 13 53 69 17 54, and when he turned the slip over, he read his fortune, one of Ignatius's creations.

"'Repent before it is too late,'" the rookie cop read aloud. "'Learn proper theology and geometry. Turn to Boethius,'" but instead of saying Boethius correctly, the rookie cop pronounced it BO-AYE-TEE-US.

"What the hell does that mean?" the veteran cop asked.

The rookie cop shrugged, crumpled the slip of paper, and tossed the halves of the cracked-open fortune cookie into his mouth.

"I told you not to eat that," the veteran cop said. "You never what know these queers are going to put in the food."

"Told you," the rookie cop said, munching, "these ain't made by queers. I've had several of 'em, and this one is the tastiest I've ever had."

"You sure these queers didn't make 'em?"

"Absolutely sure," the rookie cop said. "Like I said, me and wife eat 'em all the time."

The veteran cop removed his fortune cookie from its wrapper, tossed aside the fortune, and popped the halves into his mouth and munched them.

"Not bad," the veteran cop said. "Say, don't the colors look a lot brighter in here?"

"They do, they do," the rookie cop replied, frowning because he was surprised at the lilt in his voice. He motioned with a limp wrist at the portrait of Judy Garland. "Oh, let's go have a look at that beautiful painting. Isn't she just gorgeous?"

"I should say so," the veteran cop said, and the two moved among motley arrayed people who, upon seeing the two cops holding hands, surmised that the two weren't actual cops but were in costume and applauded the two, who giggled gleefully in reply.

In the back office, El Lobo Macho put the finishing touches on a dynamite bomb that he, Guapo, and Chico had planted in Grenadine's new novelty, Rex the Robot.

"You are sure we are going to get out in time?" Guapo asked in Spanish.

"Right after we finish our Rockettes-style kicking, we are going to flee," El Lobo Macho replied in Spanish. "You are not afraid, are you? You are a man, are you not? You are a macho man, are you not?"

"I am a real man," Guapo said proudly, slightly unsteady on his high heels (he had wondered how his mother and his sisters had ever learned to walk in the things), and he tugged at the side of his bright red dress. "A real man who is going to do away with the faggots so that we can live in peace once for all."

"The Final Solution," Chico said in Spanish.

"The Final Solution," Guapo said.

"Yes, the Final Solution," El Lobo Macho said, and he set the timer and zipped up the pants of the robot.

A few blocks away, Ignatius, Myrna, Lady Laye, and Sir Sid emerged from the bowels of the subway onto a wintry street, and adrenaline was gushing into their bodies and keeping them from feeling the cold. From an apartment window slightly cracked open came the sound of "Jingle Bells" played on a static-plagued radio. Ignatius's heart was pounding, and he gagged when he thought about Mr. Minkoff's firing the snub-nosed .38.

"He wanted to kill me," Ignatius, who was shaking his head in disbelief, said to Myrna. "Why on earth would he want to do that?"

"He snapped," Myrna replied seriously. "It was all of those years of sexual repression, thanks to all that Walter Cronkite he watched."

Ignatius nodded. "Yes, too much Walter Cronkite. And those Laurel and Hardy films. He couldn't seem to get enough of those. The modern world must have proved too strong for his sensibilities, and he was retreating into a world where Laurel and Hardy could protect him."

"Are we going to get out of here or what, man?" Sir Sid asked. He made a face, like that of an irritated child denied an extra dessert. "We gotta keep moving, man."

From the distance came the wailing of police sirens, which seemed to be coming closer and closer.

"Sid's right," Lady Laye said. "The entire Ed Sullivan thing was a complete shipwreck. It wouldn't surprise me if they call in the National Guard. If we don't get out of here, some serious shit is going to hit our fan."

"That's why we're here in the Village," Myrna said, attempting to assuage their fears. "Dr. Ingloss knows tons about sexual repression."

"What's this got to do with getting us to safety, man?" Sir Sid said, irritated and agitated, hopping from one foot to the other, as if he were getting ready to join a conga line.

Myrna sighed. "Besides being an expert on sexual repression, Dr. Ingloss has lots of money and a place to hide."

"Why didn't you say so, man?" Sir Sid said. "Dough's definitely something we can use right now, man. Lead the way, man."

And Myrna led the way, Lady Laye and Sir Sid keeping up with her, Ignatius struggling to do so. Not only had his pyloric valve almost sealed, but his adrenal glands had almost exhausted their supply of adrenaline. He had never felt so terrified in his life.

Myrna looked over her shoulder. "Come on, Ignatius, you're not keeping up."

"I am doing my utmost to do so," Ignatius said cantankerously. "I am not built for moving quickly in these climes. Furthermore, I still have yet to get acclimated to the bitter cold of Gotham. Fortuna willing, we will be heading to a warmer area, say, New Orleans."

"There you go again, Ignatius," Myrna said, piqued. "New Orleans, New Orleans, New Orleans! What good did that miniscule, crescent-shaped city ever do for you, Ignatius!"

"It gave me my worldview," Ignatius said in Falstaffian protest. "It helped me to see that proper theology and geometry could exist, provided that the idiots who ran this world were willing for it to be so."

"I knew that I should have taken you when I had the chance," Myrna said. "You have reverted to your old nasty self. If Dr.

Ingloss is willing to come with us, I'm going to have him give you extended private sessions. Of course, I'll be there to record whatever is said."

Up the street a police cruiser rounded a corner, the cruiser's lights flashing, its sirens wailing. The cop, on the lookout after receiving an all-points bulletin, accelerated the cruiser, which swerved one way, then the other, on the icy street before crashing into a fire hydrant, which spewed water.

"We can't get to Dr. Ingloss!" Myrna shouted. "This means that this thread in the parody won't be tied!"

"This way!" Lady Laye yelled, pointing at the Stone Carver Inn. "We can hide in there!"

The four terrified people hurried towards the Stone Carver Inn, a welcome oasis in a world that was, moment by moment, becoming more and more terrifying.

Grenadine was standing out front and was wearing a mink coat that he had purchased after he had seen Jacqueline Kennedy wearing one. And he was sporting a pair of pince-nez with light green lenses. He was choosing who could enter from the scores of waiting people. He considered a lesbian wearing bangs and a bowler and fishnet stockings and was about to say no to her when Myrna, Lady Laye, Sir Sid, and Ignatius stopped in front of the Stone Carver Inn, all four huffing and puffing.

Grenadine clucked in amazement. "My, look at what the cat has dragged in."

"You've got to let us in," Myrna implored, gasping, holding out her hands in supplication. "Some very evil reactionaries are after us. They're sexually repressed, and they're blaming us for the damage on *The Ed Sullivan Show*. Walter Cronkite is bad enough, but Ed Sullivan really takes the frigging cake."

"She's right, man," Sir Sid said. "We were doing this gig, man, and I was floating high as a kite, on feelings, I mean, man, not the weed, though maybe I should've smoked more weed before it was all said and done, man, you wouldn't believe it, even a monkey was involved, man—"

"We just want to hang out for an hour or so," Lady Laye said.

"Would your establishment happen to serve hot chocolate topped off with brandy or brandy topped off with hot chocolate?" Ignatius asked, breathing stertorous.

Grenadine studied the four, especially Ignatius, and giggled. How precious, especially the largest, the man wearing the green hunting cap and clothes that looked as if they came from another universe.

"Of course, my lovelies, you are more than welcome to enter," Grenadine said. "You are so well dressed for this evening's soirée. There's a table in the back. Please make yourselves warm, and do please enjoy my establishment. By the way, we have champagne, for which you must pay, and we have Chinese fortune cookies, which are free. We were supposed to have Puerto Rican hors d'oeuvres, but my janitor went to the wrong place. One can't get good help these days, can one?"

Myrna and Lady Laye thanked Grenadine, and the four made their way to a back table, where Ignatius dropped down so quickly that his chair splintered. Had not the motley arrayed men and women been talking loudly, everyone would have peered questioningly, and perhaps even peevishly, at Ignatius.

Instead, the people continued with their conversations, and Myrna reached under her peasant's skirt and adjusted her panties, which had ridden up the crack of her ass. The throngs of people compressed into this relatively small tavern—and Myrna had been in some tight spots before—caused the air to be too hot for her, and she panted and fanned her face.

"That time of the month, man?" Sir Sid asked.

"Don't be so rude, Sid," Lady Laye said. To Myrna: "He's socially awkward. Please forgive him. But you do look like maybe you should go to the restroom."

Myrna's bladder was telling her much the same.

"See you guys in a bit," Myrna said. Before leaving, Myrna leaned over and whispered to Ignatius, "Care to come with me?"

"Oh, my God!" Ignatius bellowed. "How could you even think of such a thing at a time like this!"

"Because of stress relief," Myrna said, and she glowered, angry that she had not been able to take Ignatius's virginity. "I've really got to go. Don't run off and cause any trouble, Ignatius."

Ignatius groaned loudly and pretended that he was hanging himself. Myrna hurried off to the back of the tavern.

Ignatius studied the red stage curtains, which were illuminated by several footlights.

"This must be one helluva an act, man," Sir Sid said, looking about. "These queers and dykes, they know a good show, man."

"Unfortunately, this reminds me of a time in New Orleans, at a night club in the French Quarter," Ignatius said. "You wouldn't believe what happened that evening."

"What did happen, Ignatius?" Lady Laye said as she put a stick of gum into her mouth.

Ignatius told them about his failed attempt at starting his degeneracy revolution at Dorian Greene's apartment and his, Ignatius's, subsequent misadventures at the Night of Joy, the highlight of the story being the bird that attacked Ignatius's earring. Lady Laye's eyes crossed in amazement.

"And that's why I have trepidation about my coming into any establishment similar to that one in New Orleans," Ignatius said. "With my worldview, I have enough trouble with the monde, let alone the demimonde."

"You know Demi Mound, man?" Sir Sid said sibilantly. "Wasn't she the easiest lay you ever had, man?"

Ignatius's lips twisted into a snarl, which showed his wrath and indignation. "Demi Mound? Where, pray tell, is that?"

"Wherever the nearest mattress is, man," Sir Sid replied, laughing.

Ignatius was about to unload his wrath upon Sir Sid when Giacomo, boa constrictor wound loosely around his neck, appeared.

"We have a great quiche tonight," Giacomo said, "and a soufflé prepared by Frank, our Italian bartender. Don't know if it's any good, but if you don't want them items, we have plenty of fortune cookies. Everyone's downing them like they was hotcakes."

"Ah, yes, the fortune cookies," Ignatius asked. "Pray tell, what brand?"

Giacomo shrugged and then motioned at a waiter dressed as a French maid, who hurried over, curtsied, and dumped handfuls of Charlie Chan fortune cookies upon the table where Ignatius, Lady Laye, and Sir Sid were sitting. The waiter-French maid giggled, curtsied, and hurried off to serve other patrons.

Ignatius picked up a fortune cookie and studied its wrapper. CHARLIE CHAN CHINESE FORTUNE COOKIES the wrapper said. Ignatius raised an eyebrow; perhaps Fortuna had repented and mended her ways and was sending him a message that everything was going to be fine.

Meanwhile, to her horror, Myrna discovered that the ladies' room was filled to capacity. It felt as if she were holding the Hoover Dam between her thighs, and that that dam was about to burst. Peering around a man wearing a Venetian mask with a nose shaped like a pterodactyl's beak, Myrna saw another hallway, this one leading to what appeared to be a back office. She excused herself, pushed past the man and several other people, and hurried towards the door.

To her surprise and to her delight, she discovered that the door was unlocked. She opened the door, stepped into the back office, and closed the door behind her after turning on the light, a new and very low-wattage bulb that barely illuminated the room.

She jumped when she saw Rex the Robot.

"You scared me," she said. "I didn't think that there was anyone back here."

The robot, of course, didn't reply. She squinted and wondered why the man was being so rude to her.

"You going to say anything?" Myrna asked. "What's the matter with you? Haven't you ever seen a woman before?"

There was no response, and no longer able to contain herself, Myrna squatted, reached up into her peasant's skirt, and moved her calico panties to the side. She relaxed, finishing her business in a puddle that slowly spread across a concrete floor that Giacomo had dry-mopped that very afternoon.

Then Myrna stood and wiped her hands on her peasant's skirt. The man appeared to be very tall, at least seven feet, if not taller. And very silent. Very silent and very teratoid. Very silent and very teratoid and very sexy.

"You don't say too much, do you?" Myrna said, approaching the robot. She stuck out her hand. "Hi, I'm Myrna Minkoff. I'm hcrc to see the show with my friends. I'm in solidarity with the homosexuals and the lesbians. I even wrote a poem this year titled 'My Angry Lesbian Breasts,' though I'm not a dyke. I'm going to see if NYU's going to publish it because the student newspapers at Hunter and Columbia are way too reactionary."

The robot, of course, didn't move or reply.

Myrna, feeling rejected, lowered her hand. Because of the seeming rejection, she felt slightly humiliated and a tad bit angry.

"You think that because you work in an office you're somehow better than me," Myrna said, wagging her finger at the robot, "but let me tell you, sirs, that unlike you, I am capable of having multiple orgasms one right after the other. In fact, I don't even think that you could satisfy me, no matter how hard you tried. What do you think about that?"

Myrna tripped in the dimly lit back office. She yelped and held out her hands, one hand catching the edge of Grenadine's desk while her other hand made contact with the robot's crotch. She felt something unusually long and unusually thick. The robot jolted upon her contacting it, and its back hit a wall, which flipped the robot's on-off switch up.

The robot's patina-colored irides lit up.

"Hi, I'm Rex the Robot!" it said. "I'm at your service!"

Myrna righted herself and cleared her throat.

"Perhaps I was wrong about you," she said, and she noticed that her loins, which had already been warm and moist and eager that evening, were heating up with a concupiscence that had overtaken her entire being. "The truth is, I'm attracted to the strong, silent type. Don't tell anyone, but I even pleasure myself while thinking about Gary Cooper, that reactionary actor. Of course, from the way things seem, you'd be more to handle than Gary Cooper."

She stared at the crotch, which, because of the dim lighting, she could barely make out. She walked up to the robot and reached out.

"There ought to be a law against guys like you," Myrna said, feeling the robot's tumescence and undoing the belt that encircled the robot's waist. Myrna broke the button that held the robot's pants in place and then unzipped the pants, which slid to the floor. With both hands, she pulled down the robot's boxers and grabbed the phallus that now felt warm because of electric current flowing throughout the robot.

The clock on the dynamite bomb had been ticking, but because of the loudness in the hallways and because of her own lust, which was causing her heart to beat quickly and audibly and causing her head to throb, Myrna didn't hear the clock.

Without hesitating, Myrna reached underneath her peasant's skirt and pulled down her calico panties, stepping out of them with her left leg, then her right.

"Take me, you fool!" Myrna said, raising her peasant's skirt. "Take me now, or I'll take you, sirs!"

The robot didn't reply, of course, so Myrna yelled and leaped onto the robot. She wrapped her legs around its waist and held herself in place with one hand while she guided the phallus-missile to its target.

There was a short circuit in the phallus, which caused it to heat up to ninety-eight degrees Fahrenheit. Myrna, unaware of the short circuit and unaware that she was straddling a bomb that could level an entire city block, constricted her pubococcygeus muscle and squealed in delight as her first orgasm overtook her.

"Incredible," she panted as she rode the robot, in the bowels of which the clock ticked, the minute hand moving closer and closer to the twelve with each passing second. "Most guys I've dated would've come with me, but you're hanging in there! Keep it up, Rex! We have a long, fun ride ahead of us!"

As Myrna's passion became more ardent, she moved her hips frenziedly, riding the phallus-missile for all it was worth.

Back at the table, Ignatius was sipping a brandy.

"Wonder what's taking her so long," Lady Laye said. "Really, we need to get out of here pretty soon."

"It seems that we're safe here for the moment," Ignatius replied. "As for Myrna minx, she's probably attempting to convert one of the homosexuals into a heterosexual, or, barring that, she's engaged with one of the many lesbians on these premises."

Backstage, Grenadine observed the many homosexuals and lesbians. Near him stood Las Tres Amigas.

"We ready to do the show now!" El Lobo Macho said. "We do the show now, *puto*!"

"Easy, my dear girls, easy," Grenadine said, patting the air with his hands in an attempt to assuage the uneasiness of the three Puerto Ricans. "Patience. Look at all those lovelies out there. The suspense is building, they're buying more champagne, and my establishment is making a killing tonight, I tell you, a killing!"

Grenadine turned to kiss El Lobo Macho who, sensing what Grenadine was about to do, scowled and rolled up a hand into a threatening fist. Grenadine giggled nervously and turned to look at the audience. The bare-chested Giacomo appeared, boa constrictor around his neck, tray of fortune cookies in his hand.

"What are you doing here, you ass?" Grenadine hissed at his janitor. "Get out there and disseminate those lovely fortune cookies, which are having such a wonderful effect on our audience."

"I thought Las Tres Amigas might want to read their fortunes," Giacomo said. "Plus, the way you been fasting 'em, they're probably starving."

"*Tengo hambre*," Chico said, and he scooped up a handful of the Charlie Chan fortune cookies.

Guapo followed suit, followed by El Lobo Macho, all three Puerto Ricans unwrapping and wolfing down handfuls of the Charlie Chan fortune cookies while Grenadine put his hands to his face and clucked in disapproval.

"My show, my show!" Grenadine squealed. "You're ruining my show! If you lovelies don't keep your girlish figures, you're going to ruin my show! And if you ruin my show, you ruin my establishment! And if you ruin my establishment, you ruin me!"

"Shut up, *puto*," El Lobo Macho said, pushing aside a strand of hair from his blond wig. His pink tongue darted from his mouth and removed fortune cookie crumbs from his black mustache. "We don't eat all week. We hungry. We want to eat, we gonna eat."

Grenadine tutted. "Oh, it shouldn't be that bad, I suppose. What harm can fortune cookies do? Go ahead and splurge, my dears. But remember, tighten those guts before you go on, and ensure that your heels are steady before you go onstage."

El Lobo Macho, Guapo, and Chico ignored Grenadine and heartily partook of the fortune cookies. In fact, the more fortune cookies the Puerto Ricans ate, the more ravenous the Puerto Ricans became, so instead of cracking open the fortune cookies, the three men shoveled unwrapped fortune cookies into their mouths and gobbled handful after handful.

"Brutes," Grenadine said quietly. "What brutes. But one can have the most fun with brutes, can't one?"

In the back office, Myrna was nearing her thirteenth orgasm. As the orgasm overcame her, she screamed loudly and arched her back. Myrna squeezed her pubococcygeus muscle so hard that she almost wrenched off the robot's metallic member.

"Hi, I'm Rex the Robot!" the robot said. "I'm at your service!"

"Oh, yes!" Myrna screamed, and she bucked harder. "You're damn right you're at my service! Forever!"

In her lust, she had forgotten about Ignatius, forgotten about that evening's events at the Ed Sullivan Theater, forgotten about the Charlie Chan Chinese Fortune Cookie Company, forgotten about bringing Ignatius to the Bronx, forgotten about her trip to New Orleans to save him. She now existed in that moment for that moment. It was if she had had entered a nirvana, with no intention of ever leaving.

"I'm in love!" Myrna screamed as another orgasm overtook her.

Ignatius finished his brandy. His nerves felt as if they were settling down. Ignatius motioned at a waiter, who stopped to take Ignatius's order for another brandy. After the waiter hurried off, Ignatius looked around nervously, wondering if any cockatoos were about.

"Everything's cool, man," Sir Sid said. "I think we're blended in, man. I don't think that the man is coming after us anymore, man."

"I do wish you would drop the unnecessary apposition," Ignatius said. He spotted what looked like a parrot perched on a man's shoulder and shuddered in horror and then relaxed when he, Ignatius, saw that the bird was faux. "It's completely unnecessary."

"I'm not in opposition to nothing, man," Sir Sid said. "We almost did it, man."

"Did what?" Ignatius said. "Pray tell, tell me what we 'almost did,' Sir Sid."

"Conquered the world, man," Sir Sid said, hiccupping. "If things hadn't blown up at the gig, man, everyone would be digging us, man. We'd have a hit record, man, and life would be Easy Street from here on out, man."

Ignatius was about to scold Sir Sid when Grenadine blew air into a microphone. Feedback whined over the system, and Ignatius and everyone else in the audience cringed, many people, including Ignatius, crying out in protest.

Frank, who was manning the soundboard, adjusted a few nobs, and the feedback went away. Grenadine smiled, made a sweeping motion with his hand, and bowed.

"Ladies and gentlemen, lasses and genitals, lashed genitals, kings and queens, fags and dykes, welcome to the Stone Carver Inn!" Grenadine said in a voice rising higher and higher, as if someone had placed a burdizzo around his scrotum. "This is the evening for which you have all been waiting! Without further ado, Las Tres Amigas!"

The red stage curtains parted, and Las Tres Amigas strutted out onto the stage, El Lobo Macho in the center, Guapo to El Lobo Macho's right, Chico to El Lobo Macho's left, all three unsteady on their feet because the three men were still not used to wearing high heels. There was the sound of the stage-amplification system coming on and then the loud hiss of a needle following a groove of a record. A Puerto Rican folk song titled

"Décima" played, and Las Tres Amigas put their arms around one another and attempted to kick like the Rockettes.

To a used car salesman sitting near the stage, the three looked like out-of-time engine parts, and the patron let Las Tres Amigas know this by yelling his objections. El Lobo Macho scowled and told the man, in Spanish, to shut his trap. But because the amplification had increased, thanks to Frank, no one, not even Guapo and Chico, could hear what El Lobo Macho was yelling, and it looked to the patrons as if he were lip-synching the folk song.

"Excellent!" Grenadine exclaimed, clapping his hands. "What a stroke of genius! A drag queen lip-synching!"

People clapped and hooted and howled in appreciation. El Lobo Macho, however, thought that they were mocking him and his compatriots. He unlocked his arms from Guapo and Chico and rushed to the front of the stage, where El Lobo Macho shook his fists, swore in Spanish, and said that the audience would soon be dead.

Because of the loudness of the music, however, it still appeared to everyone that El Lobo Macho was passionately arguing with the man of his dreams not to leave.

Lady Laye was looking at Ignatius. "Myrna's missing a great show!" she shouted.

Fingers stuck in his ears, Ignatius made a petulant face. "How on earth do you expect to have a conversation in this infernal racket! This is worse than Frankie Valli and the Four Seasons! At least I could turn off the television set when those low-class Italians began their infernal caterwauling!"

"I can't hear you!" Lady Laye yelled.

Ignatius couldn't read lips, but he knew what she was saying, and this augmented his frustration.

"Obviously you can't hear me!" Ignatius screamed at Lady Laye, continuing to keep his sausage-like fingers stuck in his ears. "How could anyone hear above this din! Now, be dutiful and go find the minx! You'll probably discover her somewhere in the bowels of this establishment, either giving a lecture on the need for multiple orgasms or getting them herself from some newfound bisexual boyfriend!"

"I can't hear you, Ignatius!"

Ignatius unplugged his ears and shook his fists at her as he ranted. Sir Sid glanced at the two, then returned his attention to the stage, where a man wearing a Venetian mask and a purple cape and green tights attempted to put dollar bills into El Lobo Macho's garters. El Lobo Macho angrily snatched the dollar bills and shook his beefy fists at the man while Guapo and Chico, arm in arm, continued their Rockettes-like kicking.

"And another thing!" Ignatius yelled. "When we get out of this mess, I must spend at least two weeks in bed! I hope that you are good at making teas and foods fit for my physical, emotional, and spiritual rehabilitation, because you and your moronic twin brother and that minx have done your utmost to drive me insane!"

Frank, who was leaning against the record player, slipped and caused the needle to skip off the record. There was the whine of feedback, and Frank turned off the amplification.

Now everyone could hear El Lobo Macho. Ignatius, too, ranted and continued to shake his fists at Lady Laye.

People looked at El Lobo Macho and then at Ignatius, who stopped ranting, and then back at El Lobo Macho, who wadded up the dollar bills and threw them at the audience.

"You disgusting *putería*!" he said, and Grenadine and the audience gasped. "Do you believe that a man, a real man, would be here! Do you not know who I am!"

"You're Priscilla," Grenadine said, hopping onstage, hoping that he could quell whatever was occurring. "You are the lovely Latina Priscilla, and you are here with your two friends, and you are doing the first-ever Las Tres Amigas show at the Stone Carver Inn!"

El Lobo Macho slapped Grenadine, who squealed and fell off the stage. A lesbian dressed as Minnie Mouse rushed to his aid, as did Giacomo, who, without thinking about the consequences, removed the boa constrictor from around his neck and placed the snake on the tavern floor.

"I am El Lobo Macho!" El Lobo Macho bellowed, kicking off his high heels. "I come to deliver my people from *la putería*!"

Ignatius felt edgy. Even though he didn't understand what was going on, he knew that something was obviously very wrong. He stood, and, backing up to a wall, attempted to make himself as small as possible.

"You, *el gordo*!" El Lobo Macho yelled at Ignatius, who froze. "Where you think you going!"

"I am not one of the people whom you are addressing," Ignatius said, mustering as much dignity as he could. "Blind Fortuna has placed me here in one of her wanton vendettas. Now if you'll excuse me, kind sirrah, I will be on my way."

The Puerto Rican gang leader leaped from the stage and onto a table, causing several men and women to scream and to part the way for him. The Puerto Rican gang leader thrust an accusing finger at Ignatius.

"You *el rey de los putos*!" El Lobo Macho yelled.

"I have no idea what you're talking about," Ignatius replied, and he attempted to get closer to the door, through which several people were already fleeing. "I am a philosopher, a follower of Boethius, not a sodomite. If you must accuse anyone of this heinous sin, then accuse these others. I merely came in here to get refuge from an aborted production on *The Ed Sullivan Show*."

"You use fancy words," El Lobo Macho said, and he leaped to the floor, and women and men scattered as he strode towards Ignatius. "I do not like fancy words! A real man does not use such fancy words!"

The two cops, who had been watching in the darkness, came forward, their truncheons drawn. Then the two dropped their truncheons and embraced.

The people were silent, except for El Lobo Macho, who pushed the new lovers aside. "I can tell is you!" El Lobo Macho said, thrusting a finger in Ignatius's face. "You the one behind all this!"

Then El Lobo Macho felt a lightness overtaking him, a giddiness that he had never before experienced.

"*Qué?*" he asked no one in particular. "*Qué? Qué? Qué?*"

El Lobo Macho swooned, and he felt a lust rising within him. But not a lust for women, the kind that he had experienced each day since he was ten years old, when he began to notice the beauty of the feminine form. On the contrary, this was a lust for men, a lust that he had hated. With both hands, he covered his engorged member.

"*Qué!*" he yelled, eyes crossing in rage and eyebrows knitting together. "What is happening! Why is this happening! What you do to me, *cabrón*! You have poison me! *Qué!*"

El Lobo Macho grabbed Ignatius by his royal purple cotehardie and shook Ignatius violently.

"Do you hear me, *puto*! What you do to me! Why am I having these feelings, feelings that I have never before felt!"

"Let go of me, you Latin degenerate!" Ignatius screamed at his attacker. "What on earth are you talking about!"

"I have never felt this way," El Lobo Macho muttered, and now he felt lighter. "Now I want to listen to Judy Garland records. Now I desire to be a fashion designer. Now I desire—"

"Get away from me!" Ignatius squealed.

"I desire you, *mi amiga*," El Lobo Macho said in a sweet voice. "And only you. I only have eyes for you."

"Oh, my God!" Ignatius yelled at his Latin suitor, Ignatius wishing that a cockatoo would come to the rescue. "A bird, a bird! My freedom for a bird!"

But no bird came to Ignatius's rescue. Instead, the boa constrictor, seeking warmth and sensing it from Ignatius, and finding the scent of Ignatius's body intriguing, slithered up one of Ignatius's legs. Ignatius was too busy fending off the amorous advances of El Lobo Macho to notice the snake's caduceus-like spiraling.

"Unhand me, you vile, villainous villain!" Ignatius screamed, struggling to get away from El Lobo Macho, whose pupils were so dilated that his irides had almost turned entirely black. "This is against the natural order of worldly and heavenly things! Haven't you read Boethius, or, at the minimum, the writings of St. Paul!"

Neither El Lobo Macho nor El Lobo Macho's huge hands paid any attention to Ignatius. The snake, meanwhile, snaked its head into Ignatius's loose drawers. Ignatius's paws pushed hard against the leering Latin lothario, whose lips puckered and made kissing sounds.

Grenadine, who was watching from the stage, shook his head in disbelief. "This cannot be happening."

But it was happening: the patrons in his establishment were undressing quickly and engaging in all forms of sexual acts, thanks to the new ingredients in the Charlie Chan fortune cookies, courtesy of the palimpsest and Miss Ping's instructions. Men engaged with men, women engaged with women, men engaged with women. And in the back office, Myrna, who was eagerly nearing her eighty-second orgasm, continued her congress with Rex the Robot.

"Where's Miss Maggie?" Giacomo said to Grenadine, the janitor panicking because the boa constrictor was nowhere in sight.

"Who?" Grenadine said, and then he attempted to part two men who were sinking lower and lower to the floor as they kissed. "Stop this! You cannot do this here! We already have enough trouble with the police! If they see this, they are going to close my establishment and ruin me!"

But no matter how hard Grenadine tried to separate people, they would not stop engaging in their wanton, orgiastic, and orgasmic behaviors.

Frank, having donned his coat, now donned his fedora. He ran out from behind the bar.

"Where are you going!" Grenadine screamed at his former bartender. "You can't leave me, Frank!"

"I got a wife and three kids to take care of!" Frank yelled. "You're on your own, Grenadine! I told you that nuttin good was gonna come from this!"

And before Grenadine could say another word, Frank bolted out the door.

Out on the street, two grim-faced cops made their way towards the Stone Carver Inn. According to a dispatcher, the veteran cop and his rookie partner had not checked in, and the dispatcher had dispatched the two grim-faced cops to find out what might have happened to their fellow officers.

Frank was running towards them. One of the cops held out his hand.

"You okay, mister?" the cop said.

Frank was panting, never having run so fast or so far or so hard in his life. He leaned forward, placed his hands on his knees, and took several moments to catch his breath. He pointed down the street.

"It's crazy!" Frank said. "The place has gone crazy!"

"What place? What are you talking about, pal?" the other beat cop asked.

"The Stone Carver Inn!" Frank said. "The queers are gonna tear it up! There's two cops in there, too!"

"Thanks!" the cop said, and he ran to find a telephone to call for backup.

Back at the Stone Carver Inn, El Lobo Macho, Guapo, and Chico became part of the orgy, which looped around the interior of the tavern like a daisy chain. Grenadine poured pitchers of ice water onto the orgy's participants, but the only effect the ice water had was to encourage the participants even further. A man shouted in ecstasy, a woman groaned, and El Lobo Macho french-kissed the small East Indian waiter dressed as Carmen Miranda.

A Bowery Brew beer bottle flew across the room and smashed against Grenadine's prized possession, the gilt-framed portrait of Judy Garland. Grenadine slapped his hands to his face and screeched.

Giacomo put on a record of a Desi Arnaz conga song from RKO's *Too Many Girls,* and then Giacomo hurriedly brought his congas onstage, where he beat a loud tattoo that followed the music's lead.

Grenadine shook his head in rage and in disbelief.

"You oaf, what in the hell do you think you're doing!" Grenadine screamed. "How could you!"

"Didn't Nero play the violin while Rome burned, boss?" Giacomo said in response. "If so, and if the Stone Carver Inn is burning down, why shouldn't I thump the congas?"

Giacomo's erotemae threw Grenadine into a deeper rage, one so deep that Grenadine's already crimson face deep-purpled and then blanched. He curled his fingers into claws and rushed the stage.

"I'm going to scratch your eyes out!" Grenadine shrieked. "Just like I did Justin Martin's when we were in the eighth grade, and he called me a sissy! Nobody calls Grenadine Roe a sissy, and nobody destroys Grenadine Roe's establishment!"

Before Grenadine could leap onstage, however, Guapo and Chico tackled the tavern owner. The three rolled on the floor, Grenadine howling and clawing as the three disappeared among other bodies chained in the frenetic homosexual-heterosexual orgy.

Sir Sid and Lady Laye, who were peeking out from around the corner of the mahogany bar, stared in amazement.

"We need to get out of here before we get it in the end, man," Sir Sid said.

"What about Ignatius?" Lady Laye asked.

"Looks like our fearless leader is a fearful goner, man," Sir Sid replied uncertainly.

"We can't leave him here. He's a genius. The world needs to hear his words."

"Okay, you get him out of here, man, and I'll meet you with the van near Big Fat Fred's warehouse, man."

El Lobo Macho, finished with the East Indian waiter, embraced Ignatius, who had been fending off homosexuals and lesbians. El Lobo Macho was about to kiss Ignatius's twisting lips when Ignatius felt the head of the boa constrictor press against the crotch of the scarlet pantaloons. Ignatius looked down and saw a pulsating bulge.

"Oh, my God!" Ignatius screamed, and now he had the adrenaline-fueled strength that he needed to push away El Lobo Macho, who crashed on top of a table that gave way with a bang from the impact. "Something is in my pants! Please don't tell me that it's a bird!"

Ignatius shook his hefty leg, hopped onto his other hefty leg, and then hopped onto his other leg, doing his best to shake off the boa constrictor, which tightened its grip. Ignatius emitted several moose calls as he clawed at his crotch.

"Hey, a conga line!" a cross-eyed man wearing a loincloth and a pair of Chippewa moccasins yelled, and he placed his hands on Ignatius's shoulders and followed Ignatius's lead, the man jumping from one foot to the other. Giacomo slapped the congas louder, and, like magnets attracted one to another, homosexuals and lesbians gathered one behind the other to form an S-shaped conga line.

"Oh, my God!" Ignatius bellowed. "Something is growing in my crotch!"

El Lobo Macho now stood in front of Ignatius, and the gang leader leered at the ever-expanding, ever-undulating bulge in Ignatius's scarlet pantaloons.

"Is because you happy to see me?" El Lobo Macho asked. The gang leader leaped at Ignatius. "Come to papa!"

"Get away from me, you degenerate Latin sodomite!" Ignatius screamed. "Take your filthy hands off me!"

A man tackled El Lobo Macho, and El Lobo Macho giggled.

Ignatius shoved against the door, which fought back because of a fierce wind. He felt his perineum being probed by the tip of the boa constrictor's tail.

"Help! Help!" Ignatius screamed. "The sodomites and lesbians are raping me! Help! Help!"

Ignatius made more moose calls, and the men and women behind him repeated the moose calls in glee. The tip of the snake's tail entered Ignatius's rectum, and Ignatius's sphincter muscle instinctively locked onto the tip of the tail. The snake responded in turn, constricting tighter around Ignatius's leg. Ignatius's pyloric valve sealed, and Ignatius groaned in agony.

A Greyhound Scenicruiser headed down the street, the bus's picine, red-haired driver smiling as he spoke into a microphone. "And this, folks, is Greenwich Village, which is what we call the 'hip and happening' place of New York City," he said in his plegnic voice. "And lookie up ahead! There's a festival of some sort going on!"

Mr. Robichaux frowned. "I bet they's a bunch of communiss."

"Oh, hush up, Claude," Mrs. Reilly replied, who was beyond tears and beyond exhaustion. "I just want to get back home safe and sound. I'm tired of New York City, I'm tired of Ignatius, and I'm tired of all your talk about communiss."

The red-haired bus driver squinted. From his vantage point, it looked as if a mob of men and women were dancing in the street, with one man packing something extraordinarily hefty.

"Queers," the picine bus driver whispered to himself. "Goddamn queers. What was I thinking, taking these good folks through here?" Then he spoke into the microphone: "Please, folks, close your eyes. You don't want to get a gander at what's ahead."

The driver's warning caused the passengers to want to see what was happening, of course, and passengers in the front seats peered out their windows, and other passengers, who were in the middle seats and backseats, rushed forward to see what was going on.

The driver tapped the brakes, which didn't brake hard enough or soon enough. The Scenicruiser veered from one side of the street to the other. Mrs. Reilly and several passengers screamed, and Mr. Robichaux, remembering when he had once been in a wayward caboose off the mainline, braced himself, closed his eyes, and grunted.

Ignatius stumbled in the middle of the street and caused several of the dancing men and women behind him to tumble. The head of the boa constrictor burst forth from the crotch of the scarlet pantaloons with an extremely loud pop. Ignatius sat up on the icy street and looked down at his crotch, from which emerged not only the head of the snake but the beginnings of its pulsating body.

The men and women around Ignatius scattered when they saw the Scenicruiser. The boa constrictor slithered towards a sewer opening, and Giacomo, who had stopped playing his congas, ran to the snake, scooped it up, and hurried off before the snake could forever vanish into the New York City sewer system.

Ignatius stared like a frozen deer at the headlights of the bus, which the bus driver had turned to bright.

This can't be happening, Ignatius thought, no, not happening at all, no, I am back in my room on Constantinople Street in New Orleans, and the previous night's dinner and the bags of popcorn that I ingested are all causing me to have this nightmare, and I will awaken, and no, it is not real, it cannot be real—

And the bus, which was screeching, stopped abruptly, less than one thousandth of a millimeter away from the tip of Ignatius's weather-reddened nose.

Ignatius's blue and yellow eyes crossed, and he fainted, falling backwards, his head cushioned by his green hunting cap. Men and women who had not partaken of the Charlie Chan fortune cookies, and who were thus not engaged in the orgy occurring within the Stone Carver Inn and out on the street, rushed forward to help.

"Driver almost hit someone," Mr. Robichaux said.

"They's only one person that could be, Claude. Please don't tell me it's him."

Mr. Robichaux ruminated a moment or two. He blinked two times before he spoke. "Naw, it ain't Ignatius," he said. "It's just some bum lying out there in the middle of the street with the crotch of his pants split open. Ignatius is probably gone back to New Orleans. We should probably just go back, too. Why don't you keep your eyes closed, hon, and rest your head on my shoulder? We'll be out of this communiss place soon enough, Irene."

Not daring to look at the scene, Mrs. Reilly kept her eyes closed. "Home is not only where the heart is, it's where it's safe and sane, ain't it, Claude?"

"You said it, Irene."

On the street, a man held smelling salts underneath Ignatius's nose. The pungent odor shot up Ignatius's nostrils and fired up the neurons in Ignatius's overtaxed brain, which kicked alive like a new motor starting on a mild summer's day.

"Now, where were we?" Ignatius asked, sitting up, feeling jovial, having forgotten his recent troubles. "Ah, yes, if memory serves me correctly, Mother and I were getting ready to leave for the D. H. Holmes."

"You're in the middle of the goddamn street, that's where you is," a one-eyed cop with a coriaceous face said. His one good eye resembled a hardboiled egg because of the way the eye bulged out, and a flap of an eyelid covered the socket of his long-lost eye. "Ged up before I clobber you good."

"Obviously I'm in the middle of the street," Ignatius replied innocently to what the one-eyed cop had just said. "The question is, how on earth did I get here?"

The one-eyed cop looked around. The one-eyed cop didn't like what he was seeing. The one-eyed cop didn't like the cavorting queers, he didn't like the dancing dykes. If anyone had asked the one-eyed cop who he thought was responsible for this mayhem, the one-eyed cop would have said that it was this fat clown wearing the strange clothes and the funny green hunting cap.

The one-eyed cop eyed Ignatius and motioned with his, the cop's, truncheon. "You the one responsible for all this nonsense, pal?"

From the Stone Carver Inn came the groaning and panting of men and women and Myrna's shrieks as she had another climax.

"I, sirrah, am a victim," Ignatius said haughtily, struggling to stand. "If you want to arrest someone, there are plenty of deviants in Gotham, especially in this area formally known as Greenwich Village and colloquially known as the Village. This list includes, but is not limited to, homosexuals, lesbians, bisexuals, transsexuals, pansexuals, omnisexuals, transvestites, onanists, sadists, masochists, sadomasochists, pedophiles, autopedophiles, voyeurs, psychotics, psychopaths, sociopaths, litterbugs, jades, jesters, pornographers, addicts, alcoholics, gamblers, pimps, prostitutes, exhibitionists, vagrants, bohemians, beatniks, bums, grifters, grafters, hacks, hobos, hecklers, robbers, burglars, bombers, extortionists, bribers, arsonists, pickpockets, gigolos, B-girls, misanthropes, misogynists, misogamists, gynophobes, lotharios, castrators, flat-worlders, stabbers, pikers, plagiarists, muggers, murderers, perjurers, politicians, scammers, judges, snitches, spies, liars, unionists, trendsetters, advertisers, Antichrists, atheists, pantheists, deists, Zionists, Calvinists, Baptists, Anabaptists, Presbyterians, Methodists, Campbellites, Russellites, Pentecostals, Unitarians, spiritualists, Jansenists, Jacobins, Nazis, feminists, McCarthyites, Millerites, conservatives, neoconservatives, communists, Birchers, socialists, fascists, liberals, anarchists, libertines, republicans, democrats, monopolists, nationalists, globalists, centralists, decentralists, oligarchs, Randians, progressivists, totalitarians, Maoists, vegetarians, yogis, yoginis, jihadists, jugglers, mimes, mimics, hoydens, harridans, hosers, poseurs, viragos, and a plethora of other morons, idiots, and dunces who have isms, predilections, and other paraphilia rightfully categorized by the Church as sin but held by foolish, vapid, and vain modern man to be things categorized nosologically as so-called psychiatric disorders."

Now other cops appeared, bellowing at people and swinging truncheons. But before the cops could strike anyone, the people, in unison, pelted the cops with showers of snowballs, garbage, and Charlie Chan fortune cookies.

A fortune cookie arced over the head of the one-eyed cop and landed softly on a drift of exhaust-blackened snow.

"Them's a long list of words that make it sound like you went to some commie school, like Columbia," the cop replied angrily. "I hate commie schools because they teach people fancy words. Fancy words is dangerous. And someone who knows fancy words is dangerous. And someone who is dangerous causes trouble. And by the looks of what's going on around here, there's plenty of trouble. And trouble is always caused by a troublemaker, a troublemaker who knows fancy words. And if that be you, and I think it is, I'm going to kill you and your troublemaking ass and then haul you in."

A snowball whizzed by Ignatius's head and struck the menacing cop's heavily pockmarked face. The cop scowled, wiped away the remnants of the snowball with a gray hand the size of a boy's baseball mitt, and lurched towards Ignatius, the one-eyed cop swinging the weighted truncheon.

"You're gonna pay for that!" the outraged cop yelled. "You dirty, lousy commie—"

"I am the victim!" Ignatius yelled. "I am the one who was attacked! Blame blind Fortuna, not me!"

"I don't give a rat's ass who's to blame!" the cop yelled back. "Innocent or guilty, someone's going to get their head cracked open, and that someone's gonna be you!"

"The hell it is!" Lady Laye yelled from behind the cop.

Before the cop could turn, Lady Laye swung a frying pan she'd taken from the Stone Carver Inn and conked him. He grunted, dropped his truncheon, and slumped to the icy street. Myrna's screams of pleasure and the grunts and groans of satisfied men and women filled the night air.

Lady Laye glanced at the downed cop. She dropped the frying pan and grabbed a sleeve of Ignatius's royal purple cotehardie. "Come on, Ignatius, let's get out of here."

More cops swarmed the street and swung their truncheons, the cops so enraged that they clubbed and clawed one another.

The picine bus driver, who had hurried back into the Greyhound Scenicruiser, shifted the bus into drive. The bus groaned, like an elderly arthritic man rising from his rocking chair, and headed down the street, causing the mob that had overtaken the street to part. Ignatius thought that he saw his mother's head resting on the shoulder of Mr. Robichaux, who glanced at Ignatius and then quickly looked away. Ignatius's mouth dropped open, first in shock, then in disgust. And then Ignatius snapped his mouth shut in anger.

Three lesbians stood over a cop, trampling him.

"We've had enough!" a man dressed as Batman yelled, jumping atop a snow-covered Plymouth, tossing his cape aside, and pointing up into the air. "They've pushed us around way too long! They tax us, they fine us, they imprison us! It's time that we were left alone! It's time that we were free! It's time that we give these oinkers some of their own medicine!"

And with that, the homosexuals and lesbians increased their barrage of snowballs, garbage, and Charlie Chan fortune cookies. The outnumbered cops grouped into the center of the street, like farm animals herded into the center of a corral, and did their best to shield themselves from the assault.

Lady Laye led a huffing Ignatius through a throng of people, which was pushing against a phalanx of cops. A cop raised his truncheon and swung it at Ignatius. A snowball pelted the cop in the back, and he growled. Two men jumped the cop, and one man forced an unwrapped fortune cookie into the enraged cop's mouth and shoved hard against the cop's jaw, thereby forcing the cop to take a bite of the fortune cookie. A second or two passed, and then the cop smiled, unzipped his pants, and joined the orgiastic melee in the street.

Ignatius looked over his shoulder at the Stone Carver Inn, from which the groans and panting of men and women were growing louder. Myrna screamed "Yes!" from deep within the bowels of the tavern.

Lady Laye stumbled. She grabbed a leg of Ignatius's scarlet pantaloons to catch herself from hitting the street, and Ignatius squealed in protest but maintained his balance. Lady Laye pulled herself up an unsteady Ignatius.

Ignatius shuddered. "Just as I predicted in New Orleans, the sodomites have taken the day. Before you know it, the whole of

Gotham will be engulfed, and soon Providence and Boston and Washington D.C. and the remainder of the Eastern Seaboard will fall."

A shower of Charlie Chan fortune cookies sprayed onto Lady Laye and Ignatius, and Ignatius batted away the offensive things.

In the back office of the Stone Carver Inn, Myrna had another climax, her hundredth, and then another climax. She screamed as she had never screamed before. It was a scream of tantric delight, a scream of maximum fulfillment, a scream of holy terror, a scream of excruciating joy, a scream of utter satiation.

She had thrust so hard and clenched the robot's metallic member so hard that she had unknowingly fried Rex the Robot's circuits and deactivated the bomb that Las Tres Amigas had placed inside the robot.

Myrna, legs still wrapped around the robot, brushed her hair out of her eyes and off her sweaty brow and, looking up at Rex the Robot, smiled radiantly.

"I've never been with a man who could last so long," Myrna said, after taking a few moments to catch her breath. "Not even Ongah, that fake. I'm in love, Rex! And I'm in love with you! Dad's probably going to be gone for a while, but once he gets out of the sanitarium, I'm sure that he's going to love you. One thing we're going to have to work on is your communication skills. I know that you keep calling yourself a robot, and in this day and age we're all robots, thanks to reactionaries like my dad and Walter Cronkite. But I'll get you over that with the help of Dr. Ingloss."

The robot's motors whined in response, and then the robot's member lost its power. Myrna released her grip on the robot's waist and sank to the floor.

"I can't wait until the honeymoon," Myrna said. "By the way, are you Jewish?"

Out in the street, Magoohan, still dressed as Little Red Riding Hood, appeared with a newly arrived phalanx of ossifragant cops. Magoohan smiled. There were plenty of suspicious characters on the street. Good. Now to crack their heads open and arrest them all.

"Charge!" Magoohan yelled, raising his truncheon, and before he could say anything else, an unwrapped Charlie Chan fortune cookie thrown by a lesbian dressed as Sappho entered his mouth. Magoohan gagged and attempted to spit out the fortune cookie, but the fortune cookie broke, and Magoohan inadvertently took a bite.

And now, instead of charging warlike into the melee, Magoohan dropped his truncheon, picked up his picnic basket, and skipped merrily into the Stone Carver Inn.

II

Lady Laye led Ignatius down a street, across another, then down another, then across another, then across another. His knees were aching, and he felt like vomiting, and he wished that he had never met Myrna Minkoff or gone shopping with his mother at D. H. Holmes that fateful day or had ever come to Gotham.

"I can't, I can't, I can't—" Ignatius gagged, and Lady Laye let go of his hand. His stomach heaved, but he didn't vomit. His breathing was stertorous, like a losing horse's. "Let Fortuna take me in her depraved ways. I cannot go on, must not go on. If the world must end for me, let it end for me here and now."

Lady Laye shook her head. "We can't allow that, Ignatius."

"Why do you care about me?" he asked, and his head was swimming, and he had visions of Rex running through the front yard at the Reilly house on Constantinople Street. "And why should the world care about me?"

"Because you have much to offer," his friend replied. "Much more than you can ever imagine."

In her irides he saw a warmth, a human warmth that he had never seen or experienced before—no, not even from his own mother. Ignatius felt overwhelmed with an emotion that he had experienced only a few times in his life.

Then another emotion overtook Ignatius.

"We mustn't dawdle," Ignatius said. "You are correct. I have much to offer to the world. I do have the correct perspective on Boethius, especially his masterpiece *The Consolation of Philosophy*. Because the world must hear what he has to say, the world must hear what I have to say. Come, let us leave Gotham and see where Fortuna will take us. Perhaps this is the turning of Fortuna's Wheel once again, only this time in my favor."

"That's the spirit, Ignatius. Sid's waiting for us, and he's going to take us to a magical land on a magical coast where you can spread your magical message of proper theonomy and geology."

"That's proper theology and geometry," Ignatius said, and now he took Lady Laye by the hand. "Come, vixen, lead me to this Promised Land."

"We're almost there, Ignatius!"

But further physical exertion by Ignatius was nearing impossibility. "I—I don't know—I don't know how much more of this I can take—"

"We just need to get to that corner, Ignatius, and then we can stop! Sid's going to bring a van there! Please don't give up now!"

And Lady Laye tugged his sleeve, helping him to move along.

They reached the corner, and Ignatius entered an alley, where he bent over a lidless garbage can and vomited. A blue light bulb near a back door illuminated the area, and steam from Ignatius's waste rose into the air. Ignatius leaned against the alley wall. He gasped for air. He was glad that the running was over. Another minute, he suspected, and he would have a coronary.

Lady Laye placed her hands sororally on his shoulders. "Sid's going to be here any moment with the van. We're going to drive straight on through to California. In three days, you'll be lying on the beach in Santa Monica and soaking up rays."

"I do not like beaches," Ignatius said, his respiration returning to normal. "First, I do not do well in the sun. And second, beaches terrify me. Terrible things happen there. There are terrible mites in the sand, and people drown, and sometimes, on lonely nights, people too good for this world commit suicide at beaches."

"Not at the beaches where we're going," Lady Laye said. "You wait and see. Freedom's just around the corner, Ignatius. And remember, the darkest hour is just before dawn."

"I do wish that you wouldn't quote platitudes and bromides, particularly if they come from so-called pop music," Ignatius replied testily. "It's most unbearable."

"But what I'm saying is true," she protested.

"Perhaps, but even if it is, it is trite."

Two headlights appeared in the winter fog, like the eyes of a fierce predator. The fog separated before the headlights, and Ignatius saw a white van that Sir Sid was driving. On the side of the van screamed the lettering BIG FAT FRED'S NEW & USED CARPETING. The van's brakes whined in protest as the van slid to a halt.

Shaking his head, Ignatius studied the van. This was all that Fortuna could give to him? After all that he had suffered? That harridan of a wench had played too many games with him! Enough, already, enough!

"A carpet van!" Ignatius bellowed. "You expect me to travel in that thing! That's worse than a Greyhound Scenicruiser!"

"Ballast, man," Sir Sid said, getting out of the van. "We need the carpet for ballast, man, when we cross the Rockies, man. When we get to the Nevada desert, man, we can ditch the carpet, and you can have more room, man."

"This is insane!" Ignatius said, walking circles. "Why didn't things work out in Gotham! Why didn't my revolution start! Why was I attacked by that horrid asp!"

"It was a boa constrictor," Lady Laye said judiciously. "But what does it matter now? The past's the past. All the leaves are brown, and California's waiting for us, Ignatius, like a dream."

Ignatius frowned. "Is that from Nietzsche?"

"Who knows, man?" Sir Sid said. "But the scene's out there, man. We get out there, man, and we're going to make our killing, man. You want a revolution, man, well, let me tell you, man, it's out there, man."

"It really is, Ignatius," Lady Laye said, her eyes big and luminous like those of a lemur. "There's nothing left for you here. It's time for you to move on."

Ignatius hesitated.

Lady Laye crossed her arms. "Ignatius, are you coming with us or not?"

"But California—"

"It's your safest bet, man," Sir Sid said, his breath forming clouds, and Lady Laye nodded in agreement.

"Oh, all right," Ignatius replied. "But I do not believe that I will be able to enter your vehicle without assistance."

"No problem," Lady Laye said. "Sid, open the back doors. Ignatius, go ahead and try to get in."

Ignatius's paws nervously felt around the interior of the van, in which were several rolls of carpeting redolent of one of his pet peeves, namely, newness. He grunted as he attempted to enter the van and then felt two pairs of hands push on his behemoth behind.

"Do be careful!" Ignatius bellowed. "This reminds me of a journey that I had on a Greyhound Scenicruiser. It's a story unlike any other. Not even Dante himself could have envisioned a nightmare like it."

"You'll have to tell us the story later," Lady Laye said, and she and Sir Sid continued to push Ignatius, who was as hard to handle as a four-hundred-pound sack of sand. "Seriously, you've got to lose some weight, my friend."

"It's those horrid Charlie Chan fortune cookies," Ignatius whimpered. "If only I had known what Gotham was going to do to me, I would have stayed in New Orleans and allowed my mother to take me to that charity hospital."

"Enough talking, man," Sir Sid said. "It's time to get you into the van, man."

Ignatius huffed as Lady Laye and Sir Sid continued to shove Ignatius's gargantuan ass. With their help, Ignatius entered a newfound heart of darkness.

Sir Sid and Lady Laye closed the back doors and hopped into the front of the van. Then the van took off.

Warm air circulated throughout the rattling van. Ignatius covered himself with a Navajo blanket and cupped his cold paws together and blew hot air into them. From a window, he watched New York City streets pass by and thought about the many causeways, bridges, roads, highways, and lanes that he would cross. He was fleeing New York City in much the same way that he had fled New Orleans. How ironic.

And after the van crossed a bridge into New Jersey, he drifted off into a very pleasant, and very deep, sleep.

Printed in Great Britain
by Amazon